TERMINUS

TERMINUS

Paul Melhuish

Greyhart Press

www.greyhartpress.com

TERMINUS

Published by Greyhart Press
ISBN-13: 978- 1475192131

Also available as
Kindle eBook, ASIN: B005QBSGQS
ePUB eBook, ISBN: 978-14657690461

BOUNDARY STATION 8651/0

Against the dark background splashed with stars, Terminus thought
he saw shapes moving.

He was in two minds; his palm hovered over the console as he
decided whether to hit the battle alarm. From his position at the
viewing window he peered into the depths of space. Whatever he'd
seen didn't look like meteorites and the dim shapes were moving too
fast to be freighter shells. If he activated the battle alarm and it
turned out to be junk floating around in the vacuum, he would be in
the drent with Watch Officer Crank. Crank would hoik him off the
floor by his muc-sac and swing him round the deck. Yet Terminus
had heard the tales like everyone else. Unidentified craft, strange
lights, ships materializing right in front of the boundary post and not
showing up on the scanner.

As they closed in, he counted three shapes. All of them were
accelerating towards the small station.

Sii Terminus was the sole occupant of boundary post 8651/0. He
was ensconced behind the control desk in a self-contained space
station that hung on the very edge of the Skyfirean system, scanning
the great outer darkness of space. The mighty light of the Skyfirean
sun was just a faint glow all the way out here. Terminus was working
a three cycle tour on 8651/0 because the ching was good and there
was no gannta breathing down his neck, barking orders and giving
him drent jobs to do. Most of the time he just sat here gawping at
signal casts or frequenting the limited number of sex channels that
reached this far. Sometimes he just sat gazing into space. On the level
above, the sleep-plinth and hygiene alcove of his living quarters had
already degenerated into abject squalor. This was where he spent

most of the time sleeping, out of boredom more than anything else. He'd drunk his allowance of snakki within three stretches (what a blast that had been) and was in danger of over-using his food ration as he, again, ate out of boredom. The teleported food they sent was always bland in taste but he still ate it.

It was a shame, he reflected, that they'd never learned to teleport people through space or he could nip back to Skyfire whenever he wanted.

Terminus was sixteen cycles old; this was his first time away from the world of Skyfire, and only two cycles since he'd left the backwater planet of his birth in the Sol system. He was bored. The only thing that stopped the boredom was the fear. In the bars back on edge station *Cloud Dust*, he'd laughed at the tales told by old boundary watchers, but he wasn't laughing now. Stories of voices whispering in the darkness, watchers going mad and detonating their stations (he'd noticed the self-destruct facility had been disabled when Crank's crew had dropped him here) or being found dead with strange symbols carved into their torsos. Some, it was said, cut the symbols into their own flesh before mortoing themselves. It was all vulley, digest invented to scare apprentices like him. And yet...

These tales shot through his mind as the three fuzzy unidentifieds came into sharp focus through the oval view-screen. The darkened interior of the station seemed suddenly oppressive. He looked down at the scanner panel where the circular holo-screen showed details of the three objects that were still there in real-sight. They resembled upside down fish in the way their bodies arched and bulged like the sea beasts back on Skyfire. However, they were dark, their black coloring making them hard to distinguish against the canvas of space.

Terminus gasped; they *were* ships. Three of them. The craft were unlike anything he'd ever seen. Certainly they weren't of Skyfirean design. As they neared he could pick out more detail of the closest intruder. The ship had no exhaust nozzle as such, although a dark, circular hole cut through the front of the craft. The body was serrated and its sides were like blackened ribs. It looked as if a large black-boned carcass were being piloted through space. The base of the ship was made from the same type of bone as the ribs, locking together like vertebrae, and flattened to serve as a deck. A narrow spine ran the ship's length from nose to tail. He couldn't see a propulsion system but an inky-black, smoke-like substance oozed from its rear. The whole ship looked as if it had been grown, not constructed, and then stripped of flesh and muscle.

Terminus shuddered. The first craft was close enough for him to see that between the ribs, exposed to the vacuum of space, bipedal creatures moved within the cage. The lead ship was nearly on top of the boundary station and Terminus still hadn't hit the alarm. The craft came to a stop. The intruder was still over a click away, just sitting there, watching. The three ships dwarfed the space station and Terminus stared dumbly into the inky blackness of the ship's nose.

Then he slammed his fist into the battle alarm.

Nothing happened.

The alarm didn't sound and the computer's whining nasal voice didn't inform him that a signal had been sent and Skyfire Sundogs, packed with armed ministro clone-soldiers and carrying rapid re-load blast-cannons, would arrive as soon as possible. If a patrol happened to be in the area then it might be only minutes until it arrived; if not then Terminus could be looking at anything up to three stretches before help came.

While he stared into the dark maw of the invader, something fired out from the hole. He slammed his fist into the console again and again. A dark mass was speeding its way right towards the viewing point. The thing would crash into the window, or through it, in seconds. Terminus flung himself to the floor. This was it, this was drenting it, an out-world invasion and he would be the first casualty. Panic gripped his young mind. He managed to compose himself enough to reach the armory cabinet where he keyed in the code and waited for the doors to slide open. The boy gripped a fire-blaster and

3

primed it. The chunky gun whined in his hand and he felt heat in the hand-grip as the internal elements came alive.

Terminus turned just in time to see the black mass slide through the window, leaving it undamaged as if it had been teleported through. The intruder assembled itself in the center of the station's interior a few feet away from Terminus, the formless blackness shrinking into a figure which stood like a man. Terminus's mind was on the point of throwing the insanity switch as he stared at this enemy towering over him. He tried to angle his vision to the face hidden under the hood of the figure's dark robe. The boy's heart pounded while the shape stood impassively regarding him. Terminus gathered his thoughts. He raised the gun and spoke.

'Listen, I know there's some protocol to deal with these sort of situations but I don't know what the drent it is, so get off this station or I'll blow you back into the vacuum!'

The creature ignored him. It simply inclined its head and the hood fell back slightly. Terminus backed off when he saw the face. The narrow head was made of black exo-skeleton interspersed with thick, ugly hairs that protruded from jumbled orifices. Above the mandibles, where the mouth should have been, six pairs of eyes stared out at him. The hooded invader looked arachnid in appearance. Terminus fired... but the blasts of fire passed through the visitor and hit the wall behind.

For long moments after the noise of the blasts had died down, the figure stood unmoving, waiting for the moment when terror had rendered Terminus doubly incontinent. That didn't take long.

The creature extended its left arm and a black finger, like a spider's leg, pointed at Terminus. At that moment, his mind was taken. Involuntarily, he dropped the gun and realized in that half-second that his nerves had been commanded to relax his muscles, to loosen his grip. Darkness filled his mind as his will sapped away. The arachnid was willing the boy to go to him, even giving him a glimpse of what awaited him: pain and darkness such as he had never experienced. It wanted to use the boy, to inflict unimaginable horror upon him. Terminus had no choice but to go with the creature; succumbing to the beast's dominion was all he existed for now, to endure defilement at the creature's hands and to suffer for its pleasure. He kicked the gun away and managed only to whimper when his body slowly crossed the floor towards the arachnid demon. Terminus felt every nuance of screaming agony as the demon's superior mind began to crush his humanity, diligently reducing him to nothing.

Without warning, light blasted through the viewing port, snapping the intruder's hold on the boy. A *fourth* ship had emerged. This one was totally different from the three that had engaged the station. The size was immense; a brilliant white hull filled the view screen. The front and rear end disappeared into nothingness as if they had been cut away. Something told the boy that the ship wasn't damaged but had partially materialized from somewhere else. From its smooth, white, vastness it fired three bolts of yellow sunlight that instantly consumed all three black boneships in a holocaust of pure light. The ship the intruder had arrived from was the last to be vaporized. Its bones imploded in a vortex of white fire. All solidity belonging to the figure before Terminus began to shimmer and was drawn from its footing on the space-station floor, sucked though the solid window and out into space where the fiery death took it. As the black bone structures were blasted out of existence, the larger ship began to shudder. With a blinding lightning flash Terminus's otherworldly rescuer disappeared.

The boy was left standing in his soiled skids, staring into space. Shortly after, the sound of the battle alarm started and the computer's nasal whine informed him that Skyfire warcraft would be arriving in the next few minutes.

PART I

THANATOS ONE

Deep Spaced

Terminus was shaken awake by the intermittent bleeping of the homeworld line. The holo-image sprang out at him from the console, alerting him to the incoming message. He stretched out from the sleep area and sat up. Two more seconds passed before he shifted his torso round and his feet thumped firmly on the floor. Through his heels he could feel the dull shuddering of the ship's engine and his muscles flexed in response to the slightly out of sync gravity enhancer. Holding forth his arms, he again studied the intricate tattoos of the newly installed phys-tech. The microscopic liquid metal slept beneath the epidermis. Physiological technology served many purposes. For instance, with one code word a multifunction comm would unfold across the anterior aspect of his wrist like a steel flower blooming at rapid speed. Knowing this tech was inside him made his limbs feel weighty as he transferred from sitting to standing to move over to the console.

His quarters were a mess of discarded ration cartons and drink containers. He'd only been here twelve sub-stretches and already the room was devolving into squalor. The rectangular viewing port showed the ship to be well out of Skyfirean orbit and, judging by the time, Terminus supposed they must be well past the boundary by now. His head throbbed with dehydration. When he'd taken command of deep space cargo shell 850 he'd been so drunk he'd just crashed into his sleep-plinth. The crew had taken care of planet-lift and boundary passage in his absence. He'd slept through the whole thing. Now Terminus desperately needed a re-hydration capsule. He drenting well knew he'd not brought any with him and would, for the first time in a long while, just have to ride this hangover out.

'Terminus here,' he barked into the console and her image flashed up. She was smiling so he couldn't have said or done anything too bad last night. 'Clannel, I suppose you've called to give me an audio-bashing.'

'How's your head, Terminus?' She smiled.

'Like someone's poured liquid metal into my thinker.'

'Do you remember you telling me you loved me last night?'

Drent! 'No.'

'And how many liters of snakki you were downing with the boys?'

'Yeah, well I won't be doing that again for a few sub-cycles. This is a dry run. There's a block on any alcohol coming through the teleport.'

'Have you met the politico yet?'

'No. I had an instruction not to disturb him. I probably won't see him at all for the entire flight, which suits me fine.'

'Who is he? Has he been on the info-blast?'

'I don't know. He's just some functionary, some diplomat. We won't bother him, he won't bother us.'

Her face shifted expression. Her mouth turned down in that mock expression of sadness she put on. Even scores of pulses away she was still annoying. If it weren't for her fantastic curves he would have spun her out cycles ago. Her red hair, back-lit by the dying Skyfirean sun shining through the window of their apartment, reminded him of how physically stunning she was. The way she pouted her lips right now reminded him of how infuriating she could be.

'I don't see why you have to go, anyway. Why d'you have to leave your luxury kitten all alone?' Argh! She was using that stupid, drellocking lover's nickname for herself again.

'I've told you; because it's good ching, well paid. They actually head-requested me for this job. The only time I get requested to do anything is to step into Crank's office for a swing round by the muc-sac 'cos I've vullied up again. This will look good on my record.'

'But I'm all alone.' *Oh yeah, you're all alone all right. You'll be flooring with every vulley that sniffs round you while I'm away, you skang-gat!* 'We've only been Linked for three sub-cycles and you're leaving me already. Is this how it's going to be for the rest of our lives? What am I going to do without you?'

'Not really my problem, is it?'

'I still don't see why they chose you.'

'You know why.'

That shut her ration-hole. But it had only been a sub-cycle since he'd told her his version of the boundary station nightmare, and Clannel wasn't as neuro as she sometimes made out.

'That was ten cycles ago,' she said after thinking a few moments. She was a clever geema when she could be bothered to engage her thought box. 'They want you on this job because of what happened to you when you were sixteen?'

'Yeah. Maybe they want me on this in case I spot them again, eh? Besides, my life turned to drent after the incident. Watch Officer Crank must've wanted to make up for that. So now that you know, I'd better go. I *am* supposed to be in charge of this vacuum tub.'

Terminus cut the connection, hoping that he'd said enough to keep Clannel from contacting him again before they were out of range.

The 850 was gliding through the star fields. Her wings stretched out to full capacity, the outer hull weapons cache that rested at each tip primed in response mode. Her pulsers burned steadily, creating a pink glow that teleported her forward in stuttering jumps across relatively short distances, or *pulses*, through space. Each of the five crew sat positioned at instruction panels that cast a dim red glow onto their faces and spilled over the navigation cabin. Terminus's quarters were nothing but a small bulge above and to the rear of the nav cabin.

Then there was the cargo. Hunched over the freighter's shell like a gorged parasite, the politico's habitation unit sat fixed to the cargo couplings on the superior aspect of the ship's carcass. Its gray, rounded organic look contrasted the space freighter's own rust-red, angled, mechanical features. Viewing ports, mere slits cut into the hab-unit's sides, were illuminated by a soft glowing light from within.

Terminus appeared on the steps above the navigation stations. He was tempted to pause for dramatic effect as the five crew, all fitted out in functional, scuffed work issue clothes, stopped what they were doing and looked up at him. He clattered down the steps and took his command post; a once-comfortable leather-effect chair. They all continued to stare at him. He could see that they were trying to work him out. Was he going to be a right strentner of an operative coordinator or was he a gannta, like them? He broke the silence at last and nailed his colors to the mast.

'Has anyone got any re-hyde capsules? I've got one vulley of a hangover.'

Terminus felt the cabin breathe a sigh of relief as one of the ganntas went to fetch a capsule from his bunk at the back of the navigation cabin, where five man-shaped horizontal alcoves were cut into the wall for the crew to sleep in when off-duty.

These men were hardened vacuum-farers; probably spent half their lives on deep run space jobs. All of them carried the typical Skyfirean olive-skinned complexion, apart from the scanner runner, Tulk. He was dark, almost black in skin color, with a bob of tangled dreads. Terminus wondered if he was from Sol; a Martian or even an Earther like himself. Terminus had enough time to find out; they were going to be on this ship for the next half-cycle.

'Incoming on line one, Coordinator,' a wiry black-haired gannta informed him. Terminus jumped down and joined the man at his console. In the gloom the holo-message flickered into amber-colored life.

'It's our coordinates from Control at *Cloud Dust*,' Terminus confirmed. 'Plug them into the flight plan and predict any obstacles. Asteroid fields, gas clouds, stellar events, that sort of drent.'

'Do you know where we're going?' asked the dark-skinned man. 'We haven't been briefed yet.'

'I don't know much. All I know is this: we've got to take our guest upstairs to a system out past Babel.'

'Which system?'

Terminus shrugged. 'All I know is its name: Thanatos.'

Babel

The crew possessed functional Skyfirean names. There was Fuse, the drive repair operative; Culp, the first navigator; Dich and Sank, the general operatives; and the main engineer, Tulk. All of them were male; the Watch only used single sex crews on long-hauls like this. Mixed sexes could not be trusted with each other in deep space, or so the politicos back on Skyfire thought. He studied the crew once more, trying to work them out. Terminus was eager to get to know the dark-skinned gannta who he thought might be from home. Sol was a sparsely populated system now and he liked to catch up with anyone who knew the place.

After a time, Terminus began to notice the sly glances and sniggering among his crew. He could guess what this was about. Two sub-stretches passed before he decided to put it to rest and get this digest out in the open.

'All right then. I've heard the remarks and I've been given the nicknames before. Come on, let's get it over with. Ask me about the boundary station.' Terminus scanned each face from his place at the command chair. They all went quiet. Culp openly smirked, Dich and Sank following suit.

'We heard you were once found on a boundary station screaming something about ghosts,' said Culp, laughing.

'And who told you that?'

'Some ganntas back on Skyfire, before we came out. They heard it was you co-coordinating and told us.'

'Ghosts?' Terminus spat. He stood and came down to the navigation level. 'They weren't ghosts. They were out-worlders. The one I saw was.'

'So it's true?' Tulk cut in.

'Yes, it's true. Something boarded my station. I don't know what it was and I'm not sure I want to find out. If you get me vullied enough one night, I'll tell you all about it and you can laugh your muc-sac off. But right now I just want you to get our cargo to this Thanatos place, clear?'

'As water, Coordinator.' Culp was still smirking. Terminus knew if he waited a couple of stretches the operative would get bored with trying to pull his nazbolt. Terminus re-took his seat and fiddled with his comm panel, his mind now unsettled.

Shortly after leaving Skyfire, Tulk had managed to double-ident the teleport system to deliver some snakki to the ship. Alcohol was banned on deep space flights but Tulk had fooled the dispatch computer into thinking they were a boundary station and the golden liquid had been delivered. They were now down to the last containers. Four of the crew had drunk themselves into sleep and now snored in their bunks while Tulk and Terminus finished a game of Shift, betting their wages which hadn't yet been paid into their ching-sacs back on Skyfire. Both men were too pacified by the drink to know who had won and who'd lost. The game had been abandoned while the vacuum-farers talked.

'Well, you're almost right,' said Tulk. 'I'm from Skyfire but my ancestors were Martian. Several decades ago they'd tried to settle on Venus but, you know... the terra-forming accident. They got picked up by a Skyfire relief effort and there they stayed. I knew you weren't from Skyfire, Terminus; you're too pale. You look like you've never even seen the sun. What's your story?'

Terminus took a swig of snakki. 'I grew up on Earth. My pat still lives there, in a colonists' dwelling in the Northern Hemisphere.'

'Vulley man, that's an old, old planet. Lot of history there.'

'All these vacuum ganntas, our ancestors, everyone from Skyfire came from there. Having grown up there I can see why they drenting left.'

'I heard they're disputing that. They say we came from the inner-galaxy.'

'Digest! We came from Earth. That's just more unction from the politicos, trying to rally the Planeterists. No, we're from Earth; everyone knows that.'

After a short pause Tulk asked, 'Why d'you leave?'

'Ever been there? It's dead. Nothing there. Freighters only visit once every six cycles. I wanted a job, ching, see the universe. All that digest.'

'You're in the wrong job if you want cash, my friend. Space travel ain't where it's at.'

'Oh yeah?' Terminus grinned drunkenly. 'You know how much they're paying me for this trip?'

'Not much more than us; one thousand fifty.'

'Three thousand.'

'Drellocks! Three thousand? That's twice the amount a normal co' gets. Why they paying you so much?'

'It ain't who you know,' he slurred cockily; 'it's what you've seen!'

Terminus spent the stretch worrying about telling Tulk how much he was getting for this trip. He didn't want to stir up bad feeling among the men — it wouldn't be good if he casped them off, but as the time passed they didn't treat him any differently so he assumed that Tulk had kept it quiet.

'We're receiving transmissions from a planet three hundred pulses clear,' Dich informed him. The young man showed a diligent concern for his duties that irked Terminus. He'd been nothing like Dich at that age. The kid was a clean-living ladder-climber. In a few years he'd be telling Terminus what to do, the little muc-sac.

'Ignore it. It'll be welcoming tracts from Babel.'

'Babel, huh?' Culp suddenly sprang to life. 'Are we gonna stop or what?'

'Oh yeah, the gannta upstairs is gonna love that,' Terminus said.

'The gannta upstairs is an anti-social drellock. Who is he, Terminus?'

'I don't know. This is a diplomatic mission. He's gonna offer these Thanatons a deal.'

'So he's a politico?' Culp spat. 'We should stop on Babel. He'd love it. They like what goes on down there, do politicos.'

'Yeah, he's probably got membership of the Red Palace.' Fuse laughed.

'Or the Punishment House. They're all interferers, these politicos. You want to watch it Dich, he'll have a bit of you!'

'That's enough!' Terminus tried to silence them but didn't do a very good job.

'So what's so special about this Babel planet?' Dich piped up to howls of derision from his shipmates.

Terminus sighed. He felt like he was explaining the repro-cycle to an infant. 'It's the pleasure planet. The whole thing is one big sex-house and what goes on there is real. Not like on the sex-channel where it's all conjured from pixels. You can get anything you want there. There are palaces; just huge pleasure houses where ganntas and geemas just get vullied in the orgies. It's said that people have literally gone insane there. All their fantasies become real and they can't handle it. They lose the line between reality and fantasy, I suppose.'

Terminus leaned forward. There was no *suppose* about it; he'd vullied himself stupid on Babel before. 'It's not all happy flooring. Different palaces cater for different tastes. You know; snuff slaves, crimming, Gomorrah-flooring, stuff that'll give you nightmares. And other stuff; things you and I and regular ganntas just can't imagine going on. Certain times of the cycle the whole planet has an orgy. The air fills with this, like, hormone intensifier and it's like animals on heat. Imagine a planet twice the size of Skyfire just flooring for twelve stretches solid.'

They brought the vast scarlet planet into real-life view. Blood-red clouds obscured boiling seas but its land masses twinkled with the lights of endless cities. Terminus tried to imagine the depravity below.

'Are they humans who live there?' asked Dich.

'It was colonized by Skyfireans a thousand cycles ago.' Terminus replied. 'Babel was the first world where they found indigenous intelligent life. Lung-men who now do the fetching and carrying for the humans, but they weren't the original inhabitants. Most of these palaces are adapted from the massive buildings they found empty when they got there. Intricate, fine structures built out of the red rock of the planet's surface. There were these strange carvings all around of bipedal figures, humanoid, and cages; cages everywhere. There must have been a vast civilization there but all that was left were the buildings and Lung-men. They were low-intelligence, possibly cooked up genetically then left to breed when the original inhabitants disappeared, carked off or whatever happened to them. We've no idea of why they disappeared. It's like they got up and left. Mind you, it didn't stop Skyfireans turning it into one big vulley house.'

'You've been there before,' said Dich, as if he were uncovering some great secret. 'Haven't you?'

Terminus just grinned. The truth was that not everything he'd seen on Babel gave him happy dreamtimes, but there was no drenting way he was going to admit that in front of these ganntas. So he said nothing and grinned as if the memories were so good they were sending him neuro. Memories that little muc-sac, Dich, didn't share.

'Then you can tell me why it's called Babel,' said Dich starting to sound casped off.

Terminus shrugged. 'They called it Babel because the first structure they saw resembled this old art work, *The Tower of Babel*. That's what they found, buildings and Lung-men.'

'So there is intelligent life out there,' Dich said optimistically, gesturing toward space.

'Yeah, but it's not that intelligent or interesting enough to bother with,' Culp cut in smirking.

Terminus sat back in his command chair and regarded Culp. This gannta was really beginning to get on his nerves. Terminus had an edge to his voice when he spoke.

'It may interest you, Operative Culp, that where we are going there are no humanoid settlers. It isn't a colony planet and there is no human life there.'

He frowned. 'But you said this was a diplomatic job.'

'Exactly!'

'So we are going to a system of out-worlders, genuine non-humans!'

'We are. How uninteresting does alien life sound now, Operative Culp?'

He looked genuinely disturbed. Terminus sat back and wanted to laugh out loud. That put the wind up him. Culp might be quiet for a bit now, thinking about that. Dich took a magno-scan of Babel, the conscientious little drellock, while the rest of the crew stared at the scarlet world in the large lateral screen until the 850 had carried on past its glowing orange sun and was back out into the void.

Politico

'Terminus, I've just had a call from our passenger. He wants us to backtrack to Babel on a predetermined landing code.'

Terminus sprang from his seat and studied the holo-message, joining Tulk at the console. 'This wasn't part of the remit. All codes usually come from Skyfire.'

'You wanna argue with a politico, go ahead. It's your job, Terminus.'

'Ha, we're going to Babel,' Culp sang. 'Gonna get some vulley after all.'

'What the drent does he wanna go to Babel for? I'm reporting this to Crank when I get back, I really am.' Terminus studied the message. There was an additional note. 'Oh, and he wants to see me now. Great. Just drenting great.'

Terminus waited in the small space where the hab-unit's portal intersected with the 850's cargo coupling. He studied the door before him; its shiny gray oval surface didn't fit aesthetically with the rust-red metal of the 850's battered, functional interior. Terminus shifted uncomfortably and, feeling oddly nervous, checked his uniform. He rarely met any person of high regard, besides Watch officers of higher rank, and had never actually met or addressed a politico. This gannta was one of the ruling elite who ran his adopted planet. Terminus knew that if the politico didn't like what he saw, he could have the coordinator ejected from the Boundary Watch, the system defense force that had grown into the State's space-faring monopoly.

The door finally opened noiselessly. White light glared out from the interior. Terminus adjusted his eyes and viewed a bare office. The white-walled room had no angles; walls curved seamlessly into the floor and ceiling. In the exact center stood a black desk on which sat a console and some info-processing keyboards. All of this was high-tech and very modern. The space-gannta was surprised he didn't have a couple of cloned ministro soldiers standing guard.

The politico paid him no attention whatsoever. When the coordinator walked over to his desk and stood deferentially before him, the strentner still ignored him, and so Terminus decided to take a good scan at the politico while he tapped away at his keyboard. He wore a gray tunic; the standard dress of a politico. His hair and moustache matched the tunic in color and even his flesh had an unhealthy-looking pale pallor. Terminus wondered if he was an Earther as well, but knew that this gannta wasn't going to converse on an informal basis. Eventually the politico looked up and regarded the coordinator as if he was a piece of digest stuck to the side of the disposal chute.

'Operative Coordinator Terminus at your service, sir.'

'I know your name, I was briefed.' His voice was clipped and accent-less. He spoke with a typical politico tone: abrasive and commanding, as heard so often on the info-blast back on Skyfire. 'I'll keep this short, Terminus. As you know we are on a diplomatic mission to the Thanatos system. I have important documents to impart to the government of that system. I take it that the coordinates were uploaded onto your flight terminal? Good.' He looked down to his console again but continued speaking. 'The Thanatos system consists of thirteen planets circling a green sun.' Terminus was taken aback. On all his travels he'd never encountered a green sun before. 'We will achieve planet-fall on Thanatos One. You will follow the landing coordinates given to you and follow them exactly. You will come down over a small sea and at three hundred degrees you will power the ship laterally at a respectful speed and land on the coast by the Thanaton Imperial Tower. The atmosphere is breathable so I do not require an atmo-suit and gravity is almost identical to that on Skyfire. However, you and the crew will remain on the ship at all times until my negotiations are completed. We will then return without delay.'

'If the planet is Skyfire-normal then can't the crew stretch their legs, only just outside the ship?'

'No!' he snapped shooting Terminus a hard look. 'Not on this planet. Not only would leaving the ship have diplomatic implications but the personal safety of the crew would be compromised. You stay on the ship. Anyone found leaving their post will be dealt the harshest of penalties.' Terminus knew what that meant. 'Is that clear?'

'Yes, sir.' *You flooring, vulleying, drent-shover!* 'One question; why are we stopping at Babel?'

'That is none of your business, Coordinator. You will land and your crew will be ready for take-off when I have completed my business there.'

'Can we stretch our legs once down there?'

'That's two questions. I've finished with you, Terminus. I don't expect to be disturbed by anyone before we reach Thanatos.' He looked down again at his keyboard. From Terminus's side-view he saw a glimpse of the screen. He was taken aback for a second time. Strange symbols filled the holo-space; symbols utterly alien to any language Terminus knew. They didn't originate from any of the colony systems or even the Sol system. Turning, he left the politico to his symbols and exited, swearing as soon as he was out of his quarters.

He should have told that vulleying veck where to get off. He hated being spoken to like he was some vulleying servant and that shankaa had done just that. The mood Terminus was in now, he felt like leaving that politico gannta behind on that flooring planet!

In the Heart of the Red Palace

The 850 entered the atmosphere of Babel and followed the preset coordinates. The crew hardly had to do anything, which disappointed Terminus as he was looking forward to practicing a manual landing. Descending into the rose-colored banks of cloud that obscured the continents, the crew were acutely aware of the presence of two ships closing in on them. Cloud Swords, ornate and vicious-looking aircraft that patrolled the skies of this world, drew alongside to escort the 850 to its landing point.

'Look at those vulleys.' Terminus gestured to the viewing portal on his left. The wings curved from the rear of the craft to almost meet the bulbous cockpit. These wings, and the tail fin, actually resembled sharp metal swords emanating from the scarlet, bejeweled body. The Cloud Swords were as beautiful as they were deadly.

'I saw one cut a Doolek scout ship in half once. They just took a swipe at it with one of those wings.'

'Really?' Dich's eyes were open wide with amazement. 'Do they have fire power?'

'More than this ship does,' said Terminus.

'Those ships epitomize this planet,' said Sank, the old space-gannta's voice dark with the richness from a lifetime of experience. 'Beautiful but will cut off your nazbolt as soon as scan you.'

'Yeah, well,' said Culp. 'I'm just gonna get some vulley when I'm down there.'

'What with, Culp?' asked Sank. 'You've got no ching. We don't get paid till we get back to Skyfire.' Sank almost spat. Terminus was beginning to think that Sank might be a First Churcher. He was

25

distinctly uncomfortable with the idea of going to a vulley-planet. Most religious ganntas got a bit tetchy about the old flooring for ching.

'He's got a point, Terminus,' Tulk said. 'If the politico gives us some planet leave, we ain't got enough money to even buy a drink let alone spend the night with a Babelite.'

'Relax,' said Terminus. He smiled. 'Leave it to me.'

Below them the continent came into view: a scarlet plain, devoid of vegetation, that was so bright it hurt their eyes to look at it. As the ship descended they could see the vast, ancient structures built by the race that first inhabited this planet. Huge pillars fronted ornate, detailed temples. The scarlet stone had been carved into intricate patterns. Five large temples dominated the city, their enormous monolithic presences shadowing the lesser constructs at their feet. Weaving among the ancient buildings of this city were the roads, landing sites, power generators and artificial living spaces of the humans who'd settled here. From this height the man-made technology appeared like a virus that spread through the ornate and the ancient.

The 850 banked over the city and hovered over one of the temples. Spread over its flat roof was a circular landing pad. With pre-programmed trepidation the 850 touched down on the landing site and at that moment the communicator bleeped.

'The politico's left us a message,' Tulk announced. 'He wants all of us to leave the ship. He wants us back in twelve sub-stretches.'

'Right,' Terminus announced. 'I need a drink. Then I need a woman.'

Tulk and Terminus led the way, followed by the others with Sank trailing behind. They'd taken the stairs from the landing site into the heart of the Red Palace below, the most popular pleasure house on the planet. A Lung-man escorted them into the reception area.

The interior of the palace was grandiose: large soft-stone pillars supported the roofs and expensive drapes and curtains hung from various heights. The Lung-man led them into an enormous hall where many rich ganntas and geemas ate, drank and — much to the surprise of some of the crew — openly vullied. Overhead, soft light emanated from huge crystal ornaments, and hypnotic, rhythmic music drifted like an audio mist. The hall's floor rose into a series of half-moons where customers sat at tables surrounded by semicircular enclaves of soft, emerald material. This gave a sort of privacy, although as they ascended past these enclaves they caught glimpses of sexual activity occurring inside them. Each of these enclaves faced the space where the floor show would take place.

'What the hell is he?' Dich nodded to the Lung-man.

'The original inhabitant of this planet,' said Culp. 'At least, what the Skyfireans found when they first got here.' The creature was bipedal humanoid in form but featureless apart from two eyes. Porous skin moved at the creature breathed. 'They breathe through their skin. It's like their skin is their lungs and they take directly from the air. They don't eat either. All their nutrients come from the air.'

The crew watched as Lung-men waited on tables and fetched and carried. There were human staff here also. Babelite whores drifted through the hall, occasionally summoned by some gannta or geema. Terminus watched as a rich Skyfirean trader summoned one of the pale, toned women over to his enclave. The Babelite slid onto his aged wife's lap and the two women began kissing while the husband watched.

'I'm not drinking anything, eating anything, and I'm certainly not engaging in any lovemaking.' There was an edginess to Sank's voice.

'Apart from anything there's still the problem of ching.' Culp actually looked anxious. Was he so desperate for vulley that he was getting uptight? It fitted with his personality, Terminus razzled.

'Just sitting here is costing us more than we earn in a sub-cycle,' Terminus informed them.

'And how are we gonna pay for it?' asked Tulk. Terminus gave him a wicked grin accompanied by a knowing look. 'Oh, no! No, Terminus. I hope you're not thinking what I think you are.'

'Yep.'

'What? What's going on?' Dich asked.

'You'll find out.' Terminus winked at the lad. 'Anyway, I wonder what the politico wants here?'

'Obvious, isn't it?' said Culp. 'He wants to vulley or pick up some suc-tac for the long journey to this Thanatos place. We're to be out the way so he can have a couple of Babelites in his quarters on the ship.'

'And he thinks we won't mouth off when we get back?' said Sank. 'It's ganntas like us that stitch politicos up. We'll inform Decision Central of him. He's an arrogant drellock, the type that thinks we'll keep our mouths shut, thinks we're just drones.'

Terminus caught the eyes of a voluptuous Babelite who smiled, summoned two of her younger sisters, and approached the men.

'I'm going straight to Decision Central when we get back,' said Sank

'Unless he can give us some ching to keep our mouths shut,' Culp suggested. 'What do you think, Terminus, could we skag him?'

The men fell silent when the hostesses entered their enclave and got close to them. The gorgeous invaders were garbed with bright red blouses with low-cut tops and short, black skirts. Sheer stockings caressed their pale skin. One of the younger hostesses articulated her legs over Dich's lap and placed herself over his hips, her scarlet lips inches from his face. The boy turned bright red. Terminus smirked. The larger, voluptuous hostess leaned over Terminus and her wet tongue left a trail over his cheek.

'Will you inform the mistress of the house—' Terminus smiled at the whore. 'That we would like to play the Table of Consequence.'

Choose Life

The Labyrinth of Desire cost more than just vulleying in the alcove while the floorshow was on. The idea of doing it next to each other didn't appeal to any of the crew, so they opted for the Labyrinth. Money was no object as they didn't have any. Expenses incurred would be cleared on the Table of Consequence.

'I can't believe we're doing this, Terminus. You know what happens if we lose on the table.' Tulk was quietly furious.

'What happens?' Dich suddenly looked very nervous.

'They shove a spike up the coordinator's grog-box.' Culp laughed, drunk on wine.

Tulk explained. 'You are put on display until you can pay up. By display I mean you stand in a narrow type of glass case, your feet raised on a couple of bricks. Jutting up from the floor is a huge spike, sharp as a Starfire. If you fall asleep, you're impaled. If you get tired and collapse, you're impaled. You sneeze and you're drenting impaled. You stay there until either someone pays up for you — a friend or family member who's somehow found out that you're in this position — or you drop.'

'It'll only happen to Terminus if he loses at the Table of Consequence,' said Culp. He smirked.

The voluptuous hostess turned to them and gave them a naughty smile. 'I'm so sorry, gentlemen. It seems your friend has been away from us for far too long. The rules have changed. If whoever plays the game loses, you will *all* be put on display.'

'Oh.' Terminus turned to his crew. 'Sorry, lads.'

'Who chooses to play?' asked the hostess.

They all pointed at Terminus.

'You follow me,' she told Terminus. 'The rest of you will go through the archway on your left to the Labyrinth of Desire.'

'Good luck, Terminus,' Dich said. 'For all our sakes.'

'Relax, I'll see you in a few beats. I've played this before, never lost.' The crew of the 850 parted and Terminus wondered what the hell he'd just got them into.

The voluptuous lady linked arms with him and Terminus found himself in a corridor just off from the main hall. The lighting was soft and dim. In darkened corners he caught glimpses of people lovemaking, their groans muffled by the claustrophobic acoustics of the corridor. They entered the chamber where the game was played. Nervous-looking punters stood around the table as another hostess read the cards. Terminus wasn't looking at them, not yet. He was too busy admiring the half-black, half-white dress this card-dealing geema wore, and the wide split down the front that opened right down past her navel. Phys-tech colored half her face white and the other black.

He shook himself and started to pay attention to the setup here. The room was circular with an exit; a dark mouth that Terminus knew led to the display cases. Positioned before each of the five ornate pillars that supported the low ceiling stood muscular, shaven-headed swordsmen. Their blades were ornate, curved, rather like the wings of the Cloud Swords. These would be the men that would lead him to the display case if he lost. Thinking about it, he should have got Dich to play. The young gannta was clever and could have anticipated which side the ball would fall: life or death. A hostess offered him a drink; that was the last thing he needed. He had to stay sharp, no matter how tempting the snakki was. A large man to his left began protesting loudly that the game was rigged. Instantly two of the swordsmen led him away, articulating his hand behind his back to make him comply. He'd obviously just lost. Terminus took his place and the game began.

While the 850's crew waited in the antechamber of the Labyrinth of Desire, the Red Palace's auto-seduction system activated the mind-search hidden in the walls. Over the next few minutes, the crews' deepest desires and memories were extracted and processed. Then the mind-search began to transmit, implanting each crewmember with the sights, sounds, and smells of a succession of sexual acts suggested by his memories. Hostesses waiting inside the labyrinth were implanted with the simulated memories that had triggered the strongest response. The hostesses would try to replicate these acts in the privacy of the pleasure suites. They rarely failed.

The hostesses emerged and pulled the half-neuroed crew into the heart of the Labyrinth of Desire. Dich was first and found himself in a purple room with a large motherly lady enticing him onto the bed. This was not how he imagined himself losing his virginity. He backed out of the room, thankfully finding the door unlocked, and stood in the corridor breathing heavily.

Fuse was greeted by two very young women who pinned him to the floor and began biting him.

Sank entered a room lit by a single lamp. A large-breasted lady oiled herself and beckoned him to her. He stared, looked to the door, and then stood before her. He stripped, pocketing the Creator symbol he wore around his neck, and fornicated with abandon.

Culp entered a room where a heavily made up, obese woman waited. She knelt naked on a circular bed smiling at him. He stopped, looked at her, and approached. She ran a pudgy hand over his chest whilst cooing obscene promises. As her hand reached his groin he slapped it away.

'Get out,' he barked. She blinked, surprised. Surveillance trackers in the hall had read that this one was the most lusty of all the cargo ship crew. 'Get out you drenting vulleyer. Get away from me and don't touch me.'

She sprang from the bed and ran out of the room. He sat at the edge of the bed, shaking.

Tulk entered a room glowing with the light from flickering candles. A dark-skinned woman in virgin white lay supine on the bed waiting for him. She looked like his former wife. He stood at the end of the bed.

'What's your name?'

'What do you want it to be?'

'Don't give me this Babel drivel. You don't have to talk to me like that. Let's get one thing straight; nothing is gonna happen between us.' She sat up, looked almost disappointed.

'You'll still have to pay, just for being here.' He was surprised at how quickly she dropped the act.

'The fact that the people who run this planet expect you to sell your body in this way is an obscenity. You are a human being. A person with talent, personality, and emotions. You're not a piece of meat. This place angers the Creator of the universe and it has been prophesied that he will bring an end to Babel very soon. I'm telling you, you don't want to be here when that happens.'

'Are you a First Churcher? I've had them before and they're no different to anyone else in the universe.'

'I am and I don't see a whore, I see a person being used and traded. I'll pay extra if you tell me your name. Your real name.'

She sat at the end of the bed and lit a lung-polluting tobacco cylinder. 'It's Zooma.'

'Thank you. Did you know, Zooma, that you are the daughter of the Creator of the universe? The Creator loves and cherishes you and his heart breaks to see you used like this.'

She thought about his words for at least five beats. Then she replied.

'Go on.'

*

The Table of Consequence resembled a landscape of black and white. Terminus would choose either life (white) or death (black). If a white ball settled on a white area, three destiny cards would be drawn by the half-black, half-white game mistress. White cards with negative symbols — death, judgment, vengeance — meant that he'd lost. If Terminus chose the black death ball and it landed on a black area, then she would draw black cards. If these contained positive symbols — love, home, comfort — then he'd also lose.

The coordinator was on a roll. He chose death every time because he theorized that since the players' lives were at stake, they would avoid choosing death. The palace knew this, so Terminus razzled they weighted the tables against life-choosers.

Already, he'd chosen death and landed on black three times in a row. He'd been dealt negative symbols on black cards, only once having a positive symbol, a flowing stream indicating cleansing. He'd paid off half the debt so far. Tulk and Dich joined him at the table.

'How are we doing?' Tulk whispered.

'Nearly there. Two more throws and we're out of here.'

Terminus threw again. The black ball landed on the black area. The cards were pulled. Two vengeances and a lover; the woman on the card with arms spread wide in a golden field, beautifully painted.

'Did you have a nice time?' The coordinator smirked.

'I spent time with a beautiful lady who shares my skin color,' said Tulk. 'Let's leave out the details.'

'And what about you, Dich? Still a pizzdeen?'

'I'm choosing to save myself. I don't want to do it this way,' Dich replied.

'A noble sentiment.' Tulk patted him on the shoulder. 'This man can proudly say he'd been to Babel and come away with his dignity intact.'

'You goomah,' said Terminus. 'We're from Skyfire. Noble sentiments count for drent.'

33

Terminus picked up the small ball and began to throw. Tulk stopped him.

'You need to choose life this time.'

'Vulley. Death's the color. These drenters never expect someone to choose death.'

'Probability dictates that you're not going to get another black.'

'Probability, my nazbolt. You watch.' Terminus threw the black ball. It rattled over the landscape, bounced off a hill and rolled into a white zone. The three of them tensed but slowly the ball rolled back and obscured itself in a dark valley. There were gasps from around the table.

'Told you.' Terminus smiled cockily. 'We're out of here.'

'There's the cards first, you drellock.'

'The ball's the main thing, the cards don't mean anything.'

The bi-chrome hostess selected the cards. The first card showed the waterfall. A positive.

'We're still in with a chance.' Terminus gripped the sides of the table. Up until now it didn't seem real. She turned the next card. The smiling woman in the golden field, true love, made his guts tighten.

'Wait,' Terminus said to the hostess, one side of her face pitch black, the other bright white. 'What happens if we get another positive?'

'You do not win,' the smooth voice would have been calming had the situation been different. 'You play one more time and then, I'm afraid, you face the consequences.'

Tulk and Terminus took a glance at the guards, wondering if they could take them. No drenting way. The Babelites looked like they could cut them in half in the time it took to blink. Even if they managed to overcome them they'd have to get back to the ship. Once in the air the Cloud Swords would shoot them down. Then there was the politico. He'd have them deep-spaced for this.

She showed the card. Death stared out at them from his night-dark cloak.

'Yes. Yes!' Terminus felt elated.

'We have to choose life this time, Terminus.' Dich sounded like he was about to go neuro. 'If we don't, we've had it.' The others joined them just then. Fuse was covered in love bites.

'Vulley. Vulley and drent. The old black death, that's the one to bet on.'

'No, Terminus. *Choose life!*' Tulk hissed.

The coordinator took a black ball. It rolled around the side of the table until it landed in a white area. And remained there. He looked to the hostess and gulped. No cards would be read, no debts paid.

'Oh dear, said Terminus. 'We're vullied.'

The Gatekeeper's Sister

The guards sensed that the crew would try to make a quick escape. With lightning speed they unsheathed their swords, hooking the blades up between the legs of the space ganntas. Sharp steel threatened to castrate.

'Take the player to the mistress,' commanded the black and white woman. 'Take the others below and await her orders.'

The blade was removed from between Terminus's legs and he walked through the dark exit. His feet met a pair of stairs and he was led up through carpeted, wide stairwells until he faced a circular door. Alongside the door was a semi-circular desk where a hostess sat perched on a chair. She lifted an anachronistic communication device to her face and informed the mistress that the player had arrived. The door swung outwards and a figure in a dark robe beckoned him in. Terminus beheld the figure of a woman but she was devoid of any sexual desirability. On her head she wore a large head-dress in a 'T' shape with two strings of jewels dripping from the upper aspects. The guards didn't accompany him, which caused him to really worry.

The mistress's office was the complete reverse of the politico's, lit with lamps that cast sensuous light across the fantastic ornaments and ancient furniture of the room. There were tables made of wood from the Ocillius forests, drapes handmade by the river women of Kesh, and blood-red vases made from Martian clay.

The woman who had beckoned him in strode across the room to stand at the shoulder of the mistress, who sat behind a desk of ochre stone that was adorned with busts of beautiful women. All around were alcoves set into the walls and obscured by mirrors of black glass. He counted ten of them, all around six feet tall, as tall as a man.

Terminus swallowed hard and got a scan of his host. She was beautiful. Her flesh was deathly white and her hair, pinned back from her forehead, spilled down her back like a waterfall made from night itself. A simple black dress accentuated the lush curves of her body. Her eyes were the feature that held his gaze. The pupils were bright red, so vivid they almost glowed in the semi-darkness. He didn't think she could be human. No human had eyes like that. She had to be an alien, she just had to be. The mistress studied him curiously then gestured that he should sit in the wide soft chair before her.

The other woman read something from a tablet before announcing: 'Mistress, this crewman had incurred debts of over one thousand felida...'

'Out.' The mistress's voice was deep, silky yet resonating. The accountant-flunky hesitated. 'Out!' The mistress screeched at the flunky, a nerve-shredding sound that couldn't possibly have come from a human throat. The woman hurried out.

Now that they were alone, she regarded him, weighing up her options. At last she held out her hand, palm out, and gestured that he should do the same. Those red eyes studied the palm, scanning the flesh. Terminus wondered if she was looking for phys-tech.

'Listen, I made a massive drent-up. It wasn't the others' fault, it was mine. If you're gonna punish anyone, do it to me.' He put his hand down. 'However, if you wish to pursue this line of action I'd better warn you that we're on a diplomatic mission, and if anything interferes with that you might just find three hundred Skyfirean Sundogs blasting this city to drent.'

She continued to stare, unmoved. That hadn't worked then.

'Are you gonna stare at me all night or put a spike up my digest-spreader?'

'Interesting.' She spoke at last. Her thin lips almost smiled. 'I sense that your destiny-line is strong. However, your life-line is short. Very short.'

'What?'

She stood, a fluid movement, and passed *through* the desk. Terminus had to look again. This woman had just walked through a solid object. Her butt now rested against the desk, choosing to allow the ochre stone to bear the weight of her now solid buttocks. Terminus found himself staring at her legs: white, smooth, perfect and long. High black shoes accentuated her figure.

'Why should I kill you? You're practically already dead. I've no need to waste my time.'

He had to think about this; her words didn't quite make sense. 'Wait. You're telling me you're letting me go because you think I've not got long to live?'

'You are very slow, Simon.'

Simon? No one had called him that in a long time. Terminus had questions to ask but the desire to get out of here and back to the 850 overrode them.

'What about the others? Are you doing this 'cos I didn't get any vulley and they did?'

'They are as damned as you. They are free to carry on with their very short lives as are you. I pity you, in a way.' She sidled up to him and cradled his chin in her left hand. The fingers and palm, he felt, were very cold. 'But I'm feeling very generous today. If you weren't so damned then you'd be paying the same way as others.' She hung her hands around the back of his neck and hoisted herself over his hips. With supernatural grace her dress slid from her shoulders, his slids and leg-socks found themselves on the floor.

'You're no virgin, Terminus, but you may as well be. You will have never experienced anything like this before.'

Her tongue found its way into his mouth and it burned gloriously. She took him fully and he felt a second burning in his stomach and groin. It lingered on the edge of pain but was eclipsed when her teeth found his neck. Red hot needles injected fire into his veins. She wrenched his head back and locked onto his eyes with hers. Those red firebrands ignited his mind and fought for control of his will. She won instantly and he felt his whole body engulfed in flames. She stared deeper into his mind and burned through memories like the forest fires of Kesh burn the wooden cities of the hill tribes. Flames licked his body and she laughed. She was a red goddess, a devil in a hell of desire burning his flesh and she wanted more.

For an eternity, the ecstasy continued until finally his life-giving seed entered her. But death was manifested within her seductive body; Terminus sensed the life in his seed snuff out as it entered that foul domain. She parted and discarded him. Terminus found himself lying between her feet. She laughed and then strode cockily back to her desk.

'We were being watched you know.'

'Eh... what?'

The dark mirrors suddenly flashed into light. Ten pairs of eyes stared at his bare form. Naked men and women, each foot planted on hot bricks, splayed, their legs over a large metal spike with vicious barbs jutting out from the central spire.

'Drenting vulley!' he said.

She was laughing, laughing manically.

'You should see them when they fall, it's exquisite.' He wanted to get out and quickly before she changed her mind. She tapped on the glass of the fat gannta he'd seen being led out earlier. Without looking at him she spoke one last time. 'See you in hell, Terminus.' He took this as his cue to leave.

The Mistress Feeds

'You're a liar, Terminus. You're the sort of gannta who comes out with this drent in the snakki bars back on Skyfire to try and impress the geemas.' Tulk was furious that Terminus had got them into this, and really angry at Terminus's explanation of how he'd got them out of it.

'We're walking, ain't we?' He grinned as they exited out of the Red Palace and onto the roof, where the 850 waited on its circular pad, silhouetted against the setting sun.

'I can't believe that the mistress of the Red Palace dropped our debt by vulleying you. Did you see some of the men on this planet? All muscles, expensive clothes, and ching. Why would she want a skinny gannta like you? I just don't buy it.'

They approached the landing pad and saw little lights twinkling in the politico's hab-unit, where on regular deep space runs there would be a cargo module. They remembered that they'd been ordered to stay away from the ship for the next twelve sub-stretches and still had three to go. The crew lazed around by the edge of the roof and looked over the city as night descended. All bad feeling had been engulfed by relief when they realized they were free. Terminus and Tulk stood away from the others as they leaned over the balcony of the Red Palace. Tulk spoke quietly.

'You don't seem overjoyed to have just vullied one of the most beautiful women in the universe,' he said.

Terminus checked that the crew couldn't hear before he replied. 'It was intense, I tell you that. Look, Tulk, she did vulley me but that was almost an afterthought. She let us go because she said that we

41

had very short life-lines. She said I was dead — *we* were dead — so it seemed pointless to kill us.'

Tulk was silent. Silent far too long for Terminus's liking. Finally he spoke. 'They're a very superstitious people, these Babelites. They have some strange customs. Tell me, did she look at your palm?'

Terminus thought, uncoiling the memory. 'Yes, she did. She said my destiny-line was rich but my life-line was short. It's all drent. Like you said, they're all neuro here. Neuro, and vulley mad.'

'The sooner we're off this planet, the better.'

'She wasn't human,' said Terminus. 'She had red eyes. And the sex, it was... well... scary. I think she's driven me a bit neuro, messed up my thought box. I'll be all right once I'm out of here.'

'It's phys-tech,' said Tulk. 'Those eyes, the weird sex. Expensive phys-tech can do that. She's human like us. That's the thing about Babel. Like you said, it unhinges the thought box. It burns you.'

Terminus was taken aback. For one moment he thought that Tulk knew something but then quickly put it down to coincidence.

'What about your good lady back on Skyfire? You've voondied on her, man.'

'Huh,' Terminus snorted. 'She'll be back in Alpha Gropolis wearing out the sleep deck with a different gannta every night. I'm not gonna feel guilty 'cos I got lucky with a red-eyed alien.'

Movement from the ship caught their eye. From the politico's private chamber the door hissed open and a heavily robed fat gannta emerged surrounded by four Lung-men.

'So that's why he didn't want us around,' Tulk murmured.

'What? Who is that fat gannta?'

'He's a flesh trader.' Tulk spat. 'He organizes for off-world Babelites to be transported to other planets. A corrupt individual, nothing more than a slave trader.'

'Yeah, well wait till the info-casts hear about this. He'll be up to his neck in digest.'

*

In her personal boudoir the mistress sucked the life from the Agathon pizzdeen. His cries choked away as he fought for breath.

Finally, the death gasp came, and he lay under her, drained, pale, lifeless. After her barbed tongue had retracted back through her mouth, she rolled the corpse from the bed. As she lay there, resting her bloated body to begin digesting the pizzdeen's life blood, the mistress thought of her distant and starving sister.

Within the soul of the Earth man she'd tasted, the mistress had laid seeds of fire infected with her personal spoor. The time would soon come when her sister would feed on the Earth man. His blood would make her whole again and she would recognize the seeds in his soul as the invitation they were meant to be. 'Come sister,' they said. 'Now you are whole, come to Babel for there are many souls here to feed from.'

Agathos

'World at three hundred pulses under the void-ward side, Coordinator.'

'Dich,' snapped Terminus. 'You're the only one on this heap that still calls me Coordinator. You don't get promotion by calling *me* Coordinator. Save it for the politicos. And don't say 'void-ward' say 'left'. Now, let's see it.'

The crew were edgy. Although they could now laugh about the Babel experience, knowing they were going to a world populated by genuine aliens had put them on edge. A look at the nearest planet might offer a distraction. He ordered Tulk to phase the ship out of pulse so they could refuel the engines. Besides, he fancied a beaky look.

Deep space cargo shells, such as the 850, were powered by pulse drives. Billions of miniscule pulse pathfinders would burrow through the quantum foam until one of them discovered a wormhole that led somewhere a tiny distance closer to their destination. The ship teleported to that new location. The jump might only be measured in millimeters but the clever thing about pulse drives was they worked drenting quickly. The ship would teleport again and again. Trillions of times every second, only completing each pulse when the engines needed to rest, reorganize, and take a quick slurp from the fuel tank.

The pulse drives didn't need chemicals or antimatter for fuel. Not much, anyway. What they needed was the richness of divergent possibilities, the places where the universe splintered and spawned into multiple variants. That divergence was what the drives required to enrich the quantum foam that filled the universe. Star systems were rich refueling points; inhabited planets were the richest fuel source of all because people were the best thing for stirring up that quantum foam. And so, like chronic voyeurs, deep space ganntas regularly lurked near planets as their pulse drives refueled.

Terminus joined Dich at his post while his terminal magnified the pale sphere as each pulse brought them closer. The display showed the dark stains of continents on the planet's surface; across the shadowed northern hemisphere, millions of lights pricked the surface indicating vast populated areas. Seven moons attended the planet, themselves possessing an atmosphere and land masses. In the skies of the nearest moon, Terminus could see a storm boiling away in an angry dark green cloud. Tiny flashes dotted the tempest as it raged in the skies. The world and its moons were mothered by a large white sun.

'Tulk, where is this?'

'Just over two thousand pulses out from the Skyfirean boundary.'

'Then it's Agathos! The Holy Planet. Bunch of goomahs.' Terminus grinned. 'At least they aren't the sort to take a pop shot at us while we refuel.'

'Dich is looking a bit confused, Terminus,' Culp said, smirking. 'You'd better give him another planet lesson.'

'Well he's out of luck. I don't know much about it. According to the files they're a small community of religious fanatics with links to the First Church of Skyfire, but those populated areas down there don't look small. They look like cities.'

'I've refueled here before,' said Culp. 'They always send a communication. It's hilarious!'

Tulk joined Terminus at the magnifier. From the viewport the planet came into real-sight.

'My mat and pat were First Churchers,' Tulk said. 'It's true, they had connections with Agathos.'

'What do you know about this world?' Terminus asked Tulk. 'Enlighten us.'

'Well, my pater always spoke about this planet like it was a mythical place. They said that in the Great Decline on Earth the Creator told this bunch of Churchers to leave Earth before the end. They left and ended up here, stuck out in space, scraping out an existence.'

'That sounds like vulley to me!' Terminus spat. 'There were no craft built back then at the time of the Great Decline that had the capability to travel this far. Your ancestors only got to Skyfire by the skin of their teeth and that was five hundred cycles after the Great Decline, five hundred cycles after these ganntas are supposed to have left.'

'That's what my mat and pat said.'

'Listen, I know about history,' Terminus insisted. 'You have to, being an Earther, and I know that the technology to take them this far into the galaxy didn't *exist* back then. How did they get here? On the back of an angel? Did the Creator lift them from Earth to here in his big old palm?' The crew were laughing now, all except Tulk who was barely managing a grin. Sank was glaring at Terminus, clutching something hanging at his chest, some pendant.

Culp cockily joined in with the banter. 'Anyone ever met an Agathon?'

'Yeah, we had one on Docking Point Five.' Fuse spoke up from his post. 'Drifting about in his white dress. Looked like a goomah. Acted like one too. He blessed the crew for guiding his primitive vacuum tub into dock. We just laughed at him. Then Span went up behind him and lifted up his robes. He wasn't wearing any slids! Nearly caused a diplomatic incident. Not that a bunch of Agathon digest-kickers are a threat to our planet.'

'What are they going to do? Bless us into the void?' Terminus laughed. He stole another look at Sank who had turned his back on them.

'Transmission coming through!' Tulk barked. 'It's from Agathos.'

'This should be funny.' Terminus sprang back into his commander's chair. 'Put it on quad-sound. Let's all hear it.'

The speakers barked into life. 'Greetings, travelers. And a warm welcome from your friends on Agathos. Could you identify your craft?' The crew sniggered at the anachronistic language of the soft-voiced speaker.

Terminus replied. 'This is deep space cargo shell 850 on classified diplomatic mission. We will not be breaching your world-space. We will be passing out of range in... Tulk... how long till we're out of range?'

'Two stretches.'

'...in two days, Skyfire time.'

'Thank you, friend. Is there any way we can assist you?'

'Yeah, give us your women!' Culp snorted. No one laughed at him.

'Negative. We are passing through.'

'Could you inform us of the nature of your diplomatic mission?'

Terminus said under his breath but clear enough for the crew to hear: 'Beaky gannta, isn't he? Wanting to know our business.' He cracked a wicked grin and addressed the communicant once more. 'Yes. We are delivering a consignment of slids. Does anyone down on your planet need slids?' The ship rocked with laughter.

'What are slids, friend?'

'You know, slids, undergarments, clothing for the mid-torso to cover your old muc-sac and digest spreader. Or do you Agathons like to let it all hang out?' Terminus could hardly speak for laughing now. However, all laughter ceased as the Agathon spoke again. He totally ignored the coarse language and continued in his soft, even tones.

'I see that your trajectory takes you into the Thanatos system. We advise that you do not enter this system as it is an area of great peril. If you wish, you can land on Agathos where we can further advise you. Again, I say, do not enter the Thanatos system.'

This statement slammed the crew into utter silence; all laughter ceased.

Terminus looked to them then addressed the Agathon one final time. 'Listen to me, you vulley. Where we go is none of your drenting business. We are more than capable of self-defense. We have weapons on this ship that you backwater planets can't even imagine. These Thanatons do not, repeat, do not pose a threat to us, got it?' Tulk ended the communication. The white robe had put the fear of the Creator into the crew. They were jumpy before, and this had sent them into an unhealthy silence like frightened chick-chaks. He could see the worry in their faces now. Terminus thought he'd better try and reassure them.

'He was a white robe. A religious neuro-basher. You gonna get scared by a religious neuro-basher? No? No! Good.' Sank glanced at Terminus and shot him a look of both doubt and disdain.

Terminus handled the fire-blaster carefully. He'd seen the damage these things could do. There were six of them, one for each crew member including Terminus. Each weapon responded only to the phys-tech of the crew member to whom it had been assigned. Skyfireans were adapted shortly after birth; they'd grown up with it. Terminus had gone without phys-tech for most of his life, and still felt discomfort at the thought of the implants swimming around in his system. It wasn't natural.

Scanning the holo-comm he saw that the guns had been issued by Crank himself. Terminus noticed that the politico didn't have one. Whether this was oversight by the administration or the pervading philosophy that guns were for the lower classes he didn't know. He had charge of them in his quarters; the others didn't even know about them. Crank had told him the sidearms were to be issued only in an emergency.

Terminus hesitated before sliding the fire-blaster back into its sheath in the wall and then closing and locking the small door to the tiny armory.

Pizzdeen

The crew had fallen into their usual habits after two sub-cycles. The warning from the Holy Planet had been forgotten, or buried, once the ship had passed beyond the range of Agathos's sun. However, now that they were nearing Thanatos they were showing signs of becoming anxious again. Terminus could think of nothing to reassure them. Well, he could think of Tulk teleporting some alcohol to the 850 because they were almost out. That would do it, but they were long since out of range. The systems practically ran themselves as there was now nothing but empty space between the ship and its destination, a destination that still remained out of real-sight.

'So the politico said nothing else about the Thanatos system, then?' Culp thought Terminus was lying, he could tell.

'All he said was not to get off the ship once we got there.'

'Why?'

'I don't drenting know. Perhaps these Thanatons are flesh eaters? Perhaps they like to impregnate deep space technicians with their eggs so they hatch out in their noosh-pipes. He didn't say and I'm not going to ask him again because I want to keep my drenting job.'

'They always overreact on these missions,' said Fuse, the older technician who rarely spoke. 'Remember that time we were sent to the Fratus system? We were told the locals were hostile when they were just old colonists who'd gone a bit neuro. We ended up trading with them while the explo-team surveyed the plant life. We sold them all the holo-comms.'

'If this Thanatos place was a high security risk then they would have sent a military team,' Dich put in.

'Oh yeah, pizzdeen? And maybe they sent us because they thought we're expendable.' Culp almost snarled. The boy glared at him, largely because Culp had referred to him as a pizzdeen.

'If anything happens to us,' Fuse said, 'then how's the politico going to get back?'

'Perhaps he's a sacrificial offering.'

'Perhaps we're all sacrificial offerings.'

'Enough!' Terminus stood and silenced the crew.

'You!' He pointed at Culp. 'Apologize to the boy. And the rest of you, I don't want to hear any talk of death or dying, man-eating off-worlders or any other drent. We do our jobs and then go home, right?'

No one said a word; they didn't have to. Terminus scanned them; the fear in their eyes spoke volumes.

Again Tulk and Terminus had out-drunk the rest of the crew. Again Tulk, who had a knack of pulling info from Terminus, was grilling him. Terminus was drunk enough to talk about his encounter and had relayed the whole thing in great detail to the dark-skinned Martian.

'...so by the time they found me I was lying in my own digest, terrified to come out of the corner I'd jammed myself into. They sedated me and Crank eventually got me to talk about what happened. He filed a report. Some ganntas from the military interviewed me. No one believed it and ten cycles on I'm still talked about.'

Tulk sat back as Terminus's story ended. 'I don't see why no one believed you. It's a big universe. We haven't explored even one tenth of this galaxy. There must be other intelligent life out there. Not just Lung-men and Parous-people. You must have wondered what it was you saw. You must have speculated.'

Terminus inhaled deeply then began to talk. 'Well, I think it could have been a time war.'

'What, you razzle these ganntas travelled time? Time travel's impossible, everyone knows that. The scilitos say it.'

'The big white craft came out of nowhere. It just appeared. There must have been tremendous energy displaced, given the flashes of power from the place it materialized from...I think that was a time ship. The scilitos don't know everything.'

'And the boneships?'

'I'd like to say I thought they were some sort of strategic assessment ships, you know, someone scanning out our system for an invasion, but...'

'But what?'

'When the... being... appeared on the bridge, it was calling me. *Me.* Not using words. It was drawing me using feelings, thoughts. Part of me wanted to go with it. The rest of me was screaming out to just hide somewhere, get away from it. I knew it was going to harm me. Worse, it wanted to *defile* me. Drent, it was horrible. If that white ship hadn't have appeared like it did I would have gone with it. Gone vulley knows where. That ship saved me, those time-travelling ganntas saved my muc-sac.' He drunkenly raised the bottle to the time travelers and then continued to talk. 'The military must have known something about them because they asked me if I was a pizzdeen; if I'd ever been with a woman. I hadn't. I did my own research afterwards. It's not a question that inspires honesty in a gannta, but as far as I could determine, I was the only pizzdeen serving on the boundary stations at that time. I reckon that *thing* was attracted by my... I dunno... my innocence.'

'Do you think it came from another sort of time ship?'

'No. That's harder to explain, but I've been thinking about this. Ten cycles these thoughts have been swimming round my lobe-pool. It doesn't make sense but the same idea keeps coming back to me. The First Churchers reckon there's a place you go to after you die where there is no light. They call it hell. I call it another dimension. People who have nearly died claimed to have gone somewhere before being pulled back. Somewhere dark, somewhere strentner.' At that moment the drink tripped Terminus's logic. 'If that boneship came from anywhere it came from hell.'

'System ahead, Coordinator Terminus.' Terminus wished Dich would stop calling him that. 'It's the Thanatos system.'

Terminus joined the boy at his station.

'Hey, you can see it in the real-view.' Sank pointed to his display where darker shapes against the dark background were illuminated by a glowing gleam. The system comprised of thirteen worlds that hung like a necklace around a dark-green glowing sphere. Impossibly, the crew realized that this orb acted as a sun for these worlds. The planets were aligned exactly to form an oval pattern around this stellar mother. Planets in most systems held random patterns in the ecliptic plane around their star, but not this one.

The planets looked to Terminus as if they had been *placed* into orbit. And what vulleying technology could possibly do that? There weren't even any other stars nearby, as if its neighbors were shunning this dark Thanatos system.

Thanatos One

At first it appeared that light failed to reach the black surfaces of the thirteen worlds. The sun's dull light seemed to hardly touch them. Terminus gawped, still awed by the artificiality of the planetary orbits around the green star, or whatever the drent it was at the center of the Thanatos system.

If these Thanatons were highly sophisticated stellar engineers, that would explain why the politico was on his way here: to negotiate a contract. Great, thought Terminus, humanity's first contact with intelligent alien life and we get them to do some construction work.

The crew members were seat-harnessed for planet-fall. Terminus himself had taken his commander's seat and from there he directed the crew. He tried to instill some authority into his voice but, after half a cycle with this lot, that wasn't going to be possible: they knew him too well. As he issued his orders, they sounded so mundane: *steady on the thrust to the void side; more stability needed on the fire side.* (Terminus still had trouble using space-traveler terms for left and right sides and decided to abandon them now they actually had some flying to do).

They powered toward the near side of Thanatos One, a dark sphere choked by smudged cloud-bands of ochre and ash. As it eclipsed its sister planets and their weak sun, Terminus peered at the surface but couldn't see anything but the banded swirls of clouds.

'Forward scanner,' he barked at Culp. 'Get a surface reading.'

'I can't get one.'

'Why not?'

'Heavy cloud formation above planet's surface. I know, Terminus, our scanners are supposed to be able to see through rock but this cloud... it's... well... not natural.'

'Scan the drenting cloud, then. Is it toxic? Will it affect our instruments? Be quick, you veck, we've only got a few seconds till we hit it!'

Culp scanned for accurate readings from his equipment, screwing his eyes up. At last he rattled off the readings. 'Nothing toxic. I've got a chemical readout, nothing I see as being harmful. Systems advise that we can penetrate cloud.'

'Bit late if we couldn't,' Terminus said under his breath. 'Right, next time we be more careful and take a scan before planet-fall, clear?'

Tulk span round from his panel in disbelief. 'You were the one who told us to go into planet-fall, Terminus. Way before you told us to scan.'

Blushing slightly, Terminus said: 'Well, we'll know for next time then, won't we? Just get on with it.'

The 850 dropped into the thick clouds. The interior of the cab darkened. They could feel their body weight getting heavier as artificial gravity systems automatically shut down. From the feel of his bones, Terminus could always tell the difference between artificial and natural gravity. His muscles were working harder than they had in the artificial gravity and he judged this planet to be pretty close to Skyfire-normal. That was odd because this planet was less than half Skyfire's size.

'Ready to go to manual, Terminus?' Culp raised his eyebrows. 'Or are you going to vulley that up too?'

'Enough of your digest, tech. Just give me manual. Now this is the best part. Watch this piloting, you ganntas.' From each side of the seat the steering gears emerged with a soft whine. Terminus took hold of them and ordered the ship to go to manual.

Terminus was steering the ship when it broke free from the cloud. All the men gazed out of the window at their first scan upon the surface of Thanatos One. The 850 steadied and cruised above a pale beige sea where waves hissed and foamed. The dark clouds glowering down gave the place a feel of perpetual twilight, though there was far more illumination than made sense. It seemed that some light must, by some unique phenomenon, be able to pass through the thick cloud. Ahead they could see a row of saw-toothed ebony cliffs and what looked to be two spires jutting up from inland. Terminus powered forward but, before he could check his readings, a vast entity rose up before the ship, its face filling the viewports.

The sea creature's head must have been several dozen meters across. Its eyes were just slots in its lizard-like flesh but its multi-toothed mouth, which was open and roaring, was certainly no slit. A vast red tongue sat within a cave spiked by thousands of ultra-sharp jagged teeth. The ship was on the point of flying into its jaws. The crew lurched in their seats as Terminus violently banked the craft to avoid the beast. The monster actually tried to snap at the ship but 850 shot over the sea before it could catch them.

'What the drent was that?'

'It looked like a night-worm but bigger.'

Fuse turned in his seat. 'You should have got a shot at it, Terminus.'

'And cause an intergalactic incident, Fuse? It might be the planetary pet; some mascot or creature of religious significance. Don't want to casp off the locals before we've even landed. On the way back, maybe.'

Terminus deviated from the coordinates ever so slightly when they soared over the cliffs, a broken line between land and sea. The cliffs were not black, as he had first thought, but hewn of dark-blue stone that had been eaten away over the cycles by the waves that lashed them. The beige water smashed to foam against the steep rock sides.

'What's covering the land?' Dich said but no one paid him any attention.

As far as the eye could see dark shapes grew out of the ground as it rose and fell steeply. In the distance, mountain silhouettes made a foreboding backdrop. Terminus banked the craft over land and Dich quickly took a reading.

'It's covered by some sort of vegetation.'

'They're trees,' Terminus said. They were looking down upon a forest of leafless, twisted trees, either dead or out of season. 'They look like oak trees, oak trees without the leaves.' The real reason Terminus was deviating from their coordinates was so he could get a look at their destination; the only purpose-built structure within sight.

Constructed right on the very edge of the cliff, and looking like it should fall into the sea any minute, was an ancient-looking tower. Two thin spires emerged from the tower to fork the sky from an almost unbroken ring of stone. The ring acted like a high protective wall, the rough surface pitted with holes that on further scrutiny could be identified as tiny windows, mere gashes slashed into the stonework. At the sea's edge the circle was broken. The effect was intentional; a thin gap had been left in the wall that allowed the viewer to peer into the darkness behind, within the enclosing wall. From up here the wall looked like the ancient omega sign, the edges of the gap scrolling out seawards. The two spires grew from that darkness and had been carved from black stone, much darker than the wall stone, which had the same hue as the cliffs on which it sat. These two fingers stretched high to dominate the coastline and cast a shadow over the surrounding terrain. The structure appeared to be unoccupied.

Terminus couldn't deny how creepy this castle looked. The final features to complete the eeriness of this edifice were the ragged groups of lizard-birds that hovered around the tower like the black carrion eaters indigenous to Skyfire. They created an ever-shifting crown of malice encircling the spires.

Terminus re-engaged with his coordinates and set the 850 into landing status. Spotting a clearing in the trees within spitting distance of the castle, he brought the ship to the ground. The gloomy forest swallowed them as the crew finally touched upon the surface of Thanatos One.

'What the hell were you doing, Terminus? I told you to stay within the exact coordinates given, not circle the sacred palace of our prospective clients!' Terminus slouched before the politico and fixed him with an insolent stare. He'd already decided he was not going to let this gannta intimidate him. He knew as soon as he landed he'd be called into the office for a swing round by the muc-sac. As the politico ranted he reflected that Crank was much better at this than the passenger. 'Do you realize this could have caused an inter-system incident?'

'No, or I wouldn't have done it.'

'Who knows what they are going to think?'

'And just who are they?' Terminus adjusted his seating position and leaned forward, his body language demanding an answer. 'You haven't been very forthcoming with info on these off-worlders.' He was already in trouble so he figured he might as well get himself into more trouble by being direct with the politico.

The politico stared at him. Those dead eyes were certainly unnerving.

'Your insolence is noted, Terminus.'

'Yeah, but not much sir can do about it four thousand pulses away from Skyfire. What me and the crew need are some answers. What is this place? What are these negotiations? There have been a couple of incidents that have put the digest up us and I think we deserve answers, sir.'

Ignoring Terminus's questions, the politico stood. 'I'll be gone for twelve sub-stretches. Stay here and wait until my return.' He grabbed his compact storage bag, crossed the floor in one liquid movement, and went to the exit panel of his hab-unit. Without hesitation he pressed his palm into the reader. The two sections of the door hissed open and steps extended telescopically to meet the dirt of the ground. The dense forest beyond seemed to be impacted with impenetrable darkness. Terminus experienced a pleasurable shiver; a subtle fear coupled with a strange desire to explore the planet beyond the exit portal. He drew back as a blast of cold air from outside hit him. This was the politico's exit from the ship, not his, but Terminus wished it were. The atmosphere had a musty smell despite the nearness of the sea and it was cold; frostily cold. He drank in the strange air of this planet.

'I'll need you to close the door behind me,' the politico said. 'Do not set foot off this ship.' He clanked down the steps and briskly walked toward the towering castle walls a short distance away. Terminus shivered momentarily. It was a strange sight, this formally dressed man carrying his compact case among the dark trees, a forest scene straight from Terminus's childhood nightmares; a forest he was desperate to explore.

Symbols

He always had been a nozzle; his inquisitiveness had got him into trouble many times on Earth and on Skyfire. Terminus slouched in the soft chair of the politico's white room. He glugged from a bottle of high-grade snakki he'd found in his ration chiller and now shot through his memory files, the holographic images flickering before him. He'd broken through the encryptions with no trouble. Not only did it fulfill his curiosity but he was still casped that the politico hadn't given him any straight answers. That's why he was now raiding his comm system. Most of the gannta's files were indecipherable. They consisted of strange symbols and lithographs of what looked to be semi-mythical off-world creatures. There was a vast, six-headed man on one of them and, on another, several animal-human hybrids. The symbols looked ancient, like old lettering from pre-colony cycles. Several times Terminus saw symbols that he thought he recognized from his childhood on Earth. Soon he came to the pornography.

He checked the door to see that none of the others were likely to come in, and scored through the deluge of puc-tac. However, this was not the normal sort of virtual fare that was blasted across the sex channels. For a start this looked real, not virtual. Terminus couldn't tell for sure but the images he saw looked to be happening in real life. Most of it was beyond-the-norm pain infliction, which didn't excite Terminus, but he knew the politicos liked this sort of thing. They were always getting caught on Babel with their pants down. This politico was no different. Terminus was watching a series of short shots of both young women and men getting abused and humiliated in a darkened room. If this was real then Terminus had something on him. He could bribe the shankaa. Real-view was not actually illegal on Skyfire but it wouldn't do the veck's reputation any good if this were made public. Whoever had made the short must have paid the ganntas and geemas a lot of ching to put up with this sort of treatment, a *lot* of ching.

He continued nosing through the files. There was only one shot that was guarded, classified, so this must be the really dirty stuff.

Terminus might be a lowly space-gannta, but you got to learn a thing or two during the long stretches of sobriety in deep space, such as how to fool teleports, and how to hack encryption. He tunneled through the protection circuit and starting playing the short. It was a moving image of a girl lit by night-scan; he assumed this had taken place in a darkened room. Unseen voices whispered. Terminus angled the holo-speakers so that they were nearer to his head. He couldn't make out what they were whispering to the girl, but whatever it was sent her into hysterical fits of terror. This was real; this had happened.

'Sick veck,' he said to himself.

Although nothing was actually being done to the girl it still made for unpleasant viewing. Terminus couldn't watch any more, he slammed the exit button and took another slug of the snakki. Drent, he thought, he hadn't meant to do that. He'd only meant to frac a small amount of it. Perhaps the gannta wouldn't notice. The snakki thief re-sealed the lid and put the bottle back in the chiller. They had six sub-stretches to go until the politico came back and he didn't relish the return journey. Terminus looked through the nearest viewport at the trees outside. They looked creepy, but not actually dangerous. There was a difference, and Terminus was dying to stretch his legs.

*

The crew all shared the same feeling. They wanted to explore the dark woods beyond the limit of their world. An almost unnatural impulse to leave had come over them. The only ones who didn't want to go were Sank, who sat on his bunk clutching the symbol to his chest, and Fuse whose fear of disobeying orders overrode the desire to disembark. They talked about it but no one left; they knew that if the politico found out, they could be expelled from the Watch or even executed once they returned to Skyfire. Terminus was also possessed of this unnatural restlessness. Not only did he have to resist the urge to go out but he had to try to restrain his crew from leaving too.

Terminus addressed the crew. 'It's been fourteen sub-stretches and the politico still isn't back. I want to conduct a mini-search for him. Just a quick look to stretch our legs, you understand. Who's interested?' Apart from Sank and Fuse most of them jumped at the chance to get out. All except Culp.

Culp spoke out. 'The politico told you it was dangerous out there. That's what you said.'

'Well I've watched him walk into that wood without escort and unarmed! He's talking digest about it being dangerous here. Look, I'm not saying we go far. Just stretch our legs. We'll stay within sight of the ship at all times.'

'What if he comes back?' Tulk asked.

'If he comes back we'll say we were going to look for him. He won't believe it but it will look fine on the report,' Terminus said.

Tulk shrugged. 'It's your neck on the line. As for me, I'm dying to get off this rust container.' The crew agreed.

'Just one other thing.' Terminus raised his voice above their noise. 'I want you armed. I've got a fire-blaster for each crew member, phys-tech linked. We take them with us. But do not, unless in extreme danger, use them. Not that anything's going to happen to us in a drenting wood.'

Cage

As the upper half of their cabin splayed open like a mouth, the frozen atmosphere of Thanatos One hit the crew full in the face. The ship finalized its opening procedure allowing the exit ramp to slide into the earth of the forest floor. Fuse and Sank remained determined to stay ship-bound. Fuse now wanted to go, but never went anywhere without Sank who flatly refused to leave. Culp didn't want to be left behind and was scared to go. Terminus only shamed him to join the exploring party when he asked just what the drent Culp was scared of that couldn't be sorted by the phys-tech linked fire-blaster.

So Culp joined the huddle of ganntas readying themselves to go outside. As well as the fire-blasters, they also agreed to use wrist-comms so they could contact the ship and each other if they got split up. Terminus winced as he watched each man say his code word, detonating the steel tumor to spread out over the wrist.

'Three Circle D.' He felt a nauseous sensation as he spoke his codeword and the metal slid from his pores to cling to his skin.

'Drenting stupid, still using code words for phys-tech,' Culp spat. 'Someone could fake your voice pattern. It's been done before.'

'The government could fake your voice pattern.' Tulk said. 'In fact, the government could remote-activate all sorts of implants they've put into us. Now *that's* been done before.'

They tested the comms and checked the fire-blasters, each one keeping an eye on their alien surroundings. Tulk, Dich, Culp, and Terminus were dwarfed by 850's shadow, choosing to stay close to the rust-colored craft they'd called home for the last few sub-cycles.

Now they looked into the dark forest before them. Patches of frost graced the bare ground and dusted the flexed roots of the trees. The shafts of the tree trunks looked to be very old. Each one was twisted and gnarled. The leafless branches reached out like claws, claws belonging to some deformed creature which dripped ice and exuded a pall of silence; no animals could be heard among the roots and trunks. The bark was strangled by expired vines that bit into the wood, and the roots of the ancient trees arched from the ground like contorted limbs. Terminus took another scan of their environment; it looked as if everything had just died.

'Maybe staying on the ship might have been a good idea,' Tulk observed as if reading Terminus's mind.

'We won't go far, just a few meters and come back.'

'They say,' Dich began, 'that when we've been in an artificial environment for as long as we have, we develop a fear of the natural. That's why we're a bit ghosted by this place.'

'You think this looks natural?' Culp gestured with his arms. 'I ain't ever seen anything like this back on Skyfire.'

Terminus was the first to set foot into the ground under the trees. He was consumed by their shadow; the others followed. As he walked he began to talk. Talking made him feel better, as if verbal communication helped to dispel the fear.

'On Earth the atmosphere is very much like this for several sub-cycles. They call it winter.'

No one graced him with a reply. Each man clutched his gun as they put space between themselves and the safety of the ship. Occasionally one of them would turn back to see the comforting lights glowing in the navigation cabin. The darkness increased the further they went. Each tree looked like another, which heightened the crushing awareness that the forest was utterly silent. Getting lost here was not something they wanted to think about. As they progressed there were still no signs of animal life on this dead planet.

Culp stopped and began to urinate against a tree.

'What the drent are you doing?' Terminus hissed.

'What does it look like?

'You don't know what bacteria you could be bringing to this planet by taking a siphon.'

'Place is dead. My siphon's not gonna do anything if the place is dead.'

'Shut up!' Tulk raised his weapon and crouched low to the ground. Terminus admired his instincts and made a mental note to ask Tulk if he'd been in the military. All listened. They could detect a series of thumps to their left. Without a word Tulk sprinted to the source of the sound. The others followed. Racing through the wood brought them to a scar that cut through the forest. There appeared to be a path that wound through the trees. This rutted track had been used recently and was about to be used again by the sound of it. The thumping of something unknown, a land vehicle perhaps, assailed their ears.

'Get back!' Tulk had suddenly taken charge, something that Terminus wished the other man had done sub-cycles ago, as it would have saved him a lot of drent. They crouched in the trees, seeing but themselves unseen.

The source of the sound soon appeared to them. They strained to see and found what they saw hard to believe. A bizarre creature came into view. It was pale and possessed six thin legs; its bones were just about covered by semi-translucent skin. Thin legs ended in bony points that sank into the ground as it pulled itself forward. They could see that the middle pair of legs intersected two separate rib cages, the ribs originating from one long spine that ran its length. The eerie thumping sound came from its legs hitting the ground and churning up the dark earth. How it sensed direction was beyond Terminus because the beast had no head.

Behind it trailed a carriage with spiked, black metal wheels that tore up the earth as they turned. The creature pulled its burden through a series of hooked chains that sank deep into the creature's flesh and attached to the ribs. If the creature had a nervous system then this must have been agonizing, but it had no mouth from which to express its pain. On the carriage was a cage; each bar bulged out from the cage's base to meet at the top, a design not merely crude but almost organic in structure, and strangely familiar.

'Drenting vulley!' Terminus hissed when he saw what was being carried. Five naked human females whined and sobbed within the bars of their prison. The pale, frightened prisoners clung to each other for warmth. On the planets he'd visited, Terminus had met people with many body-shades and shapes, but Skyfireans tended to look similar: darker-skinned than him but lighter than Tulk, heavy-boned and with a slight slant to the eyes. These geemas in the cage all looked young and they looked Skyfirean.

Then he noticed what was sitting in front of the girls, with its back to them, a creature they all recognized. It held the end of some of the chains in its small, three-fingered hand and directed the headless animal by pulling left or right. It wore a simple cloth covering; two large eyes looked out from his bulbous head that had no mouth or nose. Its flesh, a dark red color, was mottled with thousands of tiny holes and its entire torso seemed to swell and decrease with every breath.

'A Lung-man!' Tulk exclaimed.

When the creature, the Lung-man, and its strange contraption had passed, the four humans appeared from the trees and stood in the track.

'Did you see that?' Culp was the first to break the silence. 'Naked women! Geemas with no clothes on. I'm beginning to like this planet.'

Tulk rebuked the operator before Terminus had a chance to. 'They were terrified geemas, Culp. You saw them and it ain't funny. They were stuffed in a cage and heading Creator knows where.'

'You drellock, next time keep your ration-hole shut,' Terminus added. He turned to Tulk. 'So where are they from? This ain't a human colony planet, so they're not from here. They looked Skyfirean.'

'Bred on Babel, no doubt, and brought here,' said Tulk. 'That explains the Lung-man. I bet those girls are snuff-slaves going to some rich gannta on this planet.'

'Probably going to the tower so the politico can get his jeebers off.' Culp was grinning, oblivious to his crewmates' distain. After what Terminus had seen on the politico's comm he was inclined to agree.

Terminus stopped Culp before he could say anything offensive. 'Let's not make any assumptions,' he said. 'We don't even know that those geemas are headed for the tower.'

'I reckon we should find out,' Tulk said. Terminus was about to argue but he saw a determination in the engineer's eyes that he was loathe to challenge. 'After all, the politico might be in danger. He's been gone for fifteen sub-stretches now. We should at least look.'

'You're right.' Terminus conceded. 'It would look bad on the report if we just left him here without even a quick scan to find out what was going on. Right; we should split up. Me and Dich follow the cage, see where it's going. Tulk and Culp see where it's come from. Use wrist-comms. Meet back here in no more than twenty beats.'

'Why don't we just go back?' asked Culp.

'We're just looking. We just have a nozzle then we go back. Don't worry; we're not in any danger.'

Culp and Tulk cautiously followed the track through the tall trees either side of them. The absence of sound was even more eerie than if they'd heard small creatures crunching over branches. Tulk was beginning to remember stories from his First Churcher parents about the Destroyer and his rise to power before the worlds began.

Culp moaned on, much to Tulk's annoyance. 'I never realized how much Terminus gets up my nozzle, but since we've got here he thinks he's drenting military. He should remember the politico's nothing more than fancy cargo.'

'I think Terminus has done a good job in difficult circumstances and I think you should shut your beak.' Tulk suddenly stopped dead in his tracks. He pointed ahead and up. 'What the vulley is that? There, through the trees.'

'Drent, it's huge,' Culp agreed when he looked up and saw the spacecraft.

At the base of the tower Terminus could see a huge arched door. The Lung-man stopped, dismounted, and manually opened the ancient wood of the portal. He steered the cage inside and the doors slammed closed behind them.

'Terminus!' the communicator buzzed into life shattering the silence of the trees.

'What?' It was Tulk.

'You've got to see this... artifact. It's utterly alien.'

'Is it like anything you've seen before?'

'No, but I think you've seen it before.'

Boneship

The artifact resembled the upturned skeleton of a huge fish, though devoid of scales or fins. It was a ship, nestling upon a stout oval plinth. Ribs struck up to the black sky, protruding from its pitted base which resembled a complex of jutting vertebrae. The nose was a single gaping nostril. At the rear of the ship, an indentation like a ball-socket was cold and lifeless now, but when in motion, he recalled, held the power source that propelled the craft. Terminus couldn't see anyone inside the ribcage and decided no one was on board.

Terminus stood with his eyes wide, very much comprehending what he was now looking at. Tulk asked him if this was what he'd seen all those years ago but all Terminus could do was nod in the affirmative. He could give no verbal reply so Tulk quickly explained to the others that this was the ship Terminus had seen at the time he was stationed on the boundary when he was just a boy.

Dich punctuated the silence. 'Why didn't we see it when we came in over the sea?'

'It must have come in when we were sitting around the deck of the 850 waiting for the politico.' Tulk replied.

'Why didn't we hear it? Why didn't it show up on our scanners?'

'Does this look like the sort of ship that shows up on our damn primitive scanners? Look at it. It doesn't even look like a spaceship!'

'What are we going to do?' Culp said. 'Are we going to... er... board it?'

'No,' Terminus snapped out of his shock. 'We're getting off this planet now. We leave. We get the politico and leave.'

'That means going to that old structure.' Tulk pointed out. 'He might be in the middle of talks. He might not want to leave.'

'Especially if he's got his muc-sac into one of those geemas,' Culp smirked.

'I'll stick this fire-blaster into his back and make him come, I don't care. We get him and get out.' As he moved away he muttered, 'I don't want to meet one of *them* again.'

They stood before the ancient wooden doors in the outer wall that led into the tower. The arched doorway was so huge that Terminus briefly wondered whether the 850 might even fit through. A quick check with the ship had confirmed that the politico hadn't returned. Terminus had come up with an idea: they were to tell whoever was in charge that they needed to speak with the politico. They would tell the politico that there was an urgent message for him on the ship. Once they'd got him back, they would take off and use the next half-cycle to convince the politico that they had acted in the interests of the system.

'We don't even know what these Thanatons look like. They might not be humanoid.' Dich was obviously beginning to feel uneasy.

'They must be bipedal or at least quadrupedal. Look, there are stairs leading up to that door.' Tulk strode purposefully up to it and examined it. 'No holo-sec system. No ident-pad. Nothing. There's not even a visitor trigger. Primitive. Utterly primitive.' Terminus overtook him and banged his fist on the door. The others looked impressed.

'I come from a low-tech planet, remember. This is how we get people's attention back on Earth.' Terminus banged another three times but no one was alerted by the sound.

'Right, we try the handle.' Terminus took the large, rusted metal ring and twisted it. Slowly the heavy door began to swing inwards exposing the gloom. It creaked on its hinges, which startled the crew.

'You know what I was saying about environmental displacement syndrome?' Dich dropped his voice to a whisper. 'Well, I'm really getting it now.'

'It's just old, that's all,' Terminus said. He clutched the fire-blaster tightly in his hand and moved into the gloom. Before them a flight of ancient stone steps wound its way up into the next level. The walls were cold and made of the same dark stone as the exterior. Either side of them a hall ran into darkness. The scene was not the least bit inviting. Terminus instinctively headed for the stairs as there was a light source illuminating the flags. The others followed. As he carefully navigated each step he was gripped by the paranoid thought that a cloaked figure would emerge from the shadows. Vulley diplomacy, Terminus would blast it into bits before it could move its jaws.

Above them, in the heights of the ceiling, something moved. A pale shape scurried into a corner. Instinctively all four pointed their guns at it.

'What the drent was that?' Culp was actually beginning to look scared now.

'Some creature,' Tulk theorized. 'Not so strange when you think about it. There are lizard-birds on the walls, and then there was that sea creature.'

'But,' Dich spoke, 'it...'

'It what?'

'It looked like a woman. I thought I saw arms and legs.'

'A geema that can crawl across the ceiling?' Culp smirked at him. 'You little pizzdeen, got vulley on the brain.'

'I told you not to call him that, you drellock!' said Terminus, his edginess coming through his voice in waves. 'Now shut up and let's get on with this.'

The staircase wound round and brought them into a wide hallway that followed the curvature of the wall. Archways opened up in the left hand wall and led to further chambers. To their right, rectangular openings cut into the wall allowed meager light to shine in from from the outside. Instinctively they went to these windows and leaned over a jutting sill to look out. The clouds had thinned a little and the green sun cast its light over the planet, reflecting in the sea. It reminded Terminus of Earth moonlight, so gloomy was this sun. Before them the twin spires, the black stalagmites, rose high above the dark tower and into the sky.

'This is the inner wall, then.' Dich pointed out.

The tower rose from a well of stygian darkness. Far below they could see a bridge leading from the inner wall, spanning the darkness, to the tower. They couldn't see a single living soul anywhere below or around the tower.

'Where is he, then?' Culp angled his mouth into a cynical sneer, challenging Terminus's authority again. Terminus was so preoccupied he barely noticed Culp's sarcasm.

'Right,' he barked to them as if he were in the military. 'Culp and Dich go that way; follow the hall round to the right. Me and Tulk'll go this way, left. Set your comms for ten signal-beats. If you haven't found him by then, meet back here.'

'Then what?'

'We leave, Culp. We leave him here and go home. Ten beats, no more.'

Whispered Delights

Night had fallen very quickly over Thanatos One. On the small deck of the 850, Sank and Fuse played Shift. Fuse idly tossed the holo-counters over the table. He noticed Sank glancing over his shoulder to the viewport. All he would see were trees. When Sank wasn't glancing outside he was looking at the beat-counter. They'd been gone for forty beats and showed no sign of returning.

'They aren't back yet.' He observed for the four-hundredth time. Fuse could tell that the old man was ghosted by this place. Terminus and the others had sounded edgy when they'd called in having found that ship, the one Terminus thought he'd first seen when he was sixteen. Mad. They were all mad. This place had driven them space-crazy. Fuse had seen it happen a dozen times before. Sub-cycles spent in space had dented their sanity and once they got off the ship they went temporarily neuro-basch.

'They still ain't back yet,' the older man grumbled again.

'Do you wanna go out there and look for them?'

'I ain't going out there. You know what those Churchers from Agathos said. Stay away, they said. Once Terminus finds the politico, we're off. I knew there was something funny about this place before we even landed.'

It was Fuse's turn to take a scan out of the viewport. He got up from the table and peered into the woods.

'Fuse, what is it? Are they on their way back?'

Fuse tilted his head, listening for something. He turned to the older man, frowning. Without a word he pressed his palm into the door release panel. The upper half of the deck slid open and the front of the ship extended out to become a telescopic ramp that sloped down to the ground. Freezing air prickled Sank's skin but it didn't seem to affect Fuse who appeared to be mesmerized by something unseen.

'Can't you hear it?' Fuse was already making his way down the ramp. A faint auditory distortion tickled Sank's ears. Out there in the woods, he could hear a voice, several voices; all female. They were singing. The pitch and tone of their song drifted through the forest. The harmony was wordless but rapturous joy reverberated through the air. Fuse turned to him.

'Aren't you coming?'

'Where?'

'To hear the geemas singing.'

'Somebody should stay with the ship.' The voices were drifting through the trees. The vocal nuance lifted and fell; lilting soft voices invited them into the trees. Fuse was already setting foot on the ground. His face said it all; enraptured by the sweet voices, he was going to them. Sank wanted to go too, wanted to see and touch those beautiful geemas that waited for them in the forest, but instinct rang alarm bells. This situation was too weird. An alien planet, humanoid singing; this situation was all wrong. And Fuse, Fuse looked like he was possessed. They had got inside his mind. The operative turned once with a daft smile on his face.

'Come on!' Fuse grinned, then disappeared into the darkness.

Sank slammed the exit panel control, the ramp slid back into the ship and the cabin's upper half clicked back into place, sealing him in. He took a fire-blaster and sat clutching it in his left hand. In his right he desperately fingered a metal pendant at his chest that hung from a chain. It was the symbol of a man with his arms outstretched in embrace. He held on to this with a tighter grip than he held onto the fire-blaster.

§

Thirty beats had passed before Fuse returned. He looked physically fine but stood just inside the trees. He was still wearing that inane grin.

'Sank,' he called out. 'Come into the forest and meet my new friends!'

Adlestrop

The cavernous rooms were silent; silent and dust-covered. After parting company with Culp and Dich, Terminus and Tulk had taken the third exit on the left and discovered a network of large rooms containing a museum of discarded relics. The first room was full of beautifully preserved cycle-counters, temporal indicators with round faces and two pointers that displayed the point in the micro-cycle. Terminus had explained that they were called clocks back on Earth.

They passed through a huge, dusty bedroom; the centerpiece of which was a soft, circular bed, large enough for all the crew to fit on comfortably. The abstract patterns woven into the cloth covering were still discernable. An arched window set into the wall overlooked the forest beyond the walls.

Tulk examined a mirror placed upon an intricately carved wooden table. A human sitting on the matching chair would find the mirror to be set at face height.

Terminus opened a large wardrobe and saw many items of clothing designed to be worn by females. He'd heard of these things: dresses. The rich colors of the many dresses dazzled his vision as he sifted through the soft material. The colors ran from blood scarlet to deep ruby; all shades of red.

'These people really are alien. This looks like a geema's bedroom but not one I've ever seen before.' Tulk was sniffing an odorous, bottled liquid.

'That's it, though,' said Terminus. 'I know this stuff is anachronistic but it's also very humanoid. The gannta I saw on the boundary station, the owners of that boneship, were not human. Not at all. I couldn't imagine it wearing a dress and using scent-spray.'

'So what's that boneship doing here? Just dropping in for a visit?'

'I don't know.' Terminus closed the cupboard door. 'Come on. We're supposed to be finding the politico, not nosing through some old geema's slids.'

The next door, a heavy wooden portal, led into a vast room that glowered in the darkness. All around them were shelves piled high with items that were distantly familiar to both men.

'I've seen these before.' Tulk fingered the items on the nearest shelf. He picked one up. 'They had one of these in the First Church my mat and pat went to.' Tulk marveled at the collected tomes and flicked through the one he held.

'They're called books. They contain words, but actually written on paper, a wood-derivative. Drent, this must be worth a lot of ching. Look, there are so many.'

'You've seen books before?' Tulk asked.

'In old buildings on Earth. They were all rotted, though. Left in the cities with everything else. These,' he handled the nearest one, a heavy black tome of yellowing parchment, 'are in superb condition. But they're so old.' He opened the book but the script drawn out on the pages was indecipherable. Terminus put it down and set off into the alleys of bookshelves. He walked in among the shelves and even climbed up to some of the higher levels, which reached up to the height of the stone ceiling. There was a table in the center of the room, which Tulk sat at while Terminus explored the shelf-maze. He had a right to fulfill his curiosity, Tulk thought, but not if he took too long about it.

'Drenting vulley!' he heard Terminus exclaim from within the books. Tulk stood and raised his fire-blaster. From the shadows Terminus emerged carrying armfuls of books, his brow furrowed. They thumped onto the table as he put them down sending dust into the air.

'There's a whole load of books written in Earther. Look, these have come from Earth. Not just my planet but the Northern Hemisphere! I don't believe it!'

'Terminus, we haven't got time to go through these. We've got a job to do.'

'Just two beats, that's all I need. Two beats.'

'Right. I'll take a look around and I'll be back here in two beats, clear?'

'Clear.'

Tulk found other rooms also filled with ancient artifacts that were of little interest to him. He found his way back to the hall and took the wide stairs at the back that led down into a stygian darkness. He'd seen enough. Tulk was determined to go back, get Terminus (he could take his damn books with him if he wanted) and get out of here. Faint screams made him stop. From the nearest opening he could hear sounds of distress. Hairs stood up in the back of his neck at the harrowing intensity of anguish. Tulk leaned over the edge of the opening. The sight of the black spires rising from the darkness had begun to look familiar, but now he saw, crossing the single bridge, the tiny shape of the beast-pulled cage that had passed them in the forest. The cage was crossing to the tower. From his position he saw the thin gap of the tower doors open, spilling a faint illumination onto the bridge. Even from this distance he could see the terrified figures within, thrashing in panic and arms outstretched through the bars of the cage. The tower doors swallowed the cage and the geemas were gone.

Right, that was it, he'd seen enough. He was going to fetch Terminus and they were getting out of here.

*

When Tulk returned, Terminus was standing over a book, shaking his head in disbelief.

Tulk drew up next to him. 'We're leaving,' he said.

'I don't believe it.' Terminus ignored him. 'I don't drenting believe it at all!'

Tulk was becoming impatient. 'Right, tell me what's up and then we're getting out of here.'

So Terminus explained. 'When I grew up on Earth. I lived with my pat on the site of an old pre-Decline settlement. It was tiny. Most people in our district had never heard of it, certainly no one outside of Sol knew it existed. It was called Adlestrop. I mean, this place was a dot on the planet, insignificant. So here I am, four thousand pulses from Skyfire, twenty thousand from Earth and look, I'm reading about Adlestrop. It says where it is, how old it is and even mentions the tiny, ancient meeting building that's still standing at the center of it. Twenty thousand pulses away and I find an ancient book on my home settlement. Who the drenting hell are these Thanatons? Or, to get to the beak of it, *what* are they?'

From Flesh to Dust

At the top of the staircase, leading into the large hallway, Culp and Dich had taken a right-hand turn. Large gaping arched doorways led into a maze of chambers here too. There were other ancient sleeping quarters, and what looked to be a dining area, where a long polished table was littered with skillfully made eating handles. It was a labyrinth of architectural anomalies and was, as were the chambers Tulk and Terminus were investigating, devoid of all life.

'This is gonna take more than ten beats to nozzle through.' Culp stopped at an intersecting corridor of cold stone. 'I razzle we split up.'

'What? Go around on our own?' Dich stared in disbelief.

'Yes, on your own you digest, sliddy pizzdeen. Don't tell me you're scared?'

'Well, it's not exactly normal, this place. There could be anything here. Sonic traps, neuro-scramblers.'

'It's a relic. A zero-tech environment. They haven't even got a door-pass.'

'There's something else!' Dich was beginning to panic. 'There's something wrong with this place, an atmosphere. I think we're being watched.'

'Drent!' Culp stormed off into the nearest intersection. 'See you back here in five.'

He stomped down the corridor. At its end he passed through an aperture and found himself in a circular high-ceilinged chamber that was covered in a thin coating of dust. In the center sat a plinth, a man-sized stone oval that rose seamlessly from the flagstones to dominate the middle of the room. Culp shone his fire-blaster's flashlight at it but there was already enough natural light coming from an octagonal window set high in the ceiling.

The stone was presented so prominently that he speculated it was some kind of altar. At the head and foot of the stone hung clasps of some kind. He fitted his hand into the right one and a perverse thrill traveled his nerves. A strange thought took him; he would like to be secured in those cuffs. He would enjoy the feeling of it biting into his wrist. Disturbed, but still excited by the thought, he drew his hand out. He backed away from the altar and took a look at the walls where, under the dust, he saw metal devices secured to the walls.

'Drenting vulley!' Bolted to the stone wall was a many-bladed machine with straps to secure a humanoid inside.

Culp walked over for a closer nozzle. The blades were on hinges that articulated into place once the person had been secured. Clockwork timers would move the hundreds of sharp blades in a movement that would cut the entire body from hands to feet. While experiencing the caress of the blades, the victim would also endure a large curved blade up the digest-spreader. Very uncomfortable. Culp touched one of the blades, expecting time and oxidization to have taken its effect, but found it to be razor sharp. Blood dripped from his index finger into the dust.

He turned suddenly. Behind him he thought he'd heard a voice. A giggle as if a child had found something amusing. When he spun round he saw nothing.

'Drenting place, giving me the digests!'

Although Culp found the chamber unnerving he was in no mood to leave. The perverse thrill of being here overrode any residual fear. It was as if his mind wanted to leave but his flesh wanted to stay. The shiver of excitement he'd felt when trying on the clasp hadn't left him.

He studied other instruments. There was one where a humanoid could be placed in a crouching position and a series of fixed, curved needles would have slid in between the person's vertebra from behind. Other blades pierced in between the ribs and one large spike would penetrate the belly button. He smiled. He imagined having those needles penetrate his own spine and a warm feeling erupted in his stomach.

'virrrr.........' He turned again at hearing a woman's voice. There was definitely someone in here. He could hear a whisper. *'......giiiiiinnnn.........'*

Culp peered into the gloom. Next to a cage that could encase a human body and move it into agonizing positions, he thought he saw the dust motes swirl.

'viiiirrrr.........giiiinnn.' The whisper was all around him; he couldn't determine its source. *'tttoyyysss...... myyyy tttoooyyysss....'*

My toys? Is that what it had just said?

'Show yourself, stop drenting playing games!' He shouted into the darkness.

It repeated the last word of his sentence. *'.........gggaaammeeessss.........III liked ppplllaaayyinggg gamesss herree.........'*

Culp knew that any sane man would have run by now but his sanity was being beaten. He could feel the voice all around him. He wanted to stay here. He wanted to know the speaker. He wanted her to touch him. He dropped the fire-blaster and let it clatter to the floor.

'Cuulllppp.........you're a viiiirginnn, aaarrntt you?'

He didn't need to ask how she knew his name or that he was a pizzdeen. He was feeling light-headed now, as if each time she spoke, her influence over him increased. He didn't want to resist. He was enjoying it.

'I am. I'm a pizzdeen, a virgin. What do you want from me?'

After seconds it answered.

'It's beeeenn such a llllong time, Culp.........I'mm ssssstarvinggg, wasted to notthhhing. Nnnottt felt the wwwarrmth of a mmman for gggenerations. Lllet me ffeel you, Culp. Let me bathe in your soulll..........'

'What do you want me to do?'

'.........undressss.........'

Culp knew what he had to do then. He had to offer himself to her. Let her feed from him. She was going to defile him but he desired that defilement. There would be pain but at least he would have served her, he would have fulfilled his destiny. As he took his clothes off, he reflected that all his life he had regretted never laying with a woman but had pretended to his acquaintances that he had. He was such a space-gannta that no one had ever worked out that he hadn't. So much time spent on so many ships regretting, and all that wasted, because his destiny had always been to arrive at this time and place, to offer himself as a pizzdeen for her to defile. He was about to endure agony and terror for her, for her touch.

It was cold in this room. Culp knew what she needed so took one of the razor sharp blades from the flesh-caresser. It snapped from the device easily enough. He lay down upon the altar and waited for her touch.

The invisible creature disturbed the dust as it stalked toward him. Her icy presence sent his heart rate soaring. Good. The blood would pump through his system faster, helping her to feed. As he was about to cut he was aware for the first time of the existence of a soul, *his* soul. It was at the center of his being screaming soundlessly. She would damn him into darkness forever but he had to serve. She was crouching over him now, invisible, waiting. Without hesitation, he slowly slashed deeply into his wrists lengthways and cut into his hairless belly and chest. His blood flowed into her veins.

Tendrils grew into thin air above him. They looked as if they were sprouting from *his* body at first. Red rapidly shooting leafless vines snaked through the air until they joined into a basic human shape, its veins suspended in the air. She lay over him, just a handbreadth away, an obscene parody of a lover's embrace. It was like looking at an anatomical diagram of the human circulatory system without bones, muscles, or flesh. Capillaries were forming from her veins. As she drank from his soul, a spine took shape, each vertebra reverse-melting into existence. Moments later, ribs sprouted from the spine to form a cage for the organs that were already appearing.

For him the agony was spiritual in nature, deep and penetrating. She would soon be complete and she would be free to condemn him to the hell in her heart. The last thing he saw before the pitiless void closed over him was her dark and terrible eyes growing into her sockets.

Gatekeeper

'So where the drent are they?'

Tulk wasn't amused. He and Terminus had made it back to the rendezvous point at the top of the stairs. So where were Culp and Dich?

Tulk tried them on the wrist-comm but got only a dead line. Culp had told him that these wrist-comm implants weren't state of the art and bound to malfunction in strange environments. What the drent did Culp know, anyway?

Terminus was shifting nervously from one foot to the other. Tulk noticed his body language was different since he'd read those books. When they'd first entered this place he'd been alert and twitchy. Now something was occupying his mind.

'What is it, Terminus? Don't give me vulley answers, I wanna know what you're thinking.'

'Damn it, Tulk, I wanna know what's going on in this place. I need to see what's in the black tower.'

'Because of what you saw in that book? Terminus, this place isn't good. We need to get out. It's been five sub-stretches since the politico should've come back. That's nineteen sub-stretches he's been gone. This is an alien world, we should get out of here.'

'What about Culp and Dich?'

'They've probably gone back already. You know what Culp's like, he wouldn't wait for us.'

Something had taken Terminus's attention. He was looking over the sill to the bridge down below. Tulk joined Terminus at the window and followed his gaze to the bridge. A tiny gray figure was crossing the bridge to the dark tower, flanked by six robed figures. All of them were moving majestically, inhumanly. Tulk saw that his companion's face was frozen.

'I know it's a long way off but, are they....?'

'Yes. Look at the way they walk. They don't walk like men. They are... what I saw... all those years ago.'

'Then that's it, we're leaving.'

'What about...?'

Tulk turned to the wide space of the hall. He cupped his hands to his mouth and yelled at the top of his voice the names of the two missing crew men. There came no response. Tulk shrugged and moved off. Terminus followed him to the bottom of the stairs. The dark-skinned man was heading at speed to the still-open door when Terminus stopped dead in his tracks.

'I'm not going,' said Terminus.

Tulk stopped on hearing Terminus and, when his companion's words registered, wanted to scream.

'I've got to find out where they've taken the politico,' said Terminus. That's my official reason. Crank head-hunted me to keep a scan on the politico, report back on the out-worlders. He'll swing me round by the muc-sac if I don't do my duty.'

'When have you ever cared about duty? So what's your unofficial reason?'

'I want to know what they *are*. I can't just leave it. Curiosity'll drive me mad. I'll live my life out never knowing what it was I'd met all those years ago.'

'Curiosity will drenting kill you.' Tulk took something from the side pocket of his trousers. He handed it to Terminus. It was a flat silver representation of a man with a big head and outstretched arms with wide, abducted fingers. 'My mother gave it to me. It's the symbol of the First Church. It's supposed to represent the Creator, all his goodness, you know all that digest. She gave it to me and said to carry it in dark places. I think she was meaning space but, drent, this is a dark place, and *you're* going into the heart of it.'

'Thanks, Tulk. I'll look after it.'

'You'll bring it back to me when you get back to 850 in one sub-stretch.'

While Tulk headed for the door, Terminus followed the passage into the dark.

Her light footsteps made a trail in the dust. Naked, she moved through her domain to find that it had been violated by the presence of mortal men. From the temple antechambers she surveyed the wide passageway that ran through her habitat. Her bare feet treading on the flagstones, she took a cursory glance down in to the abyss and the bridge that spanned it. Small lights twinkled from tiny windows in the Spires of the Thirteen; they had returned from the outer dark for some purpose or another. She neither knew nor cared what that purpose had been. The memories sucked from the soul of the trespasser held no interest for her. He had been obsessed by females of his realm but had never lain with one. Oh, and he came from somewhere called Skyfire, some pitiful colony inhabited by his parasitic, wormlike race. His blood, flesh, and soul had given her substance after a millennia starving to nothing but spirit. Visitors to the Gate were infrequent and those who did come didn't last long.

As she slithered into her boudoir she was disgusted to note that other men had been fulfilling their curiosity in here, displacing her possessions; centuries-old perfume, ornaments. One curious wretch had even fondled her dresses. These bastards of Earth would suffer for this. Forgetting her upset for the moment, she admired her new flesh in the dusty full-length mirror and beheld her pale, slim beauty. Her tight white buttocks; her shapely, yet not over-endowed, bosom, and the night-dark hair that fell to her coccyx. Set in her symmetrical face, those high cheekbones ensured that she was still beautiful, and the wolf-red eyes still marked her as a Gatekeeper.

She heard a yell; one of the other men calling for his companion. They would leave soon. Never mind, they would not get far. The young companion, however — another virgin, what luck! — would be seduced and destroyed.

Dich was running through a dark chamber with a huge stone pole growing from its center, when he heard Tulk shouting. He dashed into the passage, through what looked like a torture room with a heap of dust resting on an oval plinth, and scrambled to the head of the stairs. He was expecting to see Tulk and Terminus but instead faced a strange woman.

Firstly, he was taken in by her sheer beauty. Her hair was natural and shone in the meager light. It framed her pale face and, as she smiled at him, her high cheekbones radiated warmth. She was human, he thought at first, and then spotted her bright red eyes which perfectly matched her floor-length scarlet dress. No one on Skyfire, no human, had red eyes. They could have been phys-tech, he supposed, expensive implants but he knew this was not true. The plunging neckline drew his eyes down to her cleavage and out to her pale arms, her perfect skin.

'You must be Dich.' She spoke in Earther, which Dich could understand quite well. He replied in the same language.

'Have you seen my crew? A pale gannta, sorry, man, and another one with dark skin?'

'No,' she breathed, 'but I have found you. Come.' She held out her hand and he took it. There was something in her voice that was reacting with the chemicals in his brain, releasing endorphins. He wondered if she was some sophisticated neuro-scrambler hallucination but when he took her hand he realized she was real enough.

'Are you a Thanaton? I didn't realize your species were humanoid. We weren't briefed. What's your name?'

'Centuries have passed, I don't recall. I'm the Gatekeeper. That's what I am.'

'So this wall around the tower is called the Gate? Very interesting.'

'Be silent, Dich, until we get to my boudoir. Then you will make all the noise you can.' Her voice; the tones were mesmerizing him. Was she actually going to take him into her bedroom and floor him? Was that what she'd just said? She pushed open the door of the dusty bedroom and instructed him to disrobe. He met her fiery eyes and the impulse to obey overrode any shyness he might have harbored about appearing naked before her. He discarded his clothes in seconds and was aware of a darkness in his mind, an overwhelming darkness that made him want to run, flee screaming with his nazbolt between his legs. She wouldn't let him. Escaping her was not an option.

She ordered him onto the bed and so he lay on his back. She allowed him one final rush of pleasure as she crawled on top of him like a parasite. She grabbed his face and pulled his head to look into those dreadful eyes. He knew his fate.

'Please, I have a life ahead of me. I wanted to be a pilot, have a geema, little ones, I...'

'Worthless dreams, my virgin boy,' she cooed lovingly. 'Why lay with some dull mortal wife when you have the divine blessing of my touch, my kiss. I can do more than any flesh-made woman ever could. I will drink from your soul, damn you to my hell. Your young life can give me substance. Now, isn't that so much purer and desirable than wasting your seed in some whore to spawn human bastards?'

'No...' Tears were springing from his eyes.

'No more foolish talk. I will begin your blissful agony.'

In both of her wrists three-inch slits opened like mouths. From these slid sectioned, organic lengths which resembled transparent millipedes. They encircled the boy's wrists and snaked up his arms. Her mouth opened and from her throat, another transparent appendage tightened about his neck. Two more slid out of each of her calves and wrapped themselves around his legs. Needle-like teeth from between the sections of the appendages sprang out and pierced the flesh. The tubes instantly filled with the red of Dich's lifeblood and he was siphoned into her body. A final snake oozed from her vagina and slid into his anus to rupture the bowel and drink deep from the well of blood that resided in the intestines. Dich would have screamed if he could. He felt his whole being drawn into the hell of eternal torment that waited for him inside her. Her red eyes burned as she waited to rape his soul.

The boy's carcass was reduced to ash. New dust joined the ancient dust on the floor. The Gatekeeper slid from the bed and continued the hunt.

Forest Keepers

Fuse was moving too fast through the gnarled trunks of the alien trees for Sank to follow. He became a flitting white shape a few paces ahead. Hopping over roots or stooping under branches, Sank navigated through the forest. He followed the sound of the geemas singing, which was getting closer. Ahead, he could see a clearing and a purpose-built structure, which he decided must be their destination. He checked the fire-blaster was powered up before he entered the clearing because his instincts still screamed danger. But he couldn't retreat to the 850 because he couldn't let Fuse go on alone; the way he was acting it seemed like someone had used a neuro-scrambler on him. If he found anyone had done that to his friend, they would get the sharp end of his gun all right.

Sank broke from the darkness of the trees and into the clearing, just in time to see Fuse disappear into the structure dominating the center of the open space. The building was very old and built to an arched design. Its dilapidated roof was sagging, and the rotten wooden door at the front hung precariously on rusted hinges. Sank crouched and aimed the gun. To his right he'd seen a pale shape move through the forest, some animal or creature. He scanned the twisted trees but could see nothing. Whatever it was had moved fast and gone. He focused his attention back to the black, stone structure. It reminded him of some of the First Churcher buildings back on Skyfire. His grandpat used to take him to one every seven-stretch when he was a child. He reached inside his jacket and fumbled the silver pendant of the Creator that his grandpat had given him. He often did this when he was nervous, which was a lot of the time.

Sank crossed the few meters to the building's door and stopped at the lip of the wide, dark mouth.

'Come in, Sank. Meet my friends!' Fuse called out brightly to him.

Sank could see him standing a few meters past the door in a hall. The singing was reaching a new crescendo, providing a choral soundtrack for the entrance of the new devotee. Sank stepped into the hall.

Musty air hit his nostrils. He peered into the semi-darkness. Five beautiful girls were standing around an elevated oval plinth. They wore simple, white dresses and their flesh was deathly pale. Thin red lips smirked from pallid faces; hair trailed down to their waists in night-dark waves. They were beautiful and, after sub-cycles in space devoid of women, Sank stared open-mouthed. Flanking the five were twelve of what had once been equally beautiful women. These women retained some of their former features but to Sank's horror he observed that parts of their flesh had corrupted. The nearest to him had one half of a beautiful face remaining, the other half had rotted away; great chunks of flesh were missing from her body, fallen, as if some fungal disease had eaten her away. Surrounding them, the outer circle of the singers consisted of the most horrifically decayed cadavers that Sank had ever laid eyes on. These geemas belonged in the grave. The shuffling creatures were no more than bags of bones covered by rotting epidermis. Surely they must be dead, he thought, but they were still animated despite their exposed ribs and crumbling joints. They gestured that Sank should come among them and feel their touch.

'Come on in!' Fuse smiled again from his place at the center of this cacophony of beauty and carnage.

'Yes,' one of the beautiful girls incanted. 'Come to us. Does our singing please you? We can sing for you, my love. We are the Forest Keepers and we know many songs.'

Sank felt light-headed. Her voice, her voice was dulling his senses. He could feel the Creator symbol burning into his chest. He looked up. Fuse was taking his clothes off! In seconds he was naked and lying down on the plinth. The women were crouching over him. He was smiling blissfully. Alarm klaxons were screaming out in Sank's mind. This was wrong, all wrong. Fuse was in danger; he shouldn't be smiling. These geemas meant him harm!

Sank was right about that. He saw something protrude from their mouths, a snake-like tongue or extension to the esophagus that slid from their lips and curled around Fuse's neck and limbs. Still, he lay there enraptured. Small teeth emerged from the transparent tongues and immediately the see-through tubes turned red, filled with his friend's blood. Fuse began to scream an unholy, desperate scream. The creatures nearest to him were shuffling toward him, arms outstretched for him.

Sank's attention was drawn away momentarily from Fuse's suffering as the air filled with whispers. All around him he could hear whispers calling his name.

'Ssssankkkk......... joinnnnn uusssss.........' He raised his fire-blaster. '......we cccannnn bee bbeautifull againnn......... helpp ussss.........'

The living-dead monstrosities were bearing down on him. He fired at the enclosing party, spitting bolts of flame from the fire-blaster's nozzle. To his dismay, the bolts passed right through them, as if they were holograms, and hit the far walls. He turned to run but his path was blocked by an alien horror filling the doorway. Noxious vapors drifting upwards from the creature's maggot-colored body that seemed, absurdly, to be made of two ribcages crudely sewn together. The beast didn't have a skin. Instead, the white muscles clung to exposed bones on each of its six legs that rose above its spine and ended in feet which exactly resembled human hands. On each of the five finger-toes of these hand-feet, five cracked, black fingernails bit into the earth. Sank's gaze met two wide eyes set into triangular sockets that drew down to meet its mouth. The creature's head, which hung between its forelegs, resembled an organic letter V with facial features slotted into it. With a twitch of the muscles clinging to cheekbones and jaw, its mouth opened, an elongated narrow maw filled with small razor-sharp teeth. The ugly veck wasn't going to let him pass.

Sank aimed and blasted its head wide open. Gray and black spew erupted from the smashed skull. It fell sideways and the old man leapt over its steaming corpse only to find a whole horde of them waiting outside. He'd used a fire-blaster before on many creatures and on many worlds. Usually they ran away from the noise the weapon made. Not this lot of vulleys. They closed in on him and he fired again, shooting limbs from under them and sending bolts into their ribcages. The women from the temple stood in the doorway to watch. He fired and fired until the blaster was nearly out of power. The creatures stood over their fallen comrades, their expressions impassive.

'Why don't you come inside, Sank?' one of the women suggested again, sweetly.

Mentally, he tried to block out the voice. He didn't want to hear it and certainly did not want to enter into a dialog with her or her kind.

The woman shimmied toward him, still smiling. Her red eyes couldn't disguise her hunger and yet his instincts were overridden; he wanted her embrace, to offer his soul to her.

'It doesn't have to be painful. I can make it exceptionally pleasurable for you. You're old. How long has it been since you've had a woman's caress?' She was near enough to touch him now. Her hand came up and stroked his face. The Creator symbol felt like it was on fire at his chest. 'And what a way to expire. The plaguewraiths will never let you pass. You'll die painfully, ripped to shreds or worse, they'll infect you. Use your dead cells and make you one of them. Come with me, Sank, we'll look after you.'

'Never!' he spat. He lifted the weapon and primed it to omega mode. He met her gaze as the weapon's power cells began to overload. No matter how much energy it had lost it was still able to self-destruct. The power buildup took four seconds.

Fire tore through the wood, consuming the plaguewraiths in its blast. The beautiful women and their acolytes let the flames pass through them as it tore through the structure. Fuse had already turned to a pile of ash on the altar long before the flames blew his remains into a fine, white plume that patiently settled onto the dusty floor.

The Bridge

Terminus had lost count of time-units but he knew he must have taken drenting ages to find the opening to the bridge. After walking around in the dark for beats and crunching over all manner of crawling and creeping things with only the meager light from the fire-blaster as guidance, he'd found himself in a wide indoor courtyard. He'd gone down several flights of stairs to get here and didn't relish the return journey. Nervously he crossed the stones of the deserted courtyard. Behind him a tunnel receded into darkness. The yard was featureless and his footsteps echoed against the stone walls and vaulted ceiling. He stopped. Terminus stood at the threshold of the bridge from his position under a wide, arched opening. He was looking directly at the black tower.

Suddenly his ears attuned to a loud boom, an explosion beyond the wall somewhere. He briefly wondered if it was anything to do with the crew. It couldn't have been the ship being attacked or being destroyed; the sound would have been much louder. He put it to the back of his mind as he had more important things to deal with. Terminus swallowed hard, stepped onto the bridge, and started walking. He was exposed out here in the open. Above, the black tower tipped with the twin spires glowered down on him. Behind him, the vast wall of the outer structure rose into the sky. He began to cross the bridge. It was about five meters wide and below, on either side, hung an impenetrable, unnatural darkness.

Thoughts emanated from the gloom. His mind began to be drawn toward the night below. A desire took hold of him, to look down into the darkness, and throw himself into the abyss. He sped up but the farther he progressed across the bridge, the greater the intensity of the thoughts became; wave after wave of pulling desire swept his mind. This was far more subtle than the neuro-scramblers the military used to alter the chemical makeup of the brain until the victim was hallucinating.

Terminus had tried a neuro-scrambler once, sat in the path of its beam just for a laugh. The pull from the abyss was completely different, controlling thoughts where the scrambler merely disorientated.

A sudden screeching from above drew his attention to the lizard-like birds perched on the roofs of the encircling wall. They shuffled their leathery wings and squawked from their malformed beaks. These creatures were becoming increasingly agitated the farther he went across the bridge. They scurried along the top of the walls, angling their long necks at him, sharp talons digging into the stone. Four pairs of bulbous eyes protruded from their heads, and through these they viewed him with intent. Their noise became increasingly intense, more like an aggressive warning rather than a distress call, until he noticed them take to the air. In seconds they were swooping down on him. Wide-winged black, skeletal strentners with talons like hooks. They weren't just swooping to scare, they were coming to attack. Terminus blew his chances of entering the black tower quietly when he crouched on one knee and shot three of them out of the sky. They tumbled into the black moat below. Others were dislodging from their aeries to swoop.

Terminus started to run.

Ahead, the door appeared like a slit in the black rock. A few meters to either side, light shone through small windows. He was nearly at the door when a large pair of hands grabbed the stone of the bridge from underneath. The beast heaved itself onto the bridge from below and revealed itself to be of a similar species to the thing he had seen drawing the cage earlier in the forest; except this had a head and a face and its six legs ended in human-like hands. More of these beasts hauled themselves onto the bridge and barred the way to the door, like trolls coming from under the bridge to stop passersby.

Their heads were upside-down triangles with eyes and a long mouth, and their bodies were all muscle and bone, no skin enclosing the flexors and extensors. One thing was sure; they weren't going to let Terminus pass.

A swooping lizard-bird sank its talons into his shoulders. It actually lifted Terminus from the ground until he blasted it up the digest-spreader. The white hand-monsters were advancing toward him, the birds were attacking, and the urging consciousness that wanted to meet him in the abyss was filling his head. When the next lizard-bird bore down on him, a big one with a six-meter wingspan, he finally gave in. Convinced by the voice, he launched himself off the bridge and into the black.

Web

As soon as Terminus had disappeared into the tunnel, Tulk had shot back upstairs and fetched the books his shipmate had been examining in the library. He paced back down the hallway with his fire-blaster in his left hand and the heavy books cradled under his right arm. He stopped, aware of a presence moving toward him from the dark network of labyrinths. He listened for a second but could hear nothing. Tulk decided not to hang around so began his treacherous journey down the stone steps that twisted to the ground level. From there it would be a short dash to the arched entrance and the gnarled trees beyond.

Tulk was nearly out of this Creator-forsaken place and was about to spring over the last few steps to the floor when a curtain of silky fibers dropped silently, catching him. He ran face-first into the substance and it filled his mouth spreading a poisonous taste across his tongue. His arms, legs, and torso were covered in the stuff. A second curtain of the same substance dropped behind him from above to coat his back. He thrashed and struggled but only became increasingly tangled up in the sticky net, powerless to move. Instinctively he dropped the books but held onto the fire-blaster. Tulk tilted his head up and tried to see what had dropped the web down. Far above, two thin white arms that ended in bony hooks heaved the web up from the floor, the hooks-for-arms reeling in the masses of white web. Tulk gave a little cry as he felt his feet lift from the ground, the hook-end arms still heaving the web upwards. In the nooks and crannies high above him he could see other stretches of web and, when he drew level with them, he spotted to his horror that other people had been trapped this way. All that was left of them were skeletons, hanging in their webs as they slowly crumbled to dust. The net he was trapped within stopped moving. Above, the creature sat in the darkness, its pale shape hardly visible. All Tulk could make out was that it had multiple limbs.

He couldn't believe he'd been caught this way. He was so close to getting out of this hell house. By now he should have been in the ship, sitting in the command seat with the engines in planet-lift initiation and his finger on the manual trigger for the weapons. He would have given Terminus fifteen beats, then he would be lifting off out of this cursed system. Tulk felt for his Creator symbol and realized he'd given it to Terminus. The web prisoner grimly looked up at the thing again; two red eyes stared at him. He clutched the fire-blaster. At least he still had that.

Time passed. Sweat and terror had kept Tulk company until he heard a noise and idented them as footsteps. Below, he saw shadows falling across the wall; a figure was approaching, a humanoid figure. At first he thought it might be Culp or Dich but was surprised to see it was a woman. A woman with lush, dark hair spilling down her back who wore a long scarlet dress of heavy material that trailed behind her along the stone flags like a the wedding train of a bride (Tulk had seen weddings back on Skyfire in the First Church he had been part of). At first he thought she might help him but when she stopped, a smile split her thin face, and he knew she was part of this. She found his predicament amusing. She bent down and retrieved one of the books. The one Terminus had been so fascinated by before.

'So, you've taken books from my library, have you?' She tutted like he was a naughty boy. 'I'd insist that you put them back but you're in no position to obey.'

'Listen, lady—'

'*Lady*. That is not my title. I am a Gatekeeper.'

'Gatekeeper, then. I need to get out of here. You have to help me get out of here, please!'

'And deprive my daughter of her nourishment? That would be most unfair. I've fed well tonight; to deprive her of her feast would not be polite. I'm sure you'd agree.'

She was talking archaic Earther, her voice enunciated fastidiously.

'No I don't, you drenting geema! That drenting thing is going to eat me and you're talking about vulleying manners! You obviously own this thing so call it off! I'm with the diplomatic mission and believe me, you do not want to casp off our planet!'

'You should be glad you're not female. My daughter would lay her eggs in your womb. What's to say she might not try anyway? She has been known to be confused by the humanoid sexes before. Beautiful she might be but she's none too bright. You should be honored that you are feeding a superior entity, now that your existence has no meaning. Your destiny has been fulfilled.'

And that was drenting it. Audience over! The Gatekeeper began to move off, her dress trailing down the steps as she made for the entrance.

With all the hate he could muster he snarled at her. 'Then Creator curse you, you whore of the Destroyer!'

The Gatekeeper turned slowly and moved back toward where he hung. Pure evil shone in her red eyes, and indignation was carved into her sneer.

'So, you curse me in my house using the name of the enemy. Where is your Creator now? He is absent. He will not stoop to save even his own creation, the worthless coward. I have a message for him and his children. A message of pain before my daughter consumes your worthless soul.' Her mouth opened wide and from it a swarm of black insects vomited upwards from her maw. They took to the air on tiny wings and shot toward Tulk's exposed face. Red-eyed, shiny-bodied creatures covered every inch of his face from jaw to scalp, biting and stinging mercilessly. He opened his mouth to scream and they entered, ravaging his tongue and throat.

After what seemed to be an eternity of agony, as one they began to die. When they dropped from his face his visage started to swell. Their poison had infected his nerves, making him thrash furiously in the web. The creature above began to move from her space in the rock and crawl across the web. Through the agony the instinct for survival kicked in and, when the spider-thing, this Gatekeeper's daughter, was in his sight, he fired. The creature recoiled and screeched when one of the pale legs was shot away from its joint. The limb fell to the floor and smashed on the flagstones. Through indescribable pain, Tulk continued to fire. The beast hid in the shadows above as the bolts of heat slammed into the walls and shot through web and bones. At least the noise of the firing might summon the others. A new wave of pain from the poison disorientated him; he dropped the blaster and it clattered to the floor. In the silence that followed, a gargle erupted from the creature's throat. Not a gargle of pain. Above him, the Gatekeeper's daughter was laughing.

The Eternum Codex

Terminus clung to the rough black stone of the tower. A few feet above him, the slit for a window beamed light into the darkness. The window was large enough for a man to crawl through. In the cracked, pitted surface there were enough footholds and notches to hang onto. Another flaw in the low-tech security, he thought, laughing to himself.

He'd clung onto the huge lizard-bird's leathery legs with one hand as it swooped over the abyss. When it was near enough to the wall of the tower, he'd blasted it up the digest-spreader and fallen into the wall as the bird dropped. He'd smashed into it with some force but managed to hang onto the stonework. Terminus wasn't used to such stunts and had both amazed and appalled himself. He was actually aiming for the window above, thinking the bird would fly high enough for him to magically fall through it. That hadn't happened. Terminus reflected on what a drellock he could be sometimes. Luckily, not only had he managed not to die but he'd also held onto the fire-blaster.

Now he stuffed the gun into the back of his belt and began scaling the wall. The consciousness in the abyss created a choir of insistent voices urging him to simply fall. Let them embrace him. Another volley of lizard-birds were coming in for the kill and, incredibly, the white six-legged guard creatures were now crawling across the wall like spiders, able to defy gravity. Their legs that terminated in hands were thumping across the stone toward him.

Terminus nearly slipped twice as he sought purchase from the jutting stones, but he somehow managed to keep going until he wedged his fingers into the narrow bottom of the slit. He pulled himself up, jammed one leg into the inside of the building, and sat astride the aperture. One of the beasts had followed him up the wall and was almost upon him. Terminus pulled the fire-blaster from the belt and literally blasted its head off. Its body fell into the darkness and the other creatures fled back to the bridge. Terminus swung his other leg over, his buttocks now resting on the window, and surveyed the interior.

The light from within the tower blinded him. He tried to focus and saw that the floor lay less than six feet below him. He planned to throw himself down, but as he adjusted himself he slipped, falling awkwardly and noisily to the floor. He shot to his feet and sprang to the wall, flattening himself against it. His hands touched a smooth, tiled surface which was cold to his fingers.

When he was a child he used to go into the collapsing, abandoned cities on architectural missions with his pat. Some of the old buildings were still standing. They sometimes explored old medi-facs, or hospitals, as they were called in old Earther. Terminus would wonder at the surfaces of some of the rooms inside; smooth little squares of clay composite. Shiny metal tables, white walls, and ceiling.

He stared at his surroundings and his guts tightened. The floors and walls of this place were covered in these white tiles. Before him was a large pillar that looked tree-like. The trunk reached far above and connected with other pillars via oblique beams that jutted out like branches. Trunk and branches: every surface was covered in these white tiles.

Terminus felt like he was a tiny creature looking up from the sea floor at a colony of coral. Across the wide floor he could see various metal tables such as the ones he'd seen in the hospitals back on Earth. Instruments — scalpels, scissors, and other sharp items of metal he couldn't identify — waited on metal trolleys. This place was no place of healing, he knew. He'd once spent a night in a detention room in the Kabballa system. He'd been caught with some snakki and, as alcohol was not tolerated by the regime of that oppressive planet, they'd picked him up. He spent the night stewing in his own digest, thinking they were going to snuff him when Skyfire diplos bunked him out. Skyfire was a bigger system than Kabballa and not many planets were prepared to casp off the Skyfireans. This place reminded him of that holding facility: clinical, medical, very threatening in a way that made the old digest-spreader tighten with fear. The difference was that no one was going to bunk him out of this one.

Circular gaps in the tile-walls led from one room to another. Terminus pressed on deeper into this deserted part of the tower. Each room looked much the same with an operating table and a side trolley of exquisitely sadistic tools. The tiles beneath his feet were, surprisingly, not very slippery, which was just as well as he didn't want to slip over and make a racket by falling onto his digest-spreader. At times he could hear the noise of tools clattering or the dripping of water. Whatever made that noise was not something he wanted to alert.

He crept through to another section and froze. This area was larger than the others. A central pillar rose from the ground to the murky heights of the tower, walkways intersecting from it at obtuse angles. Under the shadow of this pillar Terminus spotted the politico. What they'd done to him almost made Terminus sick.

The poor gannta was naked, and it wasn't just his clothes the politico was missing. He'd been opened up and all of his internal organs had been removed from behind his rib cage. His heart, his lungs, his liver, his kidneys, and all eight meters of his intestines were now out of his body. Terminus couldn't believe what he was looking at. All of the organs were visible, still operating and, impossibly, hanging in mid-air a few feet from their owner. His heart was still beating and his lungs were still processing oxygen to stretched veins and capillaries that fed back into his body. His legs and arms had been sliced open, nerves and muscles cut out and suspended, as he hung in a crucifixion pose, and evil-looking needles and wires had been inserted or twisted round his main nerves. Beside his feelings of horror Terminus was wondering how the drent he was going to get the politico back to the ship like this. The fact was, he wasn't. The politico was vullied.

Two catatonic-looking girls, the caged snuff-slaves they'd seen earlier, knelt at the politico's feet. From their mouths, eye sockets and ears, unnatural tubing, sectioned like a transparent millipedes, drew pinkish fluid from their brains into huge needles that had been inserted obliquely into the politico's neck. The girls looked either drugged or dead. To allow the tubes to be inserted into the eye sockets, their eyeballs had been removed and now sat in a dish on the metal trolley. Terminus was about to collapse with the awfulness of it. What those vulleys had done to the geemas was appalling enough but the question that bugged him most was how the organs hung in the air like that. Perhaps some sort of force field? Skyfire had nothing like that. The inhabitants of Thanatos One were obviously not as low-tech as they made out.

Oh, drent!

The noise of approaching footsteps flung Terminus into the wall. He tried to melt into the tiles when two Lung-men passed very close to him as they entered the room, followed by his worst nightmare. Terminus could feel his bladder expelling re-cyke.

The black cloaks and the hooded faces brought back the horror of that stretch when he was sixteen. From here he could see their odd, three-toe feet brushing arachnid-like across the floor. Two of them took a position either side of the victim. The politico's eyes didn't open.

Inside the ancient hoods of the nightmare creatures, Terminus spotted the clicking mandibles and the first few eyes of the heads.

The Lung-men deftly handled the scalpels and scissors and went in among the floating organs. Terminus would have been surprised but he was too busy waiting for the creatures from his nightmares to speak. The full terror might break him; he might just drop to his knees and begin screaming. He looked at the fire-blaster. He would set it to omega and blow himself to hell before he let those drenting shankaas even touch him. Damn it, he would blow *them* to hell. Correction, he thought, this *was* hell. Oblivion, then. He'd settle for oblivion.

The nightmare creatures spoke.

'These blood-providers are nearly depleted. I suppose two more will have to be brought here.'

'These pigs deal with matters of function, Urriss. I wanted you to be here to witness with me the crucial aspect of the Eternum Codex.'

'Crucial? The crucial part of this work comes after the crossing. The Eternum may waste our energies by engaging in mindless pleasure, squandering his new found light. It's happened before...'

'Not this one, Urriss. This one has been carefully selected. He's endured this much agony. He's proved himself. But the telling is in the heart. He must cross now.'

The first cloaked aberration took a step forward. From the folds of its dusty sleeve a five-fingered hand emerged, each finger had six joints and each digit was at least six inches long. Sparse, wiry black hairs grew from the long bones. Terminus saw the hand and the wrist. They were made of the same horrible exo-skeleton. The tapered finger caressed the beating heart.

'The test,' it said, 'comes with the cut.'

The index digit sliced the politico's pulmonary veins that served his heart. The red blood from the veins severely contrasted against the white tiles as it spurted to the floor. The creature sliced away the superior and inferior vena cava and the arteries serving the aorta. Seconds passed and the heart, totally detached from the body now, continued to beat rhythmically. The politico opened his eyes and revealed black orbs, sightless and soulless. Terminus choked back the horror. The two arachnoids heard him. Heads swiveled and he found twelve pairs of eyes staring into his being.

He had two choices now: run or fight. Terminus, whom his superior commander Crank always called brainless, realized he'd forgotten which way he'd come in. He could run but they would hunt him down. This place was full of traps, creatures, and horrors that no man could escape. He had one more option.

The coordinator straightened up and moved into the center of their vision. He raised the fire-blaster and pointed it at the creature to his left. It remained totally unfazed.

Of course, he remembered, on the boundary station the bolt from his fire-blaster had passed right through the intruder. Terminus and his fire-blaster were no threat to them. He was as vullied as the politico.

'Terminus!' The voice came from behind him. He spun and stared into the face that had haunted him for all these years: those six pairs of pupil-less eyes, the wisps of hair emerging from the exoskeleton. Beneath the split in the cloak he could see ribs, dark shades of a bumpy texture, and large insects of similar texture scurrying their bodies in and out of the gaps between the ribs.

This creature who'd called him by name was flanked by others. This was the one. This was him. There were eleven of them, thirteen if the other two were counted. The one Terminus had met before was blocking his exit. Coordinator Terminus cupped the barrel of the blaster with his free hand and pulled the trigger with his other. The beast's hand shot up, arachnid fingers splayed, and the fire hit an invisible wall, the flames dropping uselessly to the floor. He moved noiselessly across the floor to stand very close to Terminus. Almost compassionately the Thanaton extended his fingers so that the tips were touching the human. When they made contact, every nerve in Terminus's body screamed in pain.

'*Kneel!*' the Thanaton commanded. Terminus did as he was told and the pain stopped.

'I knew you would return. You are the boy from the new colony's station. Once we touch a soul, it is ours. Destiny serves us and brings our harvest back to us.'

'You remember me? From all those years ago?'

'As if seconds have passed. But you are too late. Your place has been taken. Anwar has given his flesh for us.' He nodded to the politico.

Terminus was nearly gagging at what he was hearing. 'You were gonna do that to *me*? You were gonna cut me open if I'd come with you all those years ago?'

'You would have begged us to. You would have been prepared, tutored. The darklight would have come to you and you would have torn off your own skin to serve us. Too late now. Your precious flesh has been contaminated by a woman's fetid touch. But you can still have the honor of spiritual defilement by one of the very Thirteen. Stand and follow me, Terminus.'

His head began to swim, just as it did all those years ago. Choices sapped away until his legs brought him to a halt. But he needed to take action. Terminus used all his mental strength to break this spell. He turned and fired, the bolt taking the Lung-man's head apart. Soft reddish goo exploded into the air as the body fell. In a sudden rush of inspiration he aimed the fire-blaster at the anatomically compromised politico.

'You ganntas move aside or your experiment gets it.' He shifted the sights more precisely to the politico and his mass of organs. Terminus knew this thing was mortal, was flesh, and could be destroyed.

The Arachnid stood firm. 'You have to understand your destiny. We had great work for you. You weren't the first of your kind we encountered but your destiny-line was so rich. You had to be harvested.' The member of the Thirteen took a step closer. 'We are older than your adopted world, older than your homeworld, Terminus. We are all-seeing.' The creature's voice was steady and reasonable, the delivery factual, conversational. 'You were created to suffer for us, to serve and be defiled.' It was now in Terminus's body space again. It extended its long, sharp finger, moved it almost sensuously down the side of his body. The being angled its way closer and Terminus saw the gap the Thanaton had left in the circle of the Thirteen. He suddenly drew away, back to the gap. The nearest two were closing in.

'You cannot leave Thanatos; no man leaves alive. Think about it, if I let you leave, the plaguewraiths will tear you apart. The Virgins of the Abyss will consume you in darkness. The Gatekeeper will eat your soul or the Forest Keepers will do the same. Perhaps the Spawn of the Temple Keeper or the gravesnakes will have you.' It drew closer. 'Stay, listen to my voice. I speak to your soul, Simon. I speak into your soul.'

It turned to the remaining Lung-man. *'Prepare my chamber.'*

Terminus pulled away and raised the gun to the politico again. They backed off a little.

'You shut your mandibles, not another word.' They were closing in again. There was no way in the universe he was going to go with this creature. Another idea came to him. He began to rifle through his leg-pocket with his free hand. 'I know, let's play a game.' Desperately, he fumbled in his pocket and at last found and drew out an object. 'Let's play catch.' He threw the object into the air and, with surprisingly human instincts, the creature caught it in mid-air. The silver Creator symbol nestled in its hands for a micro-second before the Thanaton dropped the thing in disgust. They recoiled, horrified by the presence of the object. The Thanaton screamed at the Lung-man to remove the symbol and totally destroy it. All focus had shifted onto the object. The Thirteen turned their attention back to the intruder; the time for words was over.

But Terminus had fled.

*

From out of nowhere, the six-legged creatures the Thanaton had referred to as plaguewraiths poured out of holes in the walls to pursue him. He fired with wild abandon at them as he ran blindly through the white-tiled hell. He dashed roughly in the direction he'd arrived in and miraculously found the door. He ripped open the metal handle and sprang out onto the bridge. To his despair he saw the bridge was covered in birds waiting for him. As he ran, he fired a few shots halfheartedly but knew he couldn't kill them all. Deciding to take his chances with the Virgins of the Abyss he went to the wall and started the climb down. There must be a way out down there, his flawed reason told him, and Virgins of the Abyss? That didn't sound too bad, unlike plaguewraiths which sounded, and looked, strentner. The consciousness below welcomed him with soothing thoughts of what awaited him down there; cooing platitudes made damnation seem almost palatable.

Terminus jumped.

The Virgins of the Abyss

The floor of the abyss served as a moat for the two towers that were the Spires of the Thirteen. These depths were dusty and possessed of an unnatural darkness. Terminus skidded from the wall, which gradually inclined the nearer he got to the ground, and jumped into the dust of the floor. The nagging voice had stopped but in the darkness he could hear movement. Above him, a sliver of faint light reached down into this oppressive and musty pit. He sprang up when he heard another sound of movement. Terminus didn't imagine for one second that these Virgins who populated the abyss were innocent, nubile geemas who'd never seen a man before. There would be something up with them, something strentner. He powered up the fire-blaster and activated its torch light.

Terminus nearly mortoed with shock. Standing before him was a spudder, a human child. Her pale face and blue eyes showed absolutely no sign of fear. She wore a pink dress of some archaic fabric that came just below the knee, and her straight, pale-blonde hair nearly touched her waist. She regarded him impassively.

'Hello,' she said at last.

Terminus didn't know what to say. He couldn't tell if this was some sort of trick or if this really was a human child. What the hell would a little spudder be doing down here?

'I said hello. Can't you speak? Oww... I would appreciate it if you could take the light from my eyes; I'm not used to it, living down here.'

'Sorry.' He shone the light away. 'What's your name?'

'Orla. What's yours?'

'Terminus.'

'That's a funny name.' She laughed. 'Where's that name from?'

She was speaking perfect Earther, Northern Hemisphere. He was actually wondering if this child just happened to live here or was allowed to live here by the Thirteen. The absurdity of this planet made the latter concept almost believable. If that was the case then perhaps this Orla could show him a way out.

'Skyfire. It's from Skyfire.' It wasn't, of course, but for some reason he didn't want to mention that he came from Earth. Everyone on this neuro planet seemed to know more about his homeworld than he did.

'Come and meet my sisters,' said Orla, and skipped off into the dark.

Terminus followed her.

'Listen, why are you down here?' he asked. 'Don't you have a mat and pat to look out for you?' He was beginning to feel uneasy again, something he was getting used to on this planet. She didn't answer his question. Something must be up with them, he thought again. This must be some trick. They had only gone a few meters when he heard other children's voices. Terminus and Orla arrived at an area where three other girls were playing some sort of complicated hand clapping game which involved shouting out numbers. They stopped when they saw him.

'This is Terminus. He's my new friend.'

'We know his name,' a slightly older looking spudder said as she sauntered toward him. She also wore clothing made from archaic fabric woven from animal hair and synthetic fibers. She also wore a dress that came down to the knee, oddly patterned with representations of some kind of animal. Terminus recognized it: an Earth rabbit.

'I'm Lucy. Why didn't you come when we called you? Didn't you hear us?'

'Er... as I was crossing the bridge I felt, not heard, something telling me to jump. Was that you?'

'Yes. Why didn't you? We were trying to stop you from going into those horrid spires with those nasty spider-men.'

Was this true? Was there something good on this planet after all? Terminus's mind was filling with confusion. One thing had changed; he no longer felt any fear. Being around these children had banished that. Perhaps their innocence protected them from the horrors of this place.

'Listen, Lucy, can you lot show me a way out? I need to get back to my ship.'

'Course we can, silly.' She smiled brightly. 'You have to turn the light off, it's hurting our eyes.'

The absence of any fear was worrying, as if his instincts had been subdued. He felt like he'd been tranquilized but that didn't matter because he was happy to play along with their game. Terminus involuntarily felt his finger brush the controls of the gun, dousing the light. He sensed a shuffling and heard them giggle. Then, to his alarm, he heard a slithering sound. Suddenly the gun was smashed from his hand by a force stronger than a child's. Terminus retreated, fear forcing itself inside him once again. As he backed away, he became aware of a second light source entering the abyss from behind. Someone was shining a pale light into the dark. However, Terminus didn't turn to see who had provided the light because the horrors before him became apparent in the dim illumination. The spudders were changing. Several pairs of pus-yellow eyes stared at him but began to recoil from the light. Their faces remained the same and the fine, straight hair still slid down their backs but now their small bodies had changed into the torsos of pale snakes. The humanoid upper torso was now supported by a reptilian trunk with a tail tapering off into a hooked appendage. At shoulder height, thin arms ending in claws protruded from maggot-white scales. Sharp fangs

121

laced their mouths. The spudders had bloated into twice the size of Terminus himself.

These were the Virgins of the Abyss.

Terminus panicked and scrambled away from them but before he got anywhere he felt a claw sink into his calf accompanied by a stinging pain as it bit into the flesh. The Virgin dragged him across the floor, plowing his face through the dirt. Then, unexpectedly, the claws withdrew as the icy light came closer, chasing away the darkness. Terminus was dropped to the floor. The Virgins backed off as the cold, blue light advanced toward them. Their bodies slithered to the periphery of the light-field and regarded the light-bearers with distain. Terminus followed their gaze.

Behind him three scabrous monstrosities with hands for feet — plaguewraiths — clung to the wall. Each held a crystal lantern which gave off the unnatural illumination that exchanged darkness for gloom.

Terminus took this opportunity to scan his environment. Opposite the plaguewraiths, in the outer wall, he could see a narrow doorway and stairs leading up. The virgin atrocities lurked between him and the escape route.

In a hideously distorted voice, one of the plaguewraiths grunted through elongated teeth.

'Virgin...man...give Earther man us... Urrseal wants... give. Give us... to tower!' It pointed upwards with its hand-foot, its dead eyes staring out the snake creatures.

'What?' The Virgin screeched in a voice that could just be recognized as female. 'It's ours. It must die bearing our children.'

Drenting what? Terminus was beginning to think he'd gone mad. How the hell was he supposed to bear their children? He was a gannta for veck's sake!

'Earther man... tower... Virgins pay if not... Virgins get killed!'

'No one takes our child-bearer from us. No one! Not even Urrseal in his spires over the tower. And you dare to threaten us, you half-breed bastard, you degenerate spawn of a gravesnake!'

The plaguewraith jumped the final few feet to confront the Virgin. It discarded the light crystal and readied itself to attack. The Virgins closed in on it. As the creatures prepared to fight, Terminus searched for the fire-blaster. One of the Virgins spotted him and dragged him to her side, but as she dragged him through the dust, he saw the weapon, and grabbed it.

The first Virgin screamed and flew into the air landing on the plaguewraith's back. She bit into the exposed muscle with her fang-laced mouth and a second plaguewraith tore her away. The first Virgin, Orla, now had Terminus in both arms and was holding him up like a baby. She was looking right into his face, cooing horribly, completely ignoring the scrap taking place behind her. He aimed the gun and blasted light into her yellow eyes, the torch function on full power. She screamed. When her hands went to cover her eyes she dropped him. He dashed through the narrow arch and into the relative safety of the hole. The small arch had a gate which looked as if it had been left open centuries ago. Crawling through, he slammed it shut behind him and set the fire-blaster to fuse mode. In seconds he had welded the gate to its frame and was scrambling away up the steps.

He froze when one of the Virgins screamed for him. The sound was so piercing that it felt as if his eardrums were tearing. But the scream's power died away, and she could do no more than rattle the gate as he scrambled up through the darkness. Her cries of rage echoed through the tunnels.

From the Bowels of the Gate

Terminus was moaning and dribbling, incanting phrases of comfort from childhood rhymes. He crawled through the darkness following the fire-blaster's light-beam. Power on the blaster was low. The gun might be capable of firing two or three more shots but it needed to charge. More terrifyingly, when it failed, the light would go out and he would be vullied. Terminus would truly go mad then.

Even if by some miracle he escaped this hell planet, the horrors he'd seen in the last couple of sub-stretches would haunt him forever. But Terminus would never escape. The rulers of this empire of darkness would never let him get away because they hadn't finished with him yet. The plaguewraith had said Urrseal desired the human for defilement.

He crawled through the tight tunnels crunching against insects that populated the bowels of the gate until at last he sprang out of his pot-hole into a wide hallway. Standing, Terminus swept the torch round and to his joy saw that he was in the hallway on the ground level. This was a place he recognized! One way would lead to the exit, the other would lead right back to the bridge. In rage and frustration he screamed an obscenity that echoed through the hall. 'Skang-gat!'

'Terminus!'

The answering voice was faint but Terminus was sure that was Tulk, or at least it was his voice. And it came from the left. Tulk called again. Tulk should be on the ship, so why was he here? Terminus didn't know or care. He just needed to see someone human, someone normal and friendly. It could of course be another

Thanaton trick but he was so lost that he refused to believe that. He raced toward the sound and saw faint light in the tunnel ahead.

When he reached the entrance, Terminus looked up to see Tulk entangled in a huge net of sticky web, hanging like a fly. Something had happened to his face; it was swollen and bloody. On the floor were three books, one of which was the one he'd seen that mentioned his home settlement, Adlestrop. Why the hell had he gone back to the library to get these books? Above him a pale, spider-like beast was descending toward its victim.

'Hold on, Tulk, I'll get you out.'

'No time. Get out. Just go. This place will kill us all, Terminus. You were right; this is hell, or a doorway to it. You have to get out. This planet is death. This is the planet of death.'

Terminus aimed the gun, fired, and left a steaming hole in one of the thing's legs causing it to retreat. He bent down and picked up the book.

'I guess you want to know why I came back for the books,' Tulk said. He seemed slightly calmer now the creature had backed off, but still hung helplessly in the web. 'You see, I'm on a mission. I'm from the First Church. We know about this place, Terminus. We know what it is. Skyfire knows what it is too. They stay away from it, don't publicize its existence. I was given the mission to find out what the politico was doing here and report back to the Church.'

'You won't drenting believe what they've done to him. They've pulled him apart.'

'I know what it is they're doing to him. Listen, get in the ship and start her up. I imagine this place has got Sank and Fuse, so don't be too surprised if they're not there.'

'I can't leave you here...'

'Chuck me my fire-blaster. It's on the floor.'

Terminus did so. It stuck in the web a few inches from Tulk who reached for it with his one free hand.

'I was getting the books as evidence,' said Tulk. 'Show exactly what Thanatos knows about the rest of the universe. Maybe you should take one. When you get back — *if* you get back — go to the Church with this. Don't go to the politicos; they don't know how to handle it. They haven't the belief the Churchers have.' He pulled the fire-blaster with his free hand to his lips and with his teeth twisted the setting dial to omega. Terminus saw what he'd done.

'Tulk, no! I can get you out of this!'

'The Creator will take my soul and I'll send this thing back to hell. Be careful, the Gatekeeper is out there. She did this to my face. She did for Culp and Dich too. You'll know her if you're unlucky enough to see her. Now go!'

Terminus wanted to say something, a goodbye, tell him what a good friend he'd been, but the words stuck in his throat. He had ten seconds before the fire-blaster detonated. Terminus ran for the door.

The Gatekeeper's daughter was not the creature her mother was. Her ten thin legs navigated the web slowly. From her bony, white exoskeleton a human face slavered and leered at Tulk. Several long tube-like tongues slid ungraciously from her mouth, eager to insert themselves into his flesh. Her red eyes glinted.

'Come on you drenting vulley. Come nearer.'

Oblivious to its imminent destruction it wrapped two of its arms around his body, lingering, trying to induce terror before the feeding began. It was mildly disappointed that the prey wasn't screaming.

Time ran out and Tulk's fire-blaster detonated, blowing them both to pieces.

Terminus heard the boom of the detonation but kept running. He ducked branches and cleared roots. At last the ship was in sight and as he boarded, running up the ramp into the navigation cabin. Sank and Fuse were gone.

However, the ship was not unoccupied.

The Old Village

The intruder draped herself like a feline queen over the command chair, her red eyes mocking him. What an anachronistic sight: this woman wearing a long and ancient velvet dress sitting between the twin steering columns and surrounded by holo-screens blinking out information. Terminus had already thudded downstairs and clanked onto the deck floor when he spotted her. The fire-blaster still had enough power to take her head off, which was just as well because he knew who she was as soon as he clapped scanners on her. This was the one Tulk had talked about. This was the Gatekeeper, and the Gatekeeper's lips pulled back into a smile.

'So you are the one who invaded my library and, as I see, saw fit to steal one of my books. Perhaps you mean to bring it back and are simply borrowing it. After all, those books did come from a library.'

Terminus looked at her with incomprehension. This woman's red eyes scanned his soul.

'You don't know what a library is, I suppose. Why that particular book, though? Or did your base colonist mind think it could be of value back on your insignificant world?'

Terminus decided it was time to reply. Although he teetered on the edge of fear-induced paralysis, he was determined not to show it.

'You won't think my planet insignificant when two hundred Sundogs turn up to smash open the worlds of this drenting system and turn it to digest. Killing the politico; big mistake by the way.'

The Gatekeeper grinned wickedly at him. 'We are above reproach. You exist to serve us; all mortal life exists to serve us. Your politician understands this and sacrificed his life accordingly. You, however, are a very rare case. You break into the Spires of the Thirteen and somehow manage to get out unscathed. Urrseal must be furious with you. How dare you throw the symbol of the enemy at him! I can feel his mind screaming out for your organs even now.' She smirked. 'Escape is impossible. No one gets away. Even the most fearless and skilled mortals always succumb, and you are neither fearless nor skilled. Just as some blunder into situations, you blunder out of them. Most unusual, Terminus.' She smiled almost brightly. 'Oh, I know your name. I briefly looked into the minds of your crewmates before I devoured them. Hardly worth reading. You come from some new backwater colony you've called Skyfire and think you are a big noise in the universe. Another festering colony planet populated by grunting swine. So tell me, why have you got my book?'

Instinct told him not to reveal the real reason; that Tulk wanted to report back to his Church about what was going on in this place. If she could read minds she could probably tell he was lying anyway. He decided to give his own reason for his curiosity about the book.

'Well, I'm four thousand pulses from Skyfire, twenty thousand from Earth, and on a black planet in an alien system. I find a book that details the settlement I grew up in back on Earth. Bit of a coincidence.'

'Which settlement is that?' She took the book from him and fingered through the pages. As she did this he was deciding exactly when to blow her head off and which exit to fling her carcass out of. Pretty soon the wraith strentners would be arriving to drag him back to the tower. His stomach tightened at the thought of it.

'Adlestrop,' he said. 'It's in the Northern Hemisphere.'

She looked up, eyes bright and smiling. 'I know it. Lovely little village. It's tucked in the Rynor Valley not far from the forest. Has a beautiful little church at its center.'

'You mean the building with the spire? Is that what it is? My pat thought it was some kind of power generator. There was a square of grass nearby.'

'The village green. They used to have a celebration every summer. Stewed apples, cider, earwig racing. And at night a barn dance. Pastor Smallwood and I would... well, what a small universe it is, Mister Terminus. And people still live there, after all this time?'

'How do you know it? Why does everyone on this drenting planet speak Earther and, more importantly, what do you mean you devoured my crewmates?'

'You question me, you impertinent swine! I've been there, you stupid little man and the language is called English, not Earther, you ignorant dolt.' Her face went back to a smile. 'However, it was good to reminisce about the old village.' She stood up from the chair and without touching any controls made the upper half of the deck open and the exit ramp slide down. 'I was going to consume you but I am replete for now. Do you know what I'm going to do? Something I don't often do. I'm going to let you go. The Thirteen will be furious, of course, but perhaps if they hadn't let me waste away to nothing for centuries on end, I might have been more co-operative. The black galleons will be after you when you take off. Perhaps this ship of yours could outrun them but I doubt it. I no longer know what mortals are capable of so you might give them a run for their money, at least. I'll bid you farewell, Mister Terminus, as I'm now going to let you live.'

'That's nice,' he replied as sarcastically as he could. 'But you killed my crewmates. You know what *I'm* going to do? I'm going to let you die.' He extended his arm, pointed the fire-blaster into her face, and fired.

The bolt passed through her head as if she were a hologram, blew a hole into the navigation seat and hit the metal steps behind.

'That was unwise; you could have damaged your little craft. Never mind. Here...' She drew close to him and her warm hands took hold of his left arm. She put her mouth to his face and her tongue drew a line up his right cheek. For a moment he relished the touch of this woman and her warm mouth. She withdrew. 'There, a little something to remember me by. A gift of pain.'

The Gatekeeper strode down the ramp toward the forest. He'd survived. She hadn't killed him. Halfway down, she paused, turned and said: 'The parasites will spread beautifully across your face. Oh, they'll live as long as you do and the pain will always make you think of me. Safe journey, Terminus.'

Her words spurned him to action. He took his seat and closed the cabin. As the engines fired up, he grabbed the steering columns and activated the weapons systems. Two blackened guns extended telescopically from the dorsal sides of the ship. The atmospheric engine whined with activity and in seconds the 850 was ready for planet-lift. The take-off thrusters hummed beneath him. As the ship rose out of the forest, Terminus felt the left side of his face itch.

Black Galleons

By the time the 850 was hovering above the trees, Terminus couldn't describe the ecstasy he felt knowing he was going to achieve planet-lift from this drenting world. Now he would declare war, getting the first blow in before leaving. All the fear he had felt turned to anger. The way they had snuffed out the lives of his crewmates, and the awful thing they had done to the politico, filled him with rage. He leveled the dorsal blasters at the walls of the castle and pressed the firing stud. White fire-bolts smashed into the side of the walls, creating gaping holes in the ancient stonework. He fired at the heavy wooden doors, fire-bolts smashing them to splinters before carving a trail of stone-shattering blows into the gate as he ascended. Large sections of wall crumbled and he saw the contents of the geema's bedroom spilling out like guts from a disemboweled stomach. Anachronistic furniture fell to the forest floor.

He would have liked to do more but he remembered the Gatekeeper telling him something called black galleons would try to stop him. The side of his face was beginning to throb now. He had to get into space, stick the 850 on auto, and take a look through the medi-holos. There must be something in there for whatever she had poisoned him with. He pulled back on the gears and the craft rose through the atmosphere. In minutes he would be clear of this place.

'Ah... drent!' He winced as a sharp pain from her lick shot across his jaw. He was on the edge of panic. Whatever she had done to him was hurting and he knew it would get worse. He pulled back on the columns and made the engine scream through the clouds and up, up until he could see the stars. Terminus was just about to grin with relief when he spotted them.

The boneships blocked his exit. They must be the black galleons. There were hundreds of them waiting in space like a shoal of fish. As one they faced him. He pivoted left, increased his speed, and then engaged the pulse thrust. The systems were going mad with no one to attend them or feed them information. The battle alarm began to emit. The nearest galleon angled its body to block his path. He fired and the white bolts hit the ribs, or so he thought. Just before they impacted, a reflective plate like a huge circular mirror bloomed out of nowhere and bounced the bolts back. They missed the 850 by a whisker.

'I'm not stopping. I'm never going back! I'll go through you, you vulleys. I'll go through you all!' he screamed to them. The ship charged at maximum velocity and the instruments went wild. He was at zero collision point. The boneship didn't move and Terminus didn't stop.

The cargo craft smashed through the ribs of the black galleon scattering the bones into space. Terminus was screaming, pain eating into his face as he blasted out of the Thanatos system. Two black galleons pulled away from the shoal in pursuit. As his man-made ship sped into the night the black galleons effortlessly matched his speed and gracefully flanked him. Above and below him, to left and right, he could see them, within their cage of bones, black shapes regarding him.

'*Did you really think you could escape us?*' Urrseal's voice filled his head.

'Of course I drenting did!'

'*Come back to us, Terminus. My servants will fetch you... they will bring you back to the Tower.*' Inside the cabin two black, many-legged shapes were beginning to form, teleported to the deck from the black galleons either side of him. Other galleons overtook and tried to block his path. He pointlessly fired and then tried to increase speed but he was already at maximum.

'No one leaves Thanatos alive. No one, Terminus... Go with my dogs and you can live...'

'No... drenting... way...'

He thrust the craft into a violent spin smashing into the galleon to his left and through the one beyond that. There was no way he was going to get out of this but he was determined to smash into as many of them as he could. He didn't think of how he was going to get out of the spin or how he was going to outrun them; panic blinded his mind. Through the screaming and the spinning his eyes were suddenly blinded by many flashes of intense light. He had seen this light before, ten cycles ago. A vast wall of steel suddenly appeared to block his chaotic trajectory, dwarfing the black galleons. Through his rotations he saw that he was going to hit it. At either end of this new ship, flashes of energy spat into the night. It looked broken but he knew better; half was in this universe, half in the next. He saw oval windows of light, observation ports set into steel walls. The closer he swung the clearer he saw them as his vision rotated at speed. He flash-saw space, boneships, steel wall, observation ports. Space, boneships, steel wall, observation ports. Space, boneships, steel wall, observation ports. Space, boneships, and then oblivion.

Terminus's universe turned to black.

PART 2

THE TERMINUS CODEX

Trinity Three

His eyes snapped open. Light flooded his mind.

'Mother! Mother! He's woken up!'

Terminus shot up into a sitting position. At first he believed he was in the gemmel he shared with Clannel back on Skyfire; that she'd been lying next to him in bed, her warm feminine form embracing him as it always did night after night. He was in *a* bed but not the one he shared with his partner. Terminus scanned the environment, sunlight hurting his eyes. The confused traveler found himself sitting up in a wooden bed, his lower half covered by white fabric sheets. He was wearing a thin, white robe. Who the hell had dressed him in this, a geema's nightie? The walls were of a sandy texture and white in color, the angles smoothed over. An oval opening in the wall gave a view of the outside; a flash of green and a blue, blue sky.

'Mother! Naomi! The man's woken up!'

A pale child, a girl, was standing at the foot of the bed. The spudder was humanoid with shining blue eyes and a dimpled face that regarded him with amusement. Terror filled his guts, making him back his way up the bed. Instinctively Terminus reached for his fire-blaster and found that the gun was nowhere near him. *Virgins. Virgins of the Abyss. They'd found him.* Other recollections erupted into his mind, the plaguewraiths, the Gatekeeper, Urrseal and the Thirteen!

He opened his mouth and screamed his lungs out. This expression of terror tore through the girl's nerves. With a squeal, the child ran out of the room.

Terminus forced himself to keep it together, breathing deeply, scanning his surroundings for an exit. He couldn't let fear take his

139

mind or he was a dead man. He had to survive. Terminus had gone space-crazy once before and he was not going to let it happen again. Dazed though he was, he pushed his last memory (the ship spinning out of control, himself succumbing to blackness) to the back of his mind and set to figuring out where he was now.

Springing from the bed, he went to the oval viewing port in the wall. Outside, green hills stretched out into the distance, and a white sun shone down into a clear blue sky. Terminus could feel the heat of the sun on his skin. His senses, instinct, and experience yelled at him: this was not Thanatos.

There were other buildings too, white squares standing against the green in the bottom of a small valley. He looked down to the fresh green grass and noticed that it was quite a few meters down, which meant that he must be on the upper floor of whatever building he was in. A quick scan to the opening of the room showed a door-less aperture in the wall and stone steps leading down. The atmosphere of this planet was peaceful and nearly silent, though now he could hear voices coming from the lower level. Human voices. Some adult, some spudder. Terminus sat on the end of the bed and tried to put the pieces of his mind together.

If he had to put ching on it, he would have wagered that he was no longer on Thanatos One. The 850 had left Thanatos One but hadn't got far. Thanaton boneships could have captured him and brought him back to the black planet. This might all be some horrible, mind-bending trick; at any moment blood might start pouring from the walls, or Urrseal appear out of thin air before him. Terminus began to panic again at the thought of this but forced the fear down. Solid reality couldn't be trusted anymore. Nothing was certain. However, when Terminus scanned the room again he saw something that dismissed the idea that he was still on Thanatos. He stood and examined the object of his salvation.

Hanging on the wall, with its arms open wide and a daft grin on its face, was a silver Creator symbol, exactly like the one Tulk had given him but larger. The Thanatons hated that symbol. The Thirteen had been utterly repulsed by it. It was unlikely that they would hang one on the wall. Underlying this feeling was the space-traveler's own instincts and experience telling him he was not on that planet. The gravity and atmosphere were completely different.

That left two other possibilities: he was dead and this was the afterlife, or he had been picked up and taken somewhere. He quickly examined his extremities. Nothing seemed damaged; he was in no pain. On a small table by the doorway he found a circular standing mirror and examined his face. The area where the Gatekeeper had infected him was pain-free and completely healed. He chose the latter of the possibilities: that he had been picked up and taken somewhere. As he was weighing this up in his mind he heard footsteps ascending the stairs. He shot back onto the bed like a child about to be caught by a parent after engaging in some misdemeanor. He knelt on the bed and looked around for something to use as a weapon. The mirror was now too far away to be grabbed and smashed against the head of the possible enemy. He was weaponless.

A geema respectfully entered the room and eyed the guest with cautious compassion. Terminus was struck by the woman's physical beauty. Her full-bodied head of white hair bounced over her pale shoulders. Her large, baby-blue eyes drew his attention and her full-lipped mouth angled easily into a smile. Her slightly tanned flesh was unblemished, a far cry from his own greasy skin, a product of bad food and excessive drinking. She wore a simple white kaftan, identical to the one he was wearing, which gave the impression that she was innocent, pure. However, when she spoke her voice carried the strength and wisdom of someone who knew her own mind and took charge of a situation.

'I heard a scream. You sounded like you were distressed. There is no need to be distressed. Whatever you have been through, I can assure you, you are safe. No one is going to harm you here.' She spoke Earther, Northern Hemisphere by the sound of it.

141

Stuck for words, he choked then said, 'Where's my drenting fire-blaster?'

'Fire-blaster? I'm guessing that's a gun of some kind. I'm afraid we don't allow weapons here.'

Allowing his former panic to return, Terminus began to bombard her with questions. 'Where the drent is this place? What happened to me and who the vulley are you?'

'Vulley? Drent? I'm sorry, I don't understand these words. You are safe. This place is called Trinity Three. It's the third moon of the planet Agathos. My name is Naomi, second daughter of Isaiah. My father will be back soon and he can enlighten you as to how you came to be here. Is there anything I can get you? A drink? Some food?'

'Yeah, my drenting fire-blaster. And a Creator symbol like that one, but smaller. If those vulleying Thanaton arachnids turn up I wanna be ready for them.' Naomi's words sank in. 'Wait. Did you say I was in the Agathos system? What the drenting vulley am I doing there?'

She put her hands on her hips and her face set into a scowl. 'Drent? Vulley? Are these swear words? We would rather you didn't use profanities on our world. Like I said, my father will be home soon. He will explain everything.'

Terminus sat on the edge of the bed and put his head in his hands. It was then that he noticed the change. He held out his arms. He brushed them a couple of times with his fingers to make sure. The intricate tattoos were absent and he could feel that there were no implants beneath his skin. The phys-tech, all of it, had been removed.

In the Shadow of Agathos

The room that Terminus had woken up in turned out to be part of a large white house with six bedrooms, two hygiene chambers and food preparation quarters that the occupants quaintly called the kitchen. Naomi had taken him to this kitchen where an older woman stood over a food preparation area chopping vegetables with a knife. She was Sarah, Naomi's mat. Two spudders, twin girls, eyed Terminus with looks of curiosity and excitement. He recognized one of them as the girl who had woken him earlier. There was also a short-haired young boy of about twelve cycles who wouldn't look Terminus in the eye. He sat at the table scribbling numbers with a carbon stick onto what looked like paper, the wood-pulp derivative he'd seen in the books in the Gatekeeper's library. This place didn't just look low-tech; it looked no-tech, which worried Terminus. If a bunch of boneships turned up here they would all be vullied.

'Isaiah is at the temple. He should be back from zenith mass soon,' Sarah said. Terminus was too stunned to really take this in. He nodded politely and hoped for the best. The silver-haired woman, whose strands were bunched behind her head in a metal fish clip, looked good for her age and possessed the same blue eyes as her daughter.

'Actually, Philip, go down to the temple and tell your father our guest has woken. He's probably gossiping with the other Elders. You can finish your mathematics later after dusk mass. Go on.' The black-haired spudder slid from the table and rushed out of the door. Terminus sat down and held his head in his hands again. His thoughts spun out of coherence. After a few beats he summoned the will to speak. Naomi slid into the seat next to him.

'Listen,' Terminus said. 'I'll get the beak of the situation off your old gannta when he gets back. Then I'll be on my way. I need to get back to Skyfire.'

Naomi laid her hand over his. 'You're going nowhere. You need to recuperate. You've been through a lot and you need to heal your soul.'

'I don't wanna be rude, but I'm wanted by out-worlders and if they turn up here you haven't got the firepower to whack 'em. You'll be up to your ears in digest.'

One of the twins asked what *digest* was as Isaiah entered his home. For some reason, a remnant of manners perhaps, Terminus stood to greet the man. He was large, much larger than Terminus, with a trimmed black beard and a mane of thick, dark hair, which possessed a single gray streak, and hung down his back in a pony tail that touched his belt. Isaiah also wore a white robe and a silver Creator symbol around his neck on a chain. His friendly blue eyes shone and he greeted Terminus by shaking his hand vigorously. The pat was followed by the boy, Philip.

'I wonder if I could have some private time with our guest.' Isaiah's voice was assertive, yet good-humored.

Sarah turned with her hands on her hips. 'I'm preparing the midday meal, husband! You and Mister Terminus can go outside to talk.' Isaiah raised his eyebrows and gave Terminus a knowing look; then he led him through the door.

The white sun in the sky blazed and Terminus was glad he was only wearing a white smock. His usual space-gear would have been too hot under this sky-blazer. Once outside, he got a good look at this abode. The house had been built on a hill and the main body of the structure was sheltered by an overhanging roof. To the space-traveler's surprise the man of the house flopped down on the grass and invited Terminus to do the same. From here the house looked like a formless, square mushroom with a bulging white roof. A path led from the house to a small collection of other dwellings huddled around a larger building; a double-spired gathering hall of some kind. Above, almost filling the sky, the massive mother-world hung over them. The huge, misty apparition of the planet looked slightly purple from the moon they were on. Terminus could see continents and oceans. Although it was a couple a pulses away it looked so close.

'When you grow up in the shadow of Agathos you grow used to it,' explained Isaiah. 'Now to business. I have some explaining to do. My son tells me your name is Terminus. You were found in what was left of your spaceship by an Agathon patrol Ark. For three days and nights you were catatonic. I estimate that to be about six days by Skyfire time.'

'You have spacecraft in this society?'

Isaiah frowned, but only for a moment before answering. 'We aren't as low-tech as the rest of the universe thinks. As I said, you were found in what was left of your ship and brought here to Agathos, to this moon. Our healers did their best with you and you were transferred to my house to recuperate.'

'What sort of state was I in when you found me?'

Here Isaiah hesitated. 'Well... you were in bad shape. You needed critical care but, Creator be praised, you were spared. The Council of Elders on the mother-world thought it best you rehabilitate in a peaceful place and now I have the honor of assisting you in your psychological and spiritual recovery. This place is a place of peace, a place where you can fit your mind back together.'

'This is all very nice but there are alien forces out there that are pursuing me. I was attempting to escape from Thanatos One when I crashed. They aren't going to just let me go. They'll find me. They'll come here and you and your family will be vullied. I don't wanna be rude but you're being a bit of a goomah about this.'

It was just his luck to get picked up by a bunch of religious pacifists. If he'd been picked up by a Sundog or a Babelite Cloud

Sword then he would be safe now. He reflected on this as Isaiah spoke.

'If you are telling me, in your vernacular language, that I am being naive then I can assure you that I am not.' His face hardened. 'The forces of that evil system will not *dare* to set foot anywhere near Agathos. We are more powerful than they will ever be. We place our faith in the Creator. I don't expect you to understand such a concept but believe me; we are more than capable of dealing with them. They fear us and, more importantly, they fear the Creator.'

'They don't like the gannta with his arms out, that's for sure. I shot a fire-bolt at one of them when I was there. Did nothing. Chuck a Creator symbol at them and they spread the digest. Not that I ever want to get close enough to the Thirteen to have to do that again. Drenting place. Wait till I tell Crank about what they did to the politico. They'll send Sundogs; turn that drenting system into an asteroid belt.'

Isaiah raised a palm to stop Terminus, 'Wait! Did you say you've *been* to Thanatos?'

'Yeah, we took a politico to Thanatos One. That's where the trouble started.'

'You've walked on the surface of Thanatos One? Actually walked there?'

'Yeah.' Isaiah was looking at Terminus like he didn't believe him.

'You have to tell me exactly what happened. Tell me everything.'

Just beginning to recall recent events was turning his flesh pale and making him feel sick. He hadn't let fear defeat him on Thanatos One and he certainly wasn't going to let fear defeat him on the religion-planet of Agathos. Terminus began his story.

He kept it brief, outlining the weird creatures he'd seen, what happened to the politico, and his escape from the Spires of the Thirteen. He was having difficulty articulating and after a few beats Isaiah told him to stop.

'We don't expect you to tell us everything now. You are in shock, I think. Relaying this story will not help you recuperate, and you are the important one here. When I think you've mentally healed enough I'll take you to Agathos and you can give an account to the Elders of Lebanon. It's nothing to fret about but we need to know what our enemies are up to. Thanatos has been silent for decades and now you say they want to start diplomatic relations with Skyfire. This isn't good.' He saw the look on Terminus's face. Isaiah's face broke into a frown of concern for his guest. 'You do not have to worry, this is our concern now. We will attend to it as we see fit. Come, the midday meal must be ready now. I hope you're hungry.'

Dive-ball

After they had eaten, the geema called Naomi offered to show him around the settlement. Still feeling uneasy about having landed among these strangers, he accepted. Terminus followed her down the path to the cluster of buildings that spread over the base of the small valley.

'What's this place called?'

'Jericho,' she said. 'The settlement hasn't been here long. When Father retired he left Agathos and founded this community. He and the other Elders wanted somewhere peaceful to raise us and so they came here.'

They passed through the boundary of the small community. The homes panned out from a large building at the settlement's center. The curious structure had a wide base that rose into a twin tower. People were sitting outside of their houses, talking or engaging in domestic tasks. Some were digging patches of garden using primitive tools. Terminus nearly laughed when he saw a man and a woman washing their robes in a wooden bucket of water. Didn't they have steri-alcoves here?

He observed another woman repeatedly pushing and pulling a sticky pale-brown mass across a wooden board coated in a fine white powder. Whether this was to prepare food or narcotics he could not tell, perhaps both.

A small herd of hairy mammals ran freely through the settlement to drink at a small and featureless fountain. There were dozens of children running around playing. He thought of those creatures at the base of the Spires of the Thirteen and shuddered.

'I can't believe that people still live like this,' he said. 'Even on the outer colonies they have some tech.'

'Well, smart-pants. We actually choose to adopt a rural, low-technology culture. The Creator has given us the gift of simplicity. Having said that, when the hillcows escape from their paddock at dusk it stops being simple then. It's no fun spending half the night trying to lure them back with honey-grass.' Naomi nodded to the small mammals running around the settlement. These, Terminus surmised, must be hillcows.

'Get a fire-blaster and stun them.'

'Are all men from Skyfire obsessed with weapons?'

'Only me and after what I'd been through, you shouldn't blame me. What's that building there?' He pointed to the double-spired structure.

'It's the temple.'

'What's it for?'

'What's it for? It's where we meet with the Creator.'

'What, he appears, does he?'

She frowned at him. He could tell she was not used to having her faith questioned.

'To hear his voice you need to clear your mind, you need silence. In the silence you feel his consciousness, his thoughts. You feel his love.'

Terminus felt the redness of embarrassment color his cheeks. She was like a First Churcher but worse. He wasn't sure if he could stand being here for long if he was going to have to listen to this sort of vulley.

Finally he said, 'If I wanted to clear my mind I'd need a refuse disposer. Can we go in?'

'You can go in, if you come to mass.'

'What, like a First Churcher day seven collective? You must be joking. You won't get me in there.'

There wasn't much else to see in the settlement. They stopped for a herb-based drink at a family friend's house where Naomi talked with the mother about people he didn't know and events he wasn't interested in. He sat and studied the white houses that sat against the backdrop of green hills and pure blue sky. Terminus couldn't take it in; his mind was a mass of confusion. On the way back Naomi asked him: 'So how are you feeling?'

'I dunno. What concern is it to you how I'm feeling?'

'Because we want to help you.'

'You can't help me. If the Thanatons turn up here, and they will seeing as you're so close to their system, then we'll all be beyond help.'

'The Thanatons will not come here. They wouldn't dare.'

'How do you know? Have you ever set foot outside this system?' She shook her head. 'Thought not.'

She stopped him in his tracks by blocking his path. She firmly but compassionately laid a hand on his shoulder. Her eyes met his.

'The Creator will not let our enemies pass. You are safe here.'

That was the second time that stretch he'd heard this said and he still didn't believe it. She could see the disbelief in his face.

'Words alone won't convince you,' she said. 'The longer you spend here the more you'll realize that the universe is not run on weapons and warfare. There are invisible powers that keep the worlds turning.'

Not only did he not feel safe here, he didn't even *want* to be here. He wanted to be back on Skyfire, the red world protected by thousands of Sundog battle cruisers each packed with a hundred Spark-fighter dart-ships. He wanted to be back on Level Five of Alpha Gropolis. He wanted Clannel. He wanted some snakki. If those boneships came for him there, the Sundogs would blast them out of the sky. This bunch of religious ganntas called their ships Arks. *Arks!* They were probably called that because they were made of drenting wood, like the ark out of the old Earth myth. The situation was bad but there was drent all he could do about it. He had to take his mind off it somehow.

At the side of the house Terminus found a large fruit amongst some fence-building paraphernalia. The skin was tough, reminded him of rubber, and the Skyfirean wasted time kicking it into the air. It was roughly spherical in shape. After a while he took one of the shorter wooden fence posts and smashed the rubbery fruit over the house. He went to the front of the house to retrieve his ball. It bounced pretty well and soon he was lost in the spudderish challenge of seeing how long he could keep it off the floor using the stick. As he did this he reveled in his healthiness. He hadn't felt this well for cycles. Muscle tone and reflexes actually seemed to have improved. And he was grateful that the phys-tech was no longer there to bother him. Whatever the Agathon physicians had done to him, it must have been thorough.

Soon the creepy twins came over to stand and watch him.

'You two aren't going to turn into giant snakes after dark, are you?' He said to them while bouncing the ball on his knees.

'No one turns into a snake, silly,' said one of the twins.

'Would you bet ching on it?'

'What's ching?' said the other.

'And what are you doing?' said her twin.

'Here,' he threw the rubber to one twin. 'You chuck this at me and I hit it. You both run. The one who gets to it first gets to hit it next. We call it dive-ball.'

The girls looked at each other, obviously puzzled.

'What, you don't have dive-ball on this moon? Come on, just wang it!'

The girl nervously threw the ball to Terminus who hit it into the green.

Automatically they bolted after it until one of them caught it and dutifully brought it back. They were soon laughing and screaming, the noise bringing Naomi and Phillip out of the house. Terminus threw the ball again and the twin hit it. Phillip and Terminus ran for it, Phillip picking up the nuances of the game instantly. Soon Naomi joined in and Terminus found himself racing with Naomi to fetch the rubbery 'ball'. As he dived for it she landed on top of him. They were both laughing as they tried to wrestle the rubber from each other's hands. At last he let her have it. As she ran to pick up the hitting stick he took a step back. For a second, just a second, he'd forgotten about Thanatos One.

That night he dreamed that he was walking on the surface of the black planet again and woke the house with his screams.

Haymaking

Naomi woke him; she shook him and offered him a herb drink. The sky was, again, cloudless and the mammals were crying contentedly in the fields.

'I'm going to give you some honey-weed tonight,' she said. 'It will relax the mind, stop those nightmares.'

He sat up. 'The only thing that'll stop my nightmares is a poke in the thought box with some neuro-spacer.'

'Neuro-spacer?' she frowned. 'Is that some sort of drug? Honey-weed will do just as well without the harmful side effects of any neurotic-spacer, or whatever you called it.'

She went to leave the room but he called after her. 'Naomi?'

'Yes?'

He got out of bed, the robe touching and tickling his feet. 'What's going on today? What are we doing?'

'Mother says you should rest, take it easy.'

His forehead creased as he frowned. 'I don't wanna take it easy. I can't sit around all day, I have to keep occupied. I have to do something to stop me thinking about... Look, I just need to keep busy.'

She shrugged. 'We're all going over to Matthew's farm to help with the hay collection. You can come with us and help if you like.'

Sweltering in the sun, Terminus could not believe what he'd let himself in for. They'd walked for clicks and clicks until they'd come to a farm in a wide valley. Dozens of people were all stabbing pitchforks into rows of cut and dried grass that striped the endless

155

field. At first he thought these workers all looked the same with their white robes, like clones. But closer up they were a right old mix. Geemas and ganntas, young and old. Well, he should've expected that because Naomi had explained that everyone was helping out. But it was the genetic jumble that surprised him. It wasn't just the variety of skin color — he'd seen that before, though not all on the same planet — but there was black and curly hair like he'd never seen, heavy duty nozzles with flared nostrils and snubby little ones like a spudder's; even nozzles that hooked like a Thanaton lizard-bird's. Perhaps the Agathon sun emitted some kind of mutating radiation, or maybe these people were so primitive that they didn't have medicinos to make sure that spudders had the right genes. The racial mix was all natural, like on Earth where ganntas and geemas from all the different continents found themselves in the Northern Hemisphere enclaves after the Great Decline.

Dotted around the field were large hoppers; containers pulled by primitive engines. The hay was being stacked into these containers and taken to a barn nestled beside a large white house similar in design to Isaiah's. Terminus had been given a long-handled tool with prongs at one end. With this he followed the example of the other white robes around him and stabbed the tool into the cut hay. They bundled it into large mounds then transferred it onto the trailers.

Terminus had never worked so hard in his life. The work was back-breaking and he had to stop for a rest at regular intervals. Naomi found his fatigue quite amusing, for which her mother rebuked her, telling her that she should not mock the visitor's willingness to help. The work might have been hard but at least it kept his mind clear. He watched a tall, dark-skinned, and handsome youth smile regularly at Naomi as he drove the primitive engine. Seeing the engine brought back memories for the space-traveler, memories of home; his real home. Old Earth. A plan also formed in his mind of how to get a rest from pitchfork duties. During the break

Terminus leapt up onto the engine; the youth looked perplexed to have this stranger share his vehicle.

'So how is this powered?' Terminus demanded to know. He'd seen antiquities like this before.

'Erm... vegetable oil, I think. My father knows more about it.'

'My pat had one of these. Drent, it's got gears and everything. I've seen them used on Razgaresh, in the Spine system. Can I have a go at driving it?'

Taken aback and confused, the kid let him drive the next load up to the barn. The kid, whose name was Ezekiel, took over from Terminus on the pitchfork duties. Terminus spent the latter half of the stretch riding the pulling engine. He winked and grinned at Naomi from the seat as she shoveled hay and he sat on his digest spreader. She did not look pleased.

As the sun began to set they retired to the house and ate a mixture of bread and fruit. They drunk some low-alcohol drink and the families talked. Matthew, an Elder from the village, introduced himself and thanked him for the work he'd done. Ezekiel did ask him about other planets he'd visited but was more concerned with talking to Naomi. The women split off to talk in the kitchen and the men sat outside in wooden chairs on a cut lawn overlooking the sloping field. They discussed people and places that Terminus knew nothing about so he sat there clutching his drink not saying a word. It was then that the darkness began to flood his mind. The feeling of being unsafe began to grip him. He broke out in a sweat and felt sick. He took himself off to the side of the house and stood with his hands on his knees.

He must have been there for quite some time because it had gone dark when he sensed someone close to him. It was Naomi.

'If they don't stop insinuating that Ezekiel and I are going to get married, I'm going to scream. He's three years younger than me.' She paused. 'Terminus, are you all right?'

He could have said he was fine or just told her to cusp off but he blurted it out. 'I'm so scared.'

Without hesitation she did the strangest thing. She approached him and put her arms around him like he was a baby. Equally strange was the sense of comfort he felt from this action.

That night he drank the herb drink she'd prescribed him. He didn't have nightmares.

Isaiah's Feast

When the sun disappeared behind the mother planet, lights flickered into life throughout the settlement. The illuminations were powered by some sort of low-tech electrical charge. It seemed that the whole settlement had arrived at Isaiah's house to eat and were crammed around the table. Included in this group were other, older men like Isaiah who were the settlement's other Elders. There were also lots of children here. Terminus was not used to there being so many spudders around. Back on Skyfire the use of contraception, or birth-stoppers, was widespread. So widespread that the scilitos had ordered an increase in the number of clones being produced simply to bolster the labor force.

Terminus kept his mouth shut and listened to the buzz of conversation, punctuated with much laughter. It seemed that all the children were conceived naturally, which meant that a lot of vulleying must be going on, enough to put Babel to shame. Also, the partners weren't shared as on Babel or, as less frequently occurred, on Skyfire. In fact, the ganntas and geemas on this planet had to undergo some sort of ceremony at the temple to become husband and wife. It worked the same way as Linking did back on Skyfire, the difference being that the marriage ceremony had some spiritual dimension; Linking was merely an administrative formality.

The last thing that he noticed was the way they talked about the Creator. They talked about him as if he was real, furthermore as if they knew him. This was manifest in an odd ceremony that took place just before the meal commenced. Conversation ceased while Isaiah talked to the Creator. As he thanked him for the food provided, Terminus noted with interest that the Creator didn't reply. They didn't really give him much chance.

Mercifully the Agathons didn't ask Terminus too many questions and he guessed Isaiah had briefed them on his delicate state of mind. Just as he was wondering how he was going to make his excuses and leave this social nightmare, they produced the snakki. It took the form of a red liquid which tasted unlike anything Terminus had drunk before. He was offered the snakki first and Naomi filled his earthenware goblet. He drained the vessel and held it out for more. Naomi looked surprised and filled his goblet again, and again he drained it. It was then he noticed how slowly the others drank. The decanter was left on the table and he filled his pot himself a third time.

Naomi admonished him from her place opposite. 'Perhaps you shouldn't drink so much wine. It can give you a sore head, you know.'

'Listen, if I don't wake up wanting a re-hydrage after a half-stretch grinding on the snakki, it don't feel right.'

'What on Trinity does that mean?'

'You never get drunk?'

'No. Never.'

'Don't know what you're missing.' He leaned back in his chair. 'So how exactly do you get your jeebers off on this moon?'

'I guess by that you mean how do we have fun? Well, certainly not by drinking excessively.'

One of the Elders cut in and asked him what it was like on Skyfire. He told them about the red night-desert that blossomed with plants when the sun rose, and about his gropolis; Alpha Gropolis, his home city. As he talked, some of the guests, mainly women, got up and began to play and dance with the children. One of the Elders produced a no-tech stringed instrument and to Terminus's amazement used it to play music. He thought that instruments needed sound-generators and a power source to operate. Continuing the conversation, he talked about the freighter docks, but skirted round discussing the defense systems, and the trash-asteroids that took the refuse from every gropolis. Terminus found he had an audience so turned to asking questions about their world.

'How many people live on this moon?'

'About a million,' Isaiah answered. 'They are all in settlements like this one.'

'What about Agathos?'

'Several billion. There are seven main cities there.'

Terminus frowned. 'Our records show that you are just this backwater, low-tech bunch of ganntas. Why would our records say that?'

'We don't advertise ourselves to others. It's not in the Creator's will. And I expect that no one from Skyfire has ever bothered to find out about us.'

Terminus helped himself to more wine. 'So what's the beak with you and the Creator? Most people on Skyfire reckon he doesn't exist, only a few neuros in the First Church. Does everybody on this planet believe?'

'Every single soul on this planet has a faith in the Creator.' The conversational circle had tightened. Isaiah and Terminus were talking now with Naomi looking on intently. Terminus was on the home-planet of the Churchers arguing with them about the existence of their god. He was going to need a lot of the red snakki to get through this one.

'There must be some doubters. I mean, it's not like you can see him, is it? When you were talking to him earlier he didn't exactly reply. Not even a "cheers, enjoy the snakki and the noosh".'

Isaiah leaned closer to him; the music had become louder and people were beginning to sing. 'The fact that I am sitting here talking to you is proof of his existence.'

'Explain.'

'Did you know that we were the first colonists to leave the Sol system? Just before the Great Decline, which nearly killed the Earth, the Creator instructed his believers to construct a ship. He gave us the knowledge to make such a vessel and equipped people with the skill to make such a ship in secret. All those who put their faith in the Creator were moved by his spirit to arrive at the place of departure. It was by his spirit that we steered a course through the stars to Agathos, the planet he prepared for us. And so here you are, Terminus, talking to me.'

Terminus leaned back in his chair. 'Drenting vulley!' he exclaimed. 'I've heard this story before. You've got it wrong somehow. No one had the tech back them to achieve interstellar travel.'

'You think we're mistaken? When I take you to Trinity, I'll show you the ship. The *Genesis* is in our first city, Nazareth, for all to see and give thanks to the Creator for delivering us safely. Then you will believe our ancestors came directly from Sol.'

'Not till I see it with my own eyes, Isaiah. Not till I've seen it with my own eyes.'

'So you'll believe it then?'

'Probably not.'

'But if you do, will you then believe the Creator exists?'

Terminus drunkenly faced the Elder. 'Again, not till I've seen him in real-sight with my own two scanners!'

The sound of singing from inside the house drifted across the valley. Even in the dark, Terminus could still feel heat where the sun had baked the ground. He was tired and drunk. It felt good. No more fear. No more mistrust. All banished by snakki. He was just about keeping bereavement at bay. This place was reminding him of Tulk. Tulk and Sank. He looked to the sky. The stars filled the sky brilliantly. After a few beats he saw it. Terminus staggered back. Against the dark of the sky something was moving, silently, like a fish through water. It was huge but it was definitely there, he wasn't imagining it.

'Drunk too much?' Naomi appeared behind him.

'What the drent is that?' He pointed to the vast, black shape. But when he turned back, it had vanished.

Again, that night he didn't dream. The house slept peacefully.

Naomi

The next morning he woke early and asked Isaiah if he could help in running the settlement in any way, since the previous day's work had provided him with occupational therapy. Isaiah had taken him to the rear side of the house where a pile of chopped tree trunks lay stacked against the wall. The older man muttered something about hard work making a happy man and then explained how the settlement's region of Trinity Three tilted away from the sun at certain times of the year and become colder; a winter sets in. The logs were used for a fire to heat the house. Terminus asked him why they didn't just get a thermo adjuster. Isaiah just smiled and asked him to cut them into quarters.

Terminus was more than willing to undertake this job until he saw the method used to cut the wood. Isaiah had produced a long wooden-handled tool with a small blade at the end. He'd called this an axe. Terminus was stunned; he'd at least expected to use a fire-slicer. Isaiah's way was energy consuming and inefficient. Not wanting to offend Isaiah, he took the axe and started chopping.

Sub-stretches later, Terminus looked out from his place by the woodpile. From here he could see that the valley stretched to the shores of a lake. Hillcows grazed in the fields beyond, wandering to the lake to drink. They were milked twice a stretch but were not slaughtered for meat, as in some societies. Terminus had eaten meat before, on other worlds, but mainly ate synthetic noosh when on Skyfire or in space.

Stoically, he chopped the logs and sweated in the sun. Eventually he stripped down to his slids and tied the robe around his waist, using it like a sarong. He thought he looked a bit of a goomah but no one was going to see him around here. Without warning a voice behind startled him.

'I thought you would be in bed with a sore head, the amount of drink you had last night.' He saw Naomi standing above him on the incline of grass.

'I drink ten times that on Skyfire. It was good snakki. Got a punch to it, not full of syntho like the digest back home.'

He noticed she was looking at his face as he spoke, her eyes trying not to look at his half-naked torso.

'What's the matter? You've seen a gannta with his top off before, haven't you?'

'No, I haven't, actually.'

'Well you've seen me now. I could stick this robe back on but that would be a bit pointless, I reckon, seeing as you've got a scan full.'

'No. It's fine.'

'Haven't you ever seen your gannta in the bush before? Have you got a gannta?'

'I have no man in my life, if that's what you mean. I've never had one.' She smiled.

'How old are you?'

'Twenty-two.'

'Twenty-two cycles and still a pizzdeena! Sorry, slip of the tongue. I meant to say, *inexperienced*. On my planet that's unheard of.'

'My father wants me to marry a man he knows from Nazareth City. My mother wants me to marry Ezekiel, Matthew's son. They're seeking the Creator's will on the matter.'

'What about you?' Terminus asked. 'What do you want to do?'

She laughed. 'You know, you're the first person that's ever asked me that. Bless you, Terminus. I'll tell you; I don't want to get married.

Actually, I've wanted to talk to you since you arrived. Tell me, what's space travel like?'

He put down the axe and thought for a moment. He wiped the sweat from his brow and sat down on a log.

'A lot of the time it's boring. You sit at your control desk and scan ahead. Occasionally you'll see something interesting, usually when we sneak close to a planet to refuel the pulse engines. You might see a gas cloud or a solar flare. When we passed *this* planet, this moon, I saw a storm raging. It looked so tiny. Then there are the planets. You land on human colonist planets and each and every one is different. The cultures and atmospheres on Mistfall or Oceanbound; they're worlds in case you didn't know. It expands your mind. Then there's the creatures. Lung-men, pod people and animals that look like something from a neuro-scrambler hallucination. It's amazing. Space travel is the most amazing thing you'll ever experience.'

'When did you first go into space?' she asked

'The first time I traveled I was fourteen. Ran away from my home on Earth, stowed away on a delivery freighter from Skyfire. I was a pizzdeen, but I soon grew up on that journey. The space-ganntas found me; put me to work, gave me noosh and snakki. After a couple of sub-cycles in the old vacuum I was hooked. Earth was just a flash in my lobe-tank; a memory. You can never go back. You just wanna go out there and see it all.'

'Are some of these planets dangerous?'

He stood and reached for the axe. Terminus resumed chopping logs. 'The one I've just come from was. Very dangerous. And creatures to bend your mind to breaking, literally.'

'My father told me not to mention your time in the Thanatos system. He said you had been through something awful.'

'Yeah, it was awful but I survived and that's the main thing.' He stood and began chopping again, splitting a large log in two with one heavy stroke. Just then a bell sounded from the settlement below.

167

'That's zenith mass. Are you coming?'

'No thanks.' He brought the axe down hard on the wood. 'I'd rather split logs.'

Candle Circle

The stretch the Elder died, Terminus slept in as usual. When he woke and came downstairs the family had just returned from dawn mass. The ceremony must have gone on a long time as it was mid-morning now. He ate the first meal of warm bread, spread with a yellow slime processed from animal milk called butter, and listened in on the conversation. They were talking about how the old dark-skinned gannta had knocked-off during the night and how his son had found him. Terminus had liked the old gannta. His name was Ben and he'd been to Earth in his youth. They'd had a conversation once about the old planet and Terminus felt he should pay his respects. It was only right.

'So, are you going to give Ben a send off? A wake?' Terminus asked them. 'I'd like to send him off.'

'Is that what you do on Skyfire?' Sarah said as she rubbed the head of a large dog sitting at her side.

'Yeah. We call it the necro-blast. We drink death-snakki till we pass out. Thinking about it, most celebrations or commiserations involve necking snakki till we pass out.'

'Here we have a mass,' Isaiah pointed out. 'The dusk mass will be dedicated to Ben's passing over to be with the Creator.'

Naomi caught Terminus's attention when she grinned as she bit into a large fruit. Once she'd swallowed she said, 'And as you said, Terminus, you would like to send him off. Does that mean you'll actually come to mass?'

'Naomi!' Isaiah rebuked. 'You cannot try and trick someone into coming to mass. They must come of their own free will. This is one of the sacred tenets of the Creator. Did you learn nothing in litany class?' Isaiah turned to his guest. 'It's entirely your choice. If you wish to come you are most welcome.'

So far he'd avoided going into the temple. However, he needed to get in with these people if he was going to get on here. Also, it would've been what old Ben would have liked.

'All right then, I'll come.'

The temple, a circular building with a double spire, was unique in the settlement due its design. The interior was cool and quiet. Any noise, no matter how small, echoed around the white walls. At the far end of the circular room were stacked a large pile of white candles. The congregation, which consisted of the entire settlement, each took one. Terminus reflected that any gannta could come into their quarters and thack away with their possessions while they were all here. However, they were so low-tech that any thief would only find tools and food, which these ganntas and geemas would give away free to them anyway.

The people formed a circle in the center of the temple and stood, each holding a candle. Terminus thought how Sank or Fuse would get digest in their slids laughing if they could see him now. He looked like a right goomah in his white robe holding his wax stick. He nearly laughed himself but the mirth was caught in his throat when he remembered that his crew were all dead, all murdered. An Elder lit his wick from a single candle burning in the left nave of the temple and then passed the flame around. Soon Terminus was standing there holding his burning wax pole. When all the candles were lit the oldest Elder spoke.

'Firstly, we would like to welcome our new friend into the Creator's house. You are most welcome among us, Sii Terminus.' Terminus nodded to the old gannta and wished he could disappear from this place; they were all looking at him. 'We also mark the passing of our brother, Ben, who was taken to the Creator's spiritual realm last night. I for one will miss my friend very much and long for the time when I can join him, but I don't relish the prospect of actually leaving my body. We here on Agathos largely die peacefully, but we must remember those in the universe who die in undignified ways or who felt pain before going to the Creator. What do others think?'

Terminus thought of his shipmates. He thought of Tulk, blasted into pieces. He was a First Churcher. He believed he would be going to the Creator. Then there were the others. Dich. Dich was so young. He would have made it to coordinator in no time. Probably would have ended up navigator on an explo-ship halfway across the old vacuum. His life had been wasted, wasted on that drenting planet.

'I will miss my friend.' Isaiah stepped forward into the circle. 'When Naomi was born I sought his advice as she had such a pale complexion that I feared she was ill. Ben told me I was right to do so as she was indeed sick. He made me a remedy from lake-weed which cured Naomi and calmed my fears. He was a wise visitor in our house and found common ground with all.'

A young, wiry man with dark eyes and black hair stepped into the circle. 'I've lost a father. I knew this day would come and I have a hole in my heart that I petition the Creator to heal.'

A woman, a frequent visitor to Isaiah's house, stood forward. 'This passing brings memories of the passing of a friend of mine, a missionary. She was lost in the outer heavens with the *Galilee*. I think about her every day and today more so.'

His mind was beginning to spin. The passing of his friends, no, the murder of his friends. He may not have liked Culp, or known Sank or Fuse, but they were brothers in space, locked in that craft for sub-cycles and never to return home. Even their remains would never reach Skyfire. They were left there, left there for eternity. And Terminus would never see them again. He would never drink snakki with Tulk, argue with Culp, or hear one of Dich's clever info-bytes. They were lost to Terminus.

Sarah was speaking now, saying how much of a father Ben had been to her after her own father had passed away. As she spoke Terminus felt his guts beginning to contract. He felt his throat going sand dry. Tears were filling his eyes. He hadn't done this since he was a spudder. He couldn't do it now, not in front of this lot. They'd die with the shock of it. On Skyfire, scanner-leak was a social taboo. It was as prohibited as taking a digest in the street. It was too late, emotion was choking him; panic gripped him. They were looking at him now, for drent's sake. Dropping his candle, he turned and ran from the temple.

Scanner-leak

There was nothing wrong with scanner-leak in the privacy of your own gemmel, but to end up with it in front of people, strangers, was not good. He allowed the tears to flow and he lay on his bed in the fetal position for what seemed like sub-stretches.

After mourning his shipmates, he remained lying there, crushed by the humiliation of crying in public. To his gut-churning horror he heard one of them coming up the stairs to confront him. It was Isaiah.

Terminus couldn't face him; his eyes were still red with tears.

'I suppose they're blasting away with laughter down there.'

'Sorry, I don't quite know what you mean,' Isaiah perched himself on a stool in the corner of the room. Terminus sat up.

'You know, they probably think it's funny, or they're disgusted. Vulley, first time in the temple and I drent it up. Might as well have flopped out my nazbolt and taken a siphon on the floor.'

Isaiah spoke with gravity and compassion. 'My friend, no one thinks ill of you. Yes, they are confused as to why you felt the need to run from the temple but they aren't judging you in the way you think they are. After you left, everyone cried. They all cried for Ben or other loved ones they'd lost just as you did.'

He felt like an infant still lying on the bed so he sat up, faced Isaiah like a man. The older host leaned forward.

'Terminus, who were you crying for? Was it someone close? You don't have to answer that question if it's still too painful to talk about.'

He sighed, 'The scanner-leak came when I thought of my shipmates. They all died on that planet. None survived. I'm stunned that I did.'

'How did they die?'

Without hesitation he said, 'I'm not sure. A woman, called herself the Gatekeeper, told me she'd... what was the word... consumed them. I think that's what happened to Culp and Dich. Tulk, he was trapped in this, well, spider's web when I last saw him. It belonged to this geema; an inhuman freak all wound up in its own threads. He set his fire-blaster to omega and blew himself and this... out-world monster to shreds.' He was beginning to choke up talking about this but stopped.

'I'm going to ask you something. I ask that you come with me to Agathos, to Nazareth, the main city on the continent of Lebanon. Would you tell the council *exactly* what happened? They may ask you to undergo Canvas to identify certain characters or individuals particular to Thanatos.'

'And after that, what are they gonna do? Pray them to death?'

'I imagine we'll finish the problem once and for all.'

The next day some other ganntas from the settlement came round to Isaiah's gemmel for lunch, which Terminus skipped. Instead, he walked out of the settlement and into the hills. The vast pink disc of the mother planet shone above him and soon, after scattering the mammals that grazed on the hillside, he arrived at the lake. From his elevated position he could see someone swimming. He crouched beside a single, green-leafed tree, hiding from view. He quickly identified the swimmer as Naomi. She was naked. He watched her for a while, instinctively trying to catch a glimpse of her naked form. He looked behind him, suddenly paranoid that her mat or pat would see him scanning. Terminus was sure Isaiah was a forgiving soul but knowing his guest was watching his naked daughter might just break his resolve. So he waited until she was out of the water and was dressing herself before coming out from his hiding place. As he skidded down the hill, he heard her singing a song to herself.

> *They say that at the center of the universe,*
> *The Creator himself resides,*
> *And holds in his hand each spacefarer,*
> *That sails the black sea.*
> *Our Genesis is rusted,*
> *But our Arks navigate the span,*
> *And one day we shall meet him there,*
> *And be lost to eternity,*
> *And be found for eternity.*

'Nice song, pretty tune,' he commented. She flashed him a smile.

'It's a song about the time when the Creator will manifest himself at the center of the galaxy. It's said that the first colonists sang it aboard the *Genesis* as it traveled here.'

'Then why are you singing it? Oh, let me guess. You want to go to the stars.' Tentatively, she nodded. 'So what's stopping you?' he asked.

'You don't understand. There's my father for a start.'

'You're twenty-two cycles old. By your reckoning, I was eight cycles younger than you when I told my pat to shove it and just left.'

'That's it; I don't want to tell my dad to shove it. You might not have had anything to lose, Terminus, but I have. I've a family, a home, loving friends, brothers and sisters. You had nothing to lose when you left Earth at fourteen years old!'

He flopped into the ground. 'You think that? You think I didn't leave a place I called my home? You're wrong. I had a pat, friends. I even lived in a settlement a bit like this. It tore my blood-pump in two leaving.'

'So why did you?'

'Same reason you want to go into the stars. They pull you. You have to go, test your limits, find out who you are. Funny, last time I had scanner-leak was when I left... until the temple.'

She hadn't mentioned his scanner-leak and he cursed himself for bringing it up.

'Father says I should wait until I'm called to mission. Then I go to the IMC...'

'What's that?'

'Interplanetary Mission Council. I go there and see if it's the Creator's will for me to go. Then I go on board an Ark for three whole years. That's three whole years away from home.' Terminus wanted to laugh; three years was drent all. On a Skyfirean explo-Sundog you were on it for life. You never went home. That's why most of them were piloted by criminals or debtors. 'I really, really want to go. I've been telling Father that you arriving here is a sign. A sign that the Creator wants me to go. And hearing your stories, although not your bad, funny language, is setting every cell of my body on fire.'

Frowning, he sat up.

'Two things; the universe don't revolve around you. I'm here 'cos of bad luck, or betrayal by my government. I still don't know which. Secondly, your Creator gave you a brain to choose with. Drenting use it and stop vulleying about.'

She did a double take. Floored by his argument, she said nothing more.

They walked and talked until dusk. Terminus talked of childhood pranks, out-worlders, snakki, pats and mats, his gemmel on Alpha Gropolis, clothes (enlightening and shocking her with details of what

Skyfirean women wore), holo-dramas, generated music, and the habitat on his homeworld. They sat together on a large hillside which overlooked domed storage sheds that resembled multicolored mechanical mushrooms.

'Look,' she pointed, 'there's a storm forming.'

He looked, but his eyes didn't focus on the green cloud swarming in from their moon's horizon; they were caught by the huge, floating machine caught in the shafts of dying sunlight. He shot to his feet.

The machine must have been the equivalent of sixty 850's lined up. Its bulging nose was pitted with tiny lights that must have been viewing portals and its long body displayed various exterior mechanisms. It drifted lazily between the moon and the mother-planet. What shocked Terminus was how the structure of its mid-deck burned into his memory. This was the ship that long ago had saved him and only a short while ago damaged and nearly killed him.

'What the drenting vulley is that?'

'Only an Ark. It's the *Sidon* I think.'

'But I thought your craft were primitive, drellocky little space-tugs.'

'Ah ha; those are the ones we let you see.' She sidled up to him and stood so close to him she was touching him. 'Now you understand why I want to go into space.'

He just stood admiring the craft that had saved him. After he had regained the power to speak he said, 'I don't think your pat's got much to worry about. Just look at that ship! Compared to those vulleys my people may as well be traveling around in buckets.' He pulled his gaze away from the Ark. 'Have you ever been in one?'

'No, but my sister has. She's a missionary. She says that the bridge is like a gathering hall and they have holds large enough to carry a thousand people at a time. The insides are white, pure white, but it's a soft white that doesn't hurt your eyes. And the engines... they can jump in and out of hyperspace like a fish hopping out of water.'

'I've seen their weapons systems in use; it was like a sun exploding,' Terminus said. 'And to think of the times I've passed this system thinking it was just some primitive religious colony. The last time I came near, refuelling the 850's pulsers, I gave the audio-greeter a beak-full of insults. You could have blasted us out of the heavens.'

'We would *never* do that,' she said, looking horrified that he'd even suggested it.

'You did it to the Thanatons.'

'The Thanatons are different.'

'Not that I'm complaining. I razzle you should go to their system and give 'em a dose of your sun-shot.'

'We would only do that if it's the will of the Creator.'

'That seems to be the cop-out excuse everyone uses around here.'

For once, Naomi didn't have a put-down answer.

Elders

Isaiah and Terminus watched the bubble shuttle approach. He was excused log-chopping duty today and was glad to be getting away for a few sub-stretches after the scanner-leak incident at the temple. He still felt like a drellock about that.

As if blown by the breeze, the shuttle's sphere drifted over the hills. Long, white fibers billowed out from every part of the transparent shell, making the transportation bubble appear almost organic in nature. Soundlessly the sphere came to rest on the top of the grassy hill behind their house, and every length of fiber disappeared back into its body. It became simply a bubble with a robed man sitting at the controls inside. Terminus followed Isaiah up the hill to the ship.

'Wait!' A sylph-like figure yelled from below. She ran up the hill toward them. Isaiah frowned with concern and some anger when he realized this was Naomi. She looked like she was carrying a hefty bag and had every intention of coming with them.

'Naomi?' Isaiah scowled.

'I've an appointment at the Mission House.'

'We talked about this...'

'I know and you said I was not to make an appointment at the IMC. Well I have!'

'But I specifically told you we need more prayer time...'

'Are we getting on this drenting shuttle or not?' Terminus cut in. 'You can argue about it once you're in Lebbon or whatever it's called. I've got Elders to see.'

'It's called Lebanon!' Isaiah stomped toward the bubble as an aperture opened in the side to allow him access to the craft. Terminus winked at Naomi and she smiled back. They joined the older man as they slipped through the slit in the membranous bubble and sat on a circle of transparent seats that ringed its bottom. The fibers extended and Terminus found that, from the inside, he could see through them as if they weren't there. He watched the settlement disappear below as they soared into the sky, noticing again the anachronistic storage domes a few clicks from the lake.

The vast continent of Lebanon covered half the planet. Very little of it was left to nature as the light, pink soil was overtaken by the encompassing city of Nazareth. The city gleamed beneath him and even from orbit Terminus could see vast tracts of greenery among the buildings. The shuttle-bubble descended easily into the atmosphere. He thought back to the 850's shuddering entrance into Thanatos One; these people had planet-fall down to a fine art and he again wondered at their technological prowess. The Skyfirean had even more chance to wonder when they neared the mass of spires and fantastic architecture that was Nazareth. He marveled at the broad boulevards that cut through spired buildings gleaming in the sun, at the lake with a multicolored fountain gushing at its center and where dozens of white-robes relaxed on its shores. All this was dwarfed by two vast hulking towers that dominated the skyline, iron monoliths tattooed with thousands of mechanical features that clung to their sides like limpets. Four ships were docked at each tower, their rears resting in the vast mouths that served as docking bays. These were Arks, the ships that had that had haunted his dreams for so long. Terminus stared at them all the way to touch-down.

The shuttle-bubble landed on a vast, polished plateau made from a patterned stone. Some paces away, the maw of a huge arch faced them and he followed father and daughter into its cool shadows.

Hundreds of white figures milled around the echoing platform. Unlike the Agathons he'd met on Trinity Three these ganntas were rushing about like politicos at the Decision House. He realized he'd become unused to all this noise and rushing; to see it all around gave him a minor thrill.

'You've made your decision,' Isaiah, relenting, said to Naomi. 'Go then, I'll meet you at the café by the effigy of Tinus after I have introduced Terminus to the Elders.'

'Thanks, Father.' She kissed him on the cheek. 'And you too, Terminus.' She leaned up and kissed him on the cheek as well. Naomi fearlessly skipped out of the hall to the Mission House across the boulevard.

Isaiah turned swiftly. 'You know, my friend; they grow up so quickly, so very quickly.'

The Elders who were so eager to meet Terminus were responsible for external affairs. Isaiah had told him that they were the ganntas in charge, the big vecks who sent out the Ark ships on missions across space. They were anxious to speak to the visitor. When the Elders were ready, a woman ushered Isaiah and Terminus from the large hall where they had been waiting for the last fifteen beats to another smaller, yet still impressive hall.

Terminus had been expecting to find a number of old ganntas sitting behind a large formal desk but instead was surprised to be met by three men and two women, all Isaiah's age, almost relaxing on soft chairs in the center of the room. They rose to greet Terminus and Isaiah. In their mannerisms, and in their jumble of skin colors and body shapes, they resembled his hosts on Trinity Three. One man had very dark skin, darker than Tulk's, but the body-configuration that most caught his attention was one of the women who had an olive complexion like a geema from Skyfire. He wondered if she had originally come from his adopted world.

The olive-skinned woman was the first to speak. 'So you are Mister Terminus. We've heard much about you. I've seen you in the flesh once before but, unfortunately, you were unconscious. I'll introduce you to the Elders for external affairs. My name is Martha. This is Joseph, Barnabas, and Paul. This lady is Ruth. We just want to ask you a few questions. There's nothing to fear, I can assure you.'

'Fear?' Terminus slouched into one of the soft, low chairs. 'I've been to Thanatos One. Don't talk to me about fear.'

'You aren't going to put him through the Canvas, are you?' Isaiah almost barked at them.

Martha smiled a placatory smile. Terminus detected something harder in those eyes, though, something he'd never seen in Isaiah before. She almost rebuked him with her reply.

'We will do as the Creator sees fit, Isaiah. You may go now. We'll send a dove when we are done here.' Terminus briefly wondered what a dove was but quickly became preoccupied by the sight of his only friend in this room disappearing through the sliding, arched doors. Martha poured him a herb-drink; a different brew from the type Naomi made. Terminus wondered what effect it would have on him, remembering the herbal concoction he'd drunk on Ragreesh that had nearly sent him neuro. Martha assured him that this leaf had no such effects.

'So, Mister Terminus,' Martha began. 'You may not know this but we have been interested in your movements for a very long time. I believe that this isn't the first time we've made contact, as it were.'

He could feel himself reddening. He remembered that broadcast sent as the 850 passed Agathos. Is this what she was talking about? Was about to get swung round by the muc-sac for asking them if they wore slids?

'Yeah, listen, I'm sorry about that. I know now that you lot don't wear slids and I can see why. Your muc-sac would get all sweaty. Drent. Sorry. Didn't mean to say that. It's just that you're a long way out in space and you get bored. Anything to relieve the thought box down-time. If I knew you were this high-tech I wouldn't have done it. We thought you were some tiny religious colony. Sorry.'

The elders were frowning, looking at each other. At last Paul, the dark-skinned man spoke. 'I think our guest is referring to the communication we directed to his cargo ship, the 850, some months ago. The reply was full of Skyfirean jargon and implied that we didn't wash ourselves properly.'

Martha smiled broadly. 'That caused a minor outrage among some of the younger, less experienced operatives. We are both experienced spacefarers, Mister Terminus, and the Elders aren't shocked by obscenity. The incident I am talking about occurred some ten years ago, when you were sixteen. You know what I'm talking about?'

'Oh yes. Like I'm gonna forget that.'

'Let me explain the incident from our angle.' She poured another cup of herb mixture then began. 'Shortly after we first arrived at this planet many centuries ago, we were at war with Thanatos. They constantly tried to ingratiate themselves into our society; seduce our leaders and decimate our culture. They failed every time as we had faith in the Creator. The Thirteen were like serpents; ever tempting, ever seeking out individuals to poison and corrupt. At last, when the Creator had revealed to us the complete science of space travel we launched an attack upon their system. We delivered all the captured people imprisoned upon the worlds of their system as our first strike, and then rained fire from the heavens of their skies upon them. They receded. The Thanatons existed in the ruins of their world and lay low. We knew they hadn't died out but they were no longer a threat. That was a long time ago. Thanatons have been largely inactive for centuries. In the last few decades we concentrated our efforts of the liberation of individuals enslaved by the Babel system. That planet almost rivals Thanatos now in acts of unspeakable evil.'

'So are you gonna shoot fire down on them from their skies?' Terminus asked.

Martha gave him one of her smiles. 'The Creator forbids it. We have no right to destroy human life like that.'

'What about the Thanatons?'

'They are far from human.'

'What are they then?'

'They, Mister Terminus, are beyond redemption. We are digressing. As I was saying; the Thanatons have laid low for centuries. When your colony of Skyfire first appeared, our ancestors feared that the Thanatons might wake, but there was no activity. The boundary station that you were working on had been running for a short time, sixty years, when to our horror we picked up activity from the Thanatos system. This was when you were stationed on the boundary post. From our observations of Thanaton movements we deduced that they had sent a scout, an invasion scout, to investigate your system. We dispatched an Ark immediately. For some reason they wanted to take you. There are reasons why they took humans to their planet but those reasons are... difficult to explain without causing acute disgust to the listener.'

'Yeah, I got the idea when I was there.'

'We couldn't let them take you. So we appeared from hyperspace and destroyed their ships.'

'But the creature, Urrseal, it didn't die. I met it again on Thanatos One.'

'The Thirteen,' Joseph spoke. 'They never die. They live forever.'

They *must* have put something in the herb drink because he felt quite relaxed when talking about Thanatos. He hadn't relayed his story to them in great detail yet so far. That's when he'd be forced to recall the memories he'd tried to bury. That's when he'd be gripped by the gut-churning fear.

'So, let me get this straight. You vecks blast about the universe in these Arks doing what, teleporting people out of sex houses on Babel?'

'That's the brunt of it, yes. You couldn't expect us to set foot on that decadent planet and see with our eyes the debauchery that occurs there. Some specialized missionaries live there but they are extremely careful not to indulge in the activities. They inform us of events and we act on that information. One hundred palaces have gone out of business in the last year alone. The masters and mistresses of that planet hate us. They also fear us; they know the sort of technology we carry. They did talk of war but realize that their Cloud Sword ships are no match for our Arks.' Martha paused and frowned. 'However, now that Thanatos is on the move again I fear that times are about to change. The situation has become darker.'

'Surely you could just blast them again. I saw the way you took care of their boneships when I was on the boundary station.'

'As I have said, we are not dealing with mortals. These creatures serve the Destroyer, the antithesis of our Creator. This is a spiritual war, not a physical battle. Tell me, Terminus, from what you saw; what do you think they are?'

He sat back. Drent, he wished he could down a big glass of Isaiah's snakki right now. 'I used to think that you were time travelers or they were, I dunno, creatures from another dimension, or hell as the First Churchers used to call it. That's what I told Tulk one night. From what I saw of their planet they are pretty low-tech but their ships are very high-tech. Even if they do look like a sky worm's skeleton turned upside down. They are old, really old. One of them, the Gatekeeper she was called, had actually lived in the settlement I'd lived in back on Earth before the Decline. She named places I'd been. That's why I razzle their civilization is old, really old.'

'What do you think they are?' Martha said. 'Where do you come from?'

'From Earth. Maybe not the Thirteen, they look too weird, but some of them are, or were, human. Some of them come from Earth and have somehow found immortality. I wasn't really thinking about it much. I was too busy trying to survive. So come on, you obviously know. Tell me.'

Martha shrugged her shoulders. 'The truth is this; we don't really know what the Thanatons are. Some aspects of their culture reflect pre-Decline Earth but it has been speculated that that is just a psychological ploy to unnerve Earth-origin races. We know that they take their metaphysical power from the Destroyer, but as to how they came into being, how they engineered their system into a perfect necklace of worlds, or doused the fire of their sun, we just do not know. They were here long before we were. That makes them the oldest race in the known universe.' She shifted expectantly. 'It's time you told your story now, Terminus. Isaiah filled us in but we need an accurate account from you. We will, despite Isaiah's concerns, need to use the Canvas. Of course, the final choice is yours. You don't have to undergo anything you don't want to. We can discuss that later. But first, tell us verbally what happened. '

Terminus wanted to help these people and that meant giving them an accurate account. This Canvas didn't sound too bad. He was sure he'd been through worse. Telling the story would be hard work, though. What he could really do with was a drink. He sighed. 'Listen, have you got any snakki?'

The Elders appeared confused, all except Paul who rose to his feet. 'I'll fetch us some wine, despite the early hour.'

Canvas

'Have you Elders got any theories as to why we were ordered to travel four thousand pulses just for a politico to get pulled to bits?'

The wine had loosened his tongue and with his mind slightly numbed by the snakki, he'd relayed the story of his time on Thanatos One with greater clarity to the Elders than he had to Isaiah a few stretches ago. As Martha and Terminus walked along the corridor, speaking as they went, the other Elders followed at a respectful distance.

'I suspect that this politician had developed an unhealthy interest in certain occult practices. In this regard, all roads lead to Thanatos. That's why he didn't charter a military craft; it would raise too many questions about the nature of his journey. Am I correct in thinking that on your world it would be a lot easier to charter a cargo ship? It would attract less attention?'

Terminus stopped in his tracks and put his hand to his head. 'Drent, I am a drellock. Of course, it makes sense. A bunch of space-ganntas like us aren't gonna make a fuss if he just wanders off. The crews of a military ship are all klonks; cloned bio-made soldiers that would guard him at all times and shoot anything that even appeared to threaten him. But why would Urrseal and his friends give him a living autopsy?'

'I believe it's called the Eternum Codex...'

'That sounds familiar,' Terminus cut in. 'I'm sure I heard one of the Thirteen talking about it.'

'...and it's believed to be a sort of initiation into the Thanaton race. Your man perhaps believed he could join them. Those who immerse themselves in the occult often lose perspective on the real world. The Eternum Codex would certainly have been fatal to a human. The Thirteen would have known this.'

'Then why did he go through with it? Why did the Thirteen do it to him?'

'Perhaps his mind was so twisted he lost the ability to choose. You said yourself that the creatures you met could control the emotions of others. As for the Thirteen, they no doubt performed the Eternum Codex for their own amusement. They are sadists, and that's putting it mildly. The fact that they have shown an interest in your planet at all concerns us. If they decided to insinuate themselves into your society then Skyfire would be in grave danger.'

'We can take care of ourselves,' Terminus almost growled, suddenly taken by acute patriotism.

'Maybe in a straight fight you might be able to, as you say, take care of yourselves. The Thanatons play dirty. Their first target is the soul and you Skyfireans haven't the spiritual faith to protect yourselves. Here we are.' They arrived at a large circular door set into the stone. The door was metal and looked to be voice-activated. This was the first high-tech piece of machinery he'd seen since leaving the shuttle, apart for the Arks, of course.

'Let me explain. The Canvas is a database. It will show you images from alien cultures, and we will ask you to identify them. It will also pull memories from your mind and add them to its database. All of the objects you will see are three-dimensional and will remain still. It would be much too disturbing for you to view moving images on the Thanatos setting. Are you ready?'

Terminus faced the door. This was odd, he thought. He felt afraid. The Skyfirean put it down to the fact that he was going to see things he'd hoped never to see again. He couldn't back out; he'd look like a goomah if he did, like he had in the temple back on Trinity Three. Besides, this was Agathos; these people were genuine. He was among friends (something he'd never thought he'd admit to). Nothing bad was going to happen here. He gave Martha the nod.

The doors slid open and Terminus followed Martha into a white space. He was partially relieved that the interior wasn't dark like the holo-shows on Skyfire. That would have put the digest right up him.

'As I name some of the... inhabitants of the Thanatos system they will appear and you can identify them. We'll be as quick as we can, then you can have another couple of goblets of wine. You can also back out at any time.'

'Let's just get it over and done with.'

She rubbed his shoulder sympathetically. 'I'll summon the first one. Simulation!'

'Deadspace or realspace setting?' spoke a disembodied voice that Terminus assumed to be the voice interface for this simulation.

'Deadspace. Setting eighteen, Thanatos One. Summon: gravesnake.'

The gravesnake appeared as a very convincing hologram. It resembled an earthworm, but for its gray color and the fact that at certain points along its side, vertical mouths opened out to reveal a cavernous interior. The gravesnake was coiled in on itself. From one end, a large orifice projected what looked to be multi-jointed humanoid arms ready to pull into its maw any gannta unfortunate enough to be in its path. Besides looking disgusting it also looked absurd.

'Do you recognize this?' Martha asked.

'No, but I heard Urrseal mention them.'

'What creatures did you see? Name them and the simulation will pick the thoughts out of your mind. Speak quite loudly; the simulation is a bit deaf. She needs a re-tune.'

'Simulation: er... plaguewraith!'

The hands-for-feet horror appeared before him, just as he'd remembered it. Against the white background the creature looked dirtier and more decayed. He briefly re-explained to Martha what this creature was.

'Name another.' She held his arm.

'Simulation: Gatekeeper!'

Terminus was sure that he'd felt something slip inside his mind. A not unpleasant feeling, rather like hoiking a long nose-string out of your sinuses after planet-fall. He assumed that the feeling was due to this database scanning his mind. He took two steps back as the scarlet-clad beauty appeared smiling before him. Her red eyes and black lips exuded none of the humanity of a living woman.

'She's beautiful,' Martha said. 'And thoroughly evil. There are millions like her in the system. Haemophites. That's what we know them as. Did you ever see anything like this? Simulation: Necrophites!'

Another woman appeared who was also pale in complexion. Her long dark dress touched the floor and her eyes were totally black. Terminus thought he was looking at a corpse. In her face several *other* eyes had opened. Black orbs stared out from her cheekbone, forehead, and neck. She held out her left hand, palm outwards and a large, black eye rested in her palm.

'One kiss and you are dead. Your body is re-animated and used. They occupy Thanatos Three. Please, Mister Terminus, summon some more.'

He showed Martha the lizard-birds and the Gatekeeper's Daughter. She was only half-formed as the last time he'd seen her she was in semi-darkness. At last she asked him to summon an image of the politico. When he appeared she bristled with recognition.

'We know him. His name is Anwar Akkbar. He's been to Babel twice to meet with some very deviant characters. So, it's led to this, has it? Poor soul. Deceived and destroyed.' Just then an intermittent bleeping interrupted the conversation. Martha pulled back the sleeve of her robe to reveal a slender, high-tech wrist-comm. She turned her back on him and with genuine anger in her voice hissed, 'Can't this wait. I'm dealing with a *very* serious issue here...'

Terminus stared into the white space. One word was all it would take. Martha was still speaking into her wrist. Some perverse voyeurism aroused a desire to see the shankaa. Just one more time.

'Simulation,' he said quietly, part of him hoping it wouldn't hear him. 'Urrseal!'

When the thing from his nightmares appeared it was naked. No cloak hid its arachnid features. Apart from the head it looked like a skeleton covered in spider's hide. Every bone from ribs to spine, carpals and tarsals, bristled with unnatural looking hair that sprouted roughly from mottled, dark brown skin. He stared at it. Urrseal stared back, unblinking, unmoving. It was just a simulation. It couldn't touch him but just its presence made him feel sick with fear. He turned. Martha was still speaking into the wrist-comm. He would have to interrupt her nattering because he wanted to get out of here and he wanted to get out now.

From behind him the voice froze his nerves.

'Terminus!'

He spun to face the creature.

'I haven't forgotten you, Terminus. Why run? I only want you to feel my touch... poisoning your flesh... fingering through your guts...'

Urrseal was upon him. Standing an inch from his shoulder. The arachnid hand moved up his arm, the hairs caressing his flesh.

'White-robed like a virgin for me.' Its mandibles moved with a perverse laugh.

Terminus backed away as the simulation took a step toward him, all six eyes blinking, and mandibles moving as it spoke. *'Very apt. You are a physical virgin again; remade, untouched. You are also a virgin to the extremities I will force you to endure.'*

This was no hallucination; Martha could see it too. She was screaming into the comm now for help. It moved closer, its hand outstretched. Terror surrendered to instinct, instinct to survive.

Terminus couldn't run. He couldn't even see the drenting door. Everything was white. Martha was panicking too.

'Simulation!' he barked. 'Setting: Skyfire. Summon: fire-blaster.'

'Deadspace or realspace.'

'Drenting realspace!' Instantly, a fire-blaster appeared in his hand. He checked settings, clicked the safety off, and then aimed. The simulation stopped dead. Urrseal extended his mandibles to say something else. Terminus fired.

The apparition exploded into pieces. Anything that escaped the initial blast was burned by smart-fire that lapped up the debris. The pieces fell to the floor still burning.

'That's impossible. That should not have happened.' Martha's voice was shaking.

Terminus lowered the weapon's nozzle to the floor. 'I really need a drink now.'

'I'm so sorry, Terminus. Are you in shock? Do you need prayer?' Martha's anxiety outstretched even his own.

Terminus drained the wine and said, 'Funny really. Shooting that simulation was actually quite cathartic. I guessed at the time that the simulation wasn't supposed to do that. I reckon that Thanaton veck somehow took remote control of the simulation.'

'Events are not always as scientific as that. On Agathos we deal in metaphysics and spirituality as much as we do in technology. Any weak spot in our faith is exploited by them. In a way the Thanatons did take control of the Canvas, but only as a consequence of your summoning Urrseal's image. We never summon the Thirteen on a simulation. We are walking on dangerous ground just by viewing images of creatures from their system. However, your quick thinking averted a potentially disastrous situation. You are to be commended, Terminus.'

'I've played fire-blaster in enough holo-halls. Much the same thing. It might have been Urrseal coming after me but he was still a simulation. The real thing couldn't be shot but that simulation could. I was working on a theory in there. Bit of a risky one. I should have summoned a Creator symbol to chuck at it but that's irrelevant now. Besides, it felt good to spanner it with a fire-blaster. Right now I'm more concerned about meeting the real thing again.'

The Genesis

Terminus found the café easily enough; tables spread out from its semicircular front under the shadow thrown by a statue of a curiously weathered-looking space-gannta. As he crossed the wide boulevard he spotted Naomi sitting at a table with two strangers. The boulevard's heavy traffic consisted solely of Agathons on foot. There wasn't a wheeled land-vehicle or levitating city-dart in sight. Any traffic seemed consigned to the air, which was filled by white flower-shuttles drifting in seemingly random patterns, almost colliding with buildings and one another.

He reached the café and got a good scan of the two sitting with Isaiah's daughter; a gannta and a geema. They weren't wearing white robes; they wore trouser suits made from the same brilliant-white cloth that everyone here, including himself, usually wore. Instead of the usual sandals, these people wore closed-toe boots. The wiry, black-haired gannta had a wide, smiling mouth and white teeth. Terminus instantly distrusted him. The stranger reminded him of the face-wing for the politicos; the publicists and info-casters. They were all smiles and digest. The geema looked astonishingly like Naomi but her black, curly hair bounced over her shoulders and contrasted with Naomi's white strands.

Naomi spotted him and waved him over.

'Terminus, this is my sister, Rebecca, and her husband, Joel.' Naomi gestured to the two. 'They're missionaries.'

Joel rose to his feet with a confidence that put Terminus ill at ease and stretched out his hand. Terminus hadn't shaken anyone's hand since he was a child back on Earth. 'Mister Terminus, our very own Lazarus!'

Naomi shot him a reproachful look. The patronizing drellock carried on. 'Pleased to meet you at last. I've heard you've had quite a time of it. Sit down, sit down.'

'Ignore him,' Rebecca said. 'So, I hear you've got my old room on Trinity. How are you finding the place?'

'Everyone has been very nice.' This placatory remark seemed to work as a reply in most of the situations he found himself in among the white-robes so he used it again here. A signal sounded on Joel's wrist-comm. Terminus noticed that it was identical to Martha's.

'Listen, we have to go.' He stood and Rebecca followed. Joel laid a hand on Terminus's shoulder, which he nearly shrugged off with an expletive. 'We have to be on board that Ark in thirty minutes. An assignment to Babel. Can't really talk about it.'

'Got to keep a secret, eh? That makes two of us.' Terminus matched Joel's winning smile, which dropped from his face, replaced by a frown. 'I'm not allowed to talk about what happened with me and Martha in the Canvas.'

Joel's face dropped even more at the mention of one of the Elders. Terminus guessed not many people got an audience with the Elders of Lebanon.

When the pair had gone, he sidled up to Naomi.

'Well?' she said. 'Are you going to tell *me* what happened? In confidence, of course.'

'Only if you get us a pitcher of wine. I haven't got any ching on me.'

'Neither have I any money.' She grinned, taking a sip of that herb drink she constantly drank. 'We don't use it on this planet. I have something to celebrate. I've been selected. I'm going to be a missionary!'

Terminus found himself hugging her as a form of congratulation. They did that a lot on this planet, he'd noticed, and without thought he was now doing it himself. He briefly felt the warmth of her body, the smell of her hair, and as he did so she returned the gesture. She let go and went to fetch some wine, leaving him feeling flushed by her touch. The feeling was not unpleasant. When she returned she poured them both a glass.

'So, what do you think of Nazareth?' she asked.

The pitcher was empty and the sun was beginning to set against the moon they called home, Trinity Three. Sub-stretches had passed. The conversation had moved on from how excited Naomi was to be a missionary, and they were now discussing procreation.

'So no one does it before marriage? Are you sure? Don't people just have a sneaky vulley when they think everyone's asleep?'

'No they don't, Terminus. Everyone would know.'

'How would anyone know? Ah, is that why you don't have doors in your houses, so you can be heard if you do try it?'

'No, you idiot! Nine months later a baby pops out or didn't your parents tell you that bit?'

'What about birth-stoppers? Take one, no one will know.'

'We don't have contraceptives here. We believe that sex exists to bring children onto the planet. We take this seriously.'

'So Joey never did it with your sister until he married her. He's over thirty cycles old. Are you telling me he was a pizzdeen for all that time?'

She rolled her eyes. 'Procreation is an experience given to us by the Creator. We have that special moment with our loved one. We mustn't waste that moment on anyone but on the one the Creator has chosen for us.'

'I should import some birth-stoppers here. I'll make mega-ching.' He looked up to the Ark drifting lazily over the city, then he returned to Naomi. 'So, is there some special person the Creator has chosen for you? Not that I believe he exists for one second, you understand.'

'No. No there isn't. And right now I don't want there to be. I want to see the galaxy first.' She too looked to the Ark that drifted above the Elders' state rooms.

'Naomi.' He moved closer to her, his face serious. 'What was I like when I first got here? Nobody's told me what sort of state I was in. I mean, which hospital did I go to?'

He detected unease in her answer, like he had just put her on the spot. 'You weren't taken to hospital. There are no hospitals. All healing takes place in the temple. You see, your ship hit the Ark that had been dispatched to save you. You were brought straight to Trinity One where the villagers, plus most of the crew, administered spiritual healing. You're not going to believe this, that's why we've been a bit hesitant about telling you. We invoked the spirit of the Creator. It only happens in the direst of emergencies. You were bleeding, your bones... you were in such a mess, Terminus. The Creator healed your wounds. We stayed all night praying until you were knit back together. This must sound strange to you but that's what happened. That's what always happens to the injured.'

He grinned slightly drunkenly. 'I want to say I don't believe you.' He grinned at her again. 'But I know you wouldn't lie. Tell me, were you there?'

'I was there all day and all night cleaning your wounds as they healed.'

For a moment he was speechless, the wine had gone to his head in the sun. He wanted to show his gratitude somehow. All he managed was a half-whispered, 'Thank you.'

They walked to the square built around the rusting hulk of their colony ship. The *Genesis* resembled a vast cathedral forged from neglected steel. Together they stood under its shadow.

'Yes it's old,' he said, 'but I still can't believe you drellocks came here in this craft four hundred cycles before we got to Skyfire.'

'You're just jealous that we got to a habitable world first. Look how *old* she is. Agathos was just a pink-soiled paradise back then. I don't know why Trinity Three has brown soil and Agathos pink but the soil here is fertile enough. They made this planet out of nothing with only the guidance of the Creator.'

'Still doesn't mean it's true, or that he's real for that matter.'

'I'm not getting into another argument about this, Terminus. All you need to know is that this ship brought the pilgrims here. That's enough for me. I want to go into space to honor the Creator, to honor my ancestors who piloted the *Genesis.*'

Almost absent-mindedly she slipped her arm through his as they stood there admiring the relic. He looked down wondering why she wanted to be close to him at that moment. He didn't withdraw or take his arm away.

Naomi's Suitors

The primitiveness of this planet still amazed him. That morning they'd herded several dozen bleating mammals from Isaiah's field to Matthew's farm on the other side of the valley. They had the technology to teleport the beasts from one place to another but still chose to coerce and shepherd them across a stretch of two clicks. Ezekiel, Matthew's youngest son, had helped. Terminus remembered him from the haymaking day. Naomi cranned Ezekiel's tank but Terminus didn't think Naomi felt the same.

Herding had been thirsty work and now Terminus, Matthew, and Isaiah sat drinking fruit beer under the shade of low trees with thick branches and wide leaves to shelter them from the sun. Ezekiel had gone off fishing with his sister, giving the men time to talk. They reclined on wide wooden seats set around a circular wooden table.

'I wanted to talk to you about something, Isaiah,' Matthew said as he poured out another glass of fruit beer.

'Oh?'

'It's about Ezekiel. He's about that age. Marrying age. He came to me last week and asked me to convey interest. You know how it is. These things can be embarrassing for the young, all uncertainty and high hopes.'

'That's why *we* negotiate on their behalf, Matthew. To spare them any embarrassment. It was the way with my daughter Rebecca and Joel's father. I went to Jordan to convey interest. Although I think by then their future was clear.' He laughed. 'They were like a pair of courting grass-birds even before the will of the Creator was sought.'

Terminus listened, feeling slightly uncomfortable. He wondered if he should be here when these two fathers were discussing their children's futures in such depth. The beaky side of him won out; he found it fascinating studying this freakish sub-culture up close.

'Ah, but things are changing,' said Isaiah. 'On Nazareth a boy and a girl will seek the will of the Creator for themselves, at temple.'

'Well, I'm a traditionalist, Matthew. I believe the parents should be involved at every stage of the process.'

Terminus smirked, causing Matthew and Isaiah to look at him. He smirked because he imagined the fathers standing over the kids while they vullied on their wedding night, giving them tips, positioning them, urging them on and the like.

'Sorry, carry on.'

'My point is...' Matthew laid his thick arms on the table. 'I'm conveying an interest, on my son's behalf, for Naomi. I know he is younger but he's a good boy.'

'You don't have to sell him to me, Matthew! It's Naomi's choice. I'm merely the go-between. However, I have to tell you that I already have a conveyance of interest from the father of Daniel, an inter-system ambassador from Nazareth.'

Matthew looked worried. His son's happiness was at stake. 'What has she decided?'

'She's yet to make her mind up. Now she has two choices to make. One thing is for certain. She's not getting any younger. She's twenty-two, well past the marrying age. Before she knows it, she'll be thirty and finding a suitor will become more difficult. Times might be changing but it's still rare to be unmarried at her age. I can count on my hand the bachelors I know of that age. There's Gideon over at Jezreel, John of the Lake—'

'So these two ganntas,' Terminus cut in, 'are they gonna wait for Naomi to come back from her missionary cycles or are they gonna sign up as well?'

Matthew frowned. Isaiah looked gob-smacked. 'I'm sorry?'

'Naomi's joined the missionaries. They've accepted her. What, hasn't she told you?'

The walk back to Jericho was silent and brooding. And long; it was very long. Two clicks was an interstellar distance with Isaiah looking so totally casped off.

At last Terminus couldn't stand the silence any longer. 'Look, Isaiah. I didn't know she hadn't told you. I'm sure she wasn't going to just frac off in the night.'

'I had other hopes for that girl.'

'Yeah, well maybe your hopes for her were all digest, Isaiah.' The father stopped in his tracks. The old man knew what that meant and wasn't used to people speaking to him in that way. Terminus carried on. 'It's not my place to interfere in your family but I can see what's going on. She wants to go into space and you want her to have spudders, you want grandkids. You said it back there; you said she's nearly past marrying age. Marrying age! Drent! Utter vulley. She's twenty-two cycles old and has her whole life in front of her. She can get Linked any time she wants. She can get Linked when she's sixty if she wants to.'

'You don't understand what it's like in this society. Family is everything.'

'Well, it's time this society changed! I know her pretty well. I razzle that she would rather walk the great vacuum and see the stars than spend her life making spudders. *Think* about it. She will spend the rest of her life wondering what's out there. Instead of ever finding out, she'll be feeding spudders and wiping their digest spreaders.'

'I've lost one daughter to the stars.' He turned and walked on. 'I don't want to lose another.'

Moon-Storm

As Terminus drifted up from deep sleep to the surface of wakefulness, he found himself caught in that twilight world between consciousness and unconsciousness. Faces and events ran through his mind. He saw the women he had known, their faces transforming in his mind's eye. He saw Naomi's face, her dimpled smile, her blue eyes and white hair. She transmuted into Clannel. Clannel was naked. It was morning and she was holding him. Her dark, cropped hair and wide mouth filled his vision. She was naked in their apartment overlooking the Sea of Dust back on Skyfire. The scene changed. She was by a lake on Agathos. She was naked. She was Naomi.

He sat up.

The bell was tolling for dawn mass. He waited for the household to go, watching as they marched down the hill to the temple. He didn't want to bump into Isaiah after last night's argument. Later on, he'd catch the old man and apologize. That would clear things up. Terminus went to the water room on the second floor and doused himself with clean, fresh water. The tap spat it out intermittently as he filled the bucket to wash. Afterwards, he cut some bread and went to sit outside. Before he left he noticed a book open at the kitchen table. The small, blue tome was surrounded by Philip's paraphernalia — carbon writing sticks and paper — so it must have been part of his educational program. It was a lot like the books that filled the library at the Gatekeeper's habitat. The book had no title and the script was Old Earther, Northern Hemisphere. As he flicked through the last two hundred pages or so he saw a familiar name: Lazarus. Joel had called him Lazarus so Terminus read on. According to this text, which must have been some sort of myth, this Lazarus died and was brought back to life by the power of the Creator. Thinking nothing of it, Terminus closed the book and went outside to eat the bread.

'Hey, Terminus, what are you doing today?' Naomi bounced up to him.

'Nothing. After yesterday's hillcow round-up I'm taking it easy.'

'How about I show you the canyon? It's a bit of a walk.'

Without having to think about it he replied. 'Yeah, fine.'

'Let's get some lunch to take with us.' She took his arm as they went to the kitchen. 'Hey, they're all talking in Jericho about you shooting that thing in the simulation room. We can't take you anywhere.'

'It least I shot it. You would have run away screaming like the geema you are.'

Naomi laughed. She was all right, that Agathon. She had a sense of humor.

He felt mild relief and a restrained excitement at the prospect of spending a whole day with her. This was better than chopping wood. They packed some fruit and set off north toward the canyon beyond somewhere called Sidon. As the two travelers passed out toward the lake, they continued beyond the domed buildings Terminus had noticed before from the air. She was so excited at the prospect of joining their space agency that she didn't shut up for eons. He didn't mind, he liked the sound of her voice. He felt envious of her, in a way, with her family and the opportunity for a safe transition from adolescence to adulthood. She reeled off seemingly trivial family events such as the day Isaiah broke his leg chasing a hillcow and had to be taken to the temple for healing. She recounted the day when her sister left the water pail from the bathroom on top of the kitchen door, a trick to play on Naomi, but instead it soaked one of the settlement Elders who had come to see Father. He heard all about her sister's wedding to Joel last year, in great detail; how the women of the house had made the dress; how they'd travelled to Trinity Two to pick wedding flowers; how she and Rebecca had climbed to the top of the temple tower at midnight when everyone else was asleep the night before the wedding. She went over in great detail how she'd danced with some boy from Sidon but he was now married to a hillcow farmer on the far side of the moon.

They crossed into the dip of a valley and passed a small stream, stopping to take a drink before the ascent ahead.

'Do people get married on Skyfire?' she asked.

'Well, they get Linked. It's a legal requirement. When a gannta and a geema decide to share a gemmel, an apartment, they get registered as being Linked. That way they share the gemmel equally. It's nothing like your ceremonies. We get snakkied afterwards, all the friends, the mat and pat.'

For one horrendous moment he thought she might ask him if he was Linked but she let the question pass. Instead she carried on talking and he actually listened. When Clannel talked he tended to switch off but when Naomi recited people and events he paid great attention. He simply told himself that through these accounts he was gaining an insight into Agathon society. This was true but there was more to it than that. Terminus felt as if he was looking through a window that looked out onto a view of paradise. He drank in Naomi's anecdotes of her near-perfect life on this moon. He was fascinated by the details of her childhood, near mesmerized by her family and its foundations; even her faith in an immortal Creator began to sound interesting. Something had opened up in him, an acceptance of this purity that only a sub-cycle ago would have grated on his nerves. He had never met, nor would ever meet again, any person quite like Naomi. She was both physically beautiful and stunningly innocent. There was something about her, an attraction that went deeper than the physical. He couldn't quite put his finger on it.

A key fact bulldozed its way through Terminus's mind; Naomi did not view the space-gannta as a prospect. She was far too sure of herself and far too in touch with her feelings to think of him in that way. They took cranning far too seriously on this moon. Look how Matthew and Isaiah had discussed their kids' futures yester-stretch, he told himself. Terminus was not one of them; he was not a prospect. As for all the physical contact, the arm linking, the play fights; they meant drent, nothing.

They were all like this on this planet; all smiles and hugs. Their religion expected it. Naomi didn't crann him; she wanted what he had — space travel — and now she had it. He could never see her — what did they call it on this planet, their word for Linking? *Marrying.* She would never marry him. Once he left this place that would be it. It was vital, then, that he enjoyed her company now.

'Naomi,' he said. 'I kind of had an argument with your pat.'

'Oh, he'll forgive you. Don't worry about it.'

'I'm not worried about it. Our words were about you.'

'Really?'

'Yes. We were over at Matthew's. That drellock, Ezekiel, has a tank-crann for you. His pat was asking your pat if you were interested.'

'Which I'm not.'

'And I let out that you were going to missionary training.'

'Oh dear.'

'Yeah, and on the way home I basically said you didn't want to get Linked but wanted to go into space. He said he's already lost one daughter to the stars and didn't want to lose another.'

She stopped, and for a second he thought she was going to casp off at him. He was pleasantly surprised when a smile creased her dimples. 'So you stood up for me? You got involved in a family argument? I'm flattered. I really am. You're a brave man, Sii. Family arguments are not something to get tangled in.'

As she walked she could not stop grinning.

They reached the next rise and she started telling him about the crazy time she'd eaten fifteen earth-fruits and was sick.

'I stood in front of a neuro-scrambler once. It was on a medium setting. That was funny,' he said.

Naomi suddenly stopped. She was staring ahead at something and didn't look too happy about what she saw. Ahead, the sun was obscured by a vast bank of green cloud. It was heading toward them. A violent sheet of lightning tore across the underside of the cloud like an electric snake.

'It's a moon-storm. We'll have to go back,' she said. 'We can't be caught out in this. They can be fatal. And we'll get soaked.'

'The rate that cloud's moving, it'll be on top of us before we get home. Do we have to get into a shelter or anything?'

'No, just undercover.'

He scanned the vista before them. Half a click away, by a field of shorn grass, stood a small building.

'There,' he said. 'We can wait it out in there.'

'But the storm will be over us before we reach it.'

'Not if we run. Come on.'

Without thinking he took her hand and they dashed down the slope toward the building, a small grass-house used by mammal farmers for grass storage. The storm roared above and Terminus felt every strand on his head become inflamed with power as a huge crackle of lightning bounced across the underside of the clouds. The rain began to fall. Heavy drops of warm water lashed them, soaking them in moments.

They burst through the wooden door of the grass-house, and threw themselves into the dry interior. Naomi started laughing, Terminus frowned but then saw how soaked she was and he started laughing too. They were still both laughing as they tried to wring their robes out. It was futile. Still laughing, she faced him and ran her fingers through his wet hair playfully.

'In the Creator's name, you're soaked!'

'Well, so are you. Your strands are wringing!' He ran his fingers through her wet hair, and then realized that she was standing very close. As he continued to wring her long hair, her hand moved down to his face. She wasn't laughing now; she was scanning his gaze. Terminus knew what this meant. He'd been in moments like this before, but never with a girl who had occupied his mind so much. She moved closer to him. Outside the lightning cracked again. Simultaneously their lips touched and for a few brief seconds Terminus was lost in her kiss, his mind silenced.

She pulled away but locked her arms around his waist and looked him in the eyes again. She led him to the soft dry grass where they lay in each other's arms. Outside, the storm raged on, forgotten.

The storm slowly silenced. Naomi slept while Terminus thought. This was no platonic caress. The strokes and embraces had been lovers' strokes and embraces. He drank in the smell of her skin and the warmth of her presence as she slumbered with her head on his chest. Then he too briefly slept until the storm passed over. Anyone seeing them would think the pair were at peace, but Terminus's mind was spinning even as he slept.

When they awoke, Naomi briskly suggested they should go. They broke off from each other and tried to act normally. Standing, he wrapped his arms around her again and they, again, kissed.

'Terminus,' she said at last, 'has there ever been anyone in your life. A woman? Has there ever been a woman to share your life?'

His arms slid around her waist once more.

'No,' he lied. 'Never.'

Wreckage

They play fought, held hands and stopped to kiss several times on the return journey.

Terminus bathed in the innocence of it all, but bubbling away beneath the surface an ocean of conflicts ran through his soul. He had just kissed Isaiah's daughter, an Agathon pizzdeena who was going to be a missionary. A girl with strict religious beliefs. For her, this kiss could signify the start of a relationship. She might even think he would marry her. Just as well their paths were separating soon. Terminus would be going back to Skyfire and Naomi would be stationed on an Ark.

What really nagged at his thought box was the fact that he'd lied. There *was* someone else; there was Clannel, and although she might be four thousand pulses away on another planet she had a habit of turning up at inconvenient times, whether in his mind or in the flesh.

Naomi didn't seem concerned. She was smiling and laughing away. She would probably return and tell her family what had happened. Terminus would then have to lie to them as well. This was just drenting fantastic.

They took a different way home. As they skirted around an outcropping of rock, Terminus noticed they were walking beside the domed constructions that he had spotted before. There were three of them and from the opening to the front of the domes he could see that the first construct housed one of the bubble shuttles. The domes weren't very big, perhaps six meters at their highest point and colored a garish yellow. As they passed he noticed Naomi's body language change slightly. She let go of his hand and hurried on as if she wanted to get away from the domes.

'What else do they keep in here?' He said. Terminus noticed her eyes widen as he asked this.

'Let's get back. I'll be late for dusk mass if we don't get a move on.'

'Hey, I just want a look. I'm a beaky gannta, always have been. What's in here?' He marched over to the second housing dome and stopped dead at the door.

Immediately all thoughts of Naomi were banished. Although she was standing a few feet behind him, she may as well have not been there. He entered the cool shade of the dome and stood over what was left of a spacecraft. It would have been unrecognizable but for the rust-red body color and the familiar control panels that were now outside of the hull, a hull that had been smashed open and gutted by the impact. The 850 was twisted and dead; most of it wasn't even here. From within the wreckage he could see the command seat crushed up against the navigation panel. Wedged against it was the book with its red leather cover still intact. He was surprised that they'd left it because they didn't tolerate any object from the enemy system here. Obviously they hadn't spotted it. He angled his head to look behind him. Naomi was sitting on the grass looking away from the dome, so he quickly seized the book and hid it more securely under the seat, out of sight from anyone who might want to inspect the wreckage. As he did this he was taken over by the oddest feeling. To get the book he had to steady himself on the command seat. The last time he had touched this seat he was sitting in it convinced he was going to die. All those emotions flooded his mind again, every muscle in his body locked in flexion. He fell to his knees and vomited.

*

Terminus lay awake all night staring at the stars through his window. The more he thought about the wreckage the more he realized that, judging by the angle the command chair had smashed into the navigation panel, he would have been crushed to death. He shouldn't have survived the crash. The only solution he could think of was that the Agathons must have teleported him out seconds before impact. That must have been what happened, it *must* have been.

Joel

Naomi hadn't said a word. When the others weren't looking she'd wink at him or touch his hand discretely. The kiss in the grass barn was their secret for now. That came as some relief.

There was much excitement and preparation in Isaiah's household. Joel and Rebecca had announced that they'd been given some time off from their missionary duties, and the couple would be arriving on Trinity in two cycle's time. Celebration feasts were usual when husband and wife arrived back at the family home, and so preparations were well underway in Isaiah's home. Other relatives from Nazareth and the outer towns located on the shores of Lebanon would be arriving on Trinity to share the meal.

The kitchen was alive with good-natured banter as the whole family prepared food. Among the sounds of chopping, Naomi and her younger brother were mocking Terminus's accent. He was busy peeling the skin from a potato, some sort of vegetable grown and harvested from the ground behind the house. He and Isaiah had spent most of the morning yanking them out the soil. During this task Isaiah had offered an apology for the previous night's argument.

Naomi held a potato in front of her and talked to it, trying to mimic Terminus's Skyfirean accent. 'Ere... lay a drellock on me you old veck.'

'My old gannta,' Philip squeaked. 'Your old gannta, drent me a potato, you old digest spreader.'

Sarah barked from the stove. 'Will you *stop* using those words.'

'Sorry Sarah, it's my fault. I taught them those words,' Terminus mock-apologized. 'But I never taught them to be such a bunch of hanging drellocks. That was your department.'

Sarah smiled and was about to say something when one of the twins burst in to the kitchen.

'Mother, the hillcows are in Elder John's pasture again!'

She threw her hands into the air and growled, exasperated. 'In the name of the Creator, they choose their times to get out! Philip, come with me. You two, keep peeling!' She grabbed a handful of honey-grass from a shelf above the spice rack and flew out of the door. The honey-grass would bring them back; they were attracted by the scent.

Suddenly, Terminus found he was alone with Naomi. He didn't know whether to kiss her or run. She immediately sensed his awkwardness.

'Look,' she began. 'I know that on your world things are different. You don't take courtship too seriously. Also, you don't want my father thinking that you are some space-traveler taking advantage of me. I know that isn't the case. You are different. You're honest. You wear your heart on your sleeve and you've told me there's no one else in your life. What I'm trying to say is; just don't worry. There's nothing to worry about. Is that clear?' He met her blue eyes with his own and felt instant relief. However, it was short-lived.

Naomi was smiling as she asked: 'So, when should we tell them? Tonight?'

Terminus froze. The idea of telling Isaiah or worse, Sarah, made his guts churn. On Skyfire you never met the mat and pat until you got linked. This was off the scanner. What the hell did it have to do with Isaiah and Sarah? But as Naomi had said, things were done differently on this planet. He panicked for a moment but quickly formulated a plan.

'I'll tell Isaiah. I'll tell him when I'm alone.'

'Do it tonight. I'll *have* to tell Rebecca. I'm dying to tell her. She'll tell Joel and then it will be all over the settlement.' Naomi looked at him with those sincere blue eyes again. 'I don't want them finding out about this through someone else.'

Terminus's mind had flipped over at the mention of Joel's name. Suddenly his predicament with Naomi was pushed aside. Terminus wanted a chat with this Joel. A private natter where they would get to the beak of this Lazarus business. Naomi leaned forward to kiss him. His mind flipped back as her lips met his. Another feeling flooded into his mind; the pleasant, blissful sensation of her kiss. Among the turmoil of his problems he felt warmth emanate from her.

'More wine, Joel?' Without waiting for a reply he filled Joel's glass. The missionary was happy enough to drink it down despite warnings from his wife across the table. The feast was now in full swing and the guests had plied the homecoming couple with questions about their missions to various systems. Joel had boasted about the worlds they had set foot on. Terminus retorted stating he'd 'been there' and listed ten other planets he'd been to that Joel hadn't. As Joel got drunker an argument between himself and Terminus brewed. Joel had boasted that the Agathon Arks were far superior to Skyfirean deep space vacuum-farers.

'That's true. But we take the risk of going into deep space with what we've got. Really, what do you see and experience from the viewport of one of those vessels? We see the lot. My old ship, the 850, you had to go to manual to initiate planet-fall. Ever landed a ship on manual, Jo? Thought not. So I razzle we've got more muck in our sack's than you Ark ganntas ever had.'

Sarah had skillfully turned the conversation to other matters, like hillcows escaping, while a female of Naomi's age — possibly her cousin, Terminus couldn't remember — quizzed him about Ragreesh, a colony world in the Doolek system. At given moments,

Terminus would fill Joel's glass again, sometimes without him realizing.

After the food had been eaten he helped to clear the plates at the water-tap. Naomi followed him.

'When are you going to tell my father?'

'I don't know. Not tonight. Look, he's surrounded by old ganntas. I'll tell him tomorrow. I'll go down to the temple with him at dawn.'

She looked less than happy but still kissed him on the cheek. Before Terminus sat down he grabbed another pitcher of wine. He returned to his seat and he saw Joel, eyes glazed, glass raised for another gulp of snakki.

'I get the feeling you don't like me much, Terminus.'

He had taken Joel outside for some fresh air because Rebecca thought he was going to be sick. The missionary was swaying discordantly so sat down on a log. This drunken Joel was ready for an argument.

'Did you hear what I said? I said you don't like me much. I know what it is, Terminus. It's not that I've been farther than you have ever been, and in a faster ship too. Now, that you can handle. What really gets you is that I have a family to come back to, a loving wife. I make you feel small, Terminus. I get the security of family *and* the rush of adventure, of risk.'

'Listen to me, you strentner. I don't like you because you're cocky, arrogant and, worst of all, you can't handle your snakki. As for risk and adventure, I've walked the surface of Thanatos One. This argument ends now!' Terminus stood over him. The gannta looked like he was going to be sick again. 'I want answers from you. That time I saw you in Nazareth, you called me Lazarus. Why did you call me that?'

'You mean they still haven't told you?'

'Told me what?'

218

'Terminus, I can't tell you. I'm sworn to secrecy. I cannot break a promise.'

'I need to know, Joel.'

'Work it out, or are all you Skyfireans brainless? Lazarus. What did Lazarus do? Damn, I've said too much.'

'According to that book, Lazarus was brought back from the dead. Are you telling me I've been brought back from the dead? That's impossible! That's drenting impossible.'

But Joel would say nothing. Terminus thought a smirk ghosted across the drellock's face but it was difficult to be sure in the gloom of the night.

The Death of Terminus

Dawn broke over the settlement as Isaiah wound his way down to the cluster of buildings. As the patriarch entered the temple, he felt a chill emanate from the open space when crossing the floor. He took the heat probe from beside the stacked pile of candles and pressed it to the wick of the thick, white candle that sat at the back of the temple. The others would be here soon. Some of the most eager inhabitants arrived even before he had sounded the bell. Although not many from his household would be early to mass after last night's celebrations. The soft light of the candle illuminating the temple revealed a figure slouched against the western wall. Dark eyes glared at Isaiah and for a moment the old man felt something he had not encountered for a long time: fear.

'Terminus, how long have you been there? Have you decided to attend dawn mass?'

So maybe Isaiah wasn't the goomah Terminus had first taken him to be, but the old man had casped him off all the same. So as to rasp in the old gannta's thought box a little, Terminus didn't reply straight away. But Terminus was too curious to play hard-gannta for long. He sprang away from the wall and faced the old man. 'No, Isaiah. I'm not here for your drenting mass. I've come to seek answers. I want the whole truth.'

'Then why lie in wait for me here? You know you can approach me at any time.'

'Naomi told me that this is the place where the Creator talks to you. I reasoned that this would be the place where he would be listening. So if you lie, he'll hear it.'

'We do not lie, Terminus. It's not a trait we foster.'

'But you do conceal truth, don't you? You don't always get to the beak of the situation, if you get my drift. I reckon that's about as close to lying as you can get.'

Isaiah was silent for a long time. Eventually he said, 'I am sorry if we have deceived you in any way.' He let silence hang in the air like a bad smell.

'So, to the beak of it. The wreck of my ship is down in one of those storage sheds. I saw it. The 850 was crumpled up like a probe in a black hole. There's no way I could have survived that crash. When we were in Nazareth, Joel called me Lazarus. So last night I asked him why he called me that. He told me to work it out. Lazarus, according to your instruction manual from the Creator, was this gannta who died and was brought back to life again.'

Terminus was about to speak when Isaiah shattered his line of interrogation. 'You were dead when they retrieved you from the space near Thanatos One.'

Terminus stood rooted to the spot. His initial instinct was to disbelieve Isaiah totally. Then a paralyzing confusion set in that raged like a storm in his mind. Isaiah carried on. 'It was Joel's ship, the *Sidon* that detected your cargo transporter. It pulled out of hyperspace and the plan was to try and teleport you out of the craft before it hit the hull of the *Sidon*. They failed. You were literally in bits aboard that ship. You had been impaled through the chest with a large girder from your own craft. An unholy disease was eating into your face; insects were actually gestating in the flesh. They light-blasted the black galleons and transported what was left of the 850 onto the *Sidon*. Our ships are huge, you've seen them. Your remains were frozen and it was decided that you would be transported to edge station *Cloud Dust*. However, when the Ark's chaplain was meditating in the spirit-room, he had a vision from the Creator. Terminus, very rarely does the Creator speak with such clarity, even to the most spiritual. The chaplain saw a vision of the man Lazarus being brought back to life. A clear vision where he could see Lazarus's features. When he came to perform the last rites over your body he recognized your face from his vision. He ordered that you be taken to Agathos. So the Ark redirected its course and the prayers for healing began.'

Terminus was too stunned to argue, sneer, or try to pick holes in the story. He simply listened with a vacant expression masking his face. Isaiah carried on.

'At the same time the chaplain had his vision, I was having a restless night. I had a dream. I never dream, Terminus, so I knew it was from the Creator. I dreamed a lost, wounded soul arrived at my door. A soul pursued by the Destroyer. When I woke, the communicator was alerting me to the arrival of an Ark. The chaplain, and a few of the others from the *Sidon*, teleported straight into the temple with your body. I and the other Elders began intercession. You lay on that plinth, just there.' He pointed to the raised platform in middle of the temple floor. 'The chaplain and I both decided that we would pray until you came to life, that being the will of the Creator. Others were not so optimistic. Perhaps the chaplain and I were so determined because we had experienced the visions, I don't know. We prayed for hours, beseeching the Creator to restore you back to life. We've never done this before. We believe that if the Creator has decided that the span of a person's life has ended, then it is time for us to give thanks for that life, not to resist the Creator's will. We use prayer to cure minor wounds or broken bones but to bring someone back to life? That has never been done before, not in this system.

'So I fetched Naomi and Sarah. Some of the others joined us. As we prayed all the candles blew out at once, which was impossible because there was no wind in here to blow them out. The darkness in the temple became impenetrable. I tell you, I was frightened. We all were. Then the room became cold, as cold as winter. I lit a candle and actually saw frost on the walls. Then my candle went out, not blown out but extinguished by this unnatural darkness. No light was allowed in this place. Our hearts nearly stopped when we heard moans all around us. They began to grow in intensity but before they could reach a crescendo a blinding white light banished all the darkness.

'You coughed, Terminus, you coughed and began to breathe. All your wounds were gone. All the implants and all the wounds, gone.'

Terminus collapsed to the floor of the temple, his mind numb, unable to take in what Isaiah had told him. Outside, the day had arrived and the sun was blazing in the sky. No one had arrived at dawn mass because Isaiah hadn't rung the bell. Even the early risers were staying away today. Anticipating his questions, Isaiah said: 'An enquiry was held. The Elders believe that your fate-line is strong, that you serve some higher purpose in your life. That's why the Creator wanted you saved.'

After some time Terminus spoke.

'Huh, funny. That's what one of the Thirteen said. He said my fate-line, my destiny-line, was strong.' He got to his feet. 'Have you told Skyfire this?'

Isaiah sighed. 'We have had no contact with them. But we do tap into their systems and a few days ago you were listed as missing. Yesterday they reported you as dead.'

'So everyone on Skyfire thinks I'm dead. All my friends, my commanders, my... friend, Clannel. They all think I'm dead.'

'We think it's best that it stays that way. The Thirteen will be looking for you. They could use any of your acquaintances on Skyfire to get to you. You are safe here. They cannot touch you here.'

Terminus stood, paced the temple, and knotted his brow. 'The Ark, what did you call him... chaplain? Him. I guess I owe him my thanks. And you, Isaiah, but I'd like to thank this chaplain gannta the most. What's his name?'

'You know him, it's Joel.'

'Then in that case I owe him an apology too.'

Second Death

Terminus threw the last of the split logs into the pile and chucked the axe into the ground. That was it; the job was finished. The logs were stacked neatly against the wall. He put his hands on his hips, satisfied to think that the family would have wood for the winter. Terminus hoped that as they burned the wood, and fire kept them warm, they would think of him. He couldn't imagine this place covered in ice and snow, frost glistening across the roof tops. It came pretty rapidly, Isaiah had said, and summer came around just as suddenly. Terminus wouldn't be here to see it, that was for sure.

He washed at the water pump and threw his whites on. The family were at the table eating the midday meal. Taking his place amongst them, he began to cut a large lump of cured yellow dairy product called cheese and pushed it into his bread. They were all there: Isaiah, Sarah, Philip, Naomi, and the twin girls who used to remind him of the Virgins of the Abyss. Now the fear was gone. Terminus had reconciled the events of the black planet and he was over it. He was cured, spiritually and emotionally cured.

'The logs are finished, Isaiah. You'll have enough for the winter.'

'Thank you, Terminus. We'll have to find another job for you.'

'I wouldn't bother, I'm leaving.' He pulled the bread apart. 'I'm going back to Skyfire.'

Isaiah stopped eating his soup and put down his spoon with great meaning. 'Don't you think we should talk about this?'

'Let's talk now. I've been living here with all of you for long enough for you all to have a say about it. Even the kids, Isaiah. I reckon they should have their say.'

'You are welcome to stay,' Sarah said. 'You can become part of the family.' Sarah wasn't stupid. She'd guessed that something was going on between Naomi and himself.

'You have to think of your own safety,' said Isaiah. 'There are… elements… out there in the universe that would show an interest in you.' Tactfully said.

'I know the Thirteen still want me. I can't hide forever. If there's one thing I've learned in this life then it's that you've got to stand up for yourself.'

'We're not talking about some childhood bully, Terminus. We're talking about very powerful beings.'

'I faced them once, I'll face them again. If I hide like some rock klep from desert scurriers they'll have won. They are not going to win.'

'Your enemies—' Isaiah ran his finger through his hair in despair '—are closer to home than you think. There are people on your home world whose sympathies lie with Thanatos. People in power, such as your cargo, Anwar Akkbar. You will be alone and defenseless. And another thing, people are going to be very surprised indeed when you arrive back on Skyfire alive and well when you are officially dead.'

'I know. That'll be funny. I'll gas my tank when I see the look in their faces.'

'Your government would probably think it better that you were dead, to avoid the embarrassment of having one of their leaders, a politico, involved with a deviant culture such the Thanatons. They'll want to cover this up and you will be living proof that it happened. You will be in so much danger.'

'The universe is a dangerous place.'

'What? Such arrogance!' Isaiah was standing up now, his face red, his chest puffing out.

'You remind me of my own pat.' Terminus laughed. 'Naomi, you put up with twenty-two cycles of this! No wonder you wanted to join the space-preachers.'

'You don't understand!'

'You're right. I don't. I was brought here to get over being on Thanatos. I'm over it, job checked and logged, over and done. What I can't get over is that I was dead. Dead as meat and now I'm alive. I don't understand that and I don't want to. It's too weird. I want to put it behind me and the only way to do that is leave.'

Exasperated, Isaiah gave in. 'Well, it's your choice. You could have been safe and happy here. You could have lived out your life with us.'

'We'll be sorry to lose you.' Sarah said. One of the twins crawled onto his lap with the tactile forwardness that only kids have, and hung around his neck. Philip, to his surprise, started crying.

Terminus scanned the faces around the table and felt scanner-leak prickle the backs of his own scan-balls. He wasn't going to run this time. It was all right, or so he thought. Naomi was looking at him, frowning.

Naomi and Terminus

'I'm coming with you!' Naomi ran after him as he boarded the bubble shuttle. She saw his astonished look. 'Only to Nazareth, I'm not coming back to Skyfire if that's what you were thinking.' She took a seat next to him and the pilot ran his palm over the light panels. As they rose into the sky he waved to the family below for the fifteen millionth time and they didn't stop waving until the bubble was out of atmosphere.

'I'm sorry if I gave you the wrong idea,' he began 'It's just that, well, I thought you were going to crew an Ark. I couldn't not return to Skyfire. For one thing I have to report to my coordinator and explain that I'm not dead. Do you understand?'

He hated exchanges like this. The pilot, a chubby black man, would hear everything for a start. He knew from experience that Naomi would neuro out any moment and start screaming at him. That's what Clannel did. He was pleasantly surprised when she replied with reasoned, calm response.

'Like my father says, choice is the most important thing. You must choose what is for the best. Personally, I'd have liked you to join me on the crew of an Ark. I think your experience and quick thinking would have been an asset. Life doesn't always turn out the way we think it should.'

A sudden sadness began to crawl into his nerves. In the confusion of the last few stretches he'd not really given much thought to the fact that he was leaving Naomi behind.

He studied her slightly freckled cheeks, her dimpled mouth, her soft golden strands and he embraced her. She relaxed in his arms and he felt that same familiar warmth countering the sadness. In that instant he realized that she'd cranned his tank. He wanted to be with her. He wanted to stay here and have a few more sub-cycles just being with her.

After touch-down they exited at the plaza. The bubble shuttle waited.

'Martha wants to see me before I go,' he said. Naomi didn't respond; she looked like she'd solidified. He added: 'I think that shuttle gannta is ready to take you back.'

'I know...' she said, but he had the feeling she wasn't answering him. 'I know I'm probably being a drellock, and you don't feel the same way as us Agathons, but I want to know one thing. If you had stayed and I'd not gone to the missionaries, would you have stayed with me? More to the point, would you have married me?'

'Of course I would have.'

His answer was too quick, too unconsidered, but Naomi didn't notice. Terminus bent down to kiss her and met her mouth. She responded, eliciting stares from passing Agathons. He held her head in his hands for a few moments longer before they parted. She boarded and he watched her drift into the sky feeling like he had lost yet escaped, was free but alone.

'So you wish to return to Skyfire. No doubt Isaiah has pointed out the dangers of such an undertaking, dangers you are already aware of and you've ignored his advice because you've made up your mind. Oh, the arrogance of youth.' Martha walked him through the large central hall of the Elders' meeting house to the diplomats' departure port. She had provided some Skyfirean clothes for him to wear; a pale body suit, also topknots, trousers and even slids. Martha had given him a small amount of ching for when he got back, to pay for transport fares and noosh. 'You know of course that once you are out of this system you are out of the protection of the Agathons. The

Thirteen were almost able to penetrate Agathos using the Canvas. They will have no problem reaching you on Skyfire, a place without spiritual protection.'

'Yes, I know.'

'However, you are never out of the Creator's protection. I don't know if your beliefs have altered in the time you spent here but I would like you to have this.' She held up a small Creator symbol on a chain. It had a big head and a wide, smiling mouth with the clumsy, childlike arms reaching out to embrace humanity.

'You haven't got a fire-blaster as well, have you?' He grinned.

'Fat lot of good it will do you. Anyway, have the Creator's blessing, Terminus, and if you ever need to return, you will always be welcome.'

He kissed her on the cheek, which she wasn't expecting but seemed to flatter her nonetheless. A Skyfirean liner was waiting on the planet-fall platform. A large red ship, twice the size of the 850 tested its grav-lift thrusters. Along with a few other ganntas, he boarded the lower deck of the ship. There was an upper deck for politicos and scilitos but it was empty. He looked to the sky as he boarded. There wasn't a single Ark to be seen. This liner only ran once a sub-cycle so Terminus estimated that they kept the Arks out of sight whenever it was here.

He was temporarily reassured by the familiar functional interior of the ship until memories of the 850 popped up in his mind. The bunks were exactly the same design as the ones aboard his old ship, except there were more of them. The gannta next to him started speaking to him.

'Drenting bunch of goomahs on this world,' he was saying. 'Gives me the neuros, all this religion, all this being nice to one another. Can't wait to leave, me. And it's too drenting hot here.'

Terminus ignored him and crawled into the man-sized space that would be home for the next four sub-cycles. He felt like he was making a grave mistake, leaving Agathos, but then Terminus was good at making mistakes; he'd turned it into an art form. He felt the grav-lift thrusters heave the ship up from the platform as he rifled through his bag. Slowly, he took out the book he'd found in the Gatekeeper's library. He held the heavy leather book in his hands and felt a chill run up his spine. Unable to put it aside, he started to read.

PART 3

THE FIRST CHURCH OF THE DESTROYER

Alpha Gropolis: Clannel and Crank

The imaginatively named Alpha Gropolis sprawled along the coast of the fourth continent, Sea Hugger, edging toward a vast green ocean. The mega-city was comprised of ten circular levels, plates on which the populace existed. Alpha Gropolis was still growing and so too were its plates, constructed from high-specification antolin; a metal whose composites were mined a graph away near to Beta Gropolis, the nine-floor capital of the third continent, Ground Wind.

A mighty central bolt reached to the sky, holding Alpha Gropolis together like a swollen metal tree trunk, a solid upright girder that kept each vast antolin disc in the air and separated from its neighbors. Girders jutted from the trunk to support each plate. As the levels rose higher, they decreased in circumference, allowing the trunk to bear the heavier weight at its lower points. At the bottom, Level One was a hundred clicks wide; Level Ten, the uppermost level, was a mere ten clicks in circumference. From a distance the city resembled ten dinner plates stacked atop each other, each ascending size smaller than the last but with space between each one to allow for buildings, streets, traffic systems, sewers, homes, and factories.

Wealth was denoted in Alpha Gropolis by how much space citizens had around them. On cramped Level Ten the destitute scraped together an existence for themselves in the slums. Overcrowded and disease-ridden, not only did Level Ten's sprawl suffer the full brunt of the sun (as there were no levels above to protect it) but it also had the least amount of living space per citizen. Another factor to its poverty was the lack of drinking water, power, and waste disposal. The main trunk served all the levels, taking processed water from the sea to all the levels via pipes running up its body. Level Ten was the last to receive any water and its pipes received the least maintenance. Children from the top level often scurried through the pipes to the lower levels to beg. Levels Nine and Eight were also poverty-stricken but the increased standards of living were noticeable, especially in the rimward districts. There was less disease and more living space, with trade occurring and the populace living nearly one person to a room in almost-furnished buildings. From Level Seven downwards, civilization came into its own in a high-tech urban environment possessing transport systems and recreation zones. Travel between levels was a frequent occurrence between these civilized levels, using elaborate lift systems between floors. However, few citizens from the upper levels spent very long in the closely guarded, elitist level at the mega-city's spacious ground level. Level One was where the elite of Skyfire flourished in luxury; the scilitos, the politicos and the filthy rich.

The harsh light of the Skyfirean sun, the scourge of the unshielded upper levels, was collected by the sunlight utility corporations and beamed through mirrors to the lowest levels where it was purchased and consumed by the rich.

When Terminus had first seen it from a distance, the gropolis had reminded him of a huge child's toy, the levels bolted together to make this curious cone out of flat pieces of metal.

Mists and vapors drifted under the lips of the upper levels into the sky, a byproduct of the crammed citizens existing there. Air-vehicles buzzed around the gropolis like bees attending a hive. On these ten plates Skyfirean humanity went about its business.

On Alpha's landward side, the vast Taylor's desert stretched to the horizon. As it was day, the desert was in full bloom; the yellow dust-weed had grown to almost ten feet in height and swayed in the winds carried from the ocean. When the sun sank, the day-plants would die, crumbling to dust by the time the sun sank into the sea. At night, the land became desert once more, and the road that stretched to Beta Gropolis would again become a nocturnal race track as traders with land vehicles raced to the next gropolis before the desert bloomed again with the next day's sun. The drivers would be high on sleep-stoppers and the desperate desire to trade with the neighboring conurbation.

At ground level, citizens from Level One even had seaside apartments as their wealth spilled out of the city and onto the beach. Lower-level traders clamored for lift space to take them to the ground in their land-cars, knowing to avoid the time of the day when the gropolis threw its shadow over the bay and the idle rich flocked to the beach. Some risk-seekers camped beyond the city walls in the desert, waiting for night to come. Not all of them were seen alive again.

On Level Five, Sii Terminus stood and watched the dawn break over the sea from his apartment. Behind him, Clannel murmured and rolled over to face him. He watched a passenger vacuum-farer, filled with lower-tier occupants, bank over the sea and head for the heavens. He was thinking of Naomi again. He couldn't get her out of his mind. Clannel had realized something was wrong; he hadn't touched her since he'd arrived, making vague excuses such as space fatigue draining his energy levels or having to get used to normal gravity again and the nausea that sometimes caused. She knew he was lying. He hadn't even told her that he'd been to Agathos.

Clannel had been quite surprised to see him turn up at the door five stretches ago. His Link partner snorted that she'd heard he was dead but nothing about him surprised her. Soon she was pulling on a pair of seductive slids and luring him to bed. He couldn't; he just couldn't do it. The memories of Naomi filled his mind.

By vulleying he would be betraying Naomi but the way he reckoned it, he was never going to see her again so what the drent did it matter? Give it a few stretches, he thought, then he might get over her. When Clannel had stopped trying to seduce him she'd slept. That's when he started thinking, staring at the ceiling, the green-tinged light of the moon shining into the apartment. He'd sacrificed safety and warmth for danger and heartbreak. He had to admit, she might have been a religious neuro and her views were at odds with his, but she'd cranned his tank all right.

'Sii, why are you up so early? Crank isn't expecting you for another two sub-stretches.' Clannel smiled lazily at him, her dark hair spilling across the pillow.

'Crank isn't expecting me at all. I didn't comm him yesterday.'

'Terminus, you can't hide out here forever, you drellock. You've got to report yourself in sometime. You aren't taking your responsibilities seriously, as usual.' He could feel anger rising in the back of his brain. She was chanking him again. Clannel climbed out of bed and slid herself behind him. He studied her perfect body in the reflection of the plasti-glass. When her fingernails touched his skin they changed color from sea green to red. She was ready for sex again. 'Is my astro-man all upset? Well, his luxury kitten can take care of it. Just you promise her one thing...' He was edgy now. She was using the childish voice that irritated him even at the best of times. Now it was infuriating him. '...you'll go and see Crank before half-stretch. Then you can come back and your luxury kitten can purr into your lap, eh?'

'Fine. I'll get sterried first.' He broke away from her, rather more suddenly than he would have liked. Inside the sterilization alcove, the sub-atomic waves removed any viruses from his body. He was pretty clean. He heard Clannel activate the info-blast in the living room so he checked the steri-alcove records to see what she'd had while he was away. The holo-display showed a genital yeast infection and an immuno-deficiency virus, one that could only have been contracted through sexual intercourse. Both complaints had been eradicated by the steri-alcove and she'd not erased the memory, stupid skang-gat. So Clannel had been vulleying some diseased gannta behind his back.

240

Not only that, but the gannta had been here with his drenting penile yeast infection, the double skang-gat! That was hardly a surprise. He should challenge her about it but she'd only give him a load of rhetoric about how she thought he was dead so had vullied around. The argument wasn't worth it. The teleport filtered any dirt away from his skin and made him feel clean. He allowed the teleport to dress him today, a luxury after months in space and having to dress manually on Agathos. Arguments with Clannel were unavoidable and, as he stepped back into the apartment, another one erupted.

'What's this?' She sat on the bed holding up the Creator symbol Martha had given him. Beside the bed sat his open bag.

'You've been through my stuff?'

'We're cohabiting, drellock. Your stuff is my stuff, that's the law.'

'So is not vulleying when I'm on missions.'

'I thought you were dead!'

'So you have a decent excuse this time. All the other times you never did. I could have reported *you* then.'

'I'm not arguing about that, Terminus. I want to know why you've got a religious symbol here. Have you become a First Churcher? Is that it? Did you get converted while you were out there?'

'Clannel, this has got drent all to do with you. I don't have to tell you where I got that or why I've got it.'

He thought she might fly into a proper rage but instead she smiled her usual devious smile. 'You might not have to tell me but you'll have to tell the ministros. This is an illegal symbol if you aren't registered.'

'Since when?'

'Since two sub-cycles ago. So you either tell me where you got this and who gave it to you or I get on the comm to the ministros.'

He snatched the symbol from her and looped the chain over his neck. 'Tell who you like, you tank of digest. I'm off!' He exited with her screaming in full rage about never calling her that and how she *knew* he was flooring some First Churcher cult whore. He disappeared into the chute and out into the street.

Level Five hadn't changed. Maybe there were more ministros standing on street corners cradling fire-blasters and there were fewer beggars from the higher levels but nothing had significantly altered. The heat of the planet was exacerbated in the city. Black, scrawny birds picked scraps and litter from the gutters and the occasional brown dog sauntered through the streets looking for food. Sellers, dwarfed by the buildings, called out to him, trying to peddle everything from engine parts to implants, banda fruit to fried labna. He dodged through the traffic on Five Circle J, a cornucopia of land vehicles, auto-horses and six-legged robotic carriers, where spiraling roads connected traffic to neighboring levels. Drivers from Level Eight offered to pull him along like he was a vulleying baby in a pram. They used rudimentary two-wheeled peddle transport, known as humi-carts. He never went by humi-cart and in his opinion only a vortick would hire one. The politicos on Level One had full-time pullers and could be seen with their whole families being pulled through the streets by muscular, glistening, bare-footed, humi-cart pullers. These pullers from Level Eight were scrawny-looking veck's with no shoes.

As he walked along the pedestrian alley to Circle H, a beggar approached him but was reprimanded with a stim-shot from a ministro's fire-blaster. That was odd, thought Terminus, the ministros never usually bothered the beggars. They weren't programmed to.

The rim of Level Five, where he lived, was still an abandoned building site, with no one prepared to stump up the ching to widen the plate. Only the sunlight corporations bothered with this rim with their arrays of collector lenses. Here, closer toward the core, the buildings were still a mish-mash of functional-looking square apartments or gleaming glass-fronted modern living cubicles interspersed with older, sagging constructs from the early days, green with moisture-fungi, architectural victims of the humid atmosphere. As he moved on he saw another ministro give another beggar two shots of stim from his weapon. The thin man was incapacitated, reeling on the ground.

'There was no need for that!' Terminus protested as he passed. The podgy clone eyed him suspiciously. Terminus hoped that he wouldn't ask for any ident because his ident implants had been lost when he returned to life. Terminus's body went cold as he thought about the Lazarus factor again. Seeing the beggar also reminded him that he had absolutely no ching at all. His credit implants, *ching-sacs*, were also gone and they'd probably disseminated the contents of his account once they'd announced him dead. Terminus still wanted to be paid for that trip to Thanatos One. They owed him that much.

The rotund, black edifice that was the Watch headquarters towered above the other, rust-colored structures of Level Five. He entered via reception and took the chute to the eighteenth floor. The offices were so busy they didn't notice another gannta breezing through the brightly lit corridors. He remembered this when he was fourteen, hungry and homeless, just off the passenger liner from station *Cloud Dust* and seeing the recruitment drive for the Boundary Watch. He'd joined that day and was given a credit implant and a bunk at the desert base near Beta Gropolis. Since then, he'd come a long way and gone further than he'd ever wanted to.

When he reached Crank's office, he was about to put his wrist up to the ident panel when he remembered it had gone the way of all his implants. Luckily the door opened and a space-gannta came out, having been shouted at by Crank. Terminus slipped in. For several minutes he stood in front of the commander's desk. The oval-shaped office was sparse and modern with a matching oval desk that sported a new holo-panel. Crank himself still had a fixed stare and an angled jaw. His red hair had been lasered into a harsh cut as always. At last he looked up.

Terminus expected him to look surprised. He didn't expect Crank to stare at him in first horror, then surprise, and then a kind of strange compassion, like he was looking at a man about to be executed. He also noticed Crank's eyes flicker to the event recorder hanging suspended in mid-air behind him.

'So, are you gonna swing me round by the muc-sac for turning up alive?' Terminus grinned.

'If you're asking if I'm pleased to see you, then I'm not. You really, really should not have come here.' He stood and came round to face the visitor. Terminus thought he was going to smack him. Crank came in very close. 'You shouldn't be here.'

'I know you've got me down as dead but you've gotta hear what I've to say.'

'No more mad stories, Terminus.' He pulled the young man into him by grabbing his clothes. 'They'll be here any beat. I'm sorry, Terminus. You should've died out there, you would have been better off.' He glanced once more to the event recorder, pulling back as he did so.

'What's going on, Crank?'

'You are in a lot of trouble, Terminus.' Behind him the door hissed open and four ministros barged in. The lead clone fired a pulse stunner at Terminus's spine and he collapsed to the floor. Crank stood over him, arms folded, a look of achievement on his face as they dragged Terminus down the corridor.

Pizzdeena

'Don't be shy, come in.'

The girl stood nervously in the doorway of the black room. It was larger than she thought it might be. Thick pillars held up a vaulted roof high above, an architecture that made it look ancient. Web-filled alcoves glowered down from extremities of the arcane hall. Once, they had been windows, but now the sparse illumination came from candlelight. In this gloom waited a semi-circle of hooded worshippers who faced the Speaker.

Hesitant, her gaze darted from one figure to another, but the Speaker beckoned her in with a gesture, and she stepped forward across the flagstones to the semi-circle of black-clad figures. As she did, the door closed behind her.

The girl was in her late teens or early twenties with light red hair worn short in the typical fashion of her contemporaries. Unlike the majority of her generation she had no body markings, and wore a simple white robe and slip-on shoes. She hardly made a sound as she finally stepped into the shadow of the Speaker, aware of the half-circle of worshippers watching her.

'You have no implants, no physiological technologies?'

'None, sir.'

'You've not indulged in neuro-stimulants or alcohol within the last cycle?'

'My mat and pat are strict First Churchers, sir. They've never let me touch snakki or go anywhere near a neuro-scrambler.'

'Good. Good. One last thing. The most important thing. The requirements state that you have to be untouched by a man.'

The girl clasped her hands before her in a knot of fingers. 'I was examined by a medicino. I have a certificate to confirm I am a pizzdeena.'

He lifted his head and addressed the twelve onlookers. 'Ladies and gentlemen, we have a pure subject. One that fits the requirements of the rite. Let the congregation be prepared.'

The Speaker moved closer to the pizzdeena. He was dressed in the black robes of his kind but wore hand-gloves that concealed a deformity of the digits. His fingers seemed to be bunched up inside the gloves. Under the cloth they looked less like fingers and more like thin twigs or folded up insect legs.

'Could you take off your clothes, please?'

She did as he asked, pulling at the neck-ribbon of the robe, letting the garment fall to her feet and standing among them naked. The Speaker slid close to her body and reached round to her buttocks. Out of her sight, he de-gloved. She could feel the breath on his face and his hand stretch over her naked buttocks. His fingers felt incredibly thin and spindly, not like fingers at all. She jerked upwards as one sharp digit found its way inside her. A couple of seconds of discomfort and it was all over. She saw his hand as he drew it away and registered a normal human hand. Five fingers and a thumb

He addressed the onlookers. 'I've administered a hypersensitivity hormone. Within seconds, the hormone will find its way into the central nervous system. Its effects are irreversible. The subject will endure this hypersensitivity for the duration of her existence.'

Already her flesh had changed to a pale color and she shifted uncomfortably, as if she was about to vomit. The Speaker stepped forward again and blew onto her face with a gentle breath.

The girl doubled up in agony. She fell to her knees and the shock of the patellas hitting the stone brought a scream to her throat — but no further, because the stretching of the mouth muscles and tightening of the throat brought such pain that her scream died half formed. She lay still, praying for the agony to subside.

The Speaker gestured for the others to join him. Soon they had all surrounded her, leering over the kneeling girl, relishing her terror. Hands reached forward to caress her.

'What have you done to me? Stop it, please, stop it!' Her pleas for mercy only excited them further. 'I don't like it, I'm frightened.' Even the gentlest caresses drew out agonizing screams.

One of the thirteen participants, a woman whose black fingernails matched the color of her eyes, dropped to her knees beside the victim and kissed her on the lips, producing further outpourings of pain. The torturers surrounded her, engulfed her. She writhed in agony beneath them. They gloried in her weakness and desired to inflict ever more suffering.

'Enough!' the Speaker barked. They withdrew leaving a huddled, broken figure. 'You are all dismissed. Withdraw, for he comes.' The robed congregation shuffled out of the hall leaving the Speaker and the brutalized girl. He turned to the rear of the chamber and bowed his head respectfully. A new figure now emerged from one of the alcoves, wearing robes blacker than the starless space between galaxies. The girl began to moan, a deep moan that mourned for the imminent loss of her soul. The robed guest passed the master of ceremonies without a word and sank to the floor beside the pizzdeena.

The Speaker watched, fascination shining from his face.

Theater

'For the last time, how were the physiological modifications removed?'

The cell was functional, as was every holding cell that Terminus had spent time in, yet there was something different about it. He'd seen the inside of enough of them to know. Twice he'd been incarcerated on other worlds for alcohol-related misdemeanors. However, he'd never been strapped into such an uncomfortable chair and had never been threatened, wordlessly, with torture. That must have been the reason for these scilitos leaving the sharps sitting within the periphery of his scanner-sight. This cell differed in the fact that it was white and spacious. At one end, an oval window peered sightlessly into the circular interior like a giant pupil-less eye. They'd taken him somewhere, another part of Alpha — where exactly, he didn't know. Terminus craned his neck and got an eyeball full of the sharps: to his left a semi-circular steel table held a variety of nasty-looking instruments. Apart from the acute psychological discomfort he felt, Terminus wondered why the hell he was being threatened with an archaic, outmoded, and useless method of interrogation. Torture simply didn't work as a means of truth-finding; it had been proved in studies. There were ways of extracting information that were far more efficient. A neuro-scan, for example, could take selected memories and download them onto a fabric-mind. Certain settings on the newer neuro-scramblers could interrupt the thought-to-speech judgment process, forcing the interrogated to spill out the truth. Terminus came to a nasty conclusion; the scilito was doing this because he enjoyed it.

The tall, wiry blond gannta in the white suit had heard the whole story from beginning to end. Then the vulley had wanted to hear it again. Then again with different parts expounded upon.

'I've told you, I don't know how the Agathons removed them. I was out of it. They said they prayed over me.'

'Prayed?' The scilito looked skeptical.

'That's what they told me. Go to Agathos and ask them how they did it if you're so desperate to know. You're talking to the wrong gannta.'

'According to my scientific knowledge I'm talking to a walking miracle. It's anatomically impossible to remove internal modifications from human beings without killing or seriously disabling them. So you see how you are of interest to us.'

'Look, I've told you what I know. You won't get any more info out of me; you know it all. And there was no need to strap me up, or put sharps in view just to put the digest up me. So if you'll just flick open these wrist clamps, we can all go home.'

A wide smile broke over the scilito's face. He laughed, the joke obviously on Terminus. His captor brushed his hand over a control panel, and the chair slid Terminus smoothly from sitting into a lying position. Terminus protested using a series of expletives.

'Do you know where you are? You're in the Science Annex on Level Three. I was just assembling background information before the research proper begins. You didn't think we'd assembled the surgical instruments for your benefit, did you? These...' he gestured to the sharps, '...are what we'll use for your autopsy.'

The scientist turned to the surgical table and selected a small mask with a tiny canister. The mask covered the nose and mouth feeding the covered orifices with whatever was waiting in the canister. Terminus recognized the device; it contained aquaform. Once breathed, the gas inside the lungs expanded into droplets of CO_2 which aggressively blocked the alveoli of the lungs, suffocating the victim.

'You drenting vulley, you can't do this! You can't snuff me; my destiny-line is too rich. I'm only twenty-six, you shankaa!' He couldn't quite believe that it was going to happen, just so they could cut him open. Still grinning, the scientist closed in on Terminus who was now thrashing on the plinth, threatening to break the clasps that held him. In his panic, he barely noticed the circular door slide open and a heavy-set ministro guard enter. The black of the clone's uniform contrasted sharply with the white of the research theater. The scilito didn't notice the ministro at all, until he spoke in the usual atonal drawl.

'Researcher Pulsch. I have a message from Decision Central. The deceased is to be transported there before experimentation begins.'

'What!' The scilito turned on him. 'What the hell does Decision Central want with *this*? I'm about to start my operations, for drent's sake!'

'Those are my orders, sir. We have a carrier waiting.'

The scilito threw the mask aside and swore. 'I better have him back by the end of my break period. And I'll be confirming this with the Vice-Prime.' The scilito stood up erect. 'Go on, take him, and hurry up. I've got limited time to examine him before the stretch ends.'

The guard gestured to Terminus and the scilito motioned toward the panel. The clasps snapped open and Terminus slid from the plinth, naked and scared.

'I'm telling the info-casts about this, you digest-spreader,' growled Terminus as the squat ministro ushered him out.

'I think you'll find I'm beyond reproach,' the scilito said.

Once Terminus had disappeared into the oval corridor, which resembled the inside of a human capillary, the scilito brought up a holo-image and directed the comm-router. 'Decision Central, Arbiter Kane's office.'

The pale face of the politico filled the screen. 'You're not going to tell me you found something?' he said.

Pulsch frowned. 'I take it you didn't send for him, then.'

'Send for whom? The deceased? No, I didn't. I wanted him dead by now, you fool.'

'A ministro just fetched him.' Realization dawned on Pulsch. 'Drent! It's a subterfuge initiative. From who, I wonder? Don't worry, he won't get far, Kane. He'll be picked up, we'll just...'

'Detect his Physiological Modifications? He has none, remember. Without phys-tech he can move around the city undetected.'

'We have his bio-ident on record. I'll satellite trace his DNA code. Oh, and he's naked. That should make him fairly easy to spot.'

'Then do it and stop wasting time! Let's scratch this itch, Pulsch.'

Pulsch stood and was about to redirect the holo-comm to issue a secondary security alert, when the door slid open. The naked experiment stood in the doorway. Behind him in the corridor, the ministro was lying stunned against the curving wall, blood running from his broken nose. Pulsch was staring down the end of a fire-blaster.

Terminus advanced on Pulsch.

'So, if you're beyond reproach,' said Terminus, 'then you must be important. Well, important man, get me some clothes. Important-looking ones.'

Calmly Pulsch pointed out: 'That gun is set to the phys-tech of ministros only. It won't work for you.' As soon as the words had fallen out of his mouth he knew he'd made a mistake. Terminus blasted the plinth and the surgical trolley apart with one sharp burst.

'I haven't got any phys-tech so it doesn't know what I am. Now get me some drenting clothes.'

Pulsch led him through the obscured entrance near the rear of the research dome. The insalubrious tunnels led to a large hangar that bordered an entertainment area. Terminus had last visited this *funzone* when he was about to leave for his eighteen sub-cycle stretch to Thanatos One. The gray, organic hulks of delivery vehicles moaned in and out of the large hangar area. Masked clones unloaded body-shaped sacks. Terminus kept the gun pointed into the scilito's back as they walked. These clones, bred to function and not to observe, ignored them. Ahead, Terminus could see the flashing lights of the funzone.

'I've heard that some of the drugged dancers end up at your work-base,' Terminus said. 'Some people have woken up after a heavy night on the snakki to find an organ missing and replaced by phys-tech. It happened to a geema I knew. Found out she was being traced for about a cycle.'

'We have to see how new tech functions in normal everyday activity. The upper-dwellers hardly live what you could call a normal life. They make poor subjects.'

'I've heard people sometimes just disappear from the funzone.'

'Don't try to moralize with me, Terminus. Do you ever take re-hyde capsules? Where do you think the research for those was carried out? All your phys-tech and mortality cures were first tested here, on humans. You want the product, but you don't want to know how it was made.'

At the gate of the research domes the scilito swiped his palm across the reader and the circular metal barrier slid like a huge wheel to reveal the back end of Three Circle D.

Terminus stepped out into the night. 'Thanks for the clothes and the strand-shave.' He ran his finger through his shortened hair. The scilito had taken him to his work-base gemmel and furnished him with clothes and a haircut. 'You did try to send me to the Creator, so... get your coverings and slids off!'

The scilito obeyed. 'This won't delay your recapture. I'm a scientist, not a religious zealot who's ashamed of his body. I'll walk back in there naked and issue a fix on your bio-readings.'

'Not if you're lying flat on your back with these clone ganntas thinking you're just another piece of meat for the lab...' he stunned the scilito with one quick blast, '...you won't.'

Assistant to the Vice-Prime

'How would you describe the deceased, this Terminus person? I, or rather the Vice-Prime, require a character analysis.'

Crank reflected that he did indeed live in strange times. A cycle ago he would never have found himself within the hallowed walls of Decision Central. The capillary-like gray corridors were designed to intimidate. It was even rumored that they pumped Cilopram, a fear agent, into the air to heighten the effect. This was the third time he'd been here, summoned by the Vice-Prime's chief assistant, a gray-skinned politico who was as cool in his mannerisms as any gray-skinned politico. In fact, all politicos looked so similar that Crank wondered if they were cloned, like the ministros. Airing such views in public was likely to get you a cycle in the desert mines.

The assistant to the Vice-Prime had his own office, a large circular affair with an oval window that gave fantastic views of Level Three. Lights from hundreds of funzones glistened below, and above — partly obscured by cloud — the underside of Level Four replaced the sky, a ceiling of red metal marked with girders and plates that stretched out to the great force field that separated the city from the desert. From here Crank could see that the desert was in full bloom.

'Why the interest? As your boss said, Terminus was an itch that needed scratching. I assume he's dead. I mean, really dead this time.'

The politico smiled humorlessly. 'I'm afraid he's got away from us. Don't worry, his recapture is imminent. My master was wondering if the itch could possibly become a sore, a minor irritation. Hence the character analysis. Well?'

Crank looked out of the window. 'Terminus is an idiot. He'll probably be necking all the snakki that he can't afford right now.'

'The people who assisted his escape did not think him an idiot. A double-ident message was sent to Decision Central. A request was made to send a ministro to fetch him from the research theater. Whoever sent this request specified that only one trooper should escort him. They obviously knew it was well within his capabilities to overpower one ministro.'

'He could. Anyone could if they thought their life was in danger, and Terminus acts when he's pushed, not like most of the people on this planet. He's a funny one. He's not from Skyfire, you know.'

'Oh?'

'He's from Earth. He stole his way here when he was fourteen cycles old. Walked into my office and said he was sixteen. Like I said, he's an idiot, but most of the people on this planet are idiots. Snakki-swilling, fun-seeking, drellocks. All that drinking and funzoning he did; I think he was just fitting in, personally.'

'Why do you say that?' The politico had found a chink in Crank's conversational armor.

He shrugged his shoulders. 'You don't find your way across seven thousand pulses of deep space for free without showing some resourcefulness. I've seen him talk and, if he has to, fight his way out of all sorts of scrapes. That's why I sent him to Thanatos One. I knew he'd be resourceful, determined.'

'Your orders were to send functionaries, human meat that would just carry out their tasks until they arrived.' His tone darkened and he glared at Crank.

'I wasn't aware of the plan a cycle ago.'

'Determined he may have been, but resourceful?' The politico continued. 'He has no military training. His physical fitness is hardly up to scratch. The Vice-Prime was very interested to know about his religious beliefs. Has he any?'

'Oh yes, he drinks. He worships at the altar of snakki like the rest of this drenting planet. I can't believe they tolerated him for so long on Agathos. They must be very forgiving. Typical of Terminus, to turn up again after being declared officially dead. He might not believe in the Creator but, for some absurd reason, the Creator smiled down on him.'

'Well the Creator can smile down upon him again when they meet face to face.' The politico stood; a signal for Crank to leave. 'I trust you'll be joining us tonight.'

'Of course.'

'I can guarantee nothing, Crank, but the Vice-Prime is, I believe, considering you for full initiation. Your services to us have not gone unnoticed.'

'Thank you, sir. I'll be honored to be accepted into the fold.'

He turned his back on Crank; that was the politico signal for dismissal. Crank left the office and proceeded down the corridor at an unusually fast pace.

The thirteen worshippers encircled the struggling figure secured to the stone plinth. The mute boy's terror increased with each second that passed. Their minds connected with his and they inflicted scenario after terrible scenario upon him. At last the Speaker commanded them to stop.

'Tonight we welcome the living embodiment of our faith, and we give this offering as a libation.'

A dark-robed figure swooped into the room with dramatic effect. The worshippers automatically fell to their knees.

The offering tried to lift his head to see who was approaching. Out of the corner of his eye he saw the hem of heavy robes sweeping the stone flags as this new tormentor advanced toward him.

To prolong these delicious waves of terror flowing from the boy, the creature inside the robes slowed its advance to a crawling pace.

Its hood hid its features but it assailed the boy with a barrage of filth from its mind. The being lifted itself over the mute boy and the black robes brushed his naked flesh.

The boy had never spoken a word in his life. His medicinos had investigated and found the mutism to be a psychological reaction to some past trauma. However, for the first and last time in his short life, he summoned a scream from his throat.

Info-blast

Terminus strolled into the funzone, looking like another gannta emerging for a break after a half-stretch working at the research theater, the organic looking monolith that shadowed the zone. He went for stealth mode, appearing to scan for a shot of mid-stretch snakki before shooting back to the theater to cut up clones or whatever they did in there. He passed over the rushing, light-filled ring system of Three Circle D via the foot bridge. The high-speed city darts shot under his feet, carrying citizens to various parts of the level, flashes of light slicing through the darkness of the track.

Terminus passed under a holo-bridge that blared promises of mid-stretch deals on snakki and noosh. The colorful figures advertising instant high-protein food made him feel quite hungry. Since he no longer had phys-tech, he no longer had credit chips. With no way of paying for any noosh, he'd just have to eat at a café and run if anyone demanded payment. His own government wanted him dead so it wasn't like he could get into any more trouble for theft.

He dodged the ganntas rushing to join friends or stepping briskly to find that mid-stretch drink. The smooth, burgundy walkway was completely pedestrianized. Only city darts were permitted, and they kept to their tracks, so the funzone had no streets as such, just spaces between structures. Either side of him the odd-shaped, multicolored buildings showed absolutely no signs of uniformity; each existed in its own architectural universe. A triangular glass snakki bar stood next to a smooth, phallic restaurant. That in turn contrasted with a super-bar, which was made up of interlocking hexagonal shapes, each a radically differing themed venue.

Since arriving back here he'd noticed how noisy everything was, even here on Level Three where a better class of cit lived. Generated gamma cut-ups blasted from a bar to his left; unidentifiable shapes danced crazily in the air in time to the fast-paced beats of the music. To his right a huge pair of bosoms looked down on him and a voice whispered seductively (in booming, sonic waves) to come; come into Madame Spine's House of Snakki. Farther up the walkway, a disembodied head in a military space captain's hat laughed at him, promising the fastest mid-stretch snakki saturation in the funzone. Another promised to make the stretch fly by with Vion, a Ragreeshean liquor that gave the sensation of drunkenness without its complications. He passed the super-bar hexagonal-matrix. Today, the super-bar ignored him.

To the residents of Level Three, Terminus might be a piece of digest from Level Five, but his ching was welcome enough and he knew this zone well. Normally, when he passed the super-bar a virtual Earther colonist spoke to him in Earther, telling him to come on in for a jug of Earth Pankkora. It knew to give him all that Earther digest because it read his history from his phys-idents. Today, as he passed by, it said nothing, as if he didn't exist.

Terminus knew exactly where he was heading. There was a bar called the Sundog which the space-ganntas used. He had gone there the night before he'd left for Thanatos One. There was always someone from the Boundary Watch drinking there. The Sundog was the only place in this city where he could get help. The only place where he might meet someone who could get him off this drenting planet and, if he couldn't find anyone to help him, at least he could get drunk. He saw the Sundog's rotund structure beyond the Preemer Café.

He cursed himself as he walked. Isaiah had been right. He should have stayed on Trinity where it was safe. Probably. Terminus had thought that when he came home everything would, just, well, be all right. People had been shifted from the planet illegally before and had returned with new identities. Ident-swaps could be done for a price. Martha had given him some high value ching-chips when he'd left Agathon. Those white-robes might think they were all smarter-than-thou, but they'd dropped a drellock on that one. Ching-chips were what you bet with in a game of Shift, what you gave your lovers to keep them eager. Sure, there were ways to legally exchange them for real ching in your ching-sac, but those ways were heavily monitored by the authorities. No way an ident-fabricator would let you near them with ching-chips.

The beak of it was he had no real ching, not that he was going to let that be a problem.

To his left he saw a smartly dressed woman in a black hood glance at him. To all intents and purposes she was an off-duty Babel-geema; a prostitute who wore a hood to disguise her appearance in case she bumped into one of her customers. The hood was a signal: leave me the drent alone! But when he looked more closely, he noticed her skirt was far too long for a respectable whore. She dropped back and he noticed her stance, the way she moved. He'd seen a woman move like that recently and the memory made his throat go dry.

If she was from the authorities and she'd spotted him then they would be here by now, dropping onto him from level-hovers. But she wasn't Skyfirean; she was from Thanatos. She had to be. Getting shot by ministros would be preferable to being caught by Thanatons. He clutched the Creator symbol to his chest and pressed on.

Terminus nearly made it to the bar when a harsh signal filled the false skies. As one, the populace groaned. The signal was a call to info-blast; an information relay that every citizen in the entire city was forced to watch. The penalty for not stopping what you were doing and looking up at the holo-screen — that now appeared some distance away — was death. He joined the fun seekers that pressed together under the screen. All other holo-displays were shut off. The face of the presenter filled the sky like a low moon.

'We now have a message from the vice-prime, your sponsor and protector.'

The gray features of a politico filled the screen, and a few snakki-saturated geemas jeered. Jeering was not illegal as long as it didn't impede information reception.

'People of all levels. I have this stretch been in talks with other decision makers, including our prime, and have allowed the following amendments to planetary governance. One; that the curfews be lifted on Level Nine dwellers. Two; that ministry police be allowed to raid First Church properties, as we believe there is a connection with the terrifying atrocities that have been occurring, namely the neuro-scrambling that occurred on Level Four last sub-cycle. Three; that increased ministry police production may be granted to assist with the capture of the criminal known as the Dust Killer. This individual will be caught and destroyed. That is all. Go about your business.'

All around him cits were complimenting the presenter for keeping it short and moving off. Terminus stared at the place where the screen had been long after it had disappeared and the crowds dispersed. He stared in disbelief. The man speaking had been none other than the politico he'd ferried all the way to Thanatos One. Terminus had last seen this gannta with his insides pulled out, the organs hanging in mid-air. Anwar Akkbar was dead but had just appeared on the screen. He was as dead as Terminus had been when leaving Thanatos.

Funzone

She was still following him but the bar he entered now, the Sundog, allowed members entrance through retinal scan only and not by phys-tech ident. A lot of space-ganntas used the Sundog because not all their implants worked that well. Off-world environments played havoc with phys-tech. The hovering laser arc hit his retinas. For a second he wondered if his unique biological make up had been altered during his resurrection. If the lasers couldn't ident him, he would be even further in the drent than he'd thought.

But the lasers must have idented him because the arched doors swung open. As she tried to follow him in, they shut in her face. Terminus saw the doors close behind him, cutting off her trail. If she was from Thanatos her retinal scan wouldn't be recognized. The geema wouldn't be following him in here this stretch.

Terminus stood over the balcony like he owned the place as snakkied-up ganntas and geemas fell about on the image-intensive floor. The trick was to keep moving normally to the pulse-generated music and stay on your feet while your scanners were bombarded with huge holo-images of increasing intensity. This was the next best thing to a neuro-scrambler and perfectly legal. Terminus was a master at it. He smiled, remembering the good times he'd had here. He would love to bring Naomi here. The Sundog would blow her naive Agathon mind.

The bar curved across the interior of the club like a half-moon. Terminus headed straight for it, passing through the invisible sound field that dulled the music around the bar area. Above, shifting images patterned the domed ceiling and holo-images sprang from the walls. He perched himself on a stool, ordered a large glass of syntol and began the long slide into alcoholic oblivion. Before him, the teleport delivered the drink with a pay advice hologram. He laughed to himself. If you didn't pay, the phys-tech locators would put a trace on you and you'd be followed home by two large clones. Terminus had no phys-tech; he could drink this digest-shifter dry if he wanted and not pay a thing. Not that he was ever going to get home. He'd be picked up and dispatched long before the night was out.

As he drank he felt a presence slide into the seat next to him. He didn't look directly at her (that could get you a shunt in the mouth in this place) but looked out from the corner of his visual field.

'Of course, back in England we had dance halls. Now they're gone forever.'

His brain unscrambled the language. Was she talking to him? He was sure that it was old Earther. Instinctively, he turned to face her.

'This reminds me of an old Northern Hemisphere city. Quaint, really. Ignorant cattle classes drinking away their sorrows, subconsciously steeling themselves for the final apocalypse. Same behavior patterns here, exactly like Earth.'

He identified her and exclaimed: 'Oh, digest!'

'Oh, shit, indeed, Mister Terminus. I've come for you.'

Her hair had been cropped short in the Skyfirean fashion which accentuated her cheek bones and her red lips. She wore a catsuit, bright scarlet of course, but also very Skyfirean. The suit's latex effect creaked as she moved like some feline predator. He could run but what would be the point? She'd catch him. Those red eyes were already making his head swim.

Calm. He had to keep calm.

'Have another drink if it calms your nerves,' the Gatekeeper said and ordered him a Babelite Orlock. He sank the golden liquid in one.

'I must say,' he said, trying to keep his cool. 'I think you look pretty hot in that suit, but I'm not sure red is your color.'

'It won't be yours, Terminus, when I've sucked it out of you.' She took a shot of snakki. 'I'm almost tempted to make it pleasurable for you, for the first five seconds, at least. Then the agony will begin. A waiting room for damnation.'

'No chance you could just let me go?'

She smiled. 'After what you did to my house? Absolutely not! And your friend killed my daughter. I've to avenge her as well. But there's no hurry. Let's have a few drinks first.'

'Did you ever visit the cities of the Northern Hemisphere? Ah, Terminus, they were beautiful before the Decline. Berlin. Salzburg. London. They were real cities. They made this set of shelves look like a rubbish dump. I mean, *Alpha*... What a name! How functional. It's not as if you haven't had time to develop a culture. And all this fuss about me, me, the *dust killer*, and I just know they're enjoying it, the novelty of murder.'

'So tell me, when did you live on Earth?'

'Oh, I don't know. My memory is hazy. I remember the fascists of the 1930s and the religious invasion of the following century, but mostly I remember the village where you grew up. Since meeting you I've remembered it more clearly. In a way it's a shame you have to die. I went back there after the Decline.'

'You remember the Decline? What was it? History draws a blank there.'

'History deleted the Decline from its memory. Neumann's experiments were nothing but an excuse to commit atrocities. All those souls, trapped in their cities, unable to leave because the Earth was sealed, the surrounding land overtaken by, what were they called? Nexus worms. Eating into the world, like maggots eating through flesh. It was beautiful.'

'Tell me,' he sidled up to her drunkenly. Her eyes were blazing with amusement and malice, her mouth curved into a poisonous smile. 'Was there a ship built during the Decline? A ship that left first, left to go to another world?'

'Questions, Questions. You are an impatient little man. There was the *Genesis*. We allowed the religious, those infected with the sickness of worshipping the Creator, to leave in a ship bound for Agathos. They left all the non-believers behind to suffer, very compassionate. Why do you ask? Have those puritans got to you? I heard about you, about how you were brought back to life by those cultists. I even know about Naomi.'

She took a sip of her drink. Terminus was shaken back into alertness. He fixed her a hard stare.

'You leave Naomi out of it.'

She uttered a sexy, throaty laugh loaded with malice. Terminus continued glaring at her.

'Let me tell you something, Earth man. One day, very soon, we will take Agathos for our own. We are growing strong in power, flexing our muscles, recruiting planets, such as Skyfire, to be our lap dogs. We will invade Agathos and I will resurrect my temple in the heart of Nazareth. Sacrifice will be made each morning to me and I will bathe in the blood of a hundred virgins. Each temple will be given over to the Destroyer, including the temple on that settlement on Trinity. Naomi will be offered as a gift to me, her back broken over the altar. I shall feast upon her soul, damning her to the caress of the Destroyer for all eternity.'

'Is that why Anwar Akkbar is here? He's been recruited by you?'

'He offered himself to us. The body politic of this planet has a limitless lust for power. Anwar was the first human to endure the Eternum Codex and Become. No human has even attempted it for what must be centuries.'

Recognition hit Terminus like a city dart. Martha had mentioned that process and said that no human could survive it. Akkbar obviously had. Resurrection at the hands of higher powers was not exclusive to Terminus himself.

'What happens next?'

'Neutralize the enemy, of course. Back on Earth it was only after the *Genesis* had left that the atrocity could really begin. Here, we can only gain a foothold once the Churches are banished. That's happening. Anwar is beginning a persecution that will live on in history.' She stopped and let out a sigh. 'These explanations are becoming most tiresome. Haven't you got to die?'

'One more thing,' he said. 'When you get to Agathos, how are you gonna cope?'

'What do you mean?'

'Well, you find these everywhere.'

He broke the Creator symbol from its chain and jammed it into her throat. She allowed herself a surprised yelp and backed away at lightning speed, putting a hand to her throat. The thing hadn't burned her badly, but when she looked up, Terminus was gone.

'You little sod!' She grinned and walked calmly away in pursuit.

Three Circle D

He ran, clutching the fire-blaster and the symbol. A clone tried to stop him exiting through the member's entrance but when Terminus raised the gun the heavy-set bio-construct shifted aside. Terminus broke out into the night. The plazas were packed with ganntas and geemas now that the work-stretch was over. He mingled with them. Through the crowds he saw the hooded pursuer.

When he was between the Dragon Bar and the Red Steamer, he let off a couple of shots in her direction, taking out two holo-displays as he did. As the crowds around him screamed and ducked he saw the pursuer dart into an alcove. He'd expected her to fire back, but she didn't. Terminus reached the edge of the funzone and took the steps down to Three Circle D. The city darts shot past him and to his horror the saw the hooded figure spring onto the barrier wall a few paces away.

Terminus raced for the second sub-level of the Circle. The traffic here was just as fast as in the above-level pass, but there was a by-lane where pay-carrier city darts waited for their fares. He would just have to board one and blow the android driver's neuro-circuits out once he'd shaken off his pursuer. Slowing his pace, he bounded up to the nearest dart. The magnetic underside hummed as it hovered above its polar opposite. The door slid open and he boarded. Before he could even state his destination, the dart was off. He took a scan of the rear window; he couldn't see the hooded woman. As the dart hit the fast lane he sensed a darkening in the interior of the cab. He was sharing the tube-like interior with another being.

'Oh, drent!'

The being bled into corporeality slowly until her body was fully formed. She smiled at him. 'Surprise!'

At that same moment, an isolated power-down hit the seaward side of Three Circle D bringing the whole system to a halt. The darts fell to the track with a clang of metal on metal. Voices were raised and threats were made but all passengers were powerless. The darts had stopped dead.

Terminus blasted his way out of the fallen dart and ran across the track. The Gatekeeper swooped down like a lizard-bird to hit the roof of the dart alongside him. She shot her snake-like tube from her mouth to give him a hint of things to come.

'Run, Earther. I like it when you try to run. Makes the heart beat faster, the blood pump.'

'Then I won't, you bag of digest. I'll not give you the satisfaction.' He slowed to a walk, moving away from the track.

She stalked him.

Between two pillars Terminus could see the door to the First Church of Three Circle D. The tall doors and spired roof looked out of place amongst the functional architecture nearby. The Gatekeeper was nearing him, casually skipping to meet him. He ran until he reached the doors.

'See this?' he shouted at the scarlet, cat-suited vampire. 'Ten ching units you won't follow me inside.'

'Your soul says I will.'

Terminus pulled the heavy door ajar and disappeared into the darkness. Once inside he briefly marveled at the interior. He'd seen First Churches from the outside but never set foot inside one before. It was remarkably similar in design to the one on Trinity that had been made of stone. This was constructed from plasti-antolin, as was everything in Alpha Gropolis, from pavements to palaces. The interior was dark and unused. Despite the heat of the planet a chill permeated the air of the church.

The Gatekeeper teased him, seductiveness oozing from her voice. 'Now, how do you want to do this? Me on top and you underneath?' She'd found her way inside and didn't seem at all repulsed. Even the huge symbol of the Creator on the far wall didn't seem to concern her.

'I can swing the experience from ecstasy to agony and back again. You won't know if you're in heaven or in hell.' The Gatekeeper was perilously close now.

'Listen,' he said, his blue eyes staring at her reds. 'I'm done with running. I'd just like to, once, you know, kiss you. No stinging, or insects. Just one last kiss.'

Her arms slipped around his waist. 'Why not? I do find you interesting and at least you're an Earther, not one of these Skyfire half-breeds.'

As his warm mouth pressed to her scarlet lips, the soft glow of candles begun to light the temple all around them. When her tongue touched his, Terminus thought it was all over. But he felt her pause when she suddenly realized that they were surrounded. She let him break away because she was intently staring at the figures encircling them, each one carrying a white candle. Terminus pulled back into the circle and was handed a candle of his own. The Gatekeeper put her hand to her chest as if she had difficulty breathing.

'You cannot do this to me! Oh no. You cannot. Not to me.' She smiled incredulously at first. Then her face twisted into a mask of hate. '*Not to me!*'

'Thanaton, we give you one last chance to repent of your evil deeds and return to the care of the Creator.' The hooded girl had emerged from the shadows, stepped into the circle and approached the demon.

271

The Gatekeeper snarled at Terminus. 'You are going to regret this.'

'I'll add it to the list!'

'Silence,' the girl said. 'Do not have dialogue with the Destroyer. Do you repent, Gatekeeper?'

The Gatekeeper screamed into the congregation. *'Never!'*

They closed in, Terminus joining them, and let the flame of their candles touch her. In an instant the Thanaton was transformed into a roaring blue fire that consigned her body to ash. The catsuit melted and the flesh burned away from the bones until the bones themselves crumbled to dust in the inferno.

The hooded girl stood over the mess. 'From dust we are made, to dust we will become.'

'Can I relax now?' Terminus snuffed his candle out. 'I mean, first she turns up in a bar, the woman of my nightmares. Then you teleport into my city dart and tell me you're going to burn her alive with drenting candles. I thought you were *her*, you know. I nearly blew your drenting head off. I'm still not sure which one of you was after me.'

The congregation dispersed and the girl trod through the ashes of the Gatekeeper and joined him in looking down at the Gatekeeper's remains. When she spoke it was out of earshot of the others.

'So,' Naomi threw the hood back revealing her face. She'd become taller, oozed confidence and looked as sexy as hell with her short, Skyfirean cropped hair. 'If she's the woman of your nightmares, what am I?'

The Creator and the Destroyer

'Explain to me how the drent the Gatekeeper went up like a stack of rags when you lot put the candles to her.'

The Agathon missionary team had rented an apartment on Level Three. It was spacious and modern, decked out in white furniture. The layout was standard and innocuous, a suitable hideout for the Agathon missionaries and their fugitive.

The one viewport overlooked the rear of the research theater where bulbous vents blasted waste air into the atmosphere. Terminus briefly wondered if Pulsch had been picked up and processed by those clones yet. Naomi leaned forward on the memory-foamed sofa. Behind her, Rebecca stood with her arms folded, and flanked by two male missionaries. Even though these missionary ganntas — whose names were Simon and Timothy — wore Skyfirean catsuits like every other mid-class cit on this planet, they shared the same wholesome looks that reminded Terminus of Joel, Rebecca's husband and Naomi's brother-in-law. The Agathons carried guns the like Terminus had never seen before. White, smooth machines that boasted an anachronistic dial fixed to the left-hand side. The dial pointed to Earther abbreviations notched into the side: *heamo, shifter, gravesnake, ecto*. Terminus recognized the word gravesnake all too well. The Agathons called these guns *lances*. Somehow it didn't have the same ring as a fire-blaster. Even their guns had a goomah name.

'Shall I explain?' Rebecca said.

'No, I can handle this.' Naomi fixed him with her blue eyes. 'Basically, the Creator and the Destroyer operate on a metaphysical, or spiritual, level. The Creator is superior to the Destroyer. The Destroyer abhors the Creator, as do his acolytes. The symbols of the Creator's power, such as the Creator's Embrace symbol and the communion candles, are anathema to anyone who employs the Destroyer's metaphysics for their or their master's gain. The candles are sacred to us, that's how they reduced the Gatekeeper to the pile of ash that's now sitting on the floor of the First Church.'

'You've already deduced that the Creator symbol burns them.' Rebecca interjected. 'Prayers also act as a defense. There are other ways to kill them, scientific methods that we are experimenting with. For instance, they cannot stand intense light.'

'Essentially, you have to believe that the Creator exists in the first place to understand and channel the power he provides,' Naomi added.

Terminus slouched back into his chair and snorted. 'How do you know that the Thanaton fear of the Creator paraphernalia isn't just psychosomatic? They could be a race of aliens that will themselves to death, because they expect that to happen when you turn up with an image of the smiley gannta with his arms out.'

'Good grief! How do you tolerate him?' Rebecca rolled her eyes and stomped into the kitchen. Naomi smiled and continued.

'I'll tell you why it isn't psychosomatic. You've seen the power that comes from the Destroyer at first hand; the Gatekeeper's unnatural longevity, the politico with his heart and lungs hanging out, the changeling children in the abyss. Is that all in the mind?'

'It might be.'

'Well you'll see what our Creator can do in the next few days, and then you'll have no choice but to believe.'

Terminus leaned forward, the comedy smile now eradicated. 'Listen, I don't *care* whether the Creator exists or not so long as I'm still here in this skin, in this universe. All I care about is surviving.'

Naomi and Rebecca briefed him while Simon and Timothy looked out of the window. The people in the church where the Gatekeeper had been dispatched were all part of the congregation of the First Church. They were in hiding because the Vice-Prime had ordered the dissolution of the First Church of Skyfire after a series of neuro-scramblers had been detonated in the city and killed hundreds. Several members of the First Church of Skyfire had claimed responsibility for the attacks, prompting Anwar Akkbar to take steps. All members of this minority had been rounded up and taken to Spike Island, a psychiatric enclave a few clicks from the coast of Beta City. It was rumored that they were being executed.

Hidden in hyperspace, an Arkship, the *Sidon*, waited in stationary orbit around Skyfire. It had teleported most of the faithful to safety on board.

'Which brings us to Akkbar,' Naomi had said. 'Since his return to Skyfire he's been active in government as well as covertly organizing the terrorist attacks. He's also gunning for the position of Prime. To line himself up for this position, Akkbar is also the president of a very secret, very influential society which counts many high-profile politicos as its members.'

'This is very worrying,' Rebecca continued. 'Thanatos is trying to get a foot in Skyfire's front door. They've eliminated the First Churches and so removed the opposition. You turning up is a minor inconvenience for him. We want to upgrade you into a headache.'

Terminus had taken that to mean that they still wanted to use him. And there he was thinking they were just being nice to him, rescuing him like that.

Later, when he was alone in the serene night light of the main room, he mulled over the afternoon's conversation. Rebecca and the two men were sleeping in their respective rooms now. Naomi came and joined him, shifting her weight onto the sofa beside him.

'Remember how we kept telling you that you were safe back on Trinity? Well, sorry to say, you're not safe now. Not here. The entire city's Watch force is looking for you.'

'I'm aware of that, Naomi. I'm also aware you want to use me to get to Akkbar.'

'That's right. Sorry. You can choose to opt out. We can teleport you to the Ark and you could be back on Trinity in three days.'

'Would you like that?'

She angled her body toward him. 'Terminus, I haven't stopped thinking about our first kiss from that day to this. You'll have to come back to Agathos when all this is over. You can't stay here. Even with Akkbar gone, your government would still want to kill you to keep you quiet about the whole embarrassing affair. Not to mention that they'll want to continue their research, try to find out why your implants suddenly disappeared.'

'I could go somewhere else. One of the colony planets...' He met her gaze. 'But I don't want to.' He didn't believe that he'd just said that. He was committing to this girl. He was letting her crann his tank. Effortlessly he moved to kiss her.

'No,' she said. 'We have to do this properly. On Agathos people, lovers, don't kiss until they're married. We shouldn't have kissed in the barn but I don't regret it. When all this is over do you think you could marry me? Do you think you could handle a big Agathon wedding?'

'Of course I could.'

'Another thing. Be honest with me. Is there anyone else? Is there someone on Skyfire that you haven't told me about? Maybe because you're nervous about telling me or think I'm some Agathon puritan who will only marry a pizzdeen. I've lived on this planet for two months. I know how it works here; it won't be the end of us if there is. You can tell me. You can decide.'

Her blue eyes were wide and searching, her face expectant.

'There is no one else.'

She fell into his arms and hugged him tight. He looked to the ceiling. He'd have to tell Clannel somehow. Tell her it was over; get the co-hab Link annulled. He was officially dead so maybe that didn't matter. There was no way he could call her; the signals were being monitored. She probably thought he was dead, properly dead, anyway. Yes, it would be all right because she thought he was dead.

851

The land-wheeler sped along the coastal road, joining the continuous stream of traffic. Above, the two moons of Skyfire reflected as pink discs in the sea, but the four people in the land vehicle were in no mood to appreciate the splendor of the night.

Rebecca had given Terminus strict orders not to leave the apartment. Other Agathon covert missionaries and First Churchers were busy laying false trails for the authorities to follow. Ahead, the port shone out into the night. Hundreds of space cargo freighters were docked there, sleeping silently on their circular pads. Rebecca speculated that the Skyfireans had built their space port by the sea in subconscious recognition of man's first forays into the unfamiliar.

'I don't think it'll be there,' Timothy said as they pulled off the coastal track into the darkness of the nearly deserted area of the port.

'Neither do I.' Rebecca retorted. 'But this is where we last traced the ethereal flow. If it isn't here then we can at least find a clue as to where it might be.'

'In Decision Central with the Vice-Prime,' suggested Simon.

'The Ark risked a deep scan there and detected no ethereal flow. Stop here.' The softly humming land-wheeler pulled up under the docking platform. Armed ministros stood to attention nearby. From here they looked more like a surly gang of youths than a governmental force. The four missionaries disembarked and approached them. Their boots crunched over the red earth at the base of the pillar from which the platform mushroomed out.

'We're closed. Come back next stretch.' The klonk on duty snapped.

Rebecca stepped up to the first ministro and stared into his squat face. From her suit she produced a holo-pad and handed it to the ministro.

He read it then said: 'We'll need to scan your phys-tech first.' He nodded to one of his doubles who came toward them, grabbed Rebecca's wrist, and thrust it under a nearby scanner. A tattoo rose to the surface of her wrist. Once the ministro was satisfied as to her identity, he then did the same to the rest of them. Whatever fakery the scientists on the *Sidon* had cooked up appeared to have fooled the clones perfectly.

'That's fine,' said the first clone, and handed back the holo-pad. 'Bring it down.'

As the platform began to descend, Rebecca asked: 'So who last commissioned this vehicle?'

'The Vice-Prime. He brought some artifacts back via Babel from some out-world. Very valuable artifacts,' the Ministro added. His squat features bulged when he talked. As she watched him, Naomi wondered why the politicos would choose such an unwieldy model as a template for their barbaric practice. She also wondered who the original ministro had been.

'Are they still in there?'

'What do you think? Security in this port is hardly high-grade.'

'We'll need to look anyway.'

'Don't expect help from us. We're programmed to guard, not open doors. Besides, the stink coming from that cargo hold is vulley!' The platform finally touched ground, revealing a deep space cargo ship waiting on its metal disc like an exhibit. The vessel's cargo hold bulged out over its back like a tumor, and its signature was, Naomi saw, the 851.

The ministros had slouched out of sight, returning to their control room on the north side of the port. Simon produced the Agathon weapon and fired an invisible energy charge at the 851. The front end immediately opened up like some large reptilian mouth.

Cautiously, they entered.

'This equipment looks so old,' said Simon.

'Everything on this planet looks old. Old or battered. As for those clones...' Timothy allowed the sentence to trail off.

'I know, they make me feel the same; a mixture of pity and disgust.' Rebecca finished his sentence for him. 'Such a tragedy. They've taken human life to its lowest level. The Creator never intended man to try to do his work for him, especially to create a race of slaves.'

'If I was the Creator I'd turn this planet into a fireball!' Timothy spat.

'Then I thank the Creator that he is compassionate,' Naomi retorted. 'And I thank him that he hasn't your mind.'

'Just because you love a man from this world doesn't mean you have to defend it.'

'Enough!' Rebecca snapped. 'We remain united here. We must not bicker. Timothy, you open the cargo seal. Simon, Naomi, ready with your lances.'

The four missionaries occupied the space where the rust-red metal of the cargo freighter's shell met the functional gray of the cargo hold. Rebecca raised her lance and turned her dial to *circuit*. With one shot, the door opened to reveal the darkness beyond. She threw a glow-ball into the space where it hovered in the air like a tiny sun. The ministros were right about the smell; it was like rotting meat had been left in there. The smooth interior of the hold was empty. What they were hoping to see was not here.

'If he's brought the Ethereal Mirror into this world and it's active...'

'The Ark would have traced it.'

Rebecca stared at him. 'We're talking about Thanaton energy here. The Destroyer can easily fool our detectors. If Akkbar is using an Ethereal Mirror then this world will be facing an apocalypse that would make the Great Decline look like a moon-storm! We're too late.'

'Drent!' Timothy's curse prompted reproachful look from the girls, 'Oh... Sorry.'

'What the hell are those?' Naomi pointed her gun into the darkened hold. The glow-ball illuminated several writhing creatures that were growing in size before their eyes. The swelling creatures were dropping from the ceiling. Each wriggling entity slid from eggs attached to the ceiling that dripped slime onto their heads. They were hatching from eggs! Hatching and getting bigger with each second. The three experienced missionaries set their dials because they recognized these life-forms. Naomi just stood there, bemused.

'Gravesnakes!' Rebecca screamed but it was too late. A gray coil had wrapped itself around her legs and pulled her to the floor. From the sides of the worm the hideous vaginal mouths were already opening. Barbed tongues aimed to sink the reproductive poison into her flesh. With lighting speed she set her dial and aimed. The narrow, gray beam reduced the whole ghastly worm to ash. The others were doing the same. In a last-ditch attempt, the gravesnakes released a yellow poison into the air. As the lances fired, they not only turned the worms to dust, but also disabled the harmful effects of the gas before it entered the lungs of the humans.

'Is everyone all right? Naomi, are you hurt?' Rebecca's voice echoed around the cargo hold.

'No, I'm fine.'

'Good. We'll reflect on this during debrief when we get back to the apartment.'

Something else moved inside the cargo hold. Standing under the light were three female children. Rebecca could see the distress in their young faces and the fear in their body language.

'Could you turn the light down, please? It hurts our eyes.'

*

Terminus reckoned he could move through Level Three undetected. He had no phys-tech to give him away and the Gatekeeper was dead; that was one enemy down. The politicos probably had better things to do than find him, so he should be able to get to the perma-case and back before the missionaries returned. Besides, he needed to see it again. He needed to see it one more time.

Springing from the sofa he took a casual glance out of the viewport. He could see the spire of the First Church poking out through the streets. The Gatekeeper was still there. Terminus hadn't finished with her yet. The fugitive made his exit, slamming his palm into the door seal and walking out into the night.

Naomi raised her gun and the others looked at her astonished.

'Naomi, they're *children*, for goodness sake. Put that thing down!' Rebecca rebuked.

'I've read the Terminus files. I think we should close the cargo store door and leave them.'

Simon raised his gun to scan. 'They're clean,' he pronounced. Rebecca gave her a reproachful look.

'Are you looking for a mirror?' one of the children said.

'A man came and took it from here. He wanted to take us too but we hid,' another said. Timothy, who a father himself, reduced his lance to thumb size and slipped it into his calf pocket. He picked the first child up and carried her in his arms.

'We have to teleport them to the Ark. We have to,' he said, his face furrowed with concern.

'We can leave them with the First Churchers for now,' Rebecca decided. 'They'll be safe there and they can have a med-scan before we teleport them up.'

'Rebecca,' Timothy retorted, 'they may need counseling urgently. Creator knows what they've been through.'

'Can we just get out of here?' Naomi said. 'We can argue about this outside.'

Rebecca took the second child's hand and led them off the ship into the night. Under the light of the moons they made their way back to the land-wheeler. Suddenly, Timothy began screaming.

The child was anatomically changing; her legs were fusing into one large, white scaly tail. The face was elongating and, before he knew what was happening, the Virgin had sunk her fangs into the flesh of his face. He dropped to his knees as his skin began to blacken. Rebecca quickly let go of the hand that she clutched as its digits and palm were absorbed into the white reptile that bore down upon her, its snake's tongue shooting in and out of its human mouth. Behind it, the two other Virgins of the Abyss were tearing Simon's clothes from his body. Rebecca and Naomi fired into their faces and chests. They tried various settings but the beams were just swallowed up by the torsos of the monstrosities. Simon's screams of panic intensified as the creatures penetrated his body with the stings that had emerged from their reptilian tails. His body began to fill with a pale substance that glowed through his skin. The snakes were speaking, urging each other to mate with him. To Naomi's horror she saw that they were laying their eggs in his body, injecting him through a reproductive appendage that emerged from just below their stings.

'What the drent is going on here?' The Virgins turned to see the ministros appear behind them. 'Have you got a holo-pass for these?' asked one of the klonks, but even his clone mind could see that they did not belong to the Agathons. Suddenly registering that the Virgins were hostile out-worlders, the ministros let rip with their fire-blasters. The pulses of fire had no effect on the Thanatons; they simply bounced away as they hit the white scales. The clones held their position, still firing, until the snakes reached them. The sisters took great delight in tearing open the bodies of the ministros. Timothy and Simon were done for, one a blackened husk and the other a bloated body filled with eggs. In the precious seconds while the creatures were dispatching the ministros, resolve deserted the surviving missionaries to be replaced by fear.

Rebecca hid; Naomi fled.

Naomi crossed the deserted coastal track, her boots clanking over the metal surface, and into the red soil of the night desert. After a few minutes she stopped and listened. The port behind her was silent. The creatures weren't following her, which was good, until the awful thought that perhaps they had cornered Rebecca jumped into her mind. She signaled Rebecca using the temporary phys-tech installed in her hand but there was no reply. For long seconds she stood praying to the Creator. She had to make a decision; she could look for Rebecca and risk meeting those things again or she could go back to the vehicle and return to Alpha. The city of ten levels burned brightly like holo-discs stacked on a stick. With a heavy heart Naomi decided to leave her sister; there was nothing she could have done to save her. The Agathon's boots scuffed through the red soil. When she returned to the apartment she would be forced to signal the Ark. The operation would be over.

Then, from out of nowhere, three beings took corporeal shape. At first Naomi thought they might have teleported somehow, but then she saw their tracks in the desert. That's how they hadn't been noticed in the cargo hold at first. They could become invisible. The Virgins of the Abyss towered over her. As one, they converged, encircling her.

Ashes

Terminus really didn't get on with these missionary ganntas. The two that were with Naomi and Rebecca — Timothy and Simon — were a pair of cocky, sneering drellocks who looked down their nozzles at him. He found it impossible to converse with them; they had nothing in common. Terminus wondered what they did with their time. They didn't have dive-ball on their planet and they never went out and got snakkied. They didn't even floor geemas, which was probably why they were so uptight. Nothing like a flooring session to release the tension, not that Terminus would be getting any soon because Naomi didn't believe in it before Linking. Terminus didn't mind, Naomi was special, worth giving up some things for.

The rain was hammering this district of Level Three, which lay near the rim and so was uncovered by Level Four. This meant he could dart through the streets with his rain-hat over his eyes, unnoticed. He clutched the container to his chest and hurried on.

In the church, they'd left a circle of candles burning around her ashes. The scene almost looked like a tribute, a vigil of mourning, though actually the candles were designed to keep her there. Now Terminus scooped up what was left of the Gatekeeper into the sealed container. At the edge of the funzone he intended to store her in a perma-case rented from one of the holding centers.

When he got there, he found the holding center deserted. Not surprising at this time of night but a relief all the same. He entered the functional, door-less building and found a locker. There were banks of them running across the curvature of the rear wall. After checking once more that no one was around, he entered his code into the keypad. The Gatekeeper's book, stored in a perma-case locker on Level Five, would automatically teleport to the locker in front of him. That was the plan, but the authorities could have taken over his account, or the holding center canceled it on the grounds that he was dead. His luck held. When he opened up the locker, there was the ancient tome just as he'd hoped. After placing the canister next to it, he took the old book in his hands and turned to the page that mentioned Adlestrop. He'd been four thousand pulses from Skyfire, twenty thousand from Earth, and he found a book that detailed his home settlement. Not only that, he met a woman who had been there. The Gatekeeper must have the answers, all the answers.

Naomi, of course, would not be pleased to know he had these items in his possession. Naomi need never know. Beyond the rectangular gap that led to the street the rain was dripping onto the metal of the pavement. He stood for a few minutes just holding the Thanaton book. When the rain stopped, he closed the book, placed it in the locker next to the Gatekeeper's ashes, and closed the door. Turning, he saw a figure silhouetted in the doorway. Drent, he'd been found. When the figure stepped into the meager light, Terminus recognized him.

'Oh digest.'

'Digest indeed.' Akkbar's voice echoed through the hall. 'You know, if you'd stayed in that apartment you would have been safe. The Creator has protected that area against any interference from the power I serve. Fortunately you had to go out, had to look at your little book. Now I can dispatch you quickly and easily.'

Akkbar was a slight figure. He retained his pale, politico complexion but wore an expensive, tailored suit. Terminus could see no ministros around. Akkbar had come alone. Terminus estimated that he could easily punch this strentner out and run. However, he still had questions unanswered. The knock-out could wait.

'Last time I saw you, you had your guts hanging out and your insect mates cut the pipes to your blood-pump. I see you've recovered.'

'And shortly after that, you were smashed to pieces against an Agathon Ark.'

'So that's something we have in common. We're both dead.'

'That's all we have in common, you vulgar little drellock. Your god also resurrects the dead, so does mine, but my god does it better.'

'Ah, well, Akkbar, you see I haven't found religion. There's no forgiveness from my end.' With that, the space-gannta swung his fist into the politico's face. He readied himself for a satisfying crack but instead his fist passed through the man's head as if he were punching air. He thrust his fist into the stomach and the same thing happened. Drent and vulley, he thought, this was like fighting a hologram. Akkbar arched an eyebrow, raised his own fist, and smashed Terminus back into the lockers.

Terminus quickly regained his balance, punched through the politico, and received two more intense poundings.

'I told you my god does it better,' sneered Akkbar. 'With the Destroyer, the resurrected enjoys added bonuses.'

He thrust his hand around his victim's neck. Terminus had time to see Akkbar's human hand change into a Thanaton limb. The arachnid digits delivered nerve-burning pain to every part of Terminus's body.

Death wasn't a common occurrence in the mission field, protected as they were by the Creator. That's what Naomi had learned in the few short months spent at the novice school. Timothy and Simon's sudden and horrifying end had quickly put that training into question. They hadn't taught her extensively about the lance's use but, due to the revived Thanaton threat, she knew more about its use than her predecessors.

Now the Virgins of the Abyss surrounded her and that limited training would have to be enough.

Facing the first snake, she set the dial to *shifter* and aimed. With lightning speed the sister furthest from her, the one she was not aiming at, shot forward and almost gracefully knocked the lance from her grip. As they closed in, they hissed threats like actors playing villains, badly.

Naomi clutched the Creator symbol and prayed.

'We were told to expect opposition from the Creator's fawning slaves,' mocked the snake who had knocked the weapon from her hand. 'We expected more than two virgin females and two males who might as well have been girls.'

Naomi felt the ground all around begin to gently undulate.

'I will have no dialogue with the servants of the Destroyer,' she announced defiantly. That was something else they taught them at novice school. The tongue of the Destroyer seduces so that the hand of the Destroyer can kill.

'I think we should fill her with poison,' said one.

'No, she has to bear our children. Her body must house our spawn.'

'No,' snapped the first. 'You heard the commands of the Thirteen. We must spread out. We cannot leave another hatchling site so close to the first. We'll go into the city and leave our eggs there. That's what the Thirteen ordered. That's what we'll do.'

'So it's poison for this one.'

All around, small mounds were being created in the red soil. Something was trying to break through. Naomi looked to the sky and saw that in the last few seconds it appeared as if every molecule of air had caught fire. From the earth, garish blue plants were unfolding, leaves uncurling to meet the flaming sky at rapid speed. She smiled, day was coming. This was the reason for the planet's grandiose name: Skyfire. The first ray of the mighty Skyfirean sun burst over the horizon with the power of a laser cannon. The rays hit the Virgins of the Abyss full in the face. They screamed in agony and flattened themselves to the ground but the sun rose rapidly and they could not escape the dawn. Naomi seized the lance from the floor and set the dial to *heamo*. Haemophites loathed any sun on any world, according to her tutor at the Intergalactic Mission Center. These creatures weren't strictly bloodsuckers but they shared the same genetic makeup and so they hated sunlight. A blast of intense light from the lance set the creatures ablaze with white fire. Naomi backed up, knelt, and fired into the writing worms again. Their substance was breaking up, their corporeal form disintegrating. Soon they would be nothing but dust. That at least was something useful they had taught her at the academy.

All around her the plants were growing at alarming speed. She noticed that they possessed sharp thorns that could cut and sting. In minutes she would be trapped in a forest of thorny day-plants. This was another Skyfirean hazard she'd been warned about. At that moment the wrist-comm sprang across the top of her hand. Someone was trying to contact her. She started to run.

'Naomi? Are you out there?' The wrist-comm spoke.

'Rebecca? Creator be praised! I'm still here, in the desert.'

'I have your position. I'm in the vehicle. Fortunately, it's fitted with a day-plant cutter. Hold on, Naomi, I'm coming!'

'Listen, Anwar, can I call you Anwar? We didn't really get to talk much on the 850.' Terminus was backing away from the advancing politico, his hand raised pathetically before him in a gesture of weak defense. 'Your bosses are the Thirteen, right? Well, I've got some news. You can't kill me because Urrseal wants me. He's pretty interested in me for some reason, so if you kill me, he'll be pretty vullied. They won't like you on Thanatos.'

'Wrong!' Akkbar smashed his fist into Terminus's face again. 'We serve the Destroyer equally. You are an irritation to the plan. You must be eradicated. Urrseal won't care; he'll soon have an entire new world to play with.'

Terminus knew that his life depended on keeping this gannta talking.

'How are they gonna get here? We've got boundary stations, Sundogs. We'll blast the boneships out of the sky.'

Akkbar stopped and leered. 'We are the government. We control the military. And we have the Ethereal Mirror.'

'What's the Ethereal Mirror?'

Akkbar started to laugh and laugh hard. If there was one thing to be said for attaining immortality through the Destroyer, it did seem to give a sense of humor.

'They haven't told you? Oh dear.' His smile ceased abruptly. He looked to his left and frowned, as if sensing something approaching. Terminus backed up against the lockers. The politico was still staring into space and when Terminus followed his gaze to a point on the horizon he couldn't see anything. If the politico had forgotten about him, maybe there was something to this Creator gannta after all.

Quietly, Terminus ran away.

The apartment the Agathon missionary team had rented possessed a steri-alcove. It was a couple of notches in quality above the one in the gemmel that Terminus shared with Clannel. This alcove performed minor cosmetic work, so he had the waves remove the bruises from his face and body. His muscles still ached with whatever Akkbar had done to him with the pain-inducing touch but he'd survive. By the time Naomi and Rebecca arrived back it was past dawn and they found him scanning a dive-ball game. They looked vullied. Naomi was covered in desert dust and Rebecca's clothes were torn.

'Where are the goomahs?' Terminus snorted.

'They're dead.' Rebecca cut the air with her announcement.

Terminus immediately regretted the remark, feeling like a veck as he watched Rebecca go into the alcove cursing the fact that they didn't have water showers on this planet. Naomi shot him a meaningful look. Her wrist-comm buzzed again and she had a brief, muffled conversation. When she was done, the phys-tech dissolved back into her wrist.

'Joel is here. He has the Eden Globe. We will have to meet.'

'Where?'

'On the Ark. The *Bethany* is in hyperspace orbit, docked with the *Sidon*. It won't be good. Simon's father is part of the crew on that ship.'

The *Bethany*

Terminus thought his stomach might turn and he'd vomit, or the effect of the teleportation would be like a blast of a neuro-scrambler. That would have been good. Disappointingly, the instantaneous journey had left him with no ill effects at all. On Skyfire, all attempts by the scilitos to perfect human teleportation had ended in disaster. Perfectly healthy clone specimens had been used in the first experiments and had been transformed into hideous, anatomically-compromised monstrosities as the molecules failed to re-assemble themselves into the correct order after teleport. Quite how the Agathons had perfected this he didn't know. All Naomi would say was that it was the Creator's will that scientific advancements were revealed to her people.

In hyperspace, the *Bethany* was docked beside the *Sidon*, Naomi's ship. He'd expected to find himself in some sort of teleportation alcove. Instead they had materialized in the center of a vast hall. The interior was sterile in appearance and white in color, apart from the silver disc set into the floor they'd found themselves standing upon. Naomi explained that the teleportation circles were set at various points around the *Bethany*. If teleportation was imminent then the disc would turn red to warn the crew to skirt around the area before the teleportees appeared.

'Come on, I'll show you the bridge.' She took his hand, leading him away. Rebecca let them go, saying that she'd meet them presently in the Discourse Lounge with some of the Elders. The *Bethany's* midsection echoed with the buzz of conversation and the sound of hurried footsteps. Despite this, a feeling of serenity and order permeated the social atmosphere of the ship. He noticed that some of the Agathons wore the familiar white robes but others scurried around the ship wearing white trouser suits. Apparently this denoted that they were engineers or missionaries. They skipped up the steps together where the hall narrowed slightly. As they passed through the narrow section he noticed open portals leading to quiet rooms. In one room, seven or eight trouser-suited Agathons sat in the circle with their eyes closed, a candle burning before them.

'Research division,' Naomi said. 'They're seeking answers from the Creator to a scientific problem.' They moved on. The corridor opened out onto a wide platform. From this, steps led to a floor where many Agathons sat at circular workstations arranged in three gentle curves like spooning brackets. They were dwarfed by the enormous viewing screen which dominated this vast space. The wide square screen showed in crystal clarity a mesmeric scene of color and movement.

'Best not look at it too long,' Naomi advised. 'It'll give you a headache.'

Terminus stared. Vivid, abstract three-dimensional shapes formed and reformed in the bright void beyond. Never the same, always changing, the random patterns formed landscapes and clouds, abysses and mountains. Naomi smiled her all-knowing smile.

'Welcome to hyperspace,' she said.

'I had a lot of growing up to do very fast,' she informed him as they journeyed to the Discourse Lounge. 'Most missionaries train for about a year before being let out in the field. Because of my involvement with you they put me to work on the Skyfire operation.'

'That's odd,' said Terminus. He frowned. 'The Watch do the exact opposite. If two crew members are emotionally involved then they split them up. They even have same-sex ships in case anything happens between men and women onboard ship.'

'What if something happens between a man and a man?' She grinned mischievously.

'It won't. Trust me, that never happens. If a coordinator found out he had a goomah on the ship he'd chuck him out, leave him on the nearest habitable or uninhabitable planet.'

'I never took you to be a homophobe.'

'A what?'

They reached the Discourse Lounge, a functional room with a side port giving a view of hyperspace. A large oval table dominated the room. 'Listen,' she said as they entered. 'Deaths are very rare on missions. Tensions are high right now. This is the beginning of a new era for our generation where the Thanatons are a real threat again. The deaths of Simon and Timothy signal that this is war. So, please, just... I don't want to sound rude... Just don't say anything in this meeting.'

Terminus followed Naomi into the Discourse Lounge and nearly ran out again. Among the robed Agathon Elders sat his black-uniformed, shaven-headed commander. Crank rose to greet him.

'What the drent's he doing here?'

'I'll handle this,' Crank told the Elders. He turned to Terminus and barked: 'Sit down, Terminus, and shut your ration-hole!' Instinctively, the Watch operative obeyed. As he sat he noticed Martha and a few of the other Elders. Opposite him he met Joel's gaze. The chaplain was cradling a smooth, cylindrical canister. Terminus stole sideways glances at Crank while Martha opened proceedings.

'Greetings all. We meet under the sad news that we have lost two of our missionaries. We are all deeply shocked by this turn of events and commend their souls to the Creator's care. A mass is being held in the Chapel after this meeting.'

'And I might interject and stress that I haven't got long here.' Crank sounded irritated. 'If they monitor my movements — which I'm certain they will — and they find I've been on an Agathon Ark, not only will it be the end of my stretches but the whole operation will be over. So shall we get a move on?'

'For those who don't know,' said Martha, glancing at Terminus, 'Watch Officer Crank is our inside agent. He is here at great personal risk so... if you'd like to impart the information.'

'Right!' Crank stood and pitched them a look bordering on contempt. Terminus shuddered. He knew Crank's tone and could tell he was going to swing this lot round by their muc-sacs. 'This inept jaunt to the port to see what was in the cargo hold of 851 was a total vulley-up. If you had contacted me when you were supposed to, instead of charging off to the out-world port, I could have told you that Akkbar has the Ethereal Mirror at the temple. I've seen it with my own eyes. The deaths of these two men could have been avoided. Of course, it doesn't help when you put kids in charge of a delicate operation like this. There's bound to be digest-spread.' Naomi opened her mouth to protest but thought better of it. 'Akkbar has recruited nearly all of the politicos and scilitos into his church. They're having a right old time, the sadistic shankaas!' Terminus winced at the language Crank was using but the Agathons didn't seem phased.

'He's being handed the documentation to become Prime in three stretches time. After that, he'll activate the Ethereal Mirror and they'll be here. Soon after, the First Church of the Destroyer will declare its existence publicly. They actually plan to take over the premises that formerly belonged to the First Churches of Skyfire.'

Terminus had heard Akkbar mention this Ethereal Mirror. It was obviously some sort of teleportation device.

'Sorry, who will be coming here?' Terminus asked.

'The Thirteen,' Martha explained. 'The Thanatons don't invade worlds as such, they corrupt them. They are taking a bottom-up approach. Corrupt a society until the populace is too weak, too seduced, to resist. Then the black galleons will land.'

'But that isn't the plan,' Crank broke in. 'Once Akkbar is Prime and the Thirteen are here, the new Prime will mobilize the military to strike Agathos.'

'With respect,' Joel piped up. 'Our Arks can easily defend our world from Skyfire Sundog attack. There won't even be any Skyfirean casualties because we can hold your fighters in stasis for up to a year. *Your* world is our concern, ours is adequately defended.'

Crank turned on him, eyes wild and sweat glistening on his forehead. 'You better wipe that digest from your mouth where you've been talking, gannta. Akkbar is planning to arm Skyfirean Sundogs with Thanaton tech. Tech equal to yours. Not only that, Skyfire will combine forces with Babel, who are already in the Thanaton payload. You've been casping them off for sub-cycles, teleporting skang-gat's off-world, putting the palaces out of business. Their Babel ships will be armed to the teeth with all sorts of metaphysical nasties. Can you really take on a fleet of Babel Cloud Sword and our Sundogs with ecto-drive fusion banks? You could hide in hyperspace until this is over, I suppose.'

Give him his ching, Joel kept his cool. 'Well if you put it like that, yes, we do have a problem.'

'Thank you,' said Crank sarcastically.

'But I think I have the answer.' Joel laid the canister on the table. 'I have the Eden Globe.'

Forged by the Mage

Joel sprang open the canister to reveal a small, glowing sphere that sat on a clasp attached to its shell. Within the sphere, light appeared to be trying to push its way out, as if part of a sun had been captured and was raging inside a prison. The whole thing could easily fit into the palm of his hand and was beautiful to look at. Terminus wondered how much it would fetch at the rarities market on Level Three, perhaps to become a brooch for some rich geema.

'The Eden Globe is unique,' Joel explained. 'The design is absolutely perfect. The research division has analyzed it and concluded that it cannot be copied. While very similar molecular constructs can be obtained from its pattern, there are always subtle flaws. The copies cannot be used in the same way as the original; they simply won't be effective. We have managed to construct a copy that looks exactly like the Eden Globe and affects the metaphysical atmosphere identically. However, it won't function in the same way as the original.'

'Why have we gone to the trouble of copying the Eden Globe?' Martha asked.

Joel explained. '*They* know we have this and they think we're going to use it. If we brought this down to the planet, they'd sense it immediately and be all over us like lake weed rash over skin. So this morning, just before dawn, I teleported down with the copy and hid it. Akkbar would have instantly sensed it, like a dog scenting meat. They'll soon be searching the city for the copy, thinking that it's the original Eden Globe.'

The ching dropped in Terminus's mind. That would explain why Akkbar was so distracted during his encounter with him earlier, giving the space-gannta time to run. Joel must have teleported down with the copy at exactly the same time as Akkbar was about to morto him. Terminus was about to open his mouth and tell them about this when he thought better of it.

'Which member of the science division made this unique object?' Martha smiled, her question loaded. Joel stood his ground and refused to be phased by the question.

'The Mage made this. I met with him on Babel.'

'Joel!' She shot him a look of disappointment. 'The Mage is not a person we should be dealing with. He has fallen away from us. He is an apostate of our faith and dabbles in dark Thanaton arts.'

'Martha, he is the only person in the cosmos who could make the Eden Globe, and the Eden Globe is the only thing that will undo the work of the Eternum Codex. No one on Agathos has the skill to undertake this work. Despite his dabbling, the Mage is still on the side of the Creator. He has no sympathy for the Thanatons'

'Yet still he practices forbidden metaphysical science.'

'The Mage is still a man, a man made with love by the Creator. No one is beyond redemption so who are we to judge? The fact is, without the Mage we would not have this!' He held the Eden Globe in his left hand.

Rebecca spoke up. 'Then the question is; how do we get close enough to Akkbar to use it? I assume it has limited range.'

'Akkbar must be less than a meter from the globe. The shell is constructed from a substance that has a very basic consciousness, sufficient to sense Akkbar's presence. When it does, its shell will become frail. The light inside will want to get to him and consume the power he holds. All the operator has to do is crush the globe to release the light. It's pretty intense, the Mage told me, so whoever holds The Eden Globe will be blinded for a few seconds. Then it will undo the particle manipulations of the Eternum Codex.'

'That means we have to get someone into the First Church of the Destroyer,' Naomi said. 'These ghastly sacrifices they have, these virgin murders. How are the unfortunate victims obtained?'

'Some come from the imprisoned Churchers on Spike Island,' Crank replied. 'Some are obtained from the human stock on Babel. Others are just poor spudders out in the funzone, captured and drugged. The sacrifices have to have one thing in common. They have to be inexperienced in the sexual act. They have to be pizzdeens or pizzdeenas.'

'I could go undercover,' Naomi said. 'I guess I would be close enough to Akkbar during whatever ceremony it is they've been carrying out.'

Terminus's guts tightened, every nerve in his body began twitching. He was staring at Naomi and his thoughts were screaming out. He remembered what the Gatekeeper had promised concerning Naomi, how she would break her back and drink her soul. The instinct to protect raged inside him.

'It would be very dangerous.' Crank put a fatherly hand upon her arm as he spoke. 'The Mirror is there, the power they draw from that thing, geema, your mind would not be your own.'

An uneasy silence fell over the room, quickly broken when Terminus asked: 'Why don't I go?'

Heads turned to look in his direction. Terminus opened his arms, offering himself.

'I've been to Thanatos. I know what they're like. They want to kill me anyway. Urrseal himself is eager to get his spidery digits on me, so I would make an ideal sacrifice.'

'You have to be a pizzdeen, Terminus.' Crank grunted.

'Well, technically I am.'

Martha frowned, indicating that he'd better explain.

'I died,' he said. 'Since coming back to life I've — well — got a new body. A new body that hasn't been near a geema so I am, as you say, a virgin.'

303

Naomi gazed at him with pride and astonishment. He had effectively taken her place to face the First Church of the Destroyer.

Joel stood. 'Then if you have chosen,' he said. 'Let the Creator bless you in your endeavor, for all our sakes.

While Naomi and Rebecca attended the mourning mass for Simon and Timothy, Terminus stared out at hyperspace.

'Unbelievable, isn't it,' Crank joined him at the viewing port. 'All this time we thought they were just a bunch of religious neuro-cases. We never razzled they were capable of all this. There's more to the universe than we'll ever know.' Crank laid a hand on his shoulder. 'I'm sorry about having you arrested, Sii. I had no choice. I thought you were dead and when you turned up at my office, well, I could have drenting well killed you again. We had to act pretty quickly to get you out of the research theater. I knew if we did our bit, you would do yours.'

'Thanks, Crank,' he replied. 'And for what it's worth I knew you wouldn't have sold me out. You've swung me round by the muc-sac enough times but I knew you weren't a vulley. So tell me, how did you get involved with the Thanatons, this Church of the Destroyer?'

He sighed. 'You know how it is. You work as Watch officer for cycles and get nothing. You see your buddies go up the ranks because they're in with one of the Societies. The old orders like the Catholics or the Baptists. You know the ones, where they're rubbing shoulders with the politicos and getting the promotions. Then a new society arrives and I get an invite. I accept. I also get a contact from a friend of mine, a Churcher, telling me to watch out. There are outer circles and inner circles. With this society you don't just get to network, you get whatever you want. They could *do* things. Cure illnesses, kill people with a whisper. I've seen things that you couldn't believe. This Destroyer church is not a society, it's a religion. Well, they must have thought me valuable because I rose up the ranks pretty quickly.

They worship this god called the Destroyer. They've got a temple made to him, right in the heart of Decision Central. The power these people wield is unbelievable but the things they do, the way they dispatch people, geemas and ganntas who have done no wrong...'

'I know.' Terminus was thinking again about what they would do to Naomi. 'How did you get in touch with the Agathons?'

'I didn't. They got in touch with me via my friend in the First Church, just before they took him to Spike Island. I arranged to meet them and told them everything. You see, to get on in this society you have to offer your soul to the Destroyer and I wasn't into that. Not at all. Something really sat uneasily with me then. Funny, I never thought about having a soul but the idea of giving it up really scanned wrong. I was in far too deep by this time, refusal meant death. So now I spy for these neuro-crackers. What a pair we make.'

'Never thought I'd be standing on an Agathon hyperspace ship looking into this light show.'

'Neither did I, spudder. Tell me, you and that Naomi geema. Is something going on between you two?'

'Well... yes.'

Terminus thought Crank might pat him on the back; tell him to get in there and the best of luck. He didn't.

'Take it easy, Terminus. They're not like us. They take their faith very seriously. You have to be careful here. You can casp them off and you don't wanna do that. We need them.'

Raid

Alone in the apartment, Terminus gazed at his wrist. The temporary implant was in there, under the skin and invisible, operating at a physiological level. He hadn't missed the phys-tech when he'd come back to life. The two tattoos on each forearm had made him feel like a marked man. Now he was clean, pure, one hundred percent human. Apart from this temporary Agathon phys-tech which could be triggered with a word: Godless. That word would summon the tiny particles to rise through his cells and assemble on his wrist. When they did, he would hit the assembled circuit and the globe that now resided in his gut would appear in his hand as if by magic. Akkbar would look horrified, crumple before him and beg for mercy. Terminus would show none. Instead, he would crush the globe and it would do whatever a magic, metaphysical globe did. Then Terminus would kick twelve shades of digest out of the politico, leave with Naomi in the big ship, marry her on Agathos in that little temple in Jericho, and there they would live forever and have a dozen spudders. It would be all right. This would be easy.

Terminus sweated with fear. He felt like he'd volunteered to go back to Thanatos One, knocked on the door of the dark tower wearing only his slids, and asked if Urrseal was in.

The door comm sounded. He froze. He sat there, didn't answer it. It rang again... then silence. The holo-panel indicated that someone had pressed the door comm but hadn't left a message. Whoever had been here might not necessarily want him but his gut instinct told him they drenting well did. If the ministros had arrived they'd have blasted the door down so someone else was looking for him. He racked his brains as to who that might be, but drew a blank.

Sub-stretches passed.

When they came for him at the apartment, they didn't ring the drenting door comm, they blasted the doors out. No less than six ministros led by Crank filed into the gemmel, surrounding him within moments.

'Where the drent are the rest of them?' Crank yelled into his face.

'I dunno... They said they'd be back later.'

Crank grabbed him by the lapels, pulling him to his feet. He raised his knee into Terminus's muc-sac. Terminus doubled over and the ministros fired a lock-field over him for good measure. Inside the invisible force field, Terminus was unable to move; not that he wanted to move, the way his balls ached. Crank had to make it look convincing, he supposed. Then he got a right battering as the clones dragged him away down the stairs to whatever fate awaited him.

The Movements Department was located on the fourth floor of Decision Central. The main desk was operated by an uncloned human; clones didn't quite have the cognitive capacity that real people needed to operate the higher-spec data recorders.

She slid into the seat opposite the operator as he tapped her request into the data-spine. Occasionally he would look her way and she would lick her lips or uncross her legs. The poor veck was a politico in the making. She recognized the type; a level descender. Probably from Level Six and eager to please, grasping for a foothold in the politico career front. He was also the type to be highly sexually frustrated. Such types never attracted decent women. In a few years he'd be using his leave time to go on furtive excursions to Babel at the city's expense. Her dark eyes sank into his soul.

'According to this he's not left the planet.'

'Then where is he?' Each word was carried as if she were talking to a naughty child.

'He's just been arrested.'

'And taken where?' She curled her legs underneath her. He swallowed hard when he got a look at her shapely calves.

'That's strange. That shouldn't happen.' He was gazing at the circular holo-screen.

'What?'

'He's gone off the scanner. He's disappeared.'

She stood up and leaned right over the desk. When she reached out for his hand he thought of running, she could tell. But when she pressed something into his hand, he brightened. This was something he understood, that he thought he could control.

'You contact me the moment he reappears,' she told him. 'Understand?'

He nodded.

She crossed the floor, walking like a cat.

When he was sure she had left him, he looked into his hand to see what she had left. It was a ring, an ancient ring that must have been worth a cargo hold of ching. He laughed. With the ching he would make from this he could afford an excursion to Babel.

Under the Influence of the Black Drug

Terminus was led through a vast network of subsurface tunnels to the place where they would sacrifice him. The tunnels reminded him of Thanatos, of his time scrambling from the abyss and its Virgins underneath the walls of the outer castle. The claustrophobic capillaries shot off in all directions. To Crank's credit he acted his part convincingly, showing nothing but contempt for his prisoner. At last they arrived at a sealed metal door. The portal slid open spilling bright light into the darkness. Terminus was thrown into a sterile room lit with a pink glow and similar to the curve-walled chambers at the research theater. Crank and the ministros followed him in.

When Terminus's eyes adjusted to the dim light, he realized that the room was actually more like a hospitality suite on Babel. A large circular bath bubbled quietly at the far end of the room; at its center, poised upon a scarlet settee, two beautiful women were waiting... for him. They wore scarlet blouses and matching above-knee skirts. Their hair shone bright blonde, the curls bunched above their heads. Their features were immaculate and Terminus could tell they weren't Skyfireans. They were Babel hostesses; prostitutes who could do unimaginable things in the bedroom for their paying customers. Terminus didn't expect to meet two of them here, on the eve of his death.

He turned to Crank. 'What, are they gonna vulley me to death?'

'Shut your protein hole. You do what they say or you'll get another knee in the muc-sac.'

'This isn't what we expected.' The geemas spoke with the smooth voices of Babelites, phys-tech manipulating vocal chords for a more seductive sound. 'You were to bring us another girl from the religious sect.' The first woman spoke as if silk was sliding from her lips.

'Besides,' the second sidled up to Terminus and splayed her hand over his chest. 'We prefer girls.'

'That's fine.' Terminus shrugged. 'I'm happy just to watch.' Crank delivered a blow to his head that knocked him to the ground.

'Careful!' said one of the Babelites. 'If he is to be the sacrifice tonight, the High Priest will want him undamaged.' A comm device spread out across her cheek like a recording of a blooming flower played at high speed. 'Anwar!'

Terminus heard the politico's voice and shivered. 'Yes, Carla, what is it?'

'The sacrifice is here. He's not what they're expecting. Crank has made a mistake. Should I punish him now or should we consult the Thirteen.' She briefly explained the situation.

'I'll be down in a second.'

Terminus began to push himself up. The high heel of Carla's boot pushed him down to the ground again. 'When the High Priest arrives, you will kneel before him.'

The second Babelite stood over him. 'As we are his acolytes, you will first kneel before us.' They giggled girlishly and the sound spread a wave of fear through Terminus.

He considered verbalizing some sarcastic remark but thought better of it. Terminus shifted into a kneeling position. As promised, seconds later Akkbar entered. The politico walked through the wall like a ghost, beheld the kneeling form of Terminus, and snorted. He turned to Crank.

'Explain.'

'Well, sir. It's no secret that Urrseal wants this particular human for his own purposes. I thought we could give Terminus to him.

After all, we do have to appease the Thirteen. It's in our best interests.'

Akkbar squared up to Crank and looked into his eyes. 'And who are you, you dog, to second-guess my decisions?'

'I am no one, master. I serve the Destroyer to the best of my abilities. If the High Priest does not think my idea worthy, then a First Church pizzdeena is waiting in the holding cells. She's terrified.'

'Hysterically terrified?'

'Yes, sir.'

Terminus could tell that Crank thought he was going to suffer for what he'd done. When Akkbar threatened him, Crank had actually gone red with fear.

'Then I'll have to take a personal visit to her cell. What of the other matter?'

'Pleased to say...' Crank ushered forward the ministro. 'This was found at the apartment where Terminus was waiting.'

Terminus risked looking up and saw Akkbar cautiously take the canister from the ministro. He looked so scared of what he thought lay inside that he dared not open it. But what Akkbar actually had was Joel's fake copy of the Eden Globe. The politico had been fooled and he hadn't sensed the real one resting in Terminus's gut. Terminus still needed to get closer to the politico before he set it off. There wouldn't be time to do it now. Crank might be undercover but the ministros weren't. Any sign that he was putting Akkbar's life in danger and they would blast him to hell.

Akkbar conquered his fear and opened the canister. For a fraction of a second he peered at the glowing ball of light before closing it. He quickly handed the canister back to Crank.

'Destroy this thing. Make sure it's been utterly atomized. I'm giving you personal responsibility for this.' He laid a hand on Crank's shoulder. 'After that, go to Minister Gopahl and end his life. You've just earned your place in the circle of the inner sanctum. Dismissed!'

Terminus was left with Akkbar and the two Babel whores. Akkbar knelt down to the prisoner's level and took his chin in his left hand. It burned but Terminus refused to scream. He might have even come out with a sarcastic comment if he could only speak.

'Listen to me,' said Akkbar. 'You cannot ever escape the Thirteen. Crank is right. We need to appease them; they are the voice of the Destroyer in the mortal universe. It doesn't mean that you are necessarily going to die. They can prolong life beyond your natural years to extend your suffering. You could be in pain for centuries. When Urrseal begins your defilement you will truly enter a physical and spiritual hell. This is why the Destroyer chose to create humanity, so that they may be playthings for his acolytes.'

'Are... they... here?' Terminus said through clenched lips. Akkbar stood and laughed.

'Has the sky turned black? Has the populace been plagued with nightmares that continue after waking? Have mothers started to kill their offspring? No, so the Thirteen have not set foot on this world, though other Thanatons have. That day will come. You won't see it. You are to be taken to them on Thanatos. You're going back.' He turned to the whores. 'Prepare him.' Then he disappeared, literally, out of the room.

Drent! Terminus could have done it. He'd been close enough. If he didn't meet Akkbar again before they transported him to Thanatos, he'd have blown his chances.

'Welcome to the First Church of the Destroyer,' said the Babelite, Carla, in a honeyed voice. 'Now take your clothes off.'

Crank entered Gopahl Simiir's personal chambers. The overweight scilito frowned at him.

'Aren't you supposed to kneel or something?' he said. 'You certainly aren't supposed to enter without my permission. Guards!'

The ministros, under new instructions from their phys-tech, ignored the now ex-inner circle minister's orders.

'Looking forward to seeing that pizzdeena vullied, eh?' Crank spat.

Oblivious to his tone Gopahl replied, 'I hope he'll use the hypersensitivity drug. I've been trying to perfect my own but the effects are only short-lived. I intend to bite her young flesh until she goes mad from the pain.'

'Well, I wish you'd had some of your own drug.'

Simiir frowned. 'Me? Why?'

'Then this would hurt twice as much as its going to but not half as much as I'd like it to.'

Abruptly, Gopahl realized the danger he was in. 'Guards!'

Crank smashed his fist into the scilito's nose knocking him back into his table covered with glass phials. He pulled the ex-acolyte to his feet and rammed his head into the wall before throwing him over to his potion collection. After administering a few more kicks he hauled him up to the table where undamaged phials of his concoctions lay.

'Right then, you digest-swilling pervert. I'm gonna make you drink each one of these nasty poisons in turn until I find out which one drenting kills you.'

The Babelites' deft hands caressed his body and Terminus quickly succumbed to their touch. They'd made him drink something they called the black drug, which sent him into an instant stupor. Now they oiled his washed, naked body arousing hitherto unknown sensorial pleasures to flood his nervous system.

'I thought I was to be killed. Death and agony and all that,' he slurred.

'Your thoughts must be impure before you meet with your fate. Pleasure always leads to pain. You must be seduced before you are destroyed.' Carla gently bit into the flesh of his back several times but never enough to make a mark. 'You should see the First Church virgins who come to us. They begin praying and rebuking but after a while, and after they've been given the black drug, they succumb, especially the girls. They are almost begging to be sacrificed after they've been stimulated.'

'Personally,' began the second Babelite, 'I think all religious pizzdeenas have Sapphic tendencies. They are taught to fear sex, sex with a man, so subconsciously I think they are drawn to other women. Other women aren't a threat to them.'

'All religious girls are emotionally stunted,' added the first.

'Not all,' said Terminus. He thought of Naomi. At the prospect that he might never see her again, his mind began to clear. He tried to focus on memories of her but his concentration wavered. The seductresses prompted him to stand and presented him with a white Agathon robe.

'The sacrificial robe and the dress of our enemies. Fitting really,' Carla sighed. 'We will escort you into the temple.'

'I thought I was going to Thanatos. Is there a spaceport in there?' He laughed. 'Hey, will Anwar be there?'

'Anwar is High Priest of the First Church of the Destroyer. Of course he'll be there.'

'Well that's all right, then.' The women slid into black robes and face masks that only covered the eyes. They took each of his arms and Terminus was led into the antechamber of the temple.

The inner sanctum of the temple gave Terminus horrible flashbacks. Still under the influence of the drug, the fear was slow to kick in. The architecture of the First Church of the Destroyer was carved of ancient stone. It had the same no-tech feel of the old, dark planet. He could have been in the Gatekeeper's boudoir or the entrance hall to the Gate. The six pillars supporting the arched roof, the intricate occult carvings around the altar at the far end, and even that huge mirror dominating the altar area: all struck up images from his time on Thanatos One.

Terminus was walked like a drugged spudder to the center of the temple to face the huge mirror that cast an eerie light over the sanctum. Melting out from the darkness, twelve dark-robed figures encircled him. Akkbar joined them, also wearing a similar cloak and Terminus could see that the players in this macabre pantomime were, thankfully, human.

Akkbar was close enough. If only Terminus's nerves could respond through the haze of the drug... He might not get another chance to get this close to the politico. The code word. He had to say the code word and the Agathon phys-tech would deliver the globe into his hand.

'Can you feel him, Terminus? Can you feel him aching for you through the mirror? Look at the Ethereal Mirror, you worm. *Stare* into it!' Akkbar turned him to face the reflecting glass.

Something was calling him from behind that glass. Just like when he was sixteen, a force was sucking the ability to choose from his mind. He peered into the Ethereal Mirror. The glass was framed and stood tall, perhaps five meters wide with intricate shapes of unnatural creatures making up its frame. Unholy. The mirror was unholy. The intricate carvings in the dark metal frame writhed and squirmed. He knew it was not the effects of the drug that made them move. Thousands of eyes and mouths blinked and opened at him. In the glass he saw an insubstantial shape take form. He recognized it instantly. It was one of the Thirteen. Probably the one that wanted to goom him. This was time to act.

'You know what you are, don't you?' Terminus slurred.

'Shut your mouth in the presence of your master. He's only interested in hearing you scream.'

Terminus stood up tall and faced Akkbar. 'You, you drenting vulley are...' Cockily he breathed the code word: 'Godless!'

Nothing happened. Terminus even held out his hand to receive the globe. He repeated the word several times but still the globe stayed lodged in his gut.

Akkbar didn't even bother to look at him as he spoke. 'Some sort of code word? No one's going to come for you here. Any implants are rendered useless by the Ethereal Mirror's presence. Whatever signal you sent won't be received. Stop wasting time, Urrseal is impatient.'

The instant Terminus heard Urrseal's name, he relinquished all resistance. The Thanaton beyond the reflection took full control of his mind and nervous system. He found one foot moving in front of the other; he was walking into the mirror. Up two short stone steps he went until he disappeared into the glass, passing through it as if he was walking into a gravity-defying pool of silver liquid.

Crank pulled his hood down and stared at the mirror in disbelief. The other members of the inner circle glared at him for disturbing protocol.

Beyond the Ethereal Mirror

Space-traveler instincts alerted Terminus to the change in gravitational pull and atmospheric pressure. He was no longer on Skyfire. He'd passed via the mirror into a temple shrouded in darkness. At first, he thought bizarrely that he'd entered the reflection of the temple they'd just left. This one had an identical layout but he was now in the genuine article; much older, a lot dustier with a distinctly Thanaton mustiness. He suddenly understood the metaphysics of this reverse church. The whole thing worked like a magic spell from a spudder's story, bound by rules that made logical sense but were beyond the belief of an adult. For the Ethereal Mirror to transport a being it must be placed in an identical, or near enough, structure to that which it reflected. Such clever realizations were shut off immediately as the Thanaton faced him. Urrseal was close enough for Terminus to see the dim light reflect off the six eyes beneath the hood. While Urrseal stood there, clicking his mandibles, Terminus heard Akkbar pass through the mirror from Skyfire to Thanatos.

'On first meeting you I never would have thought that you'd have made such trouble for us.' Akkbar smiled. 'All this trouble from a low-grade Watch operative, a drenting space monkey.'

'Oh no, wanderer. This Earther's destiny-line is rich. I sensed him when he left Earth to travel to your colony. When he made his way across the black space do you think it was by chance? No, Akkbar, this one had potential, had spirit. Do you know what he is?'

'A pain in the digest-spreader.'

'No!' He laid a spindly, arachnid finger on Terminus's shoulder. 'He is the Creator's puppet now, infected by those Agathon prostitutes, resurrected by the Creator himself. This one is so full of juices, full of succulent life. The holier he's become, the greater my lust has increased. Come, bring him to my inner chambers. I'll allow you to watch the defilement of the enemy's little soldier.'

Following behind the hooded creature like a frightened dog, Terminus could see beyond the arched windows to the dark, endless forest beyond. Before he knew it, he was being navigated down steps to the inner courtyard where the mouth-like maw opened out to the bridge. Terminus made a whining noise of fear as they exited the gate. Before them rose the Spires of the Thirteen, wreathed in circling lizard-birds that barked their alert. The black skies above glowered down upon the three figures that marched stoically to the slit-like entrance of the tower.

Their bodies lay around him groaning their last. Their flesh was burned and those still living writhed in agony under their cloaks. One of them was crawling away, her legs broken and burnt. Crank stood over her and aimed point-blank at her head. This one had enjoyed inserting needles into the spines of her victims until their nerves were stimulated to agony. She looked up now with pleading eyes.

'Where's he gone?' yelled Crank.

'Than...' blood filled her throat, '...Than... atos...'

Looking at that weird mirror, Crank could believe it. One of the Babelites poked her head through the door. Crank tried to shoot it off but she was too quick. Drent! The ministros would be here soon, alerted by those Babel geemas. Since being in the temple put the digest up any phys-tech, he used the comm on his fire-blaster to contact the ship.

'What's happening?' Naomi's voice came through.

'It's all gone brown. The temple has some sort of phys-tech scrambler. He couldn't even get the globe out of his insides. Now they've taken him. The vulley here tells me they've taken him to Thanatos. It's over. I'm going through that thing, that mirror, to get him.'

'Crank, no!'

He shut her voice off and blasted the geema beneath him. Wasting no time he ran for the mirror. The borders squirmed and blinked at his approach. He hit the glass at speed. He hadn't noticed how slowly, how carefully Akkbar and Terminus had taken the passing. As he crossed from one world to another, the Ethereal Mirror cut through his meat in places he couldn't imagine he could be cut.

Urrseal's Theater

There were new voices in the abyss to replace the three sisters who had ventured out on Akkbar's ship, the *851*, to spawn on the planet Skyfire. They'd found some poor gannta to lay their eggs in before they'd left, creating more horrors to take their place.

Terminus knew this because Urrseal placed the knowledge in his head, taking extra care to dwell on the moment when the eggs hatched from inside the body of their still-living host. Urrseal's alien gait looked almost regal as he walked to the spires. Terminus razzled that meant the Thanaton was feeling pleased. Terminus followed his master through the door into the sterile, tiled network of walkways. From different directions he could hear screams and didn't even try to imagine what was being done to those poor vecks. Terminus remembered the operating tables from the last time he'd been here. A couple of plaguewraiths padded by.

Terminus was led up this time, away from the torture rooms, up the stairs to Urrseal's chamber. As much as his brain wanted to engage his muscles to run he was still bound by the Thanaton's mental grip. As they ascended, the winding stairwell grew darker, the screams fainter. They at last reached the top, where five passages intersected. Urrseal took the first passage which darkened until it opened out, illuminated by the dim light from the dull Thanaton sun.

Urrseal's low-ceilinged chamber looked no different from the operating theaters below in terms of layout. However, shelves seemed to grow out of the sterile, tiled walls of the circular room. A large window, nothing more than a gap in the stone, allowed the Thanaton to see right over the tower gate to the stretches of forest, and what looked like blood-colored hills beyond. He could still swivel his head so Terminus took a quick scan of the chamber. The shelves were filled with jars of human heads, hundreds of them, their features pushed at absurd angles to the glass. His jaw would have dropped if Urrseal had allowed it when he saw the heads move. Mouths cried out, pleas drowned by the fluid that preserved them.

Urrseal gracefully sank down into a polished metal throne positioned under the window. The throne looked utterly uncomfortable to sit on. To the left stood a man-sized cage. Beside that was a table full of surgical tools.

'Anwar, strip him. Let me see this resurrection in its nakedness.'

Fire burst forth from Akkbar's gaping mouth and engulfed Terminus.

'The operation is not over!' Naomi shouted. 'We cannot leave Terminus down there. If one hillcow is lost, the Creator will leave the other ninety-nine to find it. That is *His* word.'

Martha leaned across the table and took her hand. 'His fate is in the Creator's hands now. There is nothing we can do.' Naomi pulled her hand away petulantly.

'He isn't on Skyfire any longer.' Joel remained calm and logical. 'His position cannot be found on the planet. He is simply no longer there.'

'I have to go down to the surface!'

'And achieve what? If his DNA can't be detected by our sensors, then you have no chance finding him by simply going down there. Besides, the ship is already moving away.'

Martha rose to leave. 'I advise that you pray, Naomi. Seek the Creator's plans for you. Seek His truth.'

The Elders shuffled out of the Discourse Lounge leaving Joel and Naomi alone, the colors of hyperspace beyond the viewing port changing wildly. Joel put a hand on her shoulder which she was on the point of shrugging off.

'I'm in charge of this ship. My missionaries know how to handle her and I've not lost a man yet.' She turned and he grinned. 'Why do you think we're on the move?'

The fire hadn't burned Terminus, only his robe. He tried to cover himself but in vain.

'I've decided that he will take the Eternum Codex. He will suffer forever as a punishment to his master. We will use him to bait the Creator. But first...' The insectoid pushed down on the arms of the throne to bring himself into standing. 'I will defile him. Your destiny is about to be fulfilled...' Urrseal spread out his five spidery digits onto the naked captive's chest. Akkbar was standing behind, smiling. The touch purged the remains of the black drug from his system, simultaneously unlocking the muscles held in check by Urrseal's power. Terminus now felt all the terror that had welled up inside of him stream from his throat in a roar of desperation.

'Ahhh... the sweet music.' Urrseal unclasped his cloak and let it drop to the floor. 'My familiars will fill his throat first, and then the true work will begin.' The ancient creature stroked each finger as it said this.

Without a covering the Thanaton reminded Terminus of a skinny, naked old man. He appeared to be made up of old arachnid limbs that sprouted, thick, unnatural hair. Within the ribcage, insects crawled and squirmed. Terminus knew that he was going to undergo torments he couldn't imagine, that Urrseal would create a hell inside of him. Another wave of terror exploded from within and Terminus lost control of his bowels.

Akkbar jumped back but not simply because he didn't want loose digest on his clothes. Urrseal angled his six eyes to the floor and gasped from his mandibles. Terminus also looked to the floor. At his feet, glowing among his own mess, sat the Eden Globe.

Terminus bent down and snatched it.

'I had no idea!' Akkbar told Urrseal, panic evident in his voice. 'We destroyed the Eden Globe, *we destroyed it!*'

Now the very thing that could destroy him was sitting in Terminus's palm. Still Akkbar tried to explain. 'We found and destroyed it, I swear.'

Terminus had no time to revel in his newfound power. He didn't even have time for a sarcastic quip because he could feel Urrseal's mind beginning to crush his will again. Looking at the globe he saw the surface integrity change as he held it. The surface was now brittle, had sensed the Thanaton presence. This was the time. Naked and kneeling, he crushed his hand over the globe.

Light.

Light filled the chamber with the intensity of a white sun. In the screaming brightness he saw the dark shape of the Thanaton consumed by that light. He even heard a scream. When the light died away the Thanaton was burning. He was falling into himself, his arachnid hand reaching out until it fell apart mid-air. Fire consumed Urrseal's being; the black spirit which drove the exo-skeleton was burning to nothing within the ribcage.

After what seemed like an entire cycle, the light finally died down completely. Urrseal was nothing more than a heap of bones. Six eye sockets in a blackened skull stared into empty space.

Behind him, Akkbar was shaking his head, dismayed. Terminus stood to full height and faced the politico.

'That should not have happened. That... you little—'

Terminus cut off Akkbar's sentence with a punch to the stomach. The politico doubled over. He could be punched; he was flesh and bone again. The Eden Globe was supposed to do that, Joel had told him. It undid the work of the Eternum Codex. Terminus wondered if it was supposed to reduce the ruler of the system, the ancient, terrible, and unquenchable evil, to nothing but bones too. The significance of Urrseal's death was not lost on Terminus. He knew what he'd done. He'd killed the creature that was death. The whole system would more than annihilate him for this.

The politico swung pathetically at him. Terminus punched him with a right and left hook.

'You'll never get off this planet alive.'

'Oh, I dunno, I did last time.' He laughed at the politico. 'If I was you, Akkbar, I'd ask for a refund. Having your innards cut out to gain immortality is a big price to pay, and I just undid it with a glow-globe.'

'You, Terminus.' Akkbar spat. 'You should learn to know your place.'

Terminus punched him again.

'You will suffer for this. You think your Creator-worshipping friends are going to fetch you? No, you'll be a martyr to them. They've left you here to be crucified.'

He grabbed the politico by the collar and dragged him to the window.

'You,' Terminus raged, 'are a strentner.'

He threw the politico against the window. The glass shattered and Akkbar plunged screaming into the abyss below.

Crossing the Bridge for
the Final Time

Terminus looked around the chamber, desperately seeking snakki, or something that approximated it. There was nothing. The veck didn't drink.

At seeing the Thanaton die and the politico thrown out of the window, the heads in the jars began to laugh in their embalming solution. Silent, laughing faces surrounded him, freaking him out; he had to get out of here. He had to get back to the mirror and get through it before they found out that their leader, their venerated voice of the Destroyer on Thanatos, had been murdered. He bent down to pick up Urrseal's skull. That, he decided, would join the book and the Gatekeeper in his locker.

Terminus could think of only one way he could get out across the bridge. It probably wouldn't work but he was too scared to just give up and wait for the Thanatons to get him. He shook the dust and dead insects out of Urrseal's cloak and pulled it over himself. It felt odd, horribly contaminated. He hadn't got a chance of making it. They would spot him immediately, probably sense that he was not Urrseal by their neuro-power or whatever it was they used. He at least had to try.

Sweating, he navigated his way down the winding steps. He could hardly see out of the heavy hood, not that he wanted to see this stinking planet, but if he tripped he'd be vullied. He pushed fear to the back of his mind. He had to get to that mirror; that was the only important thing. Over and over he told himself that, driving out any other thought.

Don't think about how these creatures would have already sensed Urrseal's demise like they magically sensed everything else on this planet, in this universe. Don't think about how absurd he looked under the cloak, that his posture and gait resembled nothing of its former owner. Don't think that he was never going to get away with this in a million cycles.

But, of course, trying not to think about how vullied he was only made him more terrified.

In the tiled area on the ground floor he heard an unnatural whispering. From the corners of his limited vision he could see a dark sea of creatures covering every inch of the tiles. They crept like a wave across the floor and veneered the branches above him. Their dark bodies contrasted against the clinical glare of the tiles. They surrounded him, chattering, creating a nerve-shredding noise. Spiky feet and dirty bodies clamored over each other to worship at the feet of the Thanaton. Their insect minds couldn't discriminate between the cloak and its owner. When they did, he imagined they'd strip him to the bone.

They gave passage to him as he left the spires and his heart leapt to be on the bridge. Although he'd left the insects behind, the lizard-birds up above circled and cried out. Their ghastly, dark shapes hacked through the air under a bank of high, solid cloud. He thought for a second they'd attack but seeing the cloak they cleared off, obviously scared of the immortal master. Thankfully they weren't able to recognize the idiot under the cloak. Terminus walked slowly, trying to imitate the magisterial stride of its former owner. In his left hand he clutched the skull.

Ahead, the gaping mouth of the gate entrance loomed large. He was almost at it when a dirty great plaguewraith crawled out from under the bridge to meet him. The beast bowed low before him and then looked up, the rotting, steaming head cocked to one side. From inside the spires a horrific scream from a thousand throats went up, not screams of distress but of outrage. They knew! A little late, but they'd realized. The plaguewraith lurched forward and, with a foot-hand, pulled back Urrseal's hood. Terminus held out the skull defiantly and the beast pulled the remains of its lips back in shock. Two more plaguewraiths joined in, surrounding him. This was it, his life was up. He was dead, more than dead. They'd make even the cruelest sadist on this planet wince when recounted with details of his suffering. They closed in.

From above, a spear of fire cleaved the largest plaguewraith's head in two. A second shot blasted the remaining two back into the abyss. Terminus's heart leapt to see fire from a fire-blaster. Leaving the cloak, but keeping the skull, he ran. From above, the birds dive-bombed but he made it into the gate leaving some of them to smash to death on the bridge. He'd seen where the shots had come from; there was a window halfway up the wall of the gate. Someone had come from the mirror-temple, followed him through. Someone had come to rescue him! As hope blazed into his being he nearly thanked the Creator. He dashed up the stairs and into the mirror room.

'Drent!' Terminus had reached the temple room but he came to an abrupt halt. 'Drent and vulley!'

The Ethereal Mirror had been smashed into a thousand, useless shards. He wasn't going back. A noise behind made him spin round. His rescuer, bleeding, slumped against a morbid statue of some horned deity, groaned. Crank clutched the fire-blaster to his shattered chest. His intestines were hanging out and, by the looks of it, he didn't have long until he bled to death. Terminus knelt beside Crank.

'Terminus...' he breathed.

'Don't try and speak. Just... just...' Just what? Crank was dying and they both knew it. 'You shouldn't have come. This was my problem.'

'I broke the mirror, Terminus. I tried to save you and ended up killing you. I'm sorry.'

'At least you tried. I don't see those Agathon digest-spreaders here. Who would have thought, eh? Both of us dying on this vulley-hole.'

He tugged Terminus's arm. 'You aren't going to die. Not again. The Creator brought you back because your destiny-line is so rich. I always knew you weren't just some gannta from the old world. You are... you are something else...'

He laughed. 'Those Agathon goomahs have been filling your thought box with digest. I'm dead, Crank. I *killed* one of them. It went morto.' He held up the skull. Crank's eyes widened.

'You see... they said, they told me. Joel, Martha, they said your destiny-line is rich... this...' his remains of a finger pointed to the skull '...is proof...'

Terminus sensed them before he heard them. They filled the doorway. Twelve hooded figures filed into the temple.

'There's only one way out now.' Terminus took the fire-blaster from Crank. 'Time to meet this Creator.'

'No.'

'If it was good enough for Tulk, then it's good enough for us. Beats bleeding to death, eh Crank? Or being goomed to death by Urrseal's friends.'

Terminus set the fire-blaster to omega and eyed the Twelve.

With the last of his strength Crank smashed the gun out of his hand and it skidded toward them. White light filled this vision; the last time he'd died it hadn't been like this.

He blinked. Shook his head. Terminus was suddenly aware that he was being stared at, was naked while those around him were clothed. He stood. The white, sterile hall of the *Bethany* was full of Agathon missionaries scanning him. Crank's body lay beside him on the teleport disc. In the viewing port beyond he could see the planet of Thanatos One below, and tiny darts that must be black galleons launching from the surface. Naomi was pushing her way to the front of the crowd of onlookers. He had no funny quips, no sarcastic lines to spit out. Wordlessly, he made his mark on Agathon history.

He stood tall, naked, and unashamed. In his right hand he held out the Thanaton deity's skull. In his face was locked an expression of grim victory for all to see. Sii Terminus, space-gannta, loser, had killed that which could not die.

Finalities

'You can never return to Skyfire,' Martha had said. 'Yes, Akkbar's influence is broken and the First Church of the Destroyer has been, well, destroyed, but this is a chapter in your world's history that the new government would rather erase. They want no one to remember this. If you went back, they would have you killed the moment you touched down. You're an embarrassment to them, Terminus.'

Skyfire's ruling body wasn't beyond murdering its own citizens to cover up incidents and embarrassments. Terminus knew that well enough. Martha took his arm and walked him from the inauguration hall to the plaza where the bubble shuttle waited. As always, the Agathon sky was cloudless and blue. His debriefing had been long, questions upon questions piled onto him until, at last, he had a chance to talk, to off-load the stress and fear that had accumulated over the last few stretches. Now he was returning to Trinity, he was going home.

On the plaza the citizens gathered to see him. His reputation had spread. This was the man who had killed one of the Thirteen. Not only that, he had stood naked on the deck of the *Bethany* thrusting out Urrseal's skull like a trophy. His notoriety had divided Agathon opinion. Half the world thought that his display was an outrage, an offence to the Creator. The other half, the older, wiser population smiled at the thought of this space-gannta basking in his moment of glory.

Agathos's history was awash with heroes. Tinus, the engineer who heard the word of the Creator and built the *Genesis;* Alison, the Martian dignitary trapped on the Earth during the Great Decline who led the last pilgrims to the rotting metropolis where the *Genesis* sat hidden, ready for blast off; Duke, the first Agathon to journey to Thanatos where he destroyed the Gatekeeper's city of glass. Judging from the conservative round of applause from the white-robes gathered on the plaza, (Agathons were not known for displays of hysterical behavior) the planet had found another. They dispersed quietly, some shaking his hand or slapping him on the back.

As he was about to board the bubble, he turned to Martha. 'About the other matter we spoke of. What do you think I should do?'

A broad grin spread across her face. 'On this world, when one person falls in love with another person, we ask for their hand in marriage.'

The sun cracked over the planet's surface. A beautiful sight that gradually receded into the distance. Much too slowly. The Sundog was heaving itself away from Skyfire at a maddeningly slow pace. The dignitaries' lounge where she sat was humming with conversation from a mixture of politicos and senior Watch officers. Her gloved hand slid over the stem of the glass. The red-lipped woman hoisted the hem of her night-black dress an inch or two, giving a better view of her thigh to the squat politico at the neighboring table. The old pervert had been giving her furtive glances for the last sub-stretch. She brought the green glass to her lips and melted into the darkness of her corner. Big circular tables were dotted around the dimly lit lounge. People were drinking together. She was the only one drinking alone. Soon enough that squat, senior politico sidled over and offered to buy her a glass of snakki. She smiled, pulling back her hood slightly. Her eyes glinted as she took in his features.

'You shouldn't be drinking alone,' he said. He tried to make his words sound smooth but he came across as oily. Even though she smiled at the politico, she could tell he was devoid of personality.

'Well I'm not alone now, am I?'

'So, where are you going?'

For an answer, she sidled up to him. He couldn't hide his excitement. Those pale cheeks were beginning to redden for the first time in cycles. This pathetic little man was going to get her passage to where she wanted to go. He had the power to do that. In exchange, she would eat him alive.

'I'm going to the holy planet,' she said. A fresh glass of snakki materialized in front of her; she sipped at the drink. 'When I get there,' she said. 'They won't know what's hit them.'

The sun smiled over the surface of Trinity Three. Terminus woke, washed, and then dressed for the most important day in his life. He stood before the mirror in his old room and looked at his reflection with disbelief. The purple and scarlet of the Agathon wedding suit seemed blindingly rich after wearing nothing but white robes for the past five sub-cycles. The intricate stitchwork made an outstanding contrast with the plain robes too.

He smiled, hoping that Tulk, Crank, and the others were looking down from the Creator's realm. Peering out of the window he could see the spire of the temple. Naomi would be waiting, wearing a beautiful dress and a white veil. All his friends, soon to be his family, would be there. He wished his pat could have been here. Joel had even offered to take the *Bethany* to Earth to find him, but something, some doubt, some grievance, had stopped him. He would find his father, one day. He and Naomi would bring their children to meet him, introduce them to their grandfather. Terminus felt happy, purely, unashamedly happy. He knew this was going to be the best day of his life.

'They're waiting for us now.' Isaiah appeared behind him and clapped a friendly arm upon his shoulder. 'Before we go I just want to say how glad I am Naomi has found a man like you. Oh, I'd lined her up with some spiritless farmer's boy but now she has you, the Agathon hero.'

'Isaiah!' Terminus blushed.

'No. She wants to fulfill her dreams of becoming a missionary and I know you'll protect her out there.'

They left the empty house and wandered down the hill to the temple under a blazing midday sun. When they reached the temple, Terminus saw it was garlanded by flowers that gave a heady perfume. The most precious and beautiful flower of all was waiting for him at the altar. Naomi's hair had re-grown quickly and her sister and mother had braided it into intricate patterns. Her pure, white dress had been adorned with jewels and lace. Naomi bloomed, so radiant with beauty that he was genuinely taken aback. Even her eyes shone. To Terminus she was the most beautiful living thing in the universe. Over the last five sub-cycles, the shackles and constraints had fallen away and he'd allowed himself to truly fall in love with her, to let her crann his tank full to bursting.

It was one day out in the fields, herding the mammals, when he'd asked Isaiah for permission to marry her. The Elder had picked Terminus up and swung him round with joy. The Earther took that to mean that Isaiah approved. Over the summer they'd built a small house bordering the hillcow field for them to live in. Naomi had stayed there for the last sub-cycle but tonight they would occupy the abode together. For the very first time they would make love with the Creator's blessing.

He joined her at the altar and she winked at him. He grinned back.

Joel stood before them and addressed the congregation.

'This day sees the joining of Sii Terminus and our dear sister Naomi in the pattern of partnership as laid out by the Creator. Their vows hold a sacred bond that cannot be broken. According to our most ancient of traditions I ask that if any person here knows of any good reason why these two should not be joined in marriage then I ask that you speak now.' A bubble of fear broke out in his guts. He calmed himself. He was thousands of pulses away from Skyfire. He was a new man now; the past was in the Creator's hands.

'Very well. I now ask Sii Terminus if he will take Naomi, our sister, into his arms, hold her, protect her...'

The doors burst open and she blasted in like a moon-storm. Terminus spun and, when his scan-balls registered her, his heart dropped out of his ribcage, smashing into his groin. The intruder's black catsuit contrasted starkly with the white robes of the congregation, her presence like black poison coursing into clear water. Green eyes blazed from her face, daring anyone to get in her way. In her hand she held something. Terminus thought it was a weapon at first but saw that it was a holo-comm. Joel indignantly asked her what she thought she was doing but the banshee ignored him and screamed into Terminus's face.

'You flooring, drenting, vulley!'

The congregation backed away from her. Naomi had pulled back her veil, her face flushed with adrenaline and confusion. Terminus managed to open his mouth and speak. Almost inaudibly, he said her name.

'Clannel.'

She circled the couple, outraged and venomous. 'Well, drenting hell. Isn't this nice? I barely got him into decent clothes when we were Linked.' She addressed Naomi. 'And if you think you're going to get any flooring done tonight, geema, forget it. He'll be too snakkied for any of that. Which one is the priest?'

Joel stepped forward. 'I am the chaplain taking this wedding.'

'This,' she spat thrusting the holo-comm into Joel's face, 'is the documentation, with footage, I might add, of our Linking back on

Skyfire. I bet he didn't tell you about this, did he? I bet he kept his mouth shut about it, eh?'

Joel, keeping his nerve, asked: 'Was the marriage consummated? Did you have sexual relations with this man?'

'Sexual relations? I was walking funny for stretches, once he'd sobered up.'

Joel stood between Terminus and Naomi. 'Then I'm sorry. I cannot authorize this marriage.'

Naomi pushed past Joel and faced her fiancé. Her face masked by many intense emotions: pity, betrayal, and disgust.

'You lied to me. You always said there was no one else. I asked you. I asked you twice and you said there was no one.' She slapped him hard around the face and made her exit. Isaiah gave Terminus a look that was also crossed with pity and disgust, and then followed his daughter out of the temple. (The children had been ushered out as soon as Clannel had begun swearing). Swiftly the guests left the building.

Terminus sunk to the floor and sat with his legs crossed. A noise was filling his head, a noise like falling metal; the sound of his life collapsing. He was dimly aware of Joel ushering the last of the guests out, Clannel screaming that it was over, that she'd had to give away some valuable heirloom, a ring, to bribe some veck so she could trace him — first time he'd ever heard of ching in her family. She'd also vullied a politico to get here and even that squat gannta was more of a man than he would ever be. Joel had practically carried her out.

He was alone in the temple, unable to move. How silent it was in the cool of the worship place. He continued to hold his head in his hands; the crashing sound began to subside.

The Usurper's Lore

From space, Thanatos One looked as dead and lifeless as it had for decades. As it had when the human ship, the 850, had arrived in the recent past. Under the cloudline, though, the planet's surface was alive with crawling, writhing, and scurrying entities.

Across the forests of the northern hemisphere, millions of creatures scrambled through the gnarled roots of the old wood. All around them the ground shuddered with seismic groans as the crust of the planet decayed rapidly. Trees crashed into cracks that opened up the ground. A planet-sized storm lashed the air so violently that many of the desperate entities were whipped into the clouds, to be pulverized in the spiraling debris of trees, rocks, earth, and flesh. Near the Tower of Spite there could be found a Deadspace; a hole in the ground that led to darkness. The vast metal lid of the Deadspace had been torn away and the creatures had plunged into the darkness of the abyss below.

The survivors yet to reach the Deadspace scrambled toward this point like desperate pilgrims: graveworms, plaguewraiths, necronymphs, garlongs, woodblight and others in various states of decay. For a normal human the sight would be disgusting to behold as slime-covered creatures crawled over one another to escape the decaying planet that had been Thantos One. The Deadspace led directly through a realm no man or creature ever wanted to enter to the second planet in the Thanatos system: Thanatos Two. The largest planet of what had once been thirteen systems would find a million migrants on its shores.

From under the northern oceans of the dying planet, the great black sea-beast, Ocahr, heaved herself onto the beach near the Deadspace and tried to ascend the crumbling cliffs to escape the dying world. To her left the walls surrounding the Spires of the Thirteen were sliding away as if they were made of sand, not million-year-old rock. The north spire shuddered first and slowly tumbled into the sea. However, the south spire still stood, defiant against the mass of swirling clouds and thunder that roared above, and the seismic shifts beneath.

Slowly and majestically the Twelve entered the cavernous meeting hall in House Thanatos, the gateway from this universe to their own eternity. The place where the Deadspaces met.

The first robed Thanaton to enter stepped forward. The remaining eleven listened.

'For too long we have sat silently, sleeping through time as mankind, the bastard spawn of the Creator, has dared to venture from the old world into the universe. He has established a kingdom, erased his past which we, we the Thirteen, gave him. Mankind was not meant to survive the Great Decline. But he has...'

'Who was it that allowed the *Genesis* to leave Earth and spawn a new colony, Urrleash? By whose decision?'

'By the Destroyer's will, Urrlock. By the Destroyer's will. The spawn of man has created colonies on a thousand worlds and that should not be. Humans should be under our command, suffering for our pleasure. We must go to war, brothers. Undermine their societies, set them against each other. It is the will of the Destroyer. The Creator is almost at the point where, as promised, he will manifest himself in physical form in this galaxy. Only our existence prevents this. We must destroy mankind before the Creator arrives.'

The seventh Thanaton stepped forward. 'Already the leaders of Skyfire have shown interest in Thanaton technology. Our role on Skyfire is not redundant.'

'A weak plan, Urrgash.' The tenth hooded figure stepped forward. 'My Gatekeepers have established themselves on Babel. They want an alliance with us, they are frightened...'

'The Babelites are frightened?'

'Yes. The Architects are returning from the depth of space. Babel wants protection from them.'

'Excellent!' the first Thanaton said. 'Frightened humans. We can always control frightened humans. Our last challenge faces us. With Urrseal dead, the first planet is collapsing. We need a Thirteenth to take his place, to enter our fold.'

'*You know the lore, Urrlock. The Usurper's Lore.*' Urrgash regarded his fellow with his six dark eyes.

'In the first days, if one of the Thirteen was murdered, the individual who carried out the deed would take his place. But this is not the same, Urrgash. Urrseal was killed by... by...'

'He was murdered by a space dog. A space dog with a rich destiny-line. Urrseal saw his potential. Only this dog can replace Urrseal.'

'Then it is agreed. He dwells now in the Forest of Thought for some crime he has committed on Agathos. The forest is the Agathons' weakest point. We have always been able to penetrate that place. We can take him from there.'

Two beautiful Gatekeepers entered the hall and bowed low. Urrlock addressed them.

'Go to Agathos, to the third moon. Fetch for us the individual known as Simon Terminus. Bring him here.' Urrlock's voice dropped low and he almost spoke to himself. 'He must meet his destiny.'

About this Story

The idea of creating a fictional universe was always a tempting one and it came to fruition one night in August 1999. I was working a night shift in a psychiatric rehab unit and it was very quiet. All the patients were asleep so I began thinking up the universe that Terminus now inhabits. Maybe other authors do this, or perhaps it's just peculiar to myself, but if I have an idea I plan it out in my head, scene-by-scene as if it were a film.

I imagined *Terminus* as a three-part TV series. I even drew, in coloured pencils I found in the art room, the location of the planetary systems. I realise now that I took the names of planets and characters from things around me. Babel; I was reading the novel *Babel* by A.S. Byatt at the time. Terminus; I was listening to the album *Wayward sons of Mother Earth* by folk/thrash band Skyclad at the time. Track 10 is a happy little ditty about nuclear war entitled *Terminus*.

I even invented terms and swear words for the crew to use. *Terminus* is full of bad language but none you've ever heard before. *Drent. Flooring. Vulley* and my personal favourite, *Skangat!*

The idea was filed in the back of my mind until 2007. In the August of that year I went to India on a voluntary mission with my church to work in a street school. Many of the ideas for Alpha Gropolis came from my experiences in Calcutta. I also came up with the name Skyfire whilst in India. On our day off we went to the college on the outskirts of Calcutta curated by William Carey, the Northamptonshire Missionary. There a museum there and I found myself looking at pictures and reading about Moulton in Northamptonshire, Carey's birthplace. There I was, four thousand miles from home and reading about a village a mere four miles away from my home. I was immediately reminded of my *Terminus* idea. In the book, Terminus is in the library on Thanatos One, four thousand pulses from Skyfire and he finds a book detailing his home settlement of Adlestrop. In that moment I decided to have a crack at writing Terminus when I got home.

(Before I went to India, my volunteer group attended a briefing at the Baptist missionary centre called the International Missionary Centre. I blatantly nicked this and changed it to the Intergalactic Missionary Centre, the place where Naomi goes for her selection interview on Agathos. However, the Baptist church obviously nicked their IMC from the 1971 Doctor Who story *Colony in Space* where the IMC stands for Interplanetary Mining Company. So there you go).

So, if Skyfire is Calcutta, then what is Thanatos One? Basically I was inspired by Hammer Horror films and various episodes of Doctor Who (*State of Decay*, *The Brain of Morbius*) to come up with the Spires of the Thirteen and the dark forests of Thanatos One. I was writing the section set on Thanatos One in those dark months between September and Christmas, and the arrival of Halloween that year definitely helped with the momentum.

So where did I come up with the specifics for the paradisiacal Agathos and Trinity Three? Well, I think that every experience is memorized in our subconscious and we draw upon these memories when writing, subconsciously or consciously. After I'd written *Terminus*, I went to my brother's house in Devon. My older brother is a big bloke with very long hair and beard. His house is always filled with people and there's always music and lots of cooking to be done. In his hallway is a carving which I swear I'd never seen before and I actually had to stop and have a look. The carving was of a bloke with a big head and his arms spread out wide to embrace the universe. The Creator symbol from my book! I must have passed this carving loads of times when I'd stayed at my brother's house and seen it every time I'd passed it to go to the loo, and never noticed it. Obviously, I had.

Paul Melhuish — Sept 2011

About the Author

Paul Melhuish has been writing since he can remember, and wrote his first novel aged fifteen. His mother typed it out and was so shocked by the language and violent content of the story that very little of the shocking element remained. He studied English, Drama and Sociology at the University of Northampton, and sometime after that qualified as an Occupational Therapist at Oxford Brookes University. Paul also inadvertently walked across a minefield whilst doing voluntary work in Lebanon, probably the stupidest thing he's ever done.

He is a member of the Northampton Science Fiction Writers' Group and has had short stories published in various magazines, and the anthology _Shoes, Ships & Cadavers_ alongside authors such as Ian Watson and Sarah Pinborough. His short stories _Fearworld_ and _Necroforms_ are available from Greyhart Press. So too is _Babel_, set in the same universe as _Terminus_ and something of a prequel.

Other Books, Films, Music and TV You Might Enjoy

Well, this is a tough one for me because when I read a science fiction novel and they visit an alien planet, that world might be creepy but it isn't Hammer Horror creepy. Weird creatures might leap out of the dark but the space marines will just shoot them down. Although I write sci-fi I defiantly lean towards horror, or more specifically, gothic horror. However, writing sci-fi isn't as easy as it looks and for inspiration on technique you can't get better than Alastair Reynolds. _Diamond Dogs_ is a fantastic story of a crew's efforts to reach the prize within an alien tower. _Chasm City_ is also a vivid epic with a real creepy factor. Four ships are on a long-term journey to another planet and they think there may be a fifth ship following that they've not been told about.

One of the best books I've ever read, and a definite inspiration for _Terminus_, is _The Monk_ by Matthew Lewis. Lewis's interplay between narrative stands is something I'd love to be able to do as a writer and the sheer atmosphere created by the writing is something I've tried to emulate myself.

Obviously religion is a strong theme in _Terminus_, and I am drawn to books that explore this theme. _Behold the Man_ by Michael Moorcock is a blasphemous but brilliant time travel story, where a man obsessed by religion returns to Palestine to have it out with Jesus face-to-face.

Mostly my fuel, not necessarily my inspiration, for _Terminus_ came from films, TV and music. The films of Jess Franco are always good to watch to get an idea of the uncanny. There's a film called Black Candles which is an Italian film, shot in Italy with an Italian cast yet supposed to be set in Britain. We had it on all the time in my student house when I was supposedly studying in Northampton. The uncanny atmosphere of the film gives it a dream like quality. Careful though, it's a bit rude! Obviously there's Seventies Doctor Who which I watch all the time (except when I have to go to work. I hate work, by the way, and I'm sure you do too). _The Daemons_ is my favourite ever story. The BBC has a crack at doing Hammer Horror and the results are really creepy. Watch out for the Morris dancing as this is a precursor for _The Wicker Man_.

Musically, Thanatos One would never have solidified into my imagination if I'd not listened to the album _Midian_ by Cradle of Filth. Yeah, yeah, yeah, I know they're pretentious goth/black metallers but listening to this album on the headphones late at night (or full blast on the speakers, depending on whether you live in a detached house) with a few ales, transports you to a trippy, nightmarish realm. Weird sound effects and Doug 'Hellraiser' Bradley's narration give life to the lyrical tales of global Chthonic takeover, A beautiful female asylum escapee and trapped souls wailing. _Her Ghost in the Fog_ is a prime example of the atmospheric experience of this album. A beautiful witch lives in the forest and the narrator falls in love with her. However, she is raped and killed by the men of the village. The narrator finds her body as well as the church bell tower key. At the next mass he locks the doors and sets fire to the church. Serves 'em right. This is Urrseal's favourite album. He used to drive the other Thanatons mental playing it all at hours. His quarters weren't detached, you see.

Paul Melhuish — Sept. 2011

Paul's given some recommendations above. I would add _Babel,_ a short story that follows Joel's mission on that planet. Paul is busy writing more short stories and novels set in the same Skyfire universe as _Terminus._ Watch out for _Skyfire Chronicles: Unauthorized Contact:_ a collection of short stories and novelettes set in the Skyfire Universe, and due to be published in paperback and eBooks formats September 2012.

Tim C. Taylor — Publisher

About Greyhart Press

Talk to us on Twitter (@GreyhartPress) or email
(editors@greyhartpress.com)

Greyhart Press is an indie publisher of quality genre fiction: fantasy, science fiction, horror, and some stories that defy description. Since our launch in spring 2011, we initially concentrated on short stories, but soon expanded into novellas and novels.

We publish eBooks and print-on-demand paperbacks through online retailers. That's great for us and for you, because we don't have to worry about all that costly hassle of stock-holding and distribution. Instead we can concentrate on finding great stories AND giving some away for free! Visit our free story promotion page for no-strings-attached free downloads.

Our motto is *Real Stories for Real People!* What's that about, then? It's about the Real Story Manifesto (credit where it's due: this is inspired by the Agile Software Development Manifesto).

We seek to tell great stories by writing them and helping others to find them.
Through this (highly enjoyable work) we have come to value:

Writing clarity over writing style.
Plots that move over plots that are clever.
Characters who make hard choices over characters who observe interesting events.

A reader left satisfied over a critic left impressed.

That is, while there is value in the items on
the right, we value the items on the left more.

Would you like to read our eBooks for free?

If so, our READ... REVIEW... REPEAT... promotion is for you.
see our website at www.greyhartpress.com for more details.

If you enjoyed this book, please consider leaving an online review at Amazon, Goodreads, or elsewhere (you don't need to have purchased this book from Amazon to write a review there, but you do need an Amazon account). Even if it's only a line or two, it would be very helpful and would be very much appreciated.

Thank you.

Printed in Great Britain
by Amazon.co.uk, Ltd.,
Marston Gate.